DREAM

By the same author

The Task
The Ceremony of Innocence
The Road to Ballyshannon

DREAM

David McCart Martin

Secker & Warburg
London

First published in England in 1986 by
Martin Secker & Warburg Limited
54 Poland Street, London WIV 3DF

Copyright © 1986 by David McCart Martin

British Library Cataloguing in Publication Data

Martin, David, 1937–
Dream.
I. Title
823'.914[F]   PR6063.A71/

ISBN 0-436-27335-7

The author wishes to thank the Trustees
of the Phoenix Trust, London, and of the
Hélène Heroys Literary Foundation, Geneva,
for financial assistance during the writing
of this novel.

Typeset in 10/11pt Linotron Baskerville by
Deltatype Ltd, Ellesmere Port
Printed in Great Britain by Billings Ltd

In memoriam

ELIZABETH HOPKINS MCCART MARTIN

*through whose tholing I glimpsed
many things of the spirit*

In dreams begins responsibility.

Epigraph to 'Responsibilities'
William Butler Yeats

It seemed that out of battle I escaped
Down some profound dull tunnel, long since scooped
Through granites which titanic wars had groined.
Yet also there encumbered sleepers groaned,
Too fast in thought or death to be bestirred.
Then, as I probed them, one sprang up, and stared
With piteous recognition in fixed eyes,
Lifting distressful hands, as if to bless.
And by his smile, I knew that sullen hall,
By his dead smile I knew we stood in Hell . . .

'Strange friend,' I said, 'here is no cause to mourn.'
'None,' said that other, 'save the undone years,
The hopelessness. Whatever hope is yours,
Was my life also . . .

I am the enemy you killed, my friend.
I knew you in this dark: for so you frowned
Yesterday through me as you jabbed and killed.
I parried; but my hands were loath and cold.
Let us sleep now . . .'

'Strange Meeting'
Wilfred Owen

Sir Wisdom's a fool when he's fou;
Sir Knave is a fool in a session:
He's there but a prentice I trow,
But I am a fool by profession.

Lines of a song from 'Love and Liberty'
Robert Burns

PART ONE

I

'Are you ferrying?'

''Cross hell or heaven. Whatever the oul' bit of water ye like.'

'Hell will do for the moment.'

'Now there's a quare stretch of the sea, so it is. And ye tell me for a moment? Now what would a moment be in hell? A million years, d'ye think? Or maybe even more than that. And what would the stretch of ocean be? A million miles or ten times the length of itself whatever the length of itself would be? Ye're asking me a brave question, John Gordon, when ye're asking me till ferry ye 'cross hell.'

'And you've given me a good enough answer. No man knows the dimension of hell. In time or in spirit.'

'And what about heaven then?'

'That too. If such exists.'

'Well I know what would do on a day like this. A drop of good spirit. Though it mightn't be the one ye were talking about.'

So saying, the ferryman pulled a half-empty bottle of whiskey from under a strut, shouldering aside the animals on board—two piglets, a calf and a sheep—took a long swig, then, standing up with the long broadbeamed rowing-boat rocking beneath him, reached the bottle up to his companion who stood on the steps of the quayside. The calf and sheep, unaccustomed to a ground that bobbed and dipped and rolled under them, began to baa and bellow loudly while the two piglets squirmed with their bellies pressed more tightly against the planking. 'Ah, quit yer bawling. Ye'll be back on land soon enough.'

John Gordon took the bottle and drank, feeling the burning sensation in his throat as he swallowed quickly. He had already consumed several glasses that afternoon in Belfast, and on the train down to Larne had almost finished the contents of a silver flask carried in his pocket. 'Thanks, Alec. The day's right and cold.'

'And colder for some by the looks of that face ye have on ye.'

'That might be so.'

'Dear God, and there's me believing all these years hell was a place

3

ye got scorched in. And now ye're telling me it's like living in one of them oul' icebergs. Sure ye'd be frize till death in a second.' Accepting the bottle as it was returned, his feet planted firmly apart on the swaying craft, he drank thoughtfully, the while tugging at the animals' ropes to see that they were still securely fastened and clipping the calf across the ear as it tried to lumber towards the steps. 'But then, if ye think about it, it wouldn't matter a damn one way or the other, would it? 'Cos if ye were burned ye'd be a cinder in a second too. Isn't that right?'

'Maybe it's both.'

'And maybe it is. Like them stories ye read about where in the North Pole and suchlike when ye touch an oul' bit of metal or the like yer fingers are burned off ye.' The ferryman laughed. 'But that'd be a quare oul' trick on the divil's part, wouldn't it? Here's us believing in hellfire and what's in store fer us is being a bit of redhot ice. I don't think any of them preachers have worked that one out yet. Not that they're stupid men, mind ye. But sometimes I think they know no more than we do. All they have is a rulebook. And as fer a moment in hell being a million years long? Maybe these oul' beasts can work that one out as well as we can.'

'And maybe what you say is right.'

'Is that so? And you a reading man?'

'Stories, Alec Dick, stories.'

'Right enough, John Gordon. Only a story. But a quare tale at that.'

'So. Are you ferrying?'

Alec, still standing, finished the bottle and dropped it into a sack at the bow and retrieved a full one which he opened and passed across. The tide mostly in, he could see over the quayside to the town of Larne where, here and there among the gaslights, coloured bunting streamed in the breeze from the sea. Now late afternoon, darkness was seeping across land and water and the line of hills was becoming imperceptible. Around the quayside itself vessels of varying kinds were moored and from some he could already hear the boisterous voices and snatches of song coming from sailors merry with drink. And perhaps from their girls too they'd smuggled on board under the eagle eye of some blustery old skipper. He smiled, turning his face away towards the sea so that the smile could not be seen, then fell serious again. There was a question he had to ask, but did not want to. And by the look on the other's countenance and his hunched bearing the answer was going to be the wrong one. A good man was John Gordon, he thought, a man everyone liked and would never say a word against. Tall and broad, quiet spoken with an educated tongue, he would never give a word of offence. Even when he went on a

4

drinking spree, which he sometimes did, there was never a word spoken in heat or anger. But what kind of man was he? He was neither farmer nor sailor, and if a man stayed at home on Islandmagee he had to work at the land or the boats. He had a good bit of land, a large farm in the middle of the island and several hundred acres on the mainland, but it was land he never worked himself. Education was the spoiling of him, when he was sent to college in the city, so people were given to say, and then added, more of a clergyman or a scholar is John Gordon.

'Ye're a man of few words, John,' Alec said, looking at the tall figure in the dusk, the black coat and suit merging with the oncoming night.

'I've asked you if you are ferrying.'

'And what if I said I'm not?'

'I'll walk.'

Alec laughed. 'Well ye're hardly able till walk on water. Not yet anyway. And it's a fair few miles walking all the way back to Ballycarry till the crossing and then up the island.' Momentarily he gazed up the length of Larne Lough which separated the peninsula from the mainland. 'Though I suppose you've done it before. Like myself when I couldn't row this oul' boat fer fear of the storm.'

'John's gone. Lost. Dead.'

'So that's yer news. I was wondering. Don't we all know him and his ship's been missing fer months.' Alec paused and drank again, his voice softer. 'When did ye learn?'

'Today. In Belfast. At the shipping offices. The ship's so long overdue now they say there's no hope. Not in those waters.'

'And where was that?'

'The South Atlantic.'

'Aye. I've heard many's the tale about that. One of the worst bits of water anywhere. Like this oul' bit out here,' Alec added, nodding towards open water. 'The Moyle's cost many a ship its doom.' Pausing, he continued: 'No hope, then?'

'None.'

'It must be bad for a man to hear of the loss of his firstborn. Wasn't he in this boat many's the time with me? A lad fer the sea if ever there was one. Couldn't keep him away from it.'

A young man's face drifted in front of John's eyes, frank and open, laughing eyes, dark hair like himself. Not a young man for schooling or books but for talking about the sea and scrambling over any ship whenever allowed by skipper or crew. The night in a storm when he'd been out round the rocks of the Maidens catching lobsters and, losing an oar, had sculled back with one. And now another storm in a different sea had taken him. 'It's seven months since I've seen him. He would be eighteen now.'

5

'I was just thinking it's a strange talk till be having about hell when it's Christmas Eve.'

But John Gordon's eyes were fixed on an image of himself and his firstnamed taking the trap to the railway station in Whitehead where the peninsula joined the mainland, the young man laughing and telling about his last ship as he gently flicked the reins of the mare. He'd been like himself, a gentle spirit, though unlike himself in his strength at dealing with others who slighted him. Where he, the father, would turn and walk away, John, the son, would stay to argue or fight it out. A drink at an hotel bar, then, kitbag over his shoulder, he had stepped onto the train. A wave through the puffing smoke and hissing steam of the engine and he was gone.

'But then maybe it isn't.'

Staring down at Alec who was now sitting with oars in hand, he asked: 'Isn't what?'

'Maybe it isn't strange to talk about hell on Christmas Eve. Maybe a better time than any. Aye, I'll ferry ye over. But you'll be the last one. Any the rest that wants till come back can swim fer it. I'm having this night fer myself.' Standing up again he slipped the rope from the bollard and said: 'I'll be back fer ye, John. This crew's hardly fer the likes of yerself. All this cow and pig dung and I don't get a penny more fer the trouble.'

'That crew will do fine. There's no point in you ferrying all the way over and then having to come back just for me. There's room enough among the beasts.'

'Well don't go blaming me if that woman of yours starts tonguing ye about getting yer clothes spoiled. It wasn't the ferryman's fault.'

'Don't worry about that.'

'And I hear she's on the way with another. Isn't that so?'

'That's right.'

'And due anytime?'

'Any day now.'

'Then don't ye have another to replace him? And maybe another son? And ye've already two others, haven't ye? Dalton and Jack?'

'There'll be no more after this one.'

'That's a fine thing to say. Ye're going till leave yer wife in a lonely bed, are ye? And her still a fine big woman needing love and warmth on an oul' winter's night? Spitting in the face of life that is, if ye ask me.'

'I'm not asking you.'

'I don't give a damn if ye're asking me or not. I'm telling ye what I think.' Beginning to feel his companion's melancholy and grief overshadow his own good spirits he turned and lit the lantern at the bow of the boat. Normally a good-natured man and willing to listen to

6

the troubles of others, and their joys, he found this particular conversation becoming too much. After all, it was Christmas Eve, as he'd remarked. Within an hour he wanted to be dressed up and in Whitehead at a bar among others where there'd be good stout and whiskey and laughter flowing, their wives left at home in peace to carry out the task of preparing the morrow's Christmas dinner. And there was tomorrow itself when he could lounge around the cottage in sleepy contemplation and in the evening go to the small pub at Millbay and listen to still more yarns. One of the few idle days in the year when there seemed to be so much time to do nothing in. Suddenly looking up at the figure still standing on the steps, he said: 'Get in, John. Else we'll be here till kingdom come. And by the looks of these oul' beasts they want a bit of turf under their feet and not be pitching about here.'

Waiting until he saw John step into the boat and settle his bulk at the stern, Alec took another sip of whiskey, passed the bottle over and slipped the rope, with his right hand manoeuvring his cargo in the direction of the other shore which was only a hundred yards away but a turbulent and treacherous stretch of water when the gales sent heavy seas crashing into the mouth of the lough, his thick sinewed hands and arms straining under the rough shirt and seaman's pullover, through the dusk watching the other's brooding shadowed face and sagging shoulders framed between the calf and sheep. Pausing for a moment and slipping an oar, he grasped a piglet by the neck and thrust it into the water, its high-pitched squealing suddenly breaking the silence between them. 'And what about this one, John? When the slaughterman comes round it'll be bacon fer yer breakfast. Won't it be our own turn one day? We all go back intil the ground in one way or another.'

John watched the piglet being tossed back into the boat, still squealing, where it again huddled down against the boards. 'If only it had been the ground. Then there'd be a place to mark his going.'

Again pulling on the oars, Alec rejoined: 'Sure there's ground at the bottom of the sea. Else what keeps the water up. And as fer being in the ground. Who'll ferry us then, will ye tell me?'

Reaching the shore Alec jumped out and looped the rope round an iron fastening used during such times as this when he had to bring cattle across, then began to haul the calf and sheep onto the shingle with the help of their owners who had been waiting. Accepting the proffered coins, he caught sight of the figure stepping silently from the boat and moving away up the shore. Going to him, he put his hand lightly on his shoulder and stared into the filmed eyes. 'Mark my words, John Gordon. Out of the oul' darkness comes life. Comes creation. Mark my words well.'

7

Returning to the boat, Alec looked down at the soiled boards, paused to scratch his beard, then muttered—'Ach, to hell with it. It can be washed and scrubbed later.' With the tide out and it lying on the shingle some of the lads would clean it for a penny. With a piglet squirming under each arm he strode up to the small harbour where the half-dazed calf and sheep were still struggling with their owners. Stopping to banter with them about the cost of bringing cattle from the mainland, he received another coin and the promise of a bit of beef when the calf was fattened up.

'And what's the matter with the big John Gordon?' asked the one who was holding the calf. 'He didn't say a word to us.'

'It's young John. He's gone fer good. The ship's lost.' Then, knowing that Dan Hawkins had a neighbouring farm, added: 'He got the news the day in Belfast. You might like to call in on him.'

'I will.'

Responding to Dan's voice, a man humorous and generous like himself, Alec said: 'He's taking it bad.'

'Aye. I'll call. But he's a strange big man.' Dan paused to light his pipe. 'Dear God. What news on Christmas Eve.'

'True. Christmas Eve,' replied Alec, suddenly changing to a less sombre tone. 'And I'll be looking till both of ye fer a drink either the day or the morrow. That was rough work with them oul' beasts and them sick even looking at the tide. Didn't I nearly get drowned with them stamping and bawling and pishing all over the boat.'

Dan laughed. 'That'll be the day. It'll take more than Larne Lough to wash you away. Or cow-pish come to that.'

Bidding them well, Alec walked towards the row of cottages sitting back from the harbour where lights shone through the gloom. Some distance away a figure caught his eye and he stopped again. It stood motionless, staring out to sea. 'Go home, go home, John Gordon,' he muttered to himself. 'Aye. Ye're a strange big man. A strange big child of a man. But mark my words well.'

II

The images in his mind would not clear. In the ensuing days they lay between himself and everything that was taking place around him, as if he were sightless. No, not quite sightless. A hazy blur of sound penetrated his ears, as did the drifting, shifting shadows that he knew must be the everyday world filtering into his eyes. Time also had fragmented. When was when and what day what he didn't really know. Hours or days passed or stood still with a volition of their own. Voices came and went, indistinctly. Even hers who lay in childbirth in the big brass bed attended by the midwife, and to whom he knew he must tell.

Only once did he recall in those few days to seemingly possess absolute clarity. He was standing on the clifftop at the Gobbins watching the sea. A fine clear day, the coastline of Scotland could be easily seen. But it was the schooner he was watching, a big three-master beating her way down Belfast Lough making seaward, her bowsprit plunging into the waves the stiff wind sent scurrying towards the city.

The city. The letter was in his hand, the bold letterheading naming the firm of solicitors whom he knew to be that engaged by the shipping company. Even before reading it he seemed able to foretell its contents. There had been an earlier one, saying that his son John's ship was overdue at a port in Argentina, but, though there was cause for concern, they were still hopeful for the ship's safety, as in those seas even the most modern ships were often delayed by hazardous weather. Two months had passed between these formal communications, during which time he had called once at the solicitors' office, only to be politely informed that the shipping company had not yet issued any final confirmation. Which meant there was still hope, obviously.

He had to go into Belfast on business, he told her, without mentioning the nature of the business concerned, and, her labour pangs making her discomfort the greater, she'd either been forgetful

9

or disinclined to ask. Then he ordered the boys to put the mare in the trap, Dalton who was home for Christmas from a school in Larne, and Jack, the younger, who was just starting school on the island. He had dressed soberly, carefully, in a dark suit and overcoat, and then taken the trap into Whitehead, the two boys with him. Was it, going this way, a superstition at work within him? He would catch the train to the city from Whitehead. And hadn't this been the last time when he'd been with his firstborn, John, taking him to Whitehead in the trap to catch the train? Because, though this newly arrived second letter offered no hope, there was still hope in him.

He told the boys to return home with the trap. He himself would return that evening. From Larne.

While waiting for the train he had a drink in the same hotel bar as they'd been in on that previous occasion. He could almost feel the young man standing at his side, hear his laughter. It was a retracing of steps, because yes, in him there was still hope.

But none.

In the solicitors' office they were courteous and polite, yet grave, speaking in a soft measured emotionless voice, each of them, speaking as men used to such occasions. Like ministers at a graveside, he thought. And so they were, in a fashion. Even though the graveside was a vast ocean at the other end of the earth. That was when his senses started to blur. There was now no hope. Wreckage had been found. And there was no possibility of survival for long in such waters. There had been two of them. The solicitor and another from the shipping company itself. A captain, now retired from sea to an office, who had seen . . . seen many such things. Condolences. The papers in his hand, the papers of his son John's signing-on, now returned to him. And the money, the money that would have been due to him. The ship had been on the last leg of a long voyage, trading from Europe down the length of the ports of the Americas. Seven pounds, seventeen shillings and sixpence. Carefully he had folded the banknotes in his wallet then, in an afterthought, slipped notes and coins into the envelope which held the papers. Gravely he thanked them, holding the retired captain's hand in a firm grip as he left.

The city was attired in coloured lights and bunting. He noticed that as he walked from the office in the centre to the LMS railway station at York Road. In the hotel bar he studied the papers as if, properly scrutinised, they were prepared to give up some secret. A secret of the sea, perhaps. In the office the silent palefaced clerks were sitting at two neat rows of desks, their pens methodically working across the documents, the solicitor saying softly: 'Of course, had he been on one of the great new steamships . . .' as if in some kind of apology, or an inference that no ocean could sink them. That year had seen the launching of the huge transatlantic steamships *Teutonic* and *Majestic* for the White Star line. With thousands of others he had watched their massive bulk move down the lough in preparation for sea trials. But young John's ship had been a schooner, one of many sailing ships which still plied for trade. The big ships would come later, he'd said, when he had reached his ambition of being a master mariner.

He stood outside the new City Hall which was in the process of being built, watching the horses plod between the shafts of the trams while thinking of the mare and the trap, then wondered what he was doing in the city. Missing the train, he went to the docks to stare at the assembly of seagoing vessels. Only once had he been there before, when his son had insisted on bringing him on board one to show him around, strange-sounding names falling from the young man's lips as he demonstrated his profession.

Christmas Day. His wife was not at table but still lay upstairs, sometimes moaning softly. Jenny, the wife of one of his farmhands who looked after the small dairy and acted as maid around the farmhouse, prepared and served the meal. It passed in a silence so heavy that he didn't notice Dalton and Jack quickly escape from his brooding solemnity. And only later did he recall Dan Hawkins come in to sit opposite him beside the big range, though what he talked of went unremembered. To relieve the midwife who was now in the house almost continuously, he sat at his wife Elizabeth's bedside staring at the dark hair on the pillow and the bulge on the patchwork quilt as she slept, framing words she could not hear and would not yet hear.

For most of the following days he wandered the shoreline and the clifftops watching the sea as if expecting some miraculous appearance from its depths. But once did a cry break from him, long and piercing, as he leathered his tongue against the razor edge of the wind.

The schooner beat down the lough, tossing, ploughing into the waves, sails taut, bowsprit sending foaming spray onto the deck and rigging. What had it been like? Now the seas were mountainous, terrifying in their savage immensity and no land in sight. No, nor seabirds. The flock of screeching crying gulls swooped away borne on the back of the wind and were gone, and then that same wind began to tear the ship apart with massive strangling hands reaching out from the storm. He saw the sails being shredded into ribbons, the masts cracking and crashing across the deck, the rigging snapping and whipping timber and crew furiously, the deck itself already a whirlpool of water thighdeep.

Alone on the shore by a calm sea he took out the envelope still carried in his overcoat pocket, examining the contents yet again.

11

Slowly the banknotes floated away on the surface of the water, and vanished. The coins spun in the air glinting in the sunlight and, with a soft plopping sound like tears into a basin, also vanished into the greenwhite deep. Scavenging gulls and cormorants, curiosity aroused, dived swiftly and wheeled skyward again emptybeaked. The dark-skinned little boys, children still, stood in their small craft alongside the ship ready to dive to the bottom for a coin worth far less than a farthing. It was great fun to watch them. Practically naked they are. And they go through the water like fishes. You can watch them hit the bottom and then scramble on their hands along the harbour bed.

Young John had told him that. What country had that been in? What port? A sailor and storyteller he had been.

No port now but an ocean breaking the timbers of the ship like wood for the kindling. A cold kindling.

The crew. Afraid? Terrorstricken? Helpless and resigned? Resigned against an elemental eruption which reduced their fumbling hands and minds and skills to a futile struggle with their own already understood and acknowledged destruction? Perhaps already half-hoped for, by some. We are going, let it be quick.

A young man's face was buoyed up on the gentle curling swell, fingers reaching forth as if in handclasp.

The schooner cleared Belfast Lough and swung towards the North Sea and the Atlantic. Straining eyes and mind he thought he could make out the tiny figures on board, the skipper booming out his orders, the bos'n puppetlike spinning the wheel on command as the others scurried to change sails. Then in the darkness they were no more, save for the winking eyes of lighthouses and the lights of the cottages and farmhouses along the foreshore. Stumbling up the narrow rocky path, gorse and hawthorn and spiky grass at moments arresting his climb, he gained the clifftop and began walking slowly. A sound from the sea halted him and he turned his face towards it. It came several times, then stopped. Furrowing his brows he remained immobile, thoughts groping for meaning. The vague shape of a woman was outlined on the cliff, features indistinct. A siren? A siren's call? Those who lured an unwary mariner to his doom? Striving, he tried to recall all that he knew of the sea, which wasn't much. An unwary mariner to his doom? Wreckers' Brae. Turning, he tried to ascertain his bearings. Yes. It wasn't far away. A story of the island, when, in one of the many famines of years gone by, the people passed down the Brae to the rocks with lights. Not warning lights. Lights that would again lure ships to their splintered rocky end so that the people could salvage the cargo for their own survival. He watched them go by, silent, wan, spectral, heard the sailors' hoarse foamfilled lungs cry to the unhearing air.

12

A low pealing of bells invaded his senses, breaking into his thoughts. Pausing, he listened. They became louder. And singing. Yes. Singing. And the more he stumbled and walked the stronger both became.

'It's a girl.'

Nothing.

'It's a girl,' Jenny repeated, looking up at the tall dark figure still in mourning clothes, he who had done nothing but walk the shore for nigh on a week and from whom no one could get an answer of any kind. Everyone now knew of young John being lost, except his wife, who would be told when her strength returned.

What was a girl?

Jenny repeated the phrase a third time, taking him lightly by the arm.

He looked around. Yes. He was standing at the inner gate of the farmhouse, the gate leading into the big yard. The farmhouse loomed bulkily out of the night, windows aglow. A group of singing figures stood at the door. And the pressure against his legs was his collie, Shadow, which he had tied up so as to be alone with his loss.

'Ye've a fine wee girl, John Gordon. A daughter that ye'll be proud of. And she'll grow up to be a beauty. She was only born a minute or two ago.'

He was in the bedroom, dazedly watching the midwife finish cleaning up. Elizabeth lay as he'd last seen her, her face pale. But she was smiling, the newborn at her left shoulder wrapped in its swaddling clothes.

'It's a girl, John. We have a daughter.'

Gently he took the child in his arms and nursed it, beginning to hum softly. 'You come like the sun in the night. Like summer in the dead of winter. Like spring from a frozen sea. Like flowers opening in a storm. My April, May and June Gordon.'

'Those are lovely names for a girl,' he heard his wife remark, the midwife joining in.

'Then she'll be May. When the flowers are breaking into bloom for the summertime.'

Elizabeth watched him, studying his face, the face of this huge childlike man who was her husband, then intuitively responded to some deep necessity she understood that lay within him. 'May she'll be. May Gordon it is.'

In an outhouse where the mare and some cattle were stabled his grief at last found full vent. There among the saddles and harnesses and reins and hay and horsedung and cowdung he wept. And only then did he remember the ferryman, Alec Dick, remembered his words. His face looked out at him from the hay and tanned leather,

13

bearded, high balding forehead ridged with veins, features weather-beaten with wind, water and whiskey, laughing. But there was another sound than that of his own sobbing. The bells were still pealing, ringing, singing. And only then did he again remember. It was New Year. She was a New Year's child. No. More than that. Much more than that. Across Ireland and Scotland and Wales and England the bells were ringing, singing, pealing out loud and clear. Across the countries of Europe and countries farther still and oceans and seas the bells, horns, voices, were ringing, singing, intoning, chanting. Because it was a new century. 'She is a child of a new century. For today, this day,' he said, talking to the mare and stroking her neck and nuzzling her some hay, 'is the first day of January, 1900.'

III

Summer came and went and winter came again, and so the first year of the century passed. The second brought great storms and floods which wrought havoc, flooding the city and surrounding countryside. Even in the middle of the island the thundering of the sea could be heard clearly, as if a tidal wave were about to crash over it. In the following year King Edward and Queen Alexandra visited the city for the ceremonial unveiling of a statue of Queen Victoria in front of the still uncompleted City Hall and the opening of the new hospital which was to be named after her, the Royal Victoria Hospital. He stood among the swaying, jostling crowds held back by rows of Royal Irish Constabulary. Being taller than most men, well over six feet, he could easily see the splendour and pageantry of the event as it unfolded. Elizabeth had refused to come. In some of her mannerisms being as though of a royal line herself, she found such occasions uninteresting. Besides, a pushing mass of bodies around her she found unpleasant and irksome. The photographs and the story in the evening *Telegraph* would be good enough, even though she had difficulty in reading and it was invariably John who would read things out to her.

May sat high on his shoulder, firmly clasped across the thighs by his left arm. Chuckling and tickling her cheek, he laughed as she laughed, was quiet when she was quiet, moved his bulk through the crowd when she became restless, stopped again when she became still, held her tightly when she seemed to become anxious. In quiet tones he pointed out the various dignitaries, repeated the words softly as her child's voice attempted to frame utterance.

It had been like that since she had first left her mother's side and been placed in the cot. A man who rarely showed emotion to others, he was now a jealous guardian, some streak in his nature that had long lain hidden having now found release. By the cot he sat when she cried, gently stroking her forehead and wiping her face. In the night it was he who would nurse her rather than Elizabeth when she was fretful in sleep. On her tumbling from the cot and crawling along the

15

floor, he would crawl with her, pushing obstacles out of the way with an indifference to household order so that practically every day the furniture had to be replaced or rearranged, a task accompanied by an angry scolding from either his wife or Jenny which went unheard. He insisted on Elizabeth breastfeeding the child herself, as she had not done with the others. And, after some initial refusals, she did so with a wondering smile, failing to recall at any time in the past her husband insisting on anything. Jenny having sent a jug crashing to the floor, he was on his knees for hours searching for the minutest speck that could inflict injury. Across the fields he carried her, talking and naming the things around them as she struggled with her growing curiosity, his faithful Shadow trotting in front sniffing amongst grass and hedgerows, the dog a stray that had followed John from a village several miles inland and had been adopted by him and so named. Along the shoreline he carried her with the pebbles and shingle crackling underfoot to play at building sandcastles under a hot sun. In the snow too he would build figures for her with smiling funny faces. And sometimes he would take her to the clifftops where, clasped tight, she would call to the wind, imitating the gulls and various seabirds as they dived and soared beneath them, kiiiyaaa kiiiyaaa scceeeheee sceeeheee kiiiyaaa. And sometimes they would be silent watching the heaving breakers and the greenflecked spume a prism of spinning colours, the landmass of Scotland and the Isle of Man jutting towards them. On occasions too, when visiting one of his farmhands' cottages near the cliffs and the wind being rough, he would sit with her by the lamp at the window telling her stories, saying that the lamp in the window was for the sailors out at sea so that they would know not to steer their ships too close to the rocks, his own eyes searching hers as she listened. And it was at such moments as these that he recalled his firstborn whose features in memory still stood out clearly. But now in his innermost being there was a feeling almost resembling peace. Baptism and burial service had been so close together as to seem inextricably bound up with one another. Elizabeth had cried and been silent but there had been May's demands to be fussed over and fed. They stood together in church amongst the solemn yet smiling faces, in his heart a tremulous emotion as though he had made a pact with the unknown and unknowable.

For now John Gordon's life was full. Or as full as he could ever possibly imagine it to be. But it was to be fuller still, though this time he did not recall the ferryman's words on that Christmas Eve. Seven years after May, another child was born, another son. 'A fighter if iver there was one, so he is. He came out of the womb wi' his wee fists up and bashing away like he was ready till take on the whole world, his mother included,' said the midwife as she finished her work with John again standing at the bedside. 'Ready fer any Goliath that one is, I'm telling ye.' And so amused had he and his wife been at her remark that they decided to call him David.

John Gordon knew that others thought him strange, or a bit odd, or not quite right in his mind. Indeed, in some way he was equivalent to being the village idiot. And if his status in life had been lower than what it was, that is probably what he would have been. That thought often came to his mind, and it amused him. Yet he also knew that everyone had more good words to say about him than bad, and, like the village idiot, there was a place for him among them.

His life was full yet he had no hand in either its creating or shaping, save for his marriage. An only child, he'd been sent to a boarding-school and college in the city, this being his father's wish, a stern-eyed figure who tolerated no other will but his own. After the latter's death his mother had returned to Belfast where she originally belonged, taking a small flat where he sometimes visited her. Inheriting everything, the farm, several hundred acres on the mainland with cattle and sheep and some property in Larne, mostly workers' cottages, he had left college to return to the farm in order to decide what to do. But, as the years passed, no decision was ever reached. Within a year he knew that he wasn't a farmer, nor did the other traditional calling of the island, the sea, appeal to him either. And, looking back upon his education, he could think of no one subject which engendered a particular interest within him. The working of the farm was taken over by the farmhands. The cattle and sheep on the mainland were gradually sold off and the land rented out. And the cottages were sold to those who occupied them for next to nothing. He wasn't rich, but very comfortably off. A gentleman farmer is John Gordon, some said, though to him this title sounded too grand.

The years following his father's death were years of a helpless and hopeless frustration of not knowing what he was or what he wanted to do, a frustration which at the time had found an outlet in the occasional few days' drinking bout during which his sober and saturnine appearance altered hardly at all despite aspects of the comic or ridiculous, such as the time he and Alec Dick and a farmhand walked through the night driving half-a-dozen cattle to the market in Ballymena, but instead of taking them to the market herded them into a bar and demanded the equivalent in whiskey, which they got. But such times were rare and the money invested for him by the bank was more than sufficient for his wants and needs. He was a man who lived mostly within himself, within his own mind and imagination and emotions. But, just as he could not put his hand to anything

17

in a skilful manner, he couldn't put his mind or imagination to anything either. His life was a gift, and the older he became the more he knew it. His wife Elizabeth he married for her beauty. A girl of rare energy and intelligence and the bearing of majesty as well, un-educated, a child of penniless parents, she was nevertheless sought after by many. She married him, he knew, for his money and the place he could give her in the world. He'd had no illusion about that. But, gradually, puzzled and in a whimsical way, he began to understand that she had fallen in love with him, that she loved him deeply. My child, she would say as they lay together in each other's arms, my big helpless hopeless child. Later, instinct told him that she had taken over the managing of everything, but, as she allowed him to wander through his mind and imagination at will and did not disturb him, he did not disturb her. Not even when she went off on lengthy trips to Belfast or Dublin, Edinburgh or Liverpool, with Jenny as a travelling companion, invariably returning with expensive clothes, but, more particularly, jewellery, which, she announced with pride, she bought for practically nothing in some pawnshop. This also amused him, this quirk of hers haunting pawnshops for whatever piece of jewellery took her fancy, and he put it down to her poverty-stricken girlhood. That she might have had a discreet love affair on such excursions never entered his thoughts.

And just such an excursion she was making now, in the late summer of 1907, leaving to spend a week in Dublin. He drove her and Jenny into Whitehead in the trap and kissed her awkwardly at the station. She was a tall imposing woman of forty-two, in full bloom, nine years his junior, nearly.

'Now take care of things while I'm away, John. And see that the young one is attended to.'

'Yes, Elizabeth,' he said, also standing awkwardly, hat in hand. 'I'll do that. And have a nice time in Dublin.'

'I'm sure I will.'

Returning to the farm he whiled away an hour leafing through some books, the poems of Ferguson, Allingham, Drennan, the novels of Scott and Dickens, in the room used by his wife who attended to daily business with the help of a retired schoolteacher. The room held a good library, but books could not hold his mind either. She, Elizabeth, would be crossing Belfast now to the Great Northern Railway for the train to Dublin. Elizabeth he had always called her, a formal manner of address he used with everyone else. There were no endearments between them. And she in turn had adopted this formality, as if in respect.

The sound of crying and hammering brought him to the cot where his new son lay. A woman was already there, another of his farmhands' wives. He peered curiously at it as the tiny hands battered against wood, then returned to his chair. This child did not hold him as May had done, and still did. Nor did the others. Idly his mind roved over them. Dalton, his face as sombre and withdrawn as his own, but with something else, something else he could not identify. Jack with his round merry face and big hands that worked with uncanny efficiency at anything, a farmer and boatman both before he was into his teens. This last one in the cot yet to be formed, shaped. And May, quick and alive, a tomboy already, with her hair a sheen like burnished copper. Sometimes before bed at night he and Elizabeth would talk of them. 'And which one of them will bring out the big child in you?' she would ask, leaning towards him across the range where he sat with his nightcap of hot whiskey in his hand. 'Perhaps not these ones, but in some future generation.' And he would smile and say nothing.

May. Always May. Clambering into the trap again he set off to Brown's Bay at the extreme end of the island, to the little school at the sands from where he would fetch her home. Mid-September, the hawthorn was in an abundance of berries. Soon October would come bringing the winter gales that would last until spring. Yes. His life had been a gift. Everything. Finding Elizabeth in Larne, a pauper's child with that beautiful coppery hair which May had inherited, and bringing her home to the island.

He brought the trap to a stop with a clicking sound of throat and reins. Out beyond the Maidens a battleship and escorts made their passage northwards, the heavy ironclads with their guns in a neutral position reminding him of chivalry and knights, horses and riders clad against a tempest of lances and arrows. War. But now in peace making their way to one of the huge naval anchorages in the north of Scotland.

A gift, he who had done nothing. Except for that searing intensity that had been young John, the firstborn of the early days of their marriage, dying still a boy. Or a young man? In the experience of life, where was the dividing line? And then, John a solitary child, ten years later Dalton had come, and close on eighteen months after that, Jack. And now May and David.

A gift except for that uncomfortable feeling which lay within him still, that he had given nothing to life, had done nothing, had had no real vocation, no real interest, as though life itself, here with him, was no more than a mere passing phantasy, phantom. Inheritance, family and all had been given. And perhaps that was why, he mused, sending the mare and trap clipping down the hill towards the expanse of Brown's Bay which looked out to the channel, Scotland, the North Sea and the Atlantic, the Irish Sea, that turbulent meeting of the

19

waters, perhaps that was the reason for the feeling that lay inside him, the feeling that he would not live out his full three-score years and ten. Even where the badger people were concerned, the foxes and the hares and the seabirds and all the creatures wild whose foraging was but struggle, his foraging had had but little tholing.

IV

'And what did the badger people do?'

'They went home.'

'Home?'

'Home.'

'How did they go home?'

'They just stopped barking and yapping and fighting and went back intil their dens. There was some quare fur flying, I'm telling ye.'

'And what did daddy do?'

'He went home too.'

'And they listened to him? To what he told them?'

'They must've done, mustn't they? Elsewise why would they've just stopped scrapping like divils and go home quiet like they did? They must've knew what he was saying till them.'

Sitting on a fence, May tried to think very hard. The world was full of wonders. And the latest wonder was this story about the badger people. She tried to think harder still.

'It's true what I'm telling ye. Didn't I see it wi' my own eyes?'

'Tell me the story again.'

Joe Jackson scratched the stubble of his chin and looked down the large field to one corner where there was a broad uneven patch of land which had lain uncultivated for years, then back towards the flushed young face which was gazing at him intently. If someone had told him the story he doubted if he would have believed it himself. But it was true, he had seen it happen. Returning home one wintry night across the fields he'd been drawn by the sound of furious fighting. At first he thought it was dogs, but there on the edge of the patch were two large badgers tearing into one another, whether over a bit of territory or mate he didn't know. But more than that. Close to them stood John Gordon, clad only in a nightshirt with an overcoat draped across his shoulders, a stormlamp in one hand and his walking stick in the other, talking to them in a normal voice saying that he hadn't given them this land to squabble over and would they stop this nonsense and go

21

home quietly. The fuss had continued for another minute or two before the badgers suddenly ceased, looked at him, then made back to their dens. His employer hadn't seen him, and he'd stood watching him stride back towards the farmhouse before continuing across the fields, thinking that he himself wouldn't have tried to interrupt two badgers in a fight in case either or both made a lunge at him. But then, that was John Gordon's way. The patch was private to the 'badger people', as John Gordon called them, and no one was allowed to disturb it. In fact, no one was allowed to disturb any of the wild creatures on his land, and any hunter found on it was to be ordered off. The dogs and cats of the farm will take care of any vermin, he'd told his hands, and what nature does is its own business. But there'll be no shooting on my land. And that's the way it had been since Joe had started working on the farm some half dozen years before. And even when he wanted some game he thought it advisable to go elsewhere.

Chewing on a blade of grass he finished the story a second time, idly thinking of his employer's odd nature, which was often the subject of conversation between him and his wife Jenny. Abruptly he asked: 'And when's yer ma coming back?'

'Mammy? I don't know. She's in Dublin.'

'I know she's in Dublin. But she was supposed till be back three days ago,' replied Joe, now beginning to feel disgruntled as he didn't like his wife being away too long. Still in his early twenties and not married long, he didn't relish the feeling of going back to an empty cottage yet another night. And the trouble wi' yer ma, he thought, glancing at the thoughtful young face and hair shining in the afternoon sun, when she says she'll be back in a week ye wouldn't know if she means it'll be this year or next. It's a wonder yer da doesn't ask her what she's been up till.

'Can I see the badger people?'

'I don't know about that. They don't exactly come out when I talk to them,' said Joe, still thinking of Jenny and a lonely homegoing. 'Maybe ye should ask yer oul' fella.'

For several minutes they were silent, Joe alternately wondering of Jenny's whereabouts and of work on the farm. He tried to think of Dublin, imagining it to be something like Belfast which he had only visited once, and that quite recently. But all the bustle and activity and clanking and clattering of the newly electrified trams had unnerved him and he was more than glad to board the train for the return journey to the island. He didn't like leaving the island, even the simple journey across Larne Lough to the mainland, which he sometimes had to make with his employer. Like most people born and bred in Islandmagee he felt himself to belong to a race apart, and when away from the island to be among foreigners. And those who

22

came to settle from outside, like John Gordon's wife, were often treated with a suspicious grudging acceptance for years before finally being considered natural members of the community. And then there were the riots in Belfast which often happened and which, for Joe, seemed to explode without warning. It all had to do with Dublin and the Nationalists and the Home Rule idea which was talked about in Parliament, something which he didn't understand much about though enough to know he didn't want it. To be ruled from Dublin, by a people he didn't know and whose political and religious inclinations were so different from his own, was wrong. He was a Presbyterian and Unionist, London was the centre of a great empire, life on the island passed peacefully and undisturbed, life in Ireland was peaceful except for a few mischiefmongers, and that is the way things should continue. Turning his mind to the farm, he thought about the remaining hay to be brought in and the fences and timbers of some of the outhouses needing to be repaired and strengthened before the winter gales set in. There'd be some cattle to single out for the slaughterman who would be coming in a few days, a task in which Joe assisted and accepted as a natural part of farm life though, he thought with an amused grin, it was a time when John Gordon went off on some business or other, he who had so little business to do. But that was changing now, soon the slaughterman would do his rounds no more because the cattle were being taken to the slaughterhouses on the mainland. Settled in his ways at an early age, change irked Joe, and again his thoughts turned to the prolonged absence of Jenny.

'So ye don't know when yer ma'll be back?'

May shook her head. 'No. But daddy says she might be back tomorrow.'

'He said that yesterday and the day before yesterday.'

'Well, she hasn't been away very very long,' said May, musing and trying to think how long her mother had been away. Was it ages or was it not ages? Sometimes time was very long and sometimes it wasn't. Was a week a very long time? But Joe had said her mother had been away longer than a week.

'Too long if ye ask me. Far too long,' said Joe, still leaning against the fence before abruptly standing upright. 'If yer da's looking for me, tell him I'm bringing in the last of the hay afore the weather turns bad,' muttering under his breath that that was about the only time John Gordon remembered he had a farm, when he suddenly started wondering what his hands were doing.

May watched as he backed a horse between the shafts of a cart and reined up, then left the yard and went down the loanan towards the outer fields, scattering a flock of loudly clucking hens. About to run after him and jump onto the cart, she checked herself. It was great fun helping to bring in the hay, particularly the journey back when she could sit at the very top with the cart swaying and bumping along the rutted lanes. She was as high as the hedges then, and could smack the hawthorn berries with a stick. But she'd done that so many times before. Besides, she understood Joe was very cross about her mother being away so long with Jenny, and he mightn't be very nice to talk to. He mightn't even allow her on the cart, saying that her father wouldn't let him. Which was sometimes true, thought May, as her father often stopped her from doing exciting things. Yet she liked him best. He was very close to her, and would always come when she wanted him to. She liked going with him to see things, to the city and other places in the country, and they would talk a lot together. But for all their talking, he seemed to her to be so quiet. Not like her mother who was always scolding her and telling her what do to and saying she should have been born a boy because she didn't behave like a little girl and was more of a tomboy. But then her mother was always telling everybody what to do. And she didn't understand that it was more interesting to climb trees than play with dolls, or go rock-jumping at the bottom of the cliffs or swing round the safety bars of the Gobbins' Path where people came from Belfast to walk on Sundays. There the sea crashed just beneath her, and she could cry and call to the seabirds that dived and swooped around her as if in answer.

Suddenly bored, May jumped down from the fence and wandered round the outbuildings, wondering what to do as there were hours yet before bedtime. She couldn't feed the hens with Granny Hopkins because that wasn't until evening. The story of the badger people still lingered in her mind and she thought of going to see if they would talk to her. But what if they wouldn't even come out? Or should she go and see the donkey that was tethered in the top field? Of all the animals surrounding her, that was her favourite. And it knew it was her favourite, because she often went to feed it, plucking grass or bringing sugar and bits of cake from the kitchen to see what it liked most. Better than any watchdog, her father had said one day as they patted and stroked it. No one puts a foot in these fields but it brays so loud you can hear it in the house. And it was true, she often heard it in her room under the thatch, even at night. Or should she go and find her father and they could go down to the sands together to play with the coloured stones and pebbles? What was the big word he'd told her? A mosaic? Yes. Making beautiful patterns in the sand with all the colours, the sun and the different light from the sea making them glint and sparkle with flecks of spray floating over them. And then the tide would come in and break them up, but not before making still more patterns. She was always very happy doing that with her father. But he always seemed to make more beautiful patterns than she did, no matter how hard she tried. She would watch his large hands with long unmarked fingers slowly push the pebbles into place, bright and gleaming like the rings he wore. He was slower than she was, but somehow finished first. And there would be a Celtic cross, or an ordinary cross, or a flag, or a fish, or a mermaid, or a starry sky, as though the sand itself had just turned it up. And once when she told her mother about their games her mother had laughed and said her father was a dreamer. And when she asked what do dreamers do, her mother, after what seemed a long while, had shrugged her shoulders and said that what can they do but dream? And May, persisting, had said can't dreams be beautiful and isn't that good, only to find herself and the subject dismissed.

Or should she go to see her new brother David in his cot beside the range? But, then, all he ever did was to sleep or yell, the latter particularly when she wakened him. And besides, she was much too old to play with babies.

Across the fields the mare galloped, mane and tail streaming behind it. She hadn't noticed it being unharnessed from the trap when her father had brought her home from school. But that meant her mother wasn't expected home today either, which would make Joe even more cross and suddenly she was glad she hadn't gone with him. Again her thoughts turned to her mother who was in Dublin. Or was she back in Belfast already? Because sometimes her mother went to the city and stayed in an hotel rather than taking the train back home at night. Wandering into a barn, she sat on one of the shafts of the trap, winding straw round her fingers. Would she, May, like to go and stay in the city? Already she'd been several times with her father. They'd gone to a picturehouse, a playhouse, had had their photographs taken together. And all the ladies seemed very glamorous in their beautiful dresses and coats and hats. Like her mother when she dressed up. It was exciting to be in the city. But it was frightening too because often the people there fought, and fought with the police. Another riot, her father had said, hastily bustling her away from a great crowd of shouting people. And when she'd asked what they were fighting about he just shook his head and said nothing.

Her mother. She didn't seem to love her mother very much, just as her mother didn't seem to bother with her except when she was angry. Particularly the time, just a few weeks ago after another visit to Belfast, when she'd tried to dress up in her mother's clothes to play at being a lady. She'd had to roll the skirt up at the top to shorten it, and the blouse was much too big. And she couldn't get the earrings to stay in her ears properly. But as she stood in front of the mirror she thought she looked quite nice. And beside her stood a man with dark hair and a curling moustache like one of the men she'd seen in the playhouse.

Through the barn door she could see the field where the mare still galloped friskily. Wasn't it time she learned to ride a horse? But she wasn't old enough yet, her father said when she asked him, and might risk a bad fall. And then he would gently chide her about not attending to her schoolbooks which didn't hold her attention. Besides, her mother didn't seem to mind whether she went to school or not.

Or should she go to see Sheila Hawkins who lived on the next farm and who was her friend? But Sheila didn't seem to be interested in the things she was interested in, though sometimes she would play at being nurses or actresses just because her friend wanted to.

And suddenly May was bored again. Eager to do something, her active mind leaping from subject to subject, there seemed to be so many things to do yet nothing she really wanted to do.

Suddenly high-spirited laughter spilled from her. 'Monkey Gordon! Monkey Gordon!'

Distraction had come in the shape of her brother Jack who had just appeared at the barn door and, at her exclamation, made a funny face at her and flapped his arms as though he were swinging from a tree.

'Monkey Gordon.'

'I'll monkey you, Mistress May.'

'And what does it mean when you'll monkey me?' asked May, sticking her tongue out at her brother's scowl.

'I'll feed you to some lions.'

'But there aren't any lions in Islandmagee.'

'Then I'll feed you to something else.'

May laughed again. She'd given him that nickname after seeing him climb the cliffs at the Gobbins. Short and square with huge hands and feet, he really had been like a monkey as he went swiftly up the rockface.

She watched as he rummaged in a sack in the loft above her, hearing the clinking of metal. 'What are you doing?'

'It's none of your business, Mistress May.'

Her mood ephemeral, she suddenly became very serious. She liked it when Jack called her Mistress May. And for all his scowls and making faces she knew he was only playing and was very warm towards her. Even though he was nearly twice her age he accepted her as his equal. Not like her other brother Dalton who was so distant that he hardly seemed to notice her. And though she was already nearly as tall as Jack, Dalton towered above her and was nearly as tall as her father even though she knew her brothers were almost the same age. Granny Hopkins called her 'little mistress', and sometimes her mother did too.

Jack clambered down from the loft and took a pair of oars that were

26

standing in a corner of the barn. In his other hand he held two rowlocks.

Quickly May jumped up. 'Can I go too? Say yes! Please say yes!'

'Well, you know what da'll say if I let you.'

'But he won't find out.'

'And what if he does? You know he gave me a quare talking till the last time when I let you come out in the boat.'

It was true. They had stood in the room with the bookshelves, father sitting behind the desk telling Jack it had been stupid and dangerous to take May out in the boat with him. Though his voice hadn't been raised, his face showed that he was very angry. And Jack was trying to explain, saying there'd been nothing to be afraid of. It was just that a wind had sprung up all of a sudden as the tide turned and had made the rowing back much slower, and weren't they back safe with a dozen good fresh herring for the kitchen. May had patiently listened to the arguing voices, so different, her father's formal and slow as always with Jack speaking more like one of the farmhands, quick and ready and rough. And she'd taken Jack's part, saying it hadn't been dangerous and she wasn't at all frightened even though she secretly had been, especially when the boat had been lifted out of the water and had fallen back with a loud smack with the waves tumbling across the bow. It had been dark when they'd returned, May attired in a heavy pullover and a pair of Jack's trousers, old clothes kept dry in the boathouse for such emergencies as this when soaked with seawater. Afterwards, with Jack dismissed, her father had talked to her quietly, showing her a photograph and telling her of a brother who had been drowned at sea. But as she looked at the photograph all she could see was the greenwhite water splashing on every side of her and feel the thrill as the shore crept closer.

'What are you going out in the boat for?'

'To see if there's any lobsters in the pots.'

'Oh! I've never done that!'

'And what happens if I feed you till the lobsters,' said Jack with a grin. 'The big ones'll bite yer head off and what'll da say when his Mistress May has no head?'

Elated, responding to his humour, May took his arm. He was going to allow her to go with him. 'Shall I help you to carry an oar?'

Jack shook his head. 'We'd better not be seen going tillgether. You take the other way round and I'll meet you at the rocking stone. I'll bring the boat across the bay.' He paused in the doorway. 'And if you see da ye'd better tell him you're doing something else.'

'I'll tell him I'm going to feed the donkey. Or to see Sheila Hawkins.'

With Jack gone, May stayed in the barn trying to count five

27

minutes on her fingers and hoping no one else would find her. Skipping across the fields she was soon at the rocking stone at the eastern side of Brown's Bay, a tall column of rock strangely balanced upright at the narrow end which was said to sway with the wind but never fall, though she had never seen it do that. It was a bit like the dolmen on the road above the farm, a massive slab of stone balanced across two others where, years and years and years ago and so many years it was difficult to think about, people were sacrificed like in a church. That was one of the stories old Granda Hopkins had told her. Sacrifice. That was another of those big words she didn't understand. And when she asked the old man to explain it, he didn't seem to know what it meant either. The Druid's Altar, the stones were called.

She watched as a steamer rounded the point of the bay, leaving Larne harbour. Farther out to sea were other ships, some with sails. A smaller sail was coming across the bay. Jack. It was pulled down as the boat nudged in among the shingle. Jumping in, she watched her brother's thickset shoulders and arms pulling on the oars as she sat opposite him, his figure outlined against the sun as it fell back inland. On the coast to the north some of the glens were already in shadow, and she shivered.

'Will we be back before dark?'

'Long before that. We'll only be out about half an hour. And ye'd better put that coat on ye if it's getting cold.'

'Where are we going?'

'We're just staying inshore there along by the rocks. That's where ye'll find the lobsters. Or out there by the Maidens. But that's too far to go today.'

The heavy coat engulfing her, May's mind wandered in a dreamy warmth. Only her face was cold and flushed as the air became chillier, the slight breeze ruffling her hair across her shoulders. In her ears was the soft chuckling sound of the water as boat and oars moved steadily over the smooth surface and, higher up, the noise of gulls calling from the clifftops. It was almost like being in bed on a still night, curled up warm and snug beside her pet donkey that Granny Hopkins had made for her from an old patchwork quilt, the soft fresh air from the fields and the sea drifting through the window to bathe her face. 'Night, night, sleep tight, Don't let the bugs bite. If they do, give them a skite, And they won't bite tomorrow night.' The old woman's face leaned over the bed repeating her laughing rhyme, hands tucking in sheets and blankets. Of course, she knew that the elderly couple weren't really her grandparents, but they adopted her in that fashion and she liked sitting with them in the little cottage with the lamp burning in the window for the sailors, listening to their stories. And sometimes she slept there when her father allowed her to, and he

28

would come across the fields in the morning calling to her and saying—And where's my wee wild one? What was it like to be as old as Granny Hopkins? Would she be old like that one day? And would she remember all this?

Gently the boat rocked her dreamy somnolence, so gently that she didn't notice Jack ship oars and begin to pull up the first of the lobster pots, the craft drifting slightly with the ingoing tide.

And what had she felt like when she had dressed up as a lady? Strange. Already she felt emotions awash inside her that she didn't understand. The blouse was too big, yet she felt as though her body was changing shape to fit it. And it was changing. Her nipples were becoming bigger, for one thing. She would grow up to be like her mother, whom she sometimes saw naked when they bathed together. Not like Jack, also whom, by accident, she'd one day seen naked, washing himself down in the yard after working in the byre, with that thing hanging between his legs. She loved Jack. Sometimes he would grab her tightly in his big arms playing at being a monkey, saying that because she called him a monkey he was going to be one and crush her, and she would pretend to be frightened and try to wriggle free. And when her father took her in his arms she liked that too, but it was different. And their bodies were so different.

Like the flowing rippling water surrounding her lay the oncoming awareness of sexual sensual difference, an experience pricking the periphery of her being sending her swirling slowly in a yet unknown selfhood, the edges of unbeguiled innocence being washed away like sand as the tides of living carried her on to the awakening of a perhaps unwanted womanhood.

The furious clicking clacking aroused her, startled and afraid, and she cried out. Jack was laughing, his merry round face flushed red, as he held the big lobster in the air then let it fall into the boat where it splattered across the boards, claws nipping, digging, gouging into the wood.

'That gave ye a quare fright. Sleeping, were ye? Dreaming?'

May tried to laugh, though she could feel her heart still thumping. 'I wasn't really asleep. I only had my eyes closed.'

'Fibber. We've been round all the pots already and there wasn't a cheep out of ye. You're a good one to take out in the boat when there's work to be done.'

'I didn't mean to. Really,' said May, feeling very angry with herself for missing all the fun. 'How many did we get?'

'Seven. And seven good ones too.' Picking the lobster up between thumb and forefinger, he examined it. 'He's a big one, this one. He'll fair steam in the pot when it's boiling. Steam red. And so ye will, my lovely,' he added, dropping it into a sack beside him which moved and

29

clicked. 'Pinch away together there. Soon there'll be no more pinching for any of yous.'

'What are you going to do with them?'

'Give a couple to the kitchen. And one of the hotels in Larne'll give me a shilling or two for the others.'

'Do they really steam red?'

'When the pot's boiling and they're still alive, they do.'

'Alive?'

'Aye. Alive. That's the way to cook them.'

May tried to think. 'But that's horrible.'

But the boat had already gained the shore, Jack standing with one foot in the shingle. 'Out, Mistress May. And away home. And don't tell da. If he asks anything about me tell him ye saw me a few hours back going till the boathouse and I'll be home about dark.'

May waited while he pulled the sail up and made back across the bay where he housed the boat, then went back over the fields, pausing for a few minutes to stroke the donkey and give it some grass. Home just in time for supper, she gave her father a story of the day's adventures, omitting the boat trip, as Granny Hopkins served the meal as she always did when her mother and Jenny were absent. In bed she felt restless, having slept in the afternoon. By the window she watched her father and Granny leave. He would walk her home before returning to bed. With a quilt pulled over her nightdress she stood there as darkness crept across the island blurring all from sight. Then the moon appeared between ragged clouds showing up the silhouettes of the outbuildings and the orchard and cattle standing motionless in the fields. In a little while a braying came over the still air to mark someone afoot, and she smiled. It was Jack. Sack in hand and oars over his shoulder, he passed the bottom of the yard towards the barn.

Yes. If ever she were as old as Granny Hopkins she would remember all this, always remember. Yes. It would always be like this, forever be like this. Forever the island, forever the island of herself, would be like this, would remain. Would remain like the rocks and the cliffs and the fields and the waves whispering to her from the shore and all the seabirds and the sea the sea the sea and scceeeheee scceeeheee kiiiyaaa kiiiyaaa scceeeheee May called, the sound being as though the seabirds had awakened in the night to send the fluttering of their wings and their wild and plaintive cries through the otherwise silent farmhouse.

V

'And how's yer oul' da? He hasn't been this way fer nigh on a month or two.'

'Father is well.'

'And that new pup ye have? Ye're a quare pack, you Gordons, I'm telling ye. Any more of yer ma and da's oul' nonsense ye'll have a tribe to take over the island. David didn't they call him?'

'The child is well too.'

Pushing off from the harbour wall and splashing the oars Alec Dick tried to hide a grin and, turning towards the grizzled elderly face of another of his passengers, asked: 'And what do you say, Len Hopkins? You work for him, don't ye?'

A smile creased the stubbly mouth. 'Ach, sure he's a good soul. And ye know that yerself. There's none the bad in John Gordon.'

'Him that's hardly done a hand's turn in his life? Have a titter of wit. And sure you wi' yer kind heart'd say the oul' divil himself has a good soul.'

'And maybe he has fer all we know. Isn't he a fallen angel?'

'Some life this when even the angels fall. Did he have a drop of whiskey on him at the time, d'ye think?' Now openly laughing, Alec turned to yet another figure in the boat. 'And speaking of the divil, what about yerself, Bertie Knox? I s'pose ye've been away blowing up half of Ireland again.'

'Aye. There was one or two wee jobs round Lough Neagh way.'

'Well I hope ye've none of the stuff wi' ye. 'Cause if ye blow up the boat I've none the money till pay fer another one. Not even fer an oul' engine and me that's getting tired rowing.'

Pausing midway to the island and lifting the oars from the water, Alec watched the steamer glide into Larne harbour before again surveying his passengers. It was a bright cool Saturday morning with little heat in the October sun rising behind him. Resuming work, and silence having fallen among them, he idly thought of the others. Len Hopkins, with a liveliness and wit that belied his some sixty years.

31

Bertie Knox who lived in an old Romany caravan on a patch of ground carefully tended with flowers and plants, his only companion an elderly mother though some said she was really his grandmother and there was a story to tell there. Hardly yet twenty, Alec thought, squinting at him, with the face of a boy and the frame of a man, a dynamiter. A quarryman and mineworker, his job was mostly in blasting rock and clay around the country. An expert, the saying was, handling the deadly charges as if like a kitten. And with a nature like the explosives he used, anger and belligerence bursting from his otherwise quiet manner without apparent reason, as Alec himself had once witnessed while drinking in a pub in Larne. Some men have strange callings, and momentarily Alec wondered how the other had learned this odd skill. Strange callings indeed. And close beside him was Dalton Gordon, growing up as fast as a weed with a nature even more silent, and brooding features that showed no trace of a boy and never really had. Perhaps they'd make a pair.

'I see ye have a stranger wi' ye,' Alec said, resuming his banter and addressing Dalton. 'Hardly an Islandmagee man.'

'He is a friend from Larne.'

'From Larne, ye say? And hardly Larne either by the sound of his tongue when I hear ye talking together.'

'No. I'm from Belfast. But now I live in Larne.'

'And yer name?'

'Samuel Ogilby.'

'Well, Samuel Ogilby, ye'll find the island a different place from Belfast. I hear all they do up there is take money out of each other's pockets so's an honest body can hardly get a living. Isn't that right, Len Hopkins?'

'Now how would I know that when I've niver been in the city in all my born days? And there'll hardly be the day when I'll want to go till it now, I'm sure.'

Alec snorted. 'Ye're a much travelled man, I see. But I wish the day would come when ye learn till agree wi' me instead of opposing my every word.' Pausing, he again addressed Samuel. 'Aye, taking money out of each other's pockets. The richer ones I mean, out of the pockets of those who have little. And wi' all these strikes of the weavers and now the carters and them up in Belfast rioting when some oul' politician stirs them up it's a wonder we don't have a revolution like in Russia a few years back.'

Len laughed. 'We'll hardly have that here.'

'And I often wonder why not,' Alec said, pulling in the oars as he reached the other side. 'C'mon, where's yer money? There's another lot waiting till be rowed across and now the sea's getting up. There'll be a storm before nightfall, I'm telling ye. In fair weather or foul

32

there's no rest for the ferryman. And maybe the only revolution that'll come is the day when I'll be rowing yous all 'cross hell.' Taking the proffered coins and slipping them into a little leather bag tied to his belt, he said to Dalton as he stepped from the boat: 'And tell that da of yours I hope that David one is the last of the pack. And a right rogue and rover he'll be, I'm sure.' But then, he thought, watching Dalton walk silently away as other passengers climbed in for the journey back to Larne, by the looks of that face ye have on ye he mightn't be as big a rogue as yerself.

'Sit down, Samuel.'

'Thank you, sir.'

'You also, Dalton.'

'Father.'

'Mmmm, yes. Dalton told me . . . mmm . . . you were coming to stay. For how long?'

'A week, father. We have a mid-term break.'

'Ah, yes. I'd forgotten. I must see Mrs Hopkins to arrange the spare room.'

'That isn't necessary, father. There are two beds in my room. Samuel can have the other one.'

'Of course. I hadn't thought of that,' said John Gordon, sitting behind the desk in the library, his hands fiddling with a pen and feeling that he must talk to the young faces in front of him though he couldn't quite think of what to say. There were days like this when his being seemed so sunk in lassitude, when life seemed so remote, and they were becoming more frequent. 'Well, I hope you enjoy your stay, young man.'

'I'm sure I shall, sir.'

'Ah, yes, Dalton,' John said, noticing his son staring at the great stag's head which hung in a niche in one corner of the room. It was something he'd often noticed before, as if the head held some strange fascination for the boy. 'You must tell Samuel the story of the stag's head.' Pausing, he continued: 'It came from a relative. A cousin. Who went to the Yukon. The gold rush, you understand. And he found enough gold to buy a great herd of deer and a farm. He sent this home before he died. An accident of some kind.'

'I'm sorry to hear that, sir,' replied Samuel, looking up at the head with its magnificent horns hanging in the shadowy recess.

'Yes. Just so.' The subject exhausted, John put the pen down and slipped on a pair of spectacles. It wasn't that he needed to. But they had a reassuring feeling, as though he could hide behind them.

'Alec Dick was asking after your health, father.'

'Yes, of course, Alec Dick. I've some business to do with Alec. I owe

33

him some money for the last batch of cattle he took over. In fact, I've business to do in Larne, so I'll be away most of the day.' His memory being jogged, he turned to Samuel. 'Which reminds me, young man, I must write to your father to thank him for allowing Dalton to stay with you during the week.'

'Oh, that's quite all right, sir. And father likes him to stay. And there's plenty of room now that my sister's gone to a hospital in Belfast to be a nurse.'

But Elizabeth had probably already done that, thought John, staring out through the window, as he seemed to recall her saying something about making a monthly payment to Mrs Ogilby because they couldn't expect her to feed a huge growing boy like Dalton for nothing.

'I was hoping we could go riding today, father.'

'Riding? Yes. And a lovely day for it. Can you ride, Samuel?'

'I've been on a horse once or twice, sir. But Dalton said he would teach me.'

'Good. Dalton's an excellent horseman.' It was true. Dalton was a fine horseman. Turning his head he again regarded his son, his thoughts drifting aimlessly, in his mind an image of horse and rider furiously galloping across the fields. But where Jack worked with animals and seemed to understand them, Dalton simply used them with a cold efficiency.

'Can we go then, father?'

'Yes. Take the two mares. They're in the bottom field. And by the way, the slaughterman's coming this morning. In fact, he's probably here already. And if I have business to do in Larne I'd better be off, so I'll walk with you and then go on to the ferry.'

'I'll fetch your coat, father.'

Standing up as Dalton left the room, John took off his spectacles and buttoned the jacket of his suit. 'And please feel free in the farmhouse, Samuel. Dalton tells me you're good at your studies. You may use the library if you wish.'

'Thank you, sir.'

'And Dalton,' he continued, as the latter returned with an overcoat and walking stick: 'Your mother is arriving home this evening. Please bring the trap to Whitehead at six o'clock. I'll take a train from Larne and join you there.'

From the window Samuel watched the two figures cross the yard, disappear behind some outbuildings and then reappear as they walked over the fields. He'd fallen in love with the farmhouse since the moment he had seen it that morning when he and Dalton had stood on the road looking down into the hollow which was like a tiny valley and at the large rambling structure that lay about a quarter way up the opposite slope, with stables and byres and other outbuildings and an orchard almost encircling it. Going through the orchard he noticed a walled garden beside it where vegetables and late roses still bloomed. Idly, his hands roamed over the volumes in the tall bookcases, but he was too excited to inspect what the library contained. Wandering across the flagged kitchen with the big range he paused beside the cot, then hastily retreated to the dining-room which looked out to the orchard when the child began to move and fret. Dalton had told him what it was like, but in Dalton's description he hadn't expected to be overwhelmed by this feeling of enchantment. Even the air seemed different. Everything seemed different from what he'd known in Belfast, or now knew in Larne, though quite how he didn't know. Perhaps one day he would. Because Dalton would invite him back again, he was sure of that. Though he was over two years younger they were each other's best friend. Retracing his steps to the library he sat at the desk, eagerly awaiting the clip-clopping sound of hoofs in the yard which would be Dalton bringing the horses to show him how to saddle up.

Though held fast, the bullock bellowed and stamped as if sensing its impending death. Quickly, efficiently, the slaughterman went to work and its life was stilled in an efflorescence of fiery crimson. In a stupor of trembling fascination May watched as the short bald figure slit and cut as he wielded the long blades, and then screamed.

Looking up from the carcass, Joe Jackson shouted: 'What are ye doing here, wee girl? Away back till the house wi' ye!'

As May screamed again she was suddenly spun round to look at the tall form of Dalton, legs encased in shiny boots and a thick cape hanging from his shoulders, who said softly: 'May. May.'

'I want Jack! I want Jack! I want daddy!'

Like a willow in the wind Dalton bended to her will and, smiling, said in an uncustomary voice: 'And where would ye find him?'

But Jack was already beside her, also drawn by her cries, and together they walked back to the yard. Lifted up to sit on a barrel, she felt her tears being dried.

'It's life,' Jack said tenderly, awkwardly, as he tried to explain. 'It's what we eat. And we have to eat.'

'Then I don't want to eat!'

'But we have to,' Jack repeated, not knowing what else to say.

'You won't let them do that to my donkey, will you?'

'No, no. The donkey'll be all right. It'll live for years and years.'

But May's attention was suddenly diverted. Standing in the yard was another person, a stranger, holding the reins of two horses. Pointing between her two brothers, she asked: 'Who's that?'

35

'A friend from Larne. He'll be staying a week,' said Dalton. 'We're going riding now.'

'Will you take me riding with you?'

It seemed a long time before Dalton answered. 'All right. You can ride in the saddle with me.'

She didn't notice Jack leaving, her thoughts now taken up with this stranger and the prospect of going riding. Being introduced, she gave him a quick impulsive kiss on the cheek, thinking he was much shorter than Dalton but very nice with his bright blue eyes and the way he smiled. Cantering out of the yard they crossed the fields to the northern tip of the island, May leaning back on Dalton's lap as the saddle jolted under her, his arms and cape around her as he held the reins, her body swaying as he occasionally leaned towards his friend to say something about horseriding. Cresting the hill sloping down to Brown's Bay they felt the full blast of the rising north wind.

'I think I'll gallop along the sands,' Dalton said as they halted close to the shore.

Samuel eased himself up from the saddle, feeling his thighs already stinging from this new exercise. 'I don't think I'll try that yet.'

'You'd better go back, then. It's too cold to stand about. And you can take May home.' Gently easing her to the ground, Dalton added: 'Ask Jack to unsaddle if you have any trouble.'

Samuel nodded, already used to such curt dismissals and aware of his friend's often solitary mood as the latter suddenly broke into a canter and then a gallop, the hoofs of the big black mare kicking up the sands. Jumping down from the horse he stood beside May. 'Shall I walk back with you?'

'That'll be nice. And I can show you my donkey on the way and we'll feed him some grass.'

At the top of the hill they stopped to look back, their faces flushed by the wind, May's hair tossing around her shoulders. Dalton was returning across the sands, still in full gallop, cape streaming behind him along the line of dark angry-seeming clouds that were scudding in from the horizon with the crashing whitetipped waves swirling and leaping at the mare's legs. 'Like Pegasus.'

'Pegasus? What's that?'

Samuel frowned. 'A great winged horse.'

'Silly! Horses don't have wings.'

Abruptly he laughed. 'I don't mean a real horse. It's a horse in a book. It's mythology.'

And yet another time May was cross with herself for not knowing such mysteries. Nor did she want to ask Samuel what 'mythology' meant because that would only show that she was the silly one and not him. 'Well then, let's feed the donkey. And then I'll show you the orchard and the garden and other things you haven't seen yet,' said May, trying to smile and feel superior to this stranger though really she still felt quite piqued.

Alone, Dalton galloped full tilt to-and-fro over the sands, body slightly raised from the saddle, thighs clasped to his charge whose vapoury breath fanned his face, hearing the mare sucking in air as he spurred her on to greater speed. Some twenty minutes later he slowed her down as they approached the middle of the bay, arriving at the other side at walking pace. From the boathouse he took cloths and a blanket, rubbing the sweat from the steaming horse before tossing the blanket across its back, then began to walk slowly along the edge of the tumbling surf staring out to sea and the darkening horizon. He was now in his thirteenth year. What was out there? And what was his future? Already he was thinking often about that and sensed that the island would not, could not, hold him. And with what people? Because for most of the people he met he had no feeling whatsoever. He and they passed by to all intents unacknowledged. They were only names to be forgotten in a moment. With his family it was different. Some emotion lay there. And with Samuel also, Samuel whom he'd befriended at school when the bully of the form had tried to pick a fight with him when he'd first arrived. But with Dalton's intervention it hadn't even begun. His feelings for Samuel he didn't understand either, he who was so aloof and withdrawn, except that there was something in the other's cheerful humorous nature that stirred him. May's screams came to mind and impassively he watched the beast die, shielding her in his arms. Russia and revolution. He'd heard the masters talk about it, had seen photographs in the newspapers, and later he and Samuel had talked about it. What did it mean? And the strikes Alec Dick had also mentioned. He'd stood listening to the speakers in Larne, standing on the opposite side of the street from the angry shouting crowd of men. What did that mean? And the talk of war in Ireland if ever there was Home Rule or the country divided.

His mother would be returning that evening. He was to be in Whitehead with the trap at six o'clock. As he recalled his father's words and turned back towards the boathouse he felt the quickening of his heart.

Back in the saddle he paused again at the water's edge, his mind still and seemingly void. At his word the mare broke into a trot as from the rocks and cliffs and sea far off came the first muted sounds of thunder.

'Fer dear sake, John. What the divil are ye talking about death fer?

And yer age is . . . What? Sure ye can't be many more years further on than me.'

'Fifty-one.'

'And that means ye've a good twenty years or more. Didn't the good Lord give us three score years and ten?'

'Not all of us, Alec. Not all of us.'

The two men sat in a pub in Larne in front of a roaring fire, the door rattling and, when another customer entered, admitting gusts of rain and sleet. Studying his companion's face as he sat, glass in hand and face reddened by the flames, Alec mentally noted that he himself was eight years younger, which surprised him. Probably because he looked the older of the two and always had done since their early days together. The unlined features in front of him were those of a man around forty, he would have judged. But then, that was undoubtedly due to the fact that where his life had been hard work since he was ten John Gordon's life had been . . . what? Not that he envied the other his years of ease. Indeed, it was quite the opposite, as he found the very idea of spending his days doing nothing unutterably boring.

'So you'll look in on the young ones if . . .' Still staring into the fire, John broke off in mid-sentence, as if uncertain as to what lay in his mind.

Alec grunted by way of explanation. 'If damn all. As fer looking in, of course. As Dan Hawkins and others would do. But what is there till look in fer? There's young May. But in a few years she'll be ready to fly the nest wi' a mate. And when that comes there'll be no stopping her. And Jack. Sure already he can work that farm of yours on his own. And that Dalton one I took over this morning, well . . .' Pausing, he signalled to the barman for another drink as the set angular impervious features of the last-named son drifted in his gaze, and shivered slightly despite the warmth of the fire. 'Well, as for him. I wouldn't like to be anyone who tries to cross him. He'd destroy ye in a wink and without a thought. You wouldn't know what to say till him in order to get an answer that has some feeling about it.'

'Yes. I've often wondered about him. About what I've given birth to in his nature. He even makes me feel that I . . . I don't exist.'

As the barman reached the glasses across, Alec grunted again. The hollowness of the other's voice meant that his words had the opposite effect of what he'd intended. Suddenly he said: 'As fer that last one, David. I hear he's been trying to pull the house down and him hardly a year born. I wouldn't be surprised if he's the joker of the pack. He'll probably learn till steal the eyes out of yer head and come back fer the blinkers.'

At this last quip John laughed quietly. 'What pack of devils are you trying to say a respectable man like me has spawned, Alec?'

38

'Sure there's a bit of the oul' divil in all of us, John,' Alec replied, about to add that in some rare ones there's more devil than human as he again thought of Dalton. Quickly he changed the subject, pleased to note his companion's mood and tone alter as they talked of their boisterous escapades in earlier days. Since they'd met in the pub in mid-afternoon John's melancholy brooding inwardness had been dampening Alec's spirits to the extent that he simply wished to leave, though he honourably couldn't just walk away from an old friend in his cups. About an hour later he looked up at the clock. 'I think it's about time till be leaving. By the sound of that wind it hasn't reached its peak yet and the mouth of that lough's a bad place when the sea's driving intil it the way it is now. And I've no wish to be stranded in Larne the night, that's fer certain.'

'Aye. Time to go,' John replied as he pulled on his coat. 'I'm taking the train to Whitehead. Elizabeth's arriving home and I've to be there at six o'clock.'

'Coming home, is she?' Alec grinned. 'Then ye'll find yer bed a bit warmer and just the night for it. Ye wouldn't try till tell me yer past a bit of the oul' sport, would ye?'

Parting in the middle of town, John walked to the station and climbed into a carriage of the waiting train. Five minutes later it puffed and hissed away from the platform, gathering speed as it ran parallel to the lough where waves on a full tide churned and spun as the gale swept across the surface. Pulling into Whitehead he noticed the train on the other platform leaving. Elizabeth had already arrived. Crossing over the footbridge he saw the mare and trap just outside the station entrance and, pausing to look over the crowd of milling passengers below, he picked out the figure of his wife. Dalton approached her and they embraced. Under the lamplight the two figures stood clasped in each other's arms, bodies entwined by flecks of rain and sleet, and as he watched a half-understood questioning began to probe his mind before he abruptly dismissed it and went down the steps.

'Elizabeth.'

'John.'

'You're overdue,' he said, kissing her lightly on the cheek.

'Oh, it was just a few things I wanted to buy and we had to stay in Belfast for a day or two.' She laughed. 'But I suppose Joe has been grumbling about Jenny being away as he always does.'

Yes. Jenny. He'd forgotten her. Hadn't noticed her from the bridge. She stood a few feet away beside a pile of cases and trunks. Turning back to Elizabeth he saw that she was still grasping Dalton around the waist.

'Well, we'd better load up. You're just in time. With this gale setting in it's a night for home and fire.'

39

Dalton, assisted by a porter, had the luggage strapped to the back of the trap within a few minutes. It could just take the four of them. Settling into the driving seat and squeezing beside Dalton, John set the mare trotting along the road, feeling the rain being driven against his face, half-listening to the chatter of the women behind him, pushing into the recesses of his mind and being those half-understood things which he knew his spirit did not dare nor have the strength to delve among.

It had been the happiest day of his life. It was a day he would always remember. Of that he was certain, thought Samuel, lying in bed listening to the storm crash across the island. The thunder, which had been ominously cracking out at sea during the afternoon and evening, was now bursting all around him. That was the only thing that disturbed his peace and made him feel a little afraid, because the farmhouse seemed so isolated, so all alone by itself. With May he had fed the donkey and strolled through the orchard and garden and, when Dalton had gone into Whitehead, had sat in the library leafing through some books though his mind had still been too excited with the newness of everything to be able to concentrate on reading. And the evening had passed in a medley of sounds and a blur of even newer faces. Dalton's mother had arrived home from Dublin. A tall beautiful woman who wore lots of bright jewellery. And Jenny and Joe Jackson who worked on the farm. Over dinner they all received presents. Even he did, a knitted winter scarf of different colours of green. And then to bed with the gale shrieking down the slopes of the hollow.

Turning, Samuel blinked his drowsy eyes, seeing his friend Dalton in bed at the other end of the room, a lamp fluttering at his elbow, a thick book in his hands. The Bible, Samuel knew, as he'd seen his friend reading it many times before. Yes. He loved this place. And perhaps one day he would come to live here. Momentarily the thought roused him, and calling out softly he said good-night, hearing the answering voice like an echo. Then, senses befuddled by the edges of sleep overtaking his consciousness, he thought he saw the door open and a woman appear. A beautiful woman in a nightdress and with a shawl over her shoulders, whose jewels sparkled even in the gloom as she crossed to his friend's bedside where they held each other for what seemed a long long time, the white bosom a silken sheen caught in the dully flickering lamp, then even the storm couldn't penetrate the depths of his slumber.

Scceeheee kiiiyaaa and May tossing in part-wakefulness in her smaller room against the gable wall at the other end of the farmhouse, the day's impressions flitting through the air in shadowy forms, her quilted donkey warm beside her and on the little table a pair of gleaming gold earrings all the way from Dublin she'd beseeched her mother for but wasn't allowed to wear yet because she would have to have her ears pierced first and the wailing singing of the hawthorn in the wind like a banshee and the mice scurrying in the thatch as the thunder rumbled with the window lit up by lightning. All the animals would be like that, like the mice, hiding from the tempest, the badger people she hadn't met yet and the cows and rabbits and the horses that had sent her bumping down to the sands at Brown's Bay. Because now all thoughts of the slaughterman had gone. And the donkey sheltering in the little copse beneath the trees where the rain can't get in. Samuel. Rosinante, he'd called the donkey, and when she'd asked him what that meant as she earnestly studied his face he'd just said it was a great romance. Which sounded nice because he knew so much more than she did. Samuel. A new face that had brought a new sense of self. Did she love him and what was love? It was all so strangely thrilling. His bright eyes and smile and the feeling of his hands that seemed so gentle and not like Jack's or Dalton's. Their faces drifted by, one by one, merged, broke apart again as a different unknown face shaped itself from the strands and splinters. And the storm still crackling across the island but couldn't touch her as she snuggled deeper in bed, for there was her dark horseman riding the sky on his beautiful blackwinged steed, riding the thunder and the lightning and the rain, riding the storm. Pegasus, protecting arms encircling her safe. All so much a lovely dream yet containing so many things the weight of passion and unendurable experience will one day obliterate from sense and memory, perhaps, perhaps, perhaps.

VI

May sat on an ancient stone wall which cut at an angle across the middle slopes of the Cave Hill—her father, Dalton and Samuel standing beside her. From their vantage point they commanded a sweeping view of Belfast Lough and the farther shore of County Down, the city itself lying just below them backed by a semi-circle of hills with the river Lagan flowing into the lough slicing it neatly in two. Still farther away over the undulating pastures of Down the Mourne Mountains could be seen, some of the peaks projecting through mist and cloudbanks. Beneath them they could also see the docks, harbour basins and channels and the great shipyards of Harland & Wolff which straddled Queen's Island and jutted into the lough in launching ramps and which, to May, seemed like long fingers trying to grasp the water. Dozens of ships lay moored or berthed alongside the various quays while others, still in the process of being built, towered above them from their platforms on land swathed in a cocoon of spidery scaffolding. Seaward towards the mouth of the lough other ships lay at anchor dwarfing several tugs which squatted on the surface, their blunt bows turned towards the shipyards. It was an event which her father had promised to bring her to Belfast to see, the launching of the newest and greatest ship in the world. Indestructible, they say, her father had told her as both pored over the newspaper as they sat beside the range. And then, despite her own excited pleadings to be taken to see it, she'd noticed the prolonged frown on his face as though he were thinking of something quite different.

The day had all the appearances of being an annual holiday. The lower and middle slopes of the hill were thronged with people, and she could see other figures standing on the craggy rock face right at the top. Most of them were in their Sunday clothes, the women and girls in bright dresses and costumes and the men in suits and ties, though some were still in working dress, having just come off the last shift in factory, timberyard or quarry. And there were bands too. From the direction of the Castle which snuggled against the hillside in turrets and battlements and courtyards and coloured windows came the sound of a marching tune. Taking the telescope from her father's hand she peered through it, the immense liner leaping to her eye as she focused the instrument. Traversing it this way and that, she inspected the crowds milling around the shipyard and yet other spectators who had found vantage points on the opposite hills.

'Well, May, it's a grand sight, isn't it?'

Looking up into Samuel's face, she asked: 'When will it be launched?'

'Very soon now, I should think,' he answered, consulting a watch. 'In about half an hour.'

'Have you seen ships being launched before?'

'Many times. And it's always like this. I mean, with all these people waiting to see it coming down the slipway.'

'Yes. I thought it looked like a holiday.'

'And why not? I'm sure many of the men here helped to build it. So why not come and see their work being put into the water?'

May nodded. When she made something good she felt proud, so why not other older people too? Just like the times with Granny Hopkins when she'd learned to crochet a shawl or make a patchwork quilt, things which were often made and given to poorer people at Christmas. Her thoughts changing course, she asked: 'Where have daddy and Dalton gone?'

'Just for a walk. I think they want to talk about something.'

Silent again, May tried to nod very wisely, and then started wondering what her father and brother were talking about. Since Dalton had left school months ago she'd noticed the two talking together several times. And it wasn't that they were talking about the farm because Dalton didn't do any work on the farm at all. Mostly he stayed in his room, and she only saw him when he occasionally came down to dinner, or went walking with father or clattering out of the yard on horseback. He was very grown-up now, nearly seventeen. But then, she was growing up too. She was eleven. Soon she would be as old as him.

Sitting quietly she tried to think about the last few years, but they seemed to have passed in a blur of ice and snow and sunshine as winter followed summer and then it was winter again, though the daily rhythm of the island and the farm seemingly passed in carefully measured steps interspaced by the rituals of Easter, Christmas and New Year. In the little school at Brown's Bay she tried hard to study her books, but there was always that wild urge within her when she heard the rocks and cliffs and seabirds calling, and she would slip away only to be later quietly admonished by her father when the

43

schoolmaster complained of her absence. Two great events were lodged in her mind. The time when the old king died and a new king had been proclaimed and everywhere there'd been a great celebration. King George. And the other time when she'd discovered that she had a real grandmother who lived in Belfast and had been taken to visit her. She had wanted to stay but wasn't allowed to because of all the fighting going on in the city. Last night was the first occasion she had stayed, and she would be staying tonight also, with her father going to a nearby hotel. And she felt sure it was the old lady's insistence which had given her this measure of freedom and was pleased, because now she felt spiteful and angry at her father who stopped her from doing so many things though she loved him and didn't want to feel that way.

Dreamily her gaze wandered over the crowds of people which had now grown even larger, some standing in groups, others in pairs. Lilting music still floated in the air and a gang of boys were yelling and kicking a ball between them. A little way down the slope and to one side a solitary figure lay lolled in the grass, hands clasped behind his head, and briefly she took in the thick mass of dark hair with a reddish tinge and the fine profile she would have thought was that of a girl had it not been for his clothes.

'There she goes!'

It was her father's voice, who had returned with Dalton and again stood beside her just as a tremendous cheer erupted from the throng and reverberated across the hillside.

With the telescope to her eye she watched as the great ship slowly, so slowly it hardly seemed to be moving at all, began to alter its position against the background of gantries and cranes, with the lines of its deck and superstructure changing shape also. Then it met the water with a tremendous surge of foamy whiteness as it plunged deep into the lough, so deep that for a moment May thought it was going to sink. But no. High in the water it floated with the tugs already swarming around it like angry wasps and, as it swung round, its sheer bulk seemed to fill half the lough with the four towering funnels blotting out part of the sky.

'And what happens now?' asked May, trying to gauge what the tiny figures were doing that had appeared on the decks.

'She'll be berthed for a last fitting-out,' said Samuel. 'Just small things like lights and cabins. And then go to sea for trials.'

'And after?'

'Across the Atlantic to America and back. That'll be her first voyage.'

Yes. Samuel knew all about these things because his father was an engineer in the railway who took charge of looking after all the big engines. Just as he knew all about everything, though this no longer piqued her.

'Come, little lady. You're not so wee now but you're still a wild one.'

It was her father's voice. Jumping down from the wall she gave him the telescope which he folded and put into his pocket, good-humouredly stroking her hair and then taking her arm. As they walked down the hill her gaze was again arrested by the solitary figure who preceded them and she looked at him curiously. Then her mind was taken up by the day's event which had consisted mostly of waiting and had been all over in a few minutes, the launching of the S.S. *Titanic*.

'We're a long-lived race, May Gordon. But when we grow old we grow old quickly.'

Was it true? Those had been her grandmother's words before kissing her good-night as they went to bed and who was now asleep in the adjoining bedroom. Her real grandmother, who seemed so old and wrinkled and even older than Granny Hopkins. She too had once lived in Islandmagee but had returned to Belfast where she'd been born and lived before she was married. That evening after the launching her father had hired a cabby and they'd gone to an hotel for dinner. All the city is celebrating, he'd said, so why shouldn't they? The hotel was very grand, so very grand with its big rooms of shining wood and broad staircases and clusters of softly glowing lights that Samuel told her were called 'candelabras'. At first she'd felt timid when faced with the array of shining cutlery with the waiters bustling around the table in smartly pressed dark suits and white shirtfronts, but with the wine flushing her cheeks and her grandmother's persistent queries of the day's happenings she'd felt her natural high spirits return. And then when Dalton and Samuel had left to return to the island, the same cabby had sent his horse clopping through the streets back to the flat in the south side of the city.

Would she ever come to live in the city like her grandmother? Standing by the window she looked out across the spacious avenue to the other houses and the lines and clumps of trees standing majestically in the dark, leaves whispering in the night breeze. Or would the island always call her back? At the table beside the bed she ran her fingers gently over the cameo and brooch and another set of earrings which would one day be hers when her grandmother was dead, and which would be in this room whenever she wanted to come and stay.

Frowning at the jewellery, she pondered. Dead?

Naked, she stood in front of the full-length mirror which formed the inside of the wardrobe door studying the protuberances of her own body which were beginning to swell her blouse and remembering the morning awakening with blood covering sheet and thighs, her thoughts and feelings now smothered in confusion as she thought of Samuel and a newer stranger face on the hillside which had aroused her senses, memory probing yet more distant days for those first perilous intimations of womanhood that had brought an exciting yet fearful awareness of intimacy of self, then, suddenly tired, climbed into bed and immediately slept.

For who, even as a child, can trace the tortuous waterways of the past and find truth?

'Sit down, Dalton. Sit down.'

'Father.'

'You've decided?'

'Yes.'

'And?'

'The ministry, father. I want to enter the Church.'

'Mmmmm. It's a difficult calling, I'm told.'

'I understand that.'

'Mmmm. Yes.'

'Do you agree?'

'Agree?' Slipping on his spectacles and lighting a pipe, John Gordon turned slightly in the chair to study the stag's head in the recess, then stood up and began to walk to-and-fro. So that was to be it. The Church. In their previous talks Dalton hadn't mentioned it, and he himself hadn't thought of it. Even during those times when he'd spoken of Dalton's future to Alec Dick, with the latter joking about Dalton's formal manner of speaking and reserved nature, the idea had not once crossed his mind. Yet why not the Church? That streak of mysticism which formed part of his own being and which, he'd often thought, was what had succeeded in blocking any distinct course of action in his own life, might now find a positive outlet in his son. And he had the bearing of one of the clergy, an aloofness mingled with a natural authority which set him apart from others, though he could almost hear Alec's tart remark when he heard the news—He's till be a preacher? Will he be of God's or the divil's oul' party, d'ye think? Fer wi' that face of his and the way he looks at ye he's sure to cross both.

'You're smiling, father.'

'Oh, it's nothing. Just something that crossed my mind.' John paused to relight his pipe. 'Tell me, do you believe in God?'

'Believe? . . . Of course.'

But, John noticed, there was a pronounced pause before his son

46

had answered in the affirmative, and the question seemed to have startled him, he who never showed any trace of emotion or inner conflict.

'Do you believe, father?'

'To tell you the truth, the thought of whether I do or not has never entered my head. If God exists, he exists. If he doesn't, he doesn't. Who am I to know?' he answered, again smiling at his own involuntary acknowledgement. Mysticism, if that's what it was, coupled with . . . what? A latent agnosticism? Two strands of energy meeting to cancel each other out, leaving a dead centre. Was he beginning to understand the truth about his own being now that his life was nearly over?

'But you go to church, father. And observe all the duties.'

'Which could mean that I do nothing but follow social custom. It's one of the few things I can do to show I'm part of the community.' Openly he smiled wryly at his son. 'My life has been mainly composed of doing nothing. So you could hardly say I'm an active member of society. This or any other. And I must admit I was beginning to worry about you doing nothing but wander about since you left school.'

'I wasn't just wandering about, father. I was receiving instruction from Reverend Kerr.'

'Well, he didn't say anything to me about it. But then, I presume that's what's called "professional silence". But I'm very glad you've found a vocation. Jack has found his life in the farm. And I hope that you now find yours in the Church.'

'I think I have, father.'

Think? In the ensuing silence John studied the side of Dalton's averted face. In those hesitations was there doubt? 'And what do you do now?'

'Reverend Kerr suggests that I go to the Presbyterian College in Belfast.'

'Then that's where you'll go. You and he can make the arrangements. And there'll be the . . . financial side of things.'

'I shan't need much, father. There'll be the fees. And I'll need to lodge in the city.'

'Of course. I wouldn't expect you to travel to the island and back every day,' replied John, mentally noting that the expense wouldn't be too great, as Dalton was as frugal in his needs as he was silent. 'I'll tell Elizabeth.'

'She already knows.'

'Oh? And she agrees?'

'Yes.'

Sitting down at the desk again John had a vision of the scene at the station a few years before. Uncomfortably he fidgeted with his pipe, then the thought was dismissed as his gaze returned to the figure in front of him whose face was still turned away. A minister of God? In those slumbering depths he sensed no trace of the bigot or fanatic and he was glad, because such he abhorred. But what else lay there? Because something else did, that he also sensed. It was like looking at himself, though where within himself lay only nullity the other seemed to be at rest in the dead centre of a cyclone, a centre which would one day shift . . . to reveal what?

'While I'm away I'd like Samuel to be allowed to visit the farm whenever he likes. Though he's going to Belfast too. To Inst.'

'Visit the farm? It's almost his home now. He's practically one of the family. He can use your room as he always does.'

Yet again silence fell between them as John fidgeted and idly thought of Samuel, whom he knew was having trouble with his father, a bluff outwardly hearty man John had met one day in Larne and who was Works Manager of the engineering shops of the LMS railway in the city. The trouble was about the boy's future profession, and why some fathers wouldn't allow their sons to go their own way he couldn't understand.

'Somehow I don't think you'll remain in the Church.'

The words were out without conscious intent, and he saw Dalton quickly look up.

'But I can go?'

'Of course.'

Suddenly he wanted to get up and go, to terminate this interview, the urge upon him being to talk to someone else over a glass of whiskey. But obviously Dalton didn't want to and he remained seated, awkwardly refilling his pipe.

'What do you think will happen in the country, father?'

'Happen?'

'In politics, I mean.'

John sucked at his pipe. 'Ah, yes. The Home Rule Bill and now this Unionist Council threatening open rebellion against the Imperial Parliament if it's passed? That's a turn of the screw. Rebelling against the Empire in order to stay in it. And Carson pledging not to acknowledge a Dublin parliament or any of its decrees if it's set up.' Pausing, he thought of the recent vast Unionist rallies which were becoming more violent in tone and manner, and the agitation in most of the rest of the country urging an opposing political direction.

'There's also talk of a separate parliament here in Ulster, with the country being divided.'

'Well, it'll hardly be the whole of Ulster as even up here there's as many Nationalists as anything else. So I'd think, anyway.'

'What would you do, father?'

'Do? Nothing.'

'Even if . . .?'

As Dalton paused, John stood up and went to the window to look out over the fields where cattle grazed in bright sunshine, the sudden desire upon him now being to talk to his son, this figure which outwardly was a replica of himself yet with a latent power he had never possessed, to use him as a kind of confessor. 'I take it that that "if" means if it comes to civil war. I've lived my days in peace and I shall die soon. No, no,' he continued, waving his hand to silence Dalton as the latter tried to speak: 'I'm not ill or anything like that. But I've had this feeling for a few years now. In fact, I've lived longer than I thought I would. And when I go you'll be the keeper. Jack's all right. The farm is really his. But there's May and that youngster David. See to them as long as necessary. Because that "if" of yours— if it's correct—means that we're all running before a storm. But I doubt if I'll be here to have to weather it. I've heard that guns are coming into the country already. And if blood's drawn it'll only be the beginning. For if ever the day comes when Ireland is divided it'll be a sad and sorry day indeed. Because it'll be friend against friend, brother against brother.'

VII

It was the clowns he liked most. They were always scampering around the ring except when the big cats, the lions and tigers, were going through their performances behind the wire netting. When the horse-riding was taking place there the clowns were at one corner of the huge ring with a diminutive pony trying to copy the exploits of the experts, but only succeeding in making the animal kick its hind legs up while hanging round its belly. It was the same when the trapeze artists were walking a tightrope and swinging from the bars suspended high up in the centre of the marquee. On came the clowns pulling a handcart with two enormously long shafts along which, after a heated debate with much pointing at what was happening over their heads and thwacking of each other's braces, they tried to walk along, most of the time hanging onto each other desperately for balance but only managing to catapult themselves through thin air to land face-down in the sawdust amidst the rumble of a drumroll. And when the cowboys and Indians were galloping around the ring demonstrating their marksmanship at the targets in the centre, the sixguns the clowns used kept blowing up in their faces until, in what one called out was the most remarkable demonstration of accuracy in the world, a cannon was brought on and loaded and a small tin can set up as a target. But, with a shudder and then a tremendous bang, the cannon also fell to pieces with the clowns, coloured arrows sticking all over them, again shooting through the air in every direction.

Sitting in the front row, Harry McKinstry laughed uproariously, as did the rest of the huge crowd which filled the tent.

It was all more or less as he'd remembered it from that time when his grandfather had taken him one Christmas to a circus at Portrush. And then he'd hired a boat and they'd gone rowing in the bay despite the freezing wind and breaking rollers. In his mind's eye he could see the old man clearly, face grizzled and greywhiskered and laughing as they recalled the various escapades of the clowns. That had been two years ago, just before his grandfather had died, though the latter had

50

been more like a father because his actual father had died so long ago he couldn't even remember him, and the only things he knew him by were the photographs hanging on the walls at home, one of his wedding day and the other a portrait which hung in the study showing a thin-faced man in a clergyman's collar.

As the ovation by the audience signalled the end of the performance, Harry saw his schoolfriends scramble from their seats and begin to leave before the exits became thronged, and moved with them.

'It was great fun, wasn't it?'

'With the clowns, yes. It was nearly as funny as that Churchill charade a few weeks ago.'

'I don't think that remark was very funny.'

Impulsively Harry laughed. 'All right, Sam, all right. I was only pulling your leg.'

But the other persisted. 'Especially when you meant that the Unionists were the clowns.'

Harry sighed, his good humour vanishing. 'It was only a joke. Forget it.' Quickly changing the subject, he asked: 'When are you going home?'

'This evening. I'm meeting father at the station.'

'Then let's have a drink.'

'But . . .'

Taking advantage of his companion's hesitation, Harry said: 'I know a place where the barman doesn't ask any questions. He'll slip us a couple of drinks in a snug. And there'll be none of the masters around that area to see us.'

'Well. As it's the last day of term . . .'

'And a good thing to celebrate. I'll be glad to get rid of that place for a while.'

Acquiescing, Samuel followed in Harry's wake as the latter ran skipping and jumping, imitating the clowns, high-spirited laughter spilling from him. Boarding a tram at the depot his amusement continued as his friend kept up the performance, other passengers joining in the laughter at this prankish schoolboy, with the tram clanking towards the centre of the city. About ten minutes later they were seated in a tiny corner snug of a public house in the docks area.

'Maybe I should join a circus,' Harry said, sipping his Guinness. 'Don't you think I'd make a good clown?'

'I think there'd be something better for you than that.'

'But what?' Harry paused. 'Does your father still want you to be an engineer?'

'Yes. But the French master is going to write to him. I think that will make him change his mind.'

Briefly Harry thought of the engineering shops at the LMS station

51

where Sam had taken him one afternoon to show him around. He'd stood watching the overalled figures clamber over and under the locomotives sitting on the pits, the clerks sitting behind the dusty windows of the ramshackle wooden offices, a grey sooty light enveloping everything. An occupation which kept him locked up in an office or a workshop wouldn't be his choice either, even though Sam's father, being a manager, had a spacious office to himself and, presumably, could come and go as he pleased. 'That's the trouble. Everyone seems to know what they want to do except me,' he said, thinking of Sam's interest in languages and his determination to study French.

'You'll find something you want to do.'

'Like being a lion-tamer. But with coloured mice.'

'They don't roar loud enough,' Samuel said, trying to imitate his friend's quick wit, a wit which both amused and puzzled him because often he wasn't quite sure of the meaning involved. It was a quick-mindedness sometimes so dazzling and explosive in verbal utterance and mimicry that trouble was the only result, to the extent that Harry had been threatened with expulsion more than once. Noticing that his friend was now staring soberly into his drink, he leaned back and sipped his own beer, thinking of the Easter vacation which lay ahead. Today was the last day of term. He would spend the weekend at home in Larne, and then find some excuse to go to Islandmagee as quickly as possible. The feeling he had about the farm was as though that were his real home, and his parents' resentment of his spending so much time on the island had gradually diminished. The September before, he'd moved from the school in Larne to the Royal Academical Institute in Belfast, where he was a boarder. And now his first year was nearly over, and to Samuel it seemed to have passed in a flash. He'd settled into his studies and new activities easily, the most interesting of the latter being a new-found love of hill-walking and rock-climbing. And there'd been the weekly meetings with Dalton which were spent in various walks around the city, and the companionship of Harry, whom he'd met shortly after arriving at Inst. Summer term was the shortest, and would go quickly. That he sensed. Yet, as he thought of the approaching long sunny days and his proposed expedition to go hill-walking in Donegal with Dalton as a companion, it held the feeling of an eternity. His attention again taken up by his companion's moody silence, he suddenly said: 'Why don't you come with me to Larne for the weekend? And then go home on Monday.'

Harry shook his head. 'Mother's expecting me home tomorrow. And you know how I feel about that.'

Samuel nodded, thinking of the demands of his own father. Harry

52

being an only child with his father dead, he understood the obligation his friend felt. 'Then what about in the summer? Coming with me and Dalton to Donegal? And you know Dalton has invited you to Islandmagee. What do you think?'

'I think if he's to be a minister he'd better do more talking. Or maybe from some pulpits a silent sermon wouldn't be a bad thing.' Harry suddenly laughed. 'Just imagine it. Some old robed figure on a dais with his mouth opening and closing like a half-dead goldfish and not a sound.'

Samuel paused, both amused at the idea and annoyed at its reference to Dalton, then asked: 'Don't you like Dalton?'

'I don't know whether I do or not. He doesn't say much, does he?'

Unwilling to pursue the point, Samuel reiterated: 'Then what about the summer?'

'You know I'm leaving Inst. to go to Trinity. So I suppose most of the summer'll be taken up with mother and trying to find digs in Dublin.' Furtively waving to the barman through the partly open door of the snug, Harry asked: 'Do you want another drink?'

'Not for me. Before I go to the station I've my things to collect from school.' Rising, he ruffled his companion's hair in a friendly gesture. 'I'll see you next term, then.'

As another drink was slipped in front of him Harry watched Samuel leave, pushing through the crowd of dockers and other workmen who stood at the bar. Elbows on the table and chin cupped in his palms, he studied his own reflection in a small mirror which was set among the wooden slats of the snug. It was a handsome face, he noted, not without satisfaction, with fine regular features crowned by reddish dark hair which fell in curls at his neck, and a face which usually attracted more than a second glance from girls and women. It was a game which amused him, this flirting with glances, and had led to a sexual encounter more than once and would have done on other occasions had it not been for his own moody temper causing a sudden disinterest in conquest. Intelligent, gregarious, passionate in nature yet with a volatile temperament which at times changed swiftly from good-humoured bantering to biting sarcasms in the course of a conversation, his friends treated him with a certain reserve yet admired his daring. Equally they admired his response to authority in any form, which was a comic obedience that just fell short of outright mockery. Knowing what others thought of him, he played the role he'd assumed, rarely allowing anyone to see any other aspect of his character.

A feeling of bored restlessness settling on him, Harry left the pub and wandered through the streets, pausing to watch a fight in progress, one of the combatants, whom he knew as Tiger Joe, having

53

the reputation of local champion and hard man. The contest ended in Tiger's favour, Harry watched them amble amicably towards the nearest bar, wiping the blood from their faces, and grinned. This he enjoyed, walking aimlessly through the city with his mind eagerly taking in detail, colour and event. Past happenings flooded his thoughts as he strolled on, the labour unrest which often erupted in violence between workers and police and sometimes between the workers themselves in their different religious groups. Having boarded in the city for several years, the latent sectarianism coiled in its by-ways he instinctively recognised when it showed itself, even though he didn't fully understand this phenomenon as it hadn't been part of his earlier experience. Born in Ballycastle, a small town on the north-east coast wedged between sea and cliffs looking across Rathlin Sound to Rathlin Island, the feeling there between people of differing religious persuasions had been one of polite tolerance. But in Belfast things were very different. Surface calm would suddenly crack to emit a pure naked hostility which was frightening yet exciting, electrifying in its sense of collective tension. It had been like that during Winston Churchill's visit when he'd come to speak on the government's Home Rule for Ireland Bill, an Act which would pass political power to Dublin on the internal affairs of the country. Barred entry to the Ulster Hall where he was to give his speech, he eventually made his address in a football field at Celtic Park to a crowd of furiously jeering Unionists who had followed him through the streets. Harry, with Dalton and Sam, had been among them, watching the bulky figure of the Boer War veteran trying to make himself heard above the hissing and yelling of his audience. There was that too. Politics. Religion and politics, a potent mixture, that his quick perception grasped. But intuition told him there were other things involved too, though what these elements were he couldn't name. Unlike Sam and the vast majority around him, he'd remained silent. As had Dalton, he'd noticed, which gave him cause to wonder, as he felt that his two companions held the same beliefs. The same beliefs which, in fact, all his school acquaintances shared, that of Unionism and Empire, subjects which found their way into most of the weekly lessons and which Harry found both infinitely boring and strangely disturbing. Repugnant almost, and a repugnance which gave vent to sarcasm.

Dalton. He remembered when they'd first met. Since his initial acquaintanceship with Sam the latter's topic of conversation had often been centred on Dalton and Islandmagee, and on his insistence the meeting had taken place. At first he'd been repelled by Sam's friend, by his aloofness and formal manner of speaking. It was as though, Harry thought, in this novitiate of the Presbyterian ministry there was a Calvinistic streak such that he assumed his sermons were to be delivered in a sepulchre. The idea amusing him, he had voiced his opinion only to have it received in silence. Antagonism had followed, during which he'd demanded to be called Harry and not Harold, a name which he hated because it sounded so pompous. Later still his feelings again changed as he recognised that he and Dalton were akin in their restlessness, though where his own found an outlet in mockery, Dalton's broke the surface in his seemingly inexplicable acts of departing from the company without a word. Where Sam's ideas and future had already been determined, his and Dalton's had yet even to be glimpsed.

Becoming aware of his surroundings he saw he was on the southern outskirts of the city, the place where he'd been that afternoon. Standing on Shaw's Bridge which crossed the Lagan, he watched the activity around the marquee and caravans and tethered animals of the travelling circus which was spread across a nearby field. A bubble of laughter broke from him as he thought of the clowns and the cannon. Perhaps that's what he really would be. A clown. What other profession gave such ample opportunity for mockery and slapstick comedy? Not even the music halls. And clowns were supposed to be very serious people. But there was more than seriousness to his own clowning, there was a rebelliousness, but a rebelliousness about . . . what? About his own uncertainty, about his contradictory sway with accumulating events pushing him towards a tomorrow he knew nothing of? About his feeling of being rootless? Yes, rootless. Homeless. Because in Harry lay the precocious sensibility of the orphan.

Home. In the morning he would take a train to Portrush and then a bus to Ballycastle and would arrive in early afternoon. The small house in the middle of the town came easily to mind, neat and tidy as he'd always known it during his mother's widowhood, the cat lying in sleepyeyed langour on the broad hearth. Going to boarding school at an early age, they'd never been close to one another. His education had been his father's wish, even to the point of stating in his will that his son was to be provided for to study at Trinity College, Dublin. His allowance was by no means substantial, but was sufficient, and would no doubt continue like that. This did not worry him because, with his charm and humour, he'd acquired the knack years before of inveigling his way into a dance, music-hall, picturehouse or some quite different function, for nothing. To date, his days had been shaped by this dead hand and he'd followed it, not out of any feeling of filial respect but simply because there was no other path to tread. But lately when going home—it began during the last long summer vacation, he remembered—he'd been drawn to the tiny study where his father had spent the last year of his life as an invalid with a severe

55

bronchial infection. The room was lined with books, in both Irish and English, mostly on theology, history, mythology. And he'd pored over the neat flowing handwriting—so like his own—which filled his father's notebooks, the subject being usually local history. The notebooks in English, that is, because he didn't know Irish though many people in the glens still spoke it and his father had begun to teach him the rudiments of the language before he'd died, as his mother had once mentioned. It was a way into the past, he intuitively understood, an attempt to find a way into his own past, because that was what had moulded him and was still. Either he would have to find his past or invent one, because the past was more necessary to the mind and imagination than present or future. Or so it seemed to him, he who felt himself to be without identity.

It was the rain spattering against his face that broke his concentration and he found that he was walking along the Lagan towpath. Across the fields the white shape of the marquee tufted the treetops. On impulse he searched through his pockets for coins to see if he had enough for the evening performance. There were always the clowns, and this time they might be blown through the air by a disintegrating blunderbuss. What better distraction?

'I hear you're leaving us.'

'Only to the university in Dublin.'

'I wasn't thinking of that.'

'Oh?' Curiosity aroused, Harry put his suitcase on the ground at his feet. 'Then what were you thinking of?'

'I don't think it's up to me to tell you.'

Harry grinned. 'Come on, Niall. What's the big secret?' Then, as the other didn't answer, said: 'Let's have a jar.'

Cutting through the narrow streets of Ballycastle to a small pub close to the shore, Harry listened to his companion's gossip about the various local characters. Friends from childhood, it was Niall McNeill he'd sought out as soon as he'd arrived some half-hour before, finding him in the cobblestoned yard he used as a base in his business of carter, mechanic and general handyman. It was a cold blustery day with snow and sleet showers whirling in from the sea across Rathlin Island, a place where they'd shared many an adventurous escapade in boyhood. Sitting by the crackling log fire, glass in hand and occasionally chuckling at some related incident, he suddenly looked into the towhaired, ruddy face of Niall and asked: 'So? The secret?'

'I hear your mother's getting married again.'

Harry felt a slight flurry of emotion prompting him to laugh, but he didn't. 'Married?'

'So I hear. And moving away. To England.'

And now there was no emotion whatsoever. Nor did any words come to mind that he wished to utter, Harry thought, as he stared into the bluish flames.

'She didn't write and tell you?'

'We hardly ever write to each other.' It was true, a whole term would pass without one line of communication passing between mother and son, and only now did Harry think it was odd. In their relationship she was more like a distant aunt. He pictured her at home, a small, slim woman of about forty, he judged, with fine features like his own, always active and bustling at doing nothing, with a constant stream of chatter as though she were talking to herself. And perhaps she did, he thought, as again only now did he try to think of the loneliness of her widowhood. And again there was that tremor of emotion whose meaning eluded him. 'And why not get married again, I suppose. It must be ten years since my father died.'

Niall nodded. 'True. And many's the one round here has asked why she didn't before.'

'Is he another clergyman?'

'I don't know whether he's in that line of business or not, but he's a cattle-dealer I hear.'

Laughing suddenly at this irreverent comparison, Harry fell silent again. He was glad Niall had told him. Confronted with the news by his mother, he wouldn't have known what to say. But now he could at least say something. 'Is he here?'

'I believe so. I saw him the other day. And I believe the house's going up for sale.' Niall paused. 'And don't worry about not having a home here in Ballycastle. You can stay with the family. Even when I get married as I s'pose I one day will. But I'll hardly leave here.'

'Thanks, Niall. But that's where we're different. I've been too long in Belfast. And now, going to Dublin . . .' Harry broke off, uncertain of his own words and mood.

'Well, with the education you're getting there mightn't be much for you in a wee place like this. But you know you're always welcome.' Smiling and putting a friendly hand on his shoulder, Niall stood up. 'I've a liming job to do so I'd better be off otherwise I won't have money for another drink.'

Harry sat alone by the fire for another hour before leaving. In the small garden outside the house there was already a notice that it was for sale. Inside he stood uncomfortably throughout the introduction as his mother fluttered briskly though nervously around the kitchen. Your new father, she said. Shaking hands with the genial heavily built individual Harry heard him say: But you don't have to call me that. James will do. Just call me James. Over the celebratory dinner his mother had arranged, future plans were discussed. James would be returning to London in a few days where he had a house and business, the latter in cattle- and sheep-trading. It was quite a large concern, he explained to Harry, and he didn't have to travel the country himself but sometimes did just to keep in touch with everything and because he sometimes liked to. Which is how he'd met Harry's mother. She would be following him to London where they would be married early in the summer. And now Harry had inherited brothers and a sister because James, widowed also, had two sons and a daughter at universities in England. Obviously Harry would be spending his vacations from Trinity—a great university, James remarked, founded by Elizabeth I and where many young English scholars went—in his new home in London. And, James continued, growing more expansive with the freely flowing wine, might there not be other brothers and sisters because his mother was still a young woman of only thirty-six and he himself wasn't too old at fifty? Wasn't he a young man now and understood these things?

Amused, Harry noticed his mother blushing at this last remark. Yet, he noted, she seemed younger than he'd ever known her. And, he thought, she would have been only eighteen, his own age nearly, at the time of his birth. Momentarily he thought of the portrait in the study of his own father. Had she been happy with him? It was only rarely, he recalled, she'd ever talked of him.

In bed he lay awake listening to the wind and the sea breaking on the shore, comforting sounds. In this north-east corner of the country there was always the wind blowing, passing by. It was like himself almost, an insubstantial sound. After dinner he'd gone to the study on the excuse that he had to look over some letters from the university which had to be answered immediately, but really it was to sit in front of the portrait of a dead face and think of this homecoming revelation. The obligation which had lain upon him and which he'd often chaffed against was suddenly gone, had been swiftly cut like an umbilical cord. He was free, but the feeling of freedom had a hollowness to it, a sense as though he were suspended in space, belonging to no one and nothing. His being was bits and pieces of seawrack bobbing and dipping on the tide to be carried this way or that, a mere chimera.

Yes. He would go to London, but only for the wedding. After that he'd return. And he'd accept Sam's invitation to join him and Dalton hill-trekking in Donegal. Why he decided to follow these instincts he didn't know, but at least the decision allowed him to drift into a somewhat fitful sleep.

58

VIII

One Man's Path lies at the top of Slieve League, a seacliff in south-western Donegal which on one side falls sheer for nearly two thousand feet into the Atlantic Ocean while on the other is an equally precipitous drop though of lesser height, the path itself being several yards in length with a treacherous surface, slippery yet pitted, hewn and sculpted by centuries of storm and hurricane driving in from the ocean's vastness. There the constant whirlpool of wind never ceases changing, gusting savagely from an unexpected quarter and threatening to dislodge anything in its way, with even the seabirds at times caught motionless before instinctively altering their plane of descent to skim over the crest. Water and sky merge to form one indistinct mass, while the white traces in those vertiginous depths are like beckoning ethereal fingers.

Dalton was first to cross, standing practically upright. Samuel followed, bent double and trying to grip the path with his hands while Harry came last, crawling along on his hands and knees. Reaching the other side they paused to look back the way they had come before moving down the broader slopes towards the bottom where they would camp that night. It was Harry who, with a laugh, broke the silence: 'I don't think I'm equipped to be a hawk. The next time I come I'll bring a pair of wings,' seeing Samuel chuckling and Dalton smile slowly as they began to move in front of him.

They had left Islandmagee two weeks before, leisurely travelling westward, sometimes walking, sometimes riding on the backs of carts when a generous farmer offered a lift, stopping at villages and farms to buy provisions. Sometimes they trekked through the night and then lazed all the next day trying to catch trout or salmon in the rivers, or Dalton would go off alone with a shotgun he'd brought and invariably bring back a hare or rabbit or some other game. They had crossed the Sperrin Mountains and passed through the Barnsemore Gap to the Blue Stack Mountains, in west Ulster. They would now travel north-east to the extreme northern point of the country at Malin Head in

Donegal, cross Lough Foyle to the coast of Derry and Antrim to Ballycastle where Harry would be leaving them while Samuel and Dalton continued south through the glens back to Islandmagee. It was Samuel who had planned the route, talking excitedly as he peered over maps during the four days Harry had spent at the Hollow Farm.

In early July Harry had gone to his mother's wedding in London, staying only a few days, the first thing he noticed being that his stepfather's talk of being a cattle- and sheep-trader had obviously been said with a self-deprecatory humour. True that he did deal in these things, but they were only a small part of a much larger business concern which included the importing of such items as tea, sugar and wines, and of dealings on the Stock Exchange. This much was imparted to him by his new relatives: James, who had just left university and was taking a commission in the army; Charles, who was still at Cambridge; and Valerie, who was studying medicine in London. In the—to him—rather grand mansion in Highgate close to Hampstead Heath he'd more than once wondered at this strange choice as he watched the display of affection between his mother and stepfather: she, once married to a minister and local scholar (and probable introvert, Harry thought), now the wife of a worldly successful extrovert, while he, his stepfather, had chosen a woman from the relatively sheltered life of the glens of Antrim when obviously there were many marriageable women in London with a very different social experience. It was a strange meeting, he thought. But there it was.

His new relatives had received him kindly, Valerie calling him 'my Irish cousin' as she happened at the time to be reading the tales of Edith Somerville and Martin Ross, a title her brothers humorously adopted. They had pressed him with questions on what was happening in Ireland now that the newspapers were so full of events there, but these he avoided, saying that as this was his first visit to the capital he was more interested in it. Only once was he drawn into a political discussion, and that was when James remarked that what was happening in Ireland was a very small affair compared to what might happen in Europe. Despite the sincerity of his welcome he felt his surroundings to be alien, and knew that these members of what was his new family found him reticent, shy, even awkward. And it was not without a sense of relief that he left to join Samuel and Dalton in Islandmagee, despite their protestations at the briefness of his visit, pleased that he could give a long-planned walking tour in the mountains with friends as the honest reason for his departure.

And it was his first visit to the farm in Islandmagee also. Jack he liked instinctively, as, Harry noticed, did everyone. The parents he only saw at dinner or glimpsed briefly around the farm, Dalton's father saying that the young men should be left alone. In those few days he played rough-and-tumble with David in the yard, laughing as much as the child did, or went horse-riding with Samuel and Dalton on the sands at Brown's Bay. Not a good horseman though he'd had ample opportunity to learn, he nevertheless fell in with the wishes of the others. It was like the family he never had, a family to which he immediately responded, though Dalton, he noticed with considerable curiosity, acted as though he didn't belong to it and again Harry felt that odd sensation of a similar ambiguity of mind and emotion. But it was May whose imprint upon his mind he felt most. He was standing at the window of the study when he first saw her, his two companions at the desk studying maps. She came skipping through the orchard, school satchel in one hand, waistlong hair swirling around the developing contours of her figure, threads of sunlight spinning from earrings and bracelet. And later he caught himself unconsciously watching her over the dinner table, the flecked eyes of indeterminate colour, the straight proud nose, her boisterous manner, the protruding shape of her blouse. Tall for her age, he thought, still watching as she helped to clear the table, her skirt creasing round her slender waist as she bent over.

Lying at Malin Head wrapped in a blanket and groundsheet, it was this confusion of recent impressions which Harry was sifting through in his mind. It had taken them three days to come from Slieve League, some of the walking being arduous. The day after tomorrow they would be at Ballycastle where they would go their separate ways. And it was as if this sense of imminent parting had lain upon all, Harry thought, because all that day their easy camaraderie had been fracturing in minor arguments and talk of separate futures, with Samuel, in a kind of nervous excitement, speaking half in French and already planning a walking tour in France for the following summer when he had finished his first year at Queen's University. Harry had refused the invitation to join, saying off-handedly that he didn't know what would happen to him in Dublin and he couldn't plan his future a week ahead never mind a year, and Dalton had been even more silent than usual, walking in brooding solitude far ahead of them.

The past few weeks had been a timeless time. It hung in a dimension unknown, inviolate, perhaps impenetrable, much like the great August harvest moon now sailing above their heads and which encircled the surrounding land and seascape in a silvery light. Farther out across the ocean myriad stars flecked the night sky, vanishing, reappearing, others as yet unseen sending a gossamer thread to focus the eye as it became aware of the depths of the darkness above, all like the flecking backs and tails of fish rising to the light from a different element. Like an arrow in the blue, Harry thought of himself, as the immensity of space gave him the impression that he was drifting without volition as would a meteorite flung through the heavens by some primordial burst of energy.

'I'm leaving the Church.'

It was a while before Harry's retort answered this unexpected exclamation. 'You can hardly say you're leaving it when you haven't entered it yet. You're still a novitiate, aren't you?'

'It amounts to the same thing.'

Samuel raised himself on his elbows and looked at Dalton who lay, hands clasped behind his head, staring upwards. 'Then what are you going to do?'

'I'm going to Queen's with you. To study physics. Astronomy. I've already been accepted.'

Involuntarily Harry's merriment gushed out as his mind seized on the apparent incongruity of the change. 'Well, Dalton, at least you can say you're still in the heavens. Up there among the stars. But is there a hell in physics, do you think? Because don't forget Swift's philosopher who was so intent on gazing at the heavens that he walked straight into a ditch.'

Despite himself Samuel laughed also then said thoughtfully, as if in reproach, 'You didn't mention anything about it to me. I thought your mind was set.'

It was a while before Dalton replied as he lay thinking of the past year, the painstaking days and nights of poring over the Bible which gradually, to him, became a work of history rather than one of divine revelation and the equally gradual disenchantment with the teleological explanations of his studies.

'And don't forget Newton,' Harry said, still chuckling. 'That apple that knocked him on the sconce might have deranged his senses for all we know.'

Dalton smiled slowly at this odd coincidence of thought, because it had been exactly that which had made him change direction. Discovering Newton's attempts at theology, he had moved from these to his scientific writings and backwards to the writings of his predecessors such as Kepler and Copernicus. And it was this quality of abstract thought which his mind had seized upon with a kind of passion. That the apparently inexplicable phenomena above him could be grasped by the rational mind and explained.

'So you're an unbeliever then?' Samuel asked, this time ignoring Harry's heretical remark.

Dalton's words were slow, careful. 'Not so much an unbeliever. It's just that I don't see the Bible as I once did. The Old Testament seems to me to be simply the history of a people. And I don't think I see Christ in the image the Church gives us.' Pausing, he added, with a note of wryness: 'So I doubt if my conviction would be strong enough to be a minister.'

'Then how do you see him? Christ, I mean?'

'Perhaps the only factual thing that can be said is that he was a kind of rebel. That is, he was against the authority of his day,' Dalton replied, attempting to make his meaning precise.

'Oh, if you mean like the moneychangers in the temple,' Samuel said, then faltered as he tried to think of some other scene. Finding his knowledge insufficient, he suddenly asked: 'Are you going to sign the Covenant?'

'Yes.'

'Even if it means civil war?'

'Yes.'

'Even war against . . . Well, you know what I mean,' Samuel continued, originally about to say 'against ourselves' before recognising it as a nonsensical statement. 'Against London. England.'

'If I sign it I presume I shall have to follow wherever it leads,' Dalton said, still enunciating his words carefully.

'Then you'll be joining the Ulster Volunteer Force?'

'If we have to fight we'll have to have a military force.'

'That's true.' How often it was like this, Samuel thought, his hesitant words seemingly without power when set against the measured emphatic statements of his friend. 'But then we'll need arms.'

'I think that that's already being arranged.'

What else did Dalton know, Samuel wondered, as he suddenly felt that the former knew much more of what was going on than he did. His own convictions were unassailable. The union between Ireland and Britain and Empire must remain. He didn't have to think about that. In a few weeks' time, September 28th had been the day chosen, a rally of hundreds of thousands of Unionists would be pledging themselves to a Covenant signed in Belfast and around the country to that purpose. And a military force would be formed, though as yet without arms. But where his thoughts could not take him was the kind of war that would follow. Where would it take place, and against whom? To ward off the feeling of anxiety rippling through him, he turned to Harry. 'And you, Harry? Will you be signing also?'

'I'll be in Dublin then.'

'Michaelmas term doesn't start until October. You'll be here on September 28th.'

'I've to go to London first to the bosom of my new family,' Harry lied, 'and then I'll be trying to find digs in Dublin. As I said. So most of my summer will be taken up.'

But Samuel persisted. 'You'll have the opportunity to sign if you want to.'

'Perhaps politics doesn't interest me that much. I prefer to talk about what happened to Newton after the apple cracked him across the skull. Or about the meaning of eternity.'

'Subjects that don't get you anywhere, mmm?' asked Dalton.

'Then if they don't get you anywhere they must be harmless,' Harry said, still trying to feign a nonchalance he didn't feel since the conversation had turned to politics, yet knowing that his voice sounded flat. 'And what I prefer most is harmlessness. As I told Sam, I'm a clown. But I wouldn't mind experiencing that *l'amour* Sam was talking about earlier. Yes,' Harry mused, 'that's what I want. A grand passion.'

'One would hardly expect that from a clown,' Samuel retorted.

'Why not? The tragic and comic rolled into one. Perhaps they're the most passionate of all.'

In spite of Harry's attempt at jocularity, an uneasy silence fell between them which continued throughout the following two days until they arrived at Ballycastle where Dalton and Samuel refused the invitation to stay overnight and continued their journey, leaving Harry to sit alone in the study of the empty house, feeling that the bonds between them had become flawed almost at the time of their forging.

The great occasion, Ulster Day on September 28th, came and went with the refutation of the government's design to allow an independent political authority to be set up in Dublin. Despite the jubilation emanating from the thousands of people thronging Belfast and the outlying towns there was also a feeling of nervous tension rippling in the air like some vitrious substance that would at any moment shatter. Even the music from the assembled bands had ceased its lilting and taken on a more martial note. Because the Pledge was a declaration of open rebellion, and what would the Imperial parliament now do? Though the thought was in everyone's mind, few voiced it outright as if its very utterance would set the spark to a chain of unforeseen consequences.

Harry had not gone south as he'd said but was in the city, sitting in a corner of the Linenhall library, inertia binding him to the chair amidst the excited tumultuous discussion and argument which filled the normally quiet rooms as people hurriedly entered or left to relate or check on the latest incident or rumour. Earlier he had witnessed the even more tumultuous reception of Sir Edward Carson and other Unionist leaders when they had arrived at the City Hall, and who would be the first to put their signatures to the Covenant. Standing among the crowd he'd been aware of the volatile force of that collective emotional stress prickling his skin, yet his own personal dread was in accidentally meeting Samuel or Dalton and again being forced to confront a choice he knew he wished only to avoid. Why he'd decided to delay his departure by remaining in Belfast he did not understand either, and assumed it was simply a wish to witness the event now taking place. And was that in fact what he was, a mere witness? A coward perhaps, afraid to declare himself and thus define his own political position? Escaping from the packed mass of bodies to the library, where he'd wrongly believed he'd find a quiet corner, it was this thought that he was struggling with. Before leaving Ballycastle he had spent some time with Niall, who had always been quite open about his Nationalist sympathies, and who told him that Sir Roger Casement would be coming north to speak for the Nationalist cause. Casement, the greatest son of Harry's own small town of Ballycastle, knighted by the British monarch for his work on behalf of the indigenous people of the Belgian Congo and who had now taken up the quite different cause of Irish Nationalism. Carson, the Dubliner, now leader of the predominantly northern movement against a separate Irish parliament. And, Harry noted wryly, the very place in which he was now sitting, the Linenhall library, had been one of the meeting places of the Presbyterian leaders of the rebellion of a century before when, allied with the southern Catholic peasantry, they had opposed English authority by force of arms. Defeated, crushed, they had been driven into exile across the seas to America, Canada, the countries of South America. Incongruity upon incongruity, disharmony, discordance, a past of such disparateness that any charismatic figure with a mythopoeic hand could carve a future. Yes. Was that not it? History as mythology? With himself, Harry, ineffectually struggling, a fly caught securely in this web which engendered both paralysis of will and movement. Not only could he not act from deliberate choice but, during those odd moments when his mind turned to the idea of creating a life for himself abroad, he instinctively knew that he had no real desire to leave Ireland and the thought itself was no more than an evanescent bubble.

And such was his mood as he collected his luggage at the Great Northern Railway and took the southbound train to begin his studies at Trinity—a mood of inertia. It was the country that was moving, the villages, towns, fields, pastures, mountains as the locomotive sped onwards in a cloud of belching black smoke, he thought, while he remained at some point of the web which was devoid of motion.

'And did ye see the great man?' As there was no immediate response, Alec Dick plied the oars for several more strokes before repeating the question.

'What?'

'I asked ye, John Gordon, if ye happened till see the great man.'

'What great man?'

'Carson. Him that was up in Belfast a while back during the signing.'

'Oh, him?' John Gordon gave an irascible snort. 'As I wasn't in Belfast I could hardly have seen him, could I?'

Alec chuckled. 'I s'pose that's a good enough answer. Else ye'd have till have eyes on ye that could travel by themselves.'

'Indestructible, they said it was. Indestructible.'

'What did you say?' But, finding that there was no response to this question either, Alec turned his attention to May, the only other occupant of the boat. Almost a strapping young woman now, he'd thought, as father and daughter had clambered in on the Larne side to be ferried across to the island with May, tall and lithe, helping her father to his seat. 'And what about you, May Gordon? Ye'll be quite the lady soon with many's the lad chasing ye.'

'I shall be a lady. But I shan't allow anyone to chase me.'

Amused at the emphatic note in her voice, Alec smiled but said nothing as he watched her trailing fingers on the surface of the water, her thoughtful face an obvious sign that she had no wish to speak either.

May, indeed, had no desire to talk, as she was thinking about something quite different. Soon it would be Christmas, and would he be coming to stay with them at the farm? Clearly she remembered their first meeting. He'd been in the yard playing helter-skelter with David, his own boisterous laughter like a child's. Harry, his name was. Slim and not very tall, not as tall as either Samuel or Dalton. She'd joined in the game, watching the quickness of his movements and the merriment in his large brown eyes. And it was true that she would soon be a lady. Already she was nearly thirteen. She was growing up quickly. Would she grow up to be taller than he was? Because she'd felt herself drawn to him in a way she hadn't known before. He'd aroused an excited yet curious feeling in her, to the extent that more than once she'd found herself dreamily looking at her own nakedness in the bedroom mirror before, giggling despite a feeling of guilty shame, she'd quickly jumped into bed to hug her donkey. The curious feeling that sometimes prevented sleep was stronger than her sense of shame and she lay listening to the night sounds drifting in through the window, Rosinante braying in an outlying field, the owl calling from its roosting place in a nearby tree, the mice in the thatch, wondering where he was and if he were with someone. He hadn't returned with Dalton and Samuel from their hiking holiday in the mountains, and she'd listened carefully to

66

Samuel's stories of their adventures together, though she hadn't dared to ask him about Harry specifically. Because she knew that Samuel was attracted to her and she was often cross at the way he tried to covet her like her father did when she was a child.

Frowning, she studied the little white patterns her fingers traced on the surface of the lough. Instantly there, and instantly gone. They were like the pebbles on the sand she and her father played with when they made beautiful pictures and designs, though they didn't do that any more. Her father wasn't the same now. Even though they still went walking together he often didn't talk at all, and the only sound was the barking of Shadow among the hedgerows or rocks. Would he, Harry, come back to stay with them at Christmas? His family was in London now but, as he didn't seem to like England, he had been invited to stay at the farm during his holidays if he wished. It was her father who'd mentioned that in a sudden remark. Perhaps the young man felt more at home in County Antrim, and as he no longer had one in Ballycastle he could come to the farm in Islandmagee. And when she'd heard his words she'd felt a quick thrill which lingered for a long time.

'Indestructible, they said it was. Indestructible.'

The abrupt comment broke across the lulling sound of softly splashing oars. So that's what it was, Alec Dick thought, still studying the faces of father and daughter, the *Titanic*, sunk in mid-Atlantic when the liner had struck an iceberg. Loss of life had been great. When the news had come the city and surrounding countryside had felt it as a personal loss as, indeed, in many ways, it had been. About to make a jocular remark about the sea being the indestructible one, he checked himself as he remembered a more distant incident. And hadn't it been at the time of the young girl's birth? The figure of John Gordon stood on the steps of the quay at Larne with the news of his son's death at sea. Some far ocean had taken him. And perhaps it was just that memory that was in his mind now, Alec mused, as he expertly swung the boat into its landing place on the island. Holding it steady as the couple climbed out, May helping her father in his stumbling awkward steps, he noticed more. The tight, lined, indrawn features of John Gordon were those of an old man. It was the face of a very old man in which life was a barely perceptible flicker. The face of an ascetic almost, Alec thought, a not unlearned man though one who preferred to keep his knowledge hidden behind rough banter. And he also recalled that afternoon not long before when they had sat talking about just this in a pub in Larne. He watched as they walked up the darkened shore with May firmly holding her father's arm. True. John Gordon was dying. And it was a long and slow death.

67

IX

'Do you think there really will be civil war in Ireland?' Valerie asked.

Harry sat staring at his dinner-plate, his brow furrowed. Why did the question make him feel so uncomfortable? He had nothing to say, no response to give. Or rather, his only response was a desire to get up and leave, and it was simply out of a sense of manners and obligation that he remained seated. This was the second Christmas he'd spent in London, and the second time he'd wished he hadn't come.

'Oh, I think the Unionists will be more than a match for the Nationalists. And besides, if anything did occur, I doubt if we would move against the North. Even if ordered to.'

We? Harry looked at the speaker, James, who sat opposite him dressed in his lieutenant's uniform, his tone a deliberate drawl to give his words emphasis. 'We?'

'Yes, we. And we have been talking about it at camp.' James smiled. ' "Be prepared", isn't that the motto?'

Of course. James was now stationed at the Curragh military camp outside Dublin. He'd half-forgotten that, Harry thought ruefully, even though they'd met twice after James's posting to Ireland. But then so much seemed to have happened during the past year, and also so little. 'But wouldn't that be . . .? No, not rebellion. Mutiny?'

'I wouldn't put it as strongly as that,' replied James, still smiling. 'It would be simply a matter of . . . what? Resigning one's commission, shall we say? And if a sufficient number of officers decide to resign their commissions, who will lead the men? A sticky problem for the government, I should think.'

Harry also smiled, though inwardly. Mutiny with velvet gloves. And suddenly he saw Niall's face in front of him, so strongly it were as though he'd appeared as an uninvited guest. You'll be with us, Harry, won't you? And then with his stepfather's laughter booming out across the table the face vanished.

'That's a good one, I must say, James. Asquith's government can hardly move against Ulster without an army.'

'And particularly when it now has an army of its own. With enough men for several battalions, I understand. Isn't that right, my Irish cousin?'

Harry nodded. 'I think so.'

'You think so? I presume you will know when you join. That's if you haven't joined already.' James's smile became conspiratorial. 'But then, I shouldn't be asking you that. Just as I shouldn't be telling what I know. So we'll look upon present company as a miniature war council and nothing is to be repeated outside this room.'

'So there won't be civil war in Ireland?' persisted Valerie.

'I don't see how there can be.'

'But isn't there an army in the south too? With the Nationalists?'

'Oh, them. We should certainly move against them all right. Though, as I said, I think the Ulstermen—and other Unionists in the south—could handle the matter alone if need be.' James paused to sip his wine, then thoughtfully stared at his glass. 'You see, my dear sister. It's more than a question of simply Ireland. It's a question of the Empire. And we cannot allow a handful of Irish Nationalists to try to damage that, can we? We'll act just as we would have to act in India or any of the other colonies. If there's any trouble in Ireland it will be seen for what it is. A storm in a teacup. After all, isn't Dublin sometimes called the second city of the Empire? And should anything happen in Europe, we shall have to have Ireland at our side. Don't you agree, Harry?'

'Must we talk of politics over the Christmas dinner-table?'

Relieved at his mother's interruption, Harry turned towards her. 'I agree. Perhaps it's not the best conversation.'

'Quite right,' James said, also deferring to her. 'Perhaps talk of war isn't suitable for ladies. Especially in . . .'

In Ireland, thought Harry, as the other broke off with a faintly apologetic cough. Yet there was a delicacy in his manner as James turned the conversation to stories of the regimental mess, encouraged by his listeners' laughter. They had spoken of the same thing when they'd met together in Dublin, James being much more emphatic in his denunciations of the Nationalist movement. Just as there had been the same unspoken assumption of Harry having a similar political outlet. Yet it was all so natural. James with his views which came spontaneously, almost without thinking, his eager desire to impress, half-hoping something would occur in Ireland so that he would have the chance to be in action. Was it this that made him feel so uncomfortable, thought Harry, his stepbrother's certainty? A sense of identity which was absolutely unquestionable? Amused now at the faint sense of quite genuine embarrassment still showing on James's face, he again looked at his mother. Yes. She was happy. She sat quietly listening, a smile puckering her lips, and for yet another time Harry found himself wondering at the ease with which she had settled into her new life, had accepted all and been accepted by all. It had been the same the previous Christmas, the first with her new husband after their marriage in the summer, when he'd watched her assume her place at the dinner table as though she had always been there and no prior life had existed. And, reticent as she'd been before in speaking of his actual father, she now never referred to him at all, which caused Harry at times to muse on the nature of love. Not that he would have expected her to remain a widow for the rest of her life. No. It was just that if she ever did think of a past life she never allowed it to be seen by others.

Dinner finished, he allowed himself to be pressed into playing a few games of bridge then excused himself saying that he wanted to walk on the heath for some air, grateful that no one suggested accompanying him. Dusk was falling as he strolled across the rolling grassland to one of the high points where he stood looking down over the city. London. There in an ocean of shimmering lights lay the centre of a great commercial and military empire. What drew him here? Was it simply out of a sense of filial obligation which he thought had been broken when he first heard of his mother's impending marriage? But then, what drew him anywhere? The digs he had found in Dublin were two small rooms above a public house close to the terminus of the Great Northern Railway. And, he sometimes thought while listening to the hubbub coming from below and the whistling and clanking from the station, it was as though his choice had been deliberate so that at any moment he could suddenly get up and go. But go where? Because that sense of being motionless while everything else moved past him had been no mere fleeting mood, it had grown stronger as weeks and months vanished into a past which had seemingly touched him not at all and could never be reclaimed. And that feeling he'd had in Ballycastle, of being suspended, had also grown more acute. Though with these visits to London the spatial dimension in which he swung like some wayward pendulum another hand had set in motion had grown much larger.

Continuing his stroll across the heath he felt the lighted windows of the houses on its periphery bring a mood of depression, of isolation. In a few days' time yet another New Year would dawn. It would be 1914. He would be twenty. Deliberately he tried to recall the past year, incident by incident. Twice he had been invited to spend Christmas in Islandmagee and on both occasions had chosen London instead. Why? Because no sooner had he arrived than he wished he were somewhere else. The previous summer Samuel had asked him to come with Dalton and himself on their walking tour in France, which

70

he'd also refused only to wish he'd gone when postcards began to arrive from Picardy, Paris and other places further south. Summer he'd spent mostly in Dublin, seeking company in pubs or with what fellow students he knew to be available, though often walking alone at Sandycove and various parts of the bay. In September, when Dalton and Samuel had returned, he'd spent a pleasant untroubled week at the Hollow Farm, mostly listening to the latter's tales of his and Dalton's adventures in France. There had been a feeling of peace at the farm, a feeling almost of belonging. He'd played with David and gone walking with May and lain in idle leisure on the shore watching fleecy white clouds drift across a blue sky. Dalton was absent, Samuel making no secret of the fact that he was drilling and on manoeuvres with the Ulster Volunteer Force, to which he himself belonged, and soon they would be armed. And it was that thought which had lain in his mind when he'd travelled north to Ballycastle to stay with Niall, his old family home having by that time been sold, and upon Niall's insistence had gone to Ballymoney to listen to Roger Casement and other Nationalist figures of a Protestant religious persuasion make their speeches.

Idly he watched his wandering feet scuff the grass. His studies were like that. Idle, desultory. Lectures and classes passed in his absence. A general degree because there was nothing which drew him with sufficient enthusiasm.

Over Hampstead Heath the air was thickening to a mist, making the lights indistinct, blurred. Other images drifted between them. The great tramway strike in Dublin earlier in the year with the labour leader Larkin imprisoned. Captain White, one of the speakers at Ballymoney and who had served in the army throughout the Boer War, coming south to urge the creation of a citizens' army, the mirror image of the UVF, and then offering his services in formation and training. Pearse's statement: An Orangeman with a rifle is a much less ridiculous figure than a Nationalist without a rifle. All over the country demarcation lines were being drawn and decisions made in this political jigsaw. Here in London also. Behind the closed doors of Downing Street the future of Ireland was being tossed this way and that. Trinity College, where he was supposed to study. A Unionist bastion becoming increasingly surrounded by a hostility which threatened its existence. The puzzle fragmented yet again, the pieces reforming in a different pattern. The leaders marched in the dark, colliding into each other or passing each other by. Civil war indeed.

But there was another sound, Harry now knew. The subterranean rumblings of a culture long since submerged yet never entirely lost.

A clown. The disintegrating cannon with himself flying through the

71

air in volitionless ephemerality as the ringmaster cracked the whip. He laughed.

'Harry.'

And with an exclamation he turned, and paused. 'James.'

A low chuckle came through the mist. 'I'm sorry to have startled you. I didn't exactly intend to play the part of a highwayman.'

He tried to conceal the note of relief in his voice, but failed. 'No. I shouldn't have thought you were.'

'Preoccupied?'

'Yes.'

'Cigarette?'

'Thanks.'

James came closer and held out a silver cigarette case. As a match flared Harry glanced at the broad handsome face, thoughtful like his own. Still in uniform, an army greatcoat now hung from James's shoulders. But when he spoke it was again with a note of amusement.

'We thought our Irish cousin had got lost. So I came out to look for you. And to get some air.' He paused. 'The heath can be tricky in fog if you don't know it well. And footpads are not unknown.'

Harry's voice was casual. 'Oh, I should imagine I'd be all right.'

'I'm sure you would. But it was an excuse to leave the family. And your mother was becoming anxious.'

That would never have occurred to me, Harry thought, as they walked together in silence, because of the remoteness that lay between them.

'And I'm sorry about that conversation at dinner,' James said, with the faintly apologetic note Harry had heard earlier. 'It was probably boorish of me to continue on the subject. I mean, with your mother . . . our mother now . . . being Irish. And yourself, of course. You must have known people who may well now be in different camps.'

'I understand.'

'Though, of course, it's natural we should talk about it.' Again there was silence before James changed tack. 'You know, we were perturbed when we heard of father getting married again. Valerie, Charles and myself, I mean. There seemed to be such a difference of . . .' James paused. 'Yet they're obviously very happy. It seems to have worked out splendidly. In fact, the old boy's even more generous than before.'

Harry smiled. It was the first time there had been this degree of intimacy between James and himself, though an intimacy not without a sense of awkwardness on both sides. And it was true that his stepfather was generous. He knew, having had several times to refuse a separate allowance which was offered to him. 'You know, I've often thought about the same thing myself. Their lives having been so completely different. But, as you say, they're obviously happy.'

'So what do you think will happen in Ireland?'

'Probably the same as you do. That civil war seems inevitable.'

'And you'll be on the side of the Ulstermen?'

Harry paused to tread the cigarette-end underfoot. 'It was just that that I was thinking about while walking here.'

'And?'

With James's presence the forces pressing in on him were much more tangible. And only now did he understand that it was the same in Islandmagee. The same, yet very different. There Samuel simply accepted his evasions as a kind of joking and thought that Harry held the same beliefs as himself. With Dalton there was an undercurrent of questioning, of suspicion, but he was not one to ask or press openly. It was his silence that was most unnerving, as if he felt that the power of his personality were sufficient for another to yield to him voluntarily. It was a kind of stoic strength forcing one to speak. But there was that other part of Dalton which Harry's intuition had grasped before, as if he too were uncertain of the foundations of his own individuality.

'I can understand your hesitations, Harry,' James continued. 'It's all very well for us here in England to talk about civil war in Ireland. For you it would be quite a different reality. After all, it would be happening in your country.'

'That's just the point. Whose country? There are many different people laying claim to it. Isn't that exactly what the civil war would be about, if it came?'

James suddenly stopped. 'But you cannot say that you would allow the Nationalist faction to have a valid claim to it?'

'Why not?'

'Harry, Ireland is your country. Part of Britain and part of the Empire. The Nationalist faction is to be seen exactly for what it is. Rabblerousers and rebels against the legally constituted Imperial parliament. And if they provoke trouble they'll be dealt with in the same fashion as other groups of their kind in the past.'

'I don't know which side I'll be on.'

It was a relief to have it out, to let his uncertainty find utterance, to adopt a stance even if it were negative. Compared to silence even indecision seemed to have substance.

'Perhaps you will know if civil war comes. Perhaps you will have to know.'

'If any side,' Harry continued. 'Because perhaps I'm not a military man like you, James.'

But the excuse was no excuse and both knew it as they returned across the heath without speaking, Harry experiencing that same

73

feeling he'd had in similar circumstances in Donegal, of an intimacy severed at its incipience.

But was there anything really fruitful in indecision, Harry kept asking himself when he returned to Dublin in the New Year. Because as the weeks passed civil war was practically a reality. Not only was it openly discussed everywhere, but the newspapers were full of photographs of both the Ulster Volunteer Force and the Nationalist Volunteers taking part in military manoeuvres in the cities and countryside, though as yet there was no display of arms. March came bringing a further heightening of tension with the reputed arrest of the Unionist leaders. But it was as James had foretold. Sitting in the bar where he had his digs one afternoon, Harry was greeted with the unexpected arrival of his stepbrother and a fellow officer, both in full uniform, the latter being introduced as Christopher Campbell and an Ulsterman like Harry himself, James said with a smile, from County Down. Harry was in no doubt as to the meaning of the insinuation, but it was the lull in the stream of talk surrounding him which was uppermost in his mind as he watched them casually stroll across the pub and approach him, the laughter and vivacity in the air being replaced by a sullen hostility. Aware of the change of atmosphere, they surveyed the scene with deliberation before ordering drinks and joining him.

'Well, Harry,' James said, lifting his glass in salute, 'you've heard the news, I'm sure.'

It was an act designed to cause embarrassment, even an act of provocation, Harry knew. Glancing around the array of now silent faces whose sympathies resented this intrusion he paused before speaking. 'I've heard plenty of rumours. And have read as many as well, no doubt.'

With an obvious satisfaction that did not conceal a sense of arrogance, James stretched out his long legs and placed them on a chair opposite, calling loudly for another round of whiskey whilst carefully brushing wisps of dust from his gleaming topboots. 'What rumours?'

Striving against a quick rebelliousness which surged up at this attempted intimidation, Harry tried to equal the other's measured tone. 'The most important, I presume, is that Carson and the other Unionist leaders have been arrested.'

Again James lifted his glass in salute, and laughed. 'I presume it would indeed be the most important, my Irish cousin. If true.'

Cat and mouse, thought Harry. But who was the cat and who was the mouse? And then he realised that their conversation on the heath in London at Christmas had gone deeper than either had known at

74

the time, and that this was a continuation. A continuation that James obviously wished the other occupants of the pub to hear, and again Harry looked around him, wryly observing these two immaculately dressed army officers against a background of roughly shod working men and shabby genteel clerks. Dublin Castle come to visit the slums and the second city of the Empire, indeed, he thought, and was amused. And then the question occurred to him as to why he had chosen this place to live. Was it simply the proximity of the railway station, somehow symbolic of his own changing moods and ability of sudden departure for another destination if he felt like it? His allowance would not have afforded him anything grand, but certainly something better than this. And yes, James was wondering, had wondered, about the same thing. He recalled the latter's first visit, though at that time out of uniform, and the quizzical expression on his face at his unexpected environment. That and the conversation on the heath and this present confrontation meshed together. Was it that James already thought of him as being a rebel?

'If true, my Irish cousin, if true,' James drawled, laughing again as he held his glass up to the light, examining the swirling amber contents. 'What do you say, Christopher?'

'It would be the most important. If true. And the most amusing.'

Cat and mouse. Mouse and cat. The thick fair moustache adorning James's face had been cultivated since their previous meeting. Quite consciously Harry allowed their exchange to lapse as he noted other details. Christopher, as tall as James, greatcoat draped from his shoulders, the broad brown belt at his waist, his northern accent rather less pronounced than Harry's own.

'James tells me you were at Inst.'

Harry nodded. His companion was trying to place him also. 'Yes. And now at Trinity.'

'I was at Campbell College myself. And then went into the army.'

'A real Irishman,' James intervened, before calling for their glasses to be refilled. 'But you're wrong, Harry. Very wrong. If you believe such rumours to be true. Christopher?'

'Our commanding officers are now in London. We refused to move against the north. Even the men.' Pausing, he added: 'Are we still in the army, James?'

Thoughtfully, though with a smile quirking his mouth, James said: 'How can a government disband a whole army? An army loyal to it? And what would happen in India? Africa? The East? Of course, one or two minor disagreements have occurred. But they have been dealt with. I believe certain commanding officers are now at conferences in England.'

Harry stared past the uniformed figures to the groups at the bar who, though talking quietly, were listening. The mutiny in velvet gloves.

James rested his elbows on the table, chin placed on clasped hands, scrutinising Harry's face. 'And so the way is open for the loyal north to do whatever it wants. Partition. Impose its will. We'll not move against you, Harry.'

Uncomfortably he sat as they left the pub, their exit like their entrance, deliberately casual, gloves flicking in one hand, his discomfort increasing in the ensuing silence and not lessening as talk and humour filled the air again.

The way was open. Yes. But which way?

The S.S. *Clydevalley* steamed slowly down the Irish Sea, hove to off the Wexford coast with the Tusker Rock to port, then altered course to a few compass points south-east. A coal boat usually plying between Glasgow and Belfast and other Irish ports, she was a familiar sight and would arouse no suspicion. From the boatdeck Bertie Knox watched the frothing water astern and felt the churning propellers vibrate through the ship, pulling the collar of his jacket tightly closed against the cold April seawind. In the odd jokes he exchanged with his companions there was a note of tension. But the men who stood watch around the ship were mostly silent as they scoured the empty expanse of sea. Because the rendezvous would take place any hour now, any minute even, if at all. Hadn't some newspapers already carried the headlines: Ulster's mystery arms-ship captured? Where was she? The ship had now been at sea for nearly three weeks, running the North Sea gales and the blockade of British gunboats and destroyers. And, once sighted, the two ships would have to transfer the cargo at sea, a hazardous operation. A landing could not be risked. The proposal had been put to him one night in Larne: would he like to join the gun-runner? It was the sense of excitement in the mission that had appealed to him. Used to travelling the country with his dynamite charges, the present enterprise had the feeling of familiarity.

And there she was, first a speck, then a vague shape and then superstructure and sides looming out of the dark water as signal lights flashed. Steaming alongside, the transhipment began with the two vessels at times rubbing together in the swell with a harsh grinding, grating noise that swamped the whizzing of derricks and cranes as the bundles and bales were swung from one to the other. And the story of her voyage was passed from crew to crew. The guns had been brought through the Kiel Canal from Hamburg by lighters. Then the ship, the S.S. *Fanny*, had been arrested by the Danish authorities at Langeland. Damaged by a gale she had to seek shelter in Great Yarmouth before crossing to the French coast to escape patrolling British destroyers, changing her name twice as she followed a zigzag course.

The reloading was carried out quickly and efficiently and the *Fanny* swung away, making a course back to Germany. With the wind spattering his face with spray, Bertie idly thought of their reception and the groups of UVF men who would be gathering nightly to watch at the various ports along the east coast of Ulster. Because their exact destination would not be known until land was in sight and they had the radio signal that all was clear to berth. And it was now they who had to be on the lookout for the white ensign which would denote a British warship trying to intercept. But they were not altogether alone on the high seas, as he'd heard there was another ship being used as a decoy which, any patrolling destroyers being sighted, would try to get them to steam in the wrong direction or would deliberately try to confuse the military and police on shore as to its cargo and landing.

Going below he joined the others who, the ship now being well under way, were carefully checking the gleaming weapons and sorting them into small easily manageable bundles in preparation for their swift dispatch to hundreds of secret locations, arms experts marking each as to its contents: brand new Austrian Mannlicher rifles, German standard infantry Mauser rifles and some Italian Vetterli-Vitali also, a cargo of some thirty thousand rifles and three million rounds of ammunition.

Four days later, with the Isle of Man in sight, their destination was announced. Not Belfast as many had thought. Larne.

X

It was the first time May had been in a motor car. It came bumping into the yard with Dalton driving, sending the flock of hens scampering wildly away from its wheels. Her father had business to do in Antrim and when she'd heard that Dalton was to hire a car for the journey she'd cajoled him into letting her accompany them. Not that it had taken much persuasion as, after an initial refusal, her father had yielded with a smile and a kiss to his mischievous tomboy, as he still sometimes called her, the refusal being no more than a display of affection which had become a ritual.

It was a sunny day in April, warm though showery. The roof of the car was partly pulled back and on her father's instructions she had brought two quilts which they could wrap round them if it became chilly. Though it would be good, he'd said, to feel the warm spring air against their faces. Holding on to his arm she helped him into the front seat beside her brother, tucking the quilt around his knees and leaning the walking stick against his lap before clambering into the rear. With a loud splutter the engine was restarted and they were off, the hens and geese clucking and hissing and flapping more madly than before, as though indignant at this second violent disturbance in the otherwise peaceful farmyard routine. Obviously, thought May, watching Dalton's gloved hands turn the steering-wheel as they swung out through the gates and climbed the path from the Hollow to the road, it was to be a great adventure.

And it was good to feel the breeze fanning her face and sending her hair flying behind her or, caught by a sudden different current of air, whisking it across her face so that she was momentarily blinded. They left the island and took the road to Carrickfergus, turning inland along much narrower roads until they gained the main road from Belfast to Antrim where, at places, she could see the great shimmering expanse that was Lough Neagh. And from all around her came that unmistakable aroma of springtime as the sun warmed the earth into new life with the grass beginning to shoot and the trees and hedges budding and the drifting scent of early flowers. Sometimes from farmhouses dogs would leap and bark furiously as they sped past and in the fields lambs would run hastily away with a frightened bleating, the sheep stumbling after them. And on several occasions she saw horses shy and rear as the motor car clanked too close.

The experience was so new and they were going so fast that Antrim was reached long before May expected it to be. Nor had she been listening very much to the conversation taking place in the front. All she knew was that her father had wanted to come on some business about cattle, and to see an old friend. When they arrived at their destination and the car stopped with a shudder in front of a farmhouse she began to feel her sense of excitement ebb, almost to a feeling of disappointment. Accustomed since birth to the life of a farm, there was nothing new to be seen, and the way her father's friends fussed over her when she was introduced only irritated her. Moodily she stood beside a horsetrough, splashing her hands in the greenish water. Dalton hadn't even got out of the car but had gone off again on some affair of his own. She'd called and run after him across the yard when she saw the car turning, but he had simply ignored her.

Wandering over a field, she climbed a small hillock to look around. Straight in front of her lay the town and on the right was the lough, glinting in places where the sun caught the breeze-blown surface. Here and there were white sails like small handkerchiefs, as though held by hands reaching up from the water to let them fluff out with the wind. They beckoned. Stooping, she plucked a blade of grass, breaking little pieces off one by one. He loved her. He loved her not. He loved her. He loved her not. He loved her. She was nearly fifteen. A woman already. Her body felt so strong and firm. So supple. And sometimes her senses felt so excited that she longed to just dance and dance and dance. And run and skip and jump. And at times when she moved quickly the weight of her breasts would cause a sudden thrilling self-awareness. Why had he never come at Christmas when he'd been invited? Not that she'd asked why. No. That would be like betraying a secret. A secret about herself the others would recognise instantly. And he was so unlike Samuel. Samuel, whom she had loved once when they'd fed the donkey and named him Rosinante. But had she really loved him even then? Because perhaps she'd been too young to love anybody. But no, that was wrong too. She had done, and still did. But she loved him in the same way she loved Jack or David or Dalton. It was like having another brother. She didn't love him in that *other* way she knew she felt but couldn't really explain. And now Samuel was beginning to make her feel shy and embarrassed, which she resented and made her speak to him crossly at times—the way he deliberately tried to seek her out and was always giving her little

79

presents. Like the lovely green scarf she was now wearing. And that time they'd gone swimming together at Brown's Bay and she'd caught him staring at her in a way that made her face all flushed and red and then he'd turned away all flushed and nervous too.

The first raindrops spattered against her face and broke. She was standing beside a river that flowed into the lough. Some fishermen were manoeuvring boats on the far side, others hauling barrels and boxes of their catches across the decks. Hurrying into the nearby woods she took shelter under the trees as the sky darkened and the rain hissed furiously down. But the shower was brief. Above her head sunlight spun gaudily coloured gossamer webs in the moisture of the treetops. Deadwood cracking softly underfoot she strolled on, seeing in the distance the arm of a rainbow arching up from Lough Neagh.

The immense stone wall rose up in front of her, its surface splintery, powdery, pitted, patterned with moss and lichen and ivy. There were flowers too, poking out from weed and spiky grass. It was like climbing the rocky face of the Gobbins, she thought, her excitement now returning as her hands and feet sought firm holds. The descent on the other side was easier. With six or seven hops she was on firm ground again, and slowly she began to walk passionately looking this way and that in these new surroundings.

It was a place of enchantment. It was a dream. She was a great lady in a place so beautiful that even her mind, she felt sure, could not have imagined it. The tall trees, in perfect line bordering the small lakes, stood like guards and dignitaries in attendance, their heads bowing to her in the ruffling yet silent air. Further on she heard a soft musical tinkling sound and rested beside a lilypond watching her own reflection break and reshape again as drops from overhead fell plipping plopping on the surface, eddying and circling out over the large green leaves and blossoming flowers to rejoin in one intricate gyre. Taking off her coat she danced along the pond's edge, feeling the rhythmic movement of her body inside the white blouse, the green silk scarf caressing her neck and the kilted skirt swinging around her hips. And once more she stopped. There in the centre of a small quiet grove was a tall Celtic cross with a bright stone in the centre. For seemingly a long time she paused with her fingers lightly crisscrossing its smooth marble pedestal. And suddenly she started, listening intently. But no. There was no one. On she went, coat clasped in one hand, turning slowly and slowly until the tall trees with their upreaching arms that turned in the sky in unison made her feel dizzy. Only once did she think she saw another figure. A dog. A great wolfhound, she knew by its shape. It stood in shadow some distance away but did not try to approach her or even move, as though it were stone. And still in the air was a sound like a lilting harp which was at one with her own senses.

What time? How many minutes, hours?

Laughing, running, she clambered over the wall and jumped straight into arms that reached out to grasp her.

'May!'

'Dalton!'

'Where have you been? We've been looking everywhere for you.'

'I was only . . .' She stopped, the sudden shock making her pant and cough.

'Quickly. Come quickly.' There was urgency in Dalton's voice and movements as he held her by the arm and they hurried to the edge of the woods where the car stood. As she climbed into the back and the engine started, her father's laughing face was turned towards her.

'And what was Mistress Tomboy May doing this time?'

But she didn't know what to say. Had she really been in such a place, a place like a fairyland, she wondered while watching the glassy surface of Lough Neagh fall behind? 'What was that place, daddy?'

'Shane O'Neill's castle.'

'No, father,' Dalton interrupted. 'It's Masserene. Shane O'Neill's is the old ruin further on.'

She heard her father tut tut testily. 'Of course. My memory's going. I forget these things.'

The journey passed in silence, a silence she did not want to break as she tried hard to go over every minute detail of her adventure. Because yes, the day had been a great adventure after all, and one greater than she ever would have thought possible. And suddenly there was Jack with the mare and trap to take them back to the Hollow and Dalton's car with its twinkling lights was vanishing into the dusk. And then, with the clip clopping of hoofs in her ears she heard her father's voice now irascible and angry in answer to a question from Jack.

'Guns. The fools, the fools, the fools. They're bringing guns in.'

Dalton drove straight to the docks at Larne to a prearranged meeting with Lance-Corporal Duncan McKinzie, a police constable in normal life who also, like many of his colleagues, was a member of the UVF. As the car jolted over the banked railway lines he noticed that dozens of other vehicles had already arrived, mostly motor cars and small lorries, though there were also horse-drawn carriages of different kinds. McKinzie was waiting for him and he saw him approach as the car stopped, a tall, broad-shouldered figure like himself from the glens around Waterfoot and old enough to be his father. When they'd first met during the formation of this military wing of the Unionist cause Dalton had found this odd, but quickly discovered that difference in rank had nothing to do with difference in

81

age. As one full-time military person had put it: with his, Dalton's, background and obvious qualities of command he was at least a lieutenant, and that was what he was.

Stepping from the car he returned the other's salute. 'What's the news, lance-corporal?'

'The ship's berthed, sir. And the unloading's begun.'

Walking to the bow of the steamer they surveyed the scene. Groups of men were swinging the cargo on to the quayside and on the seaward side bundles in huge nets were being lowered into lighters lying alongside. Lights were showing as they normally would have been, which was good. It was an ordinary operation. To have the harbour swathed in darkness would only arouse suspicion. Dalton watched the first of the smaller craft leave the ship's side and head for the narrow mouth of the lough, making for one of the arms dumps along the coast of Antrim or Down. Hearing a low chuckle from his companion, he turned.

'I've heard the police are busy in Belfast, sir. With a decoy ship, it seems.'

Dalton nodded. 'Good thinking.'

'What now, sir?'

'Start loading the car. We'll take as many rifles and as much ammunition as we can without risking being slowed down. I'll fetch some more petrol cans. We can't risk running out of fuel and being stranded on some country road. Orders are that there's to be a general announcement in the newspapers in the morning.'

'Which means the military'll be combing the country?'

'Most likely. In fact, you can be sure of it.'

Again Dalton heard his companion laugh. 'Well, sir. I'm pretty certain they'll find little of interest.'

Turning, Dalton walked the length of the ship, McKinzie automatically falling into step beside him, meticulously noting every detail as knots of men pulled boxes along the ground with others forming chains, sacked bundles being tossed from arm to arm. 'I hope you're right. But our communication line is good. And by the way, lance-corporal, should we be stopped on the road back . . . We've been what? Fishing? You'll find fishing rods in the back of the car.'

Yet again Duncan chuckled. 'Excellent foresight, sir. If I may say so.'

'Ours will be a night's journey, at least.'

'Where to, sir?'

Grasping a bundle in midair as it was being hurried along a chain of figures, Dalton placed it on the bonnet of the car and examined the contents, briefly balancing one rifle in his right hand. 'West, McKinzie. Fermanagh and Tyrone.'

*

82

The farmhouse was quiet. May, still fully dressed, sat by the window of her bedroom. Upon their return from Antrim and having dinner her father had gone out again. He seemed very angry and upset and didn't even stop to kiss her as he usually did. And she'd heard an angry exchange between her father and mother with Dalton's name mentioned several times. Yes, the farmhouse was still, yet there were other sounds like whispers drifting from across the lough. And, of course, the house being in the hollow, she couldn't see anything. What had the day's adventure been? The lilypond with the clusters of fern and flowers and the everwidening rings and circles of the gyre. It was a bit like on the sands when she was a child, watching her father's hands fitting the coloured stones into place as spiralling out from the smooth yellowness came a ship in full sail or a great fish or cross. And then came a different sound to break her concentration, the braying of Rosinante telling of someone afoot. Was it her father returning? Or Jack coming back with lobsters? Or Dalton? Pulling a shawl across her shoulders, she left the house and walked quickly through the fields in the cool night air, stopping for a moment to listen and tickle the ears of her pet who, as always on such occasions, butted her gently in the side with its muzzle. Then she climbed up the slope and stood on the road where the Druid's Altar stood closeby, her eyes intent on the lights of Larne.

'May. May Gordon.'

The voice was soft so as not to startle her. Yet startle her it did. Even though she recognised it instantly and felt the coursing of her blood and her chest heave in a quick leap.

'Harry. Harry McKinstry!'

His figure stood in the dusk. An overcoat was belted at the waist and from one shoulder dangled a travelling bag. His shoulders were broad though his form gave the appearance of slimness. And she was nearly as tall as he was. Perhaps just as tall.

'I'm sorry. I didn't mean to frighten you.'

'You didn't,' May said, hoping that the little flutter in her voice would not betray her feelings.

'I got bored in Dublin. So I thought I'd take up the invitation and come to Islandmagee for the weekend.'

Yes. It was Friday. And that meant there was Saturday and Sunday. Two whole days when she could see him again. Perhaps Monday also. Because she didn't understand what it was like being at a university but knew that sometimes you had many days free and didn't have to go back so soon.

'You know you are always welcome. Daddy has told you that.' But, May wondered in the ensuing silence, did not 'daddy' sound just a bit like being a little girl? When really she was a woman? Trying to adopt a tone that sounded like Dalton, she added: 'You know my father has told you you're always welcome.'

'Yes. I know.' There was a pause as he stood there, unmoving. 'I think he must be the kindest man I've ever met.'

'He is. And I love him very much.'

It was out without thinking, even though she tried to bite back the words. It was true. But she hadn't meant to say that, hadn't meant to show herself so openly. It was almost like standing naked.

He approached and stood beside her. 'But isn't it rather late to be out walking the fields?'

She tried to make her laugh sound casual. 'Oh, I often slip out to walk at night. It's so beautifully quiet. And you can see the hares and badgers and foxes.' She stopped speaking for a moment, wondering if she were saying the right things. 'Besides, no one around here is going to harm me.'

'No. I shouldn't think so.' It was true what she said, thought Harry. He'd felt it himself on the island, a peace that was a kind of serenity in those twilight hours when he'd been walking alone.

'And anyway,' May said, pointing in the direction of Larne, 'I wanted to see what was happening over there.'

Harry looked towards the scattered twinkling lights, some of which were moving. 'What is happening?'

'I think they're smuggling guns in. That's what daddy said.'

'So that's it!'

Just at that moment his voice was louder in tone and she turned to look at him. Part of his face was in deep shadow and on impulse her hand was half-raised to touch the lock of dark hair falling across his forehead before being quickly resisted. His presence seemed to be all around her with little incoming waves that made her skin tingle and prickle as if she were bathing in the sea feeling the stinging of salt and sand.

Now his voice was slow and soft. 'I wondered what was happening. I didn't mean to arrive so late but I was delayed in Belfast. There are police and army blocks everywhere. Obviously this is the reason.'

The moving lights were disappearing one by one as they went up over the hills on the far side of the lough, winking, beaming, suddenly snapping out like clusters of fireflies entwined in bushes as they stood silently watching.

Abruptly he turned and she felt the pressure of his hand on her shoulder, though his voice was seemingly distant. 'Let's go back to the farmhouse.'

Walking back along the road something caught her eye and she stopped at the edge of a field, feeling him bump into her with a muttered exclamation and seeing him smile in the dark as his eyes followed her pointing finger. 'Look.'

His voice, after a few minutes, was like her own, practically inaudible. 'Well, well. You know, even though I've lived along this coast all my life I've never seen anything like that. It's like . . .'

Nor had she, May thought, as she heard Harry's voice trail off and stop as though even to attempt to name this magical scene would cause it to vanish. And magical it was. Though she'd often seen the wild creatures of the island she'd never before seen them like this. There, further down the field and framed in a huge gap in the hawthorn were about a dozen huge hares in an almost perfect ring, all turned inwards as though in attendance at some grave and solemn conference. A band of moonlight kept fleetingly reappearing between the drifting clouds above as they continued to sit immobile. Again she heard his voice whisper to return to the farmhouse, yet still they stood.

XI

Harry stayed for a fortnight. Samuel arrived the following day, Saturday, for the weekend, and prolonged his visit for a week. May instinctively knew that he was jealous of Harry, even though she tried to divide her time between them both, and at moments felt so angry she could have hit him. She could have hit Harry too, but out of a different feeling she didn't know how to cope with, because often when she went to find him where he usually sat thinking in the study, he wasn't there. He was just like Dalton, she thought, going off by himself because he didn't care about anyone or anything. And then Dalton arrived in mid-week and she heard more angry words between him and her father. And there was David too. Now seven years old, growing up tall and broad like Dalton, he was forever getting into trouble with someone on the island, and twice within a week she saw her mother hit him with a belt in the yard. But off he would run again, and back would come another complaint. It was a time of turmoil.

Only with Jack was there peace. Surefooted as he skipped along the Gobbins cliffs with his big hands and feet, he skipped out of any trouble that was brewing, disappearing instantly on some farm or fishing errand. And no less than five times that fortnight she had to go and seek him out because she wanted some hours of peace for herself, knowing that, after several minutes of scratching his chin and trying to look stern, his big brown eyes would laugh as he gave way to her pleading requests. So it was that she found herself as far out as the Maidens where the lighthouse was pulling up the lobster pots dripping with water and slime and seaweed or herding some cattle across the fields to Alec Dick's ferry. And often she would slyly watch him when he wasn't looking, because now she *knew* that she was getting to know her menfolk as a woman and would ask herself why he looked so different from her father or other brothers, so very different it was as if he didn't come from the same family. Smaller than she was, thick-bodied, monkeylike and going bald even though he could hardly be twenty. Yet she would give him a hug without thinking and feel a warm hug in return. Not like Dalton, whom she was almost afraid to approach and had to think hard before touching him. Or David. Because, even though he was still a child and only half her age, with that fighting look always on his face she didn't know whether he would just turn round and punch her on the nose as she'd seen him do with a boy much older than himself. And then there was Samuel, gentle like Rosinante whom she loved like Rosinante and wanted to be kind to. And Harry, whom she now hated and didn't want to see.

Yes. It was a time of turmoil, and one much greater than that she felt in the farmhouse.

The warships appeared in Belfast Lough. Destroyers, her father said, a destroyer flotilla sent by Winston Churchill as Lord of the Admiralty in the government in London, because of the gun-running. The greyhounds of the sea, her father also said, as they both stood on the cliffs watching the slim shapes cruise this way and that across the lough and intercept other ships. There were more of them further out on the horizon. They would be patrolling the whole coastline from Down to Donegal. But they wouldn't find anything now. They were too late. Her father's laughter was caught by the wind and tossed among the rocks and subterranean caves and in the sound May recognised both sadness and pride. The Ulstermen might be fools but they weren't altogether fools. The guns had been landed without one wrong move and it would now take Winston Churchill and his government twenty armies and navies in order to find where they were hidden. Besides, hadn't they cocked the snook at London by openly displaying a Lewis machine-gun in Belfast?

And sometimes she felt that it was her father who was the child and she the grownup. Sitting in Alec Dick's ferry crossing to Larne, her father's spluttering voice was at times childlike, at times raucous like a crow's, and she would lean forward to wipe the spittle from the edge of his mouth with her handkerchief. Besides, there was something else. Samuel was again going to France for the summer months, to finish his studies, and wanted her to accompany him on the first part of the journey from Larne to Stranraer. But this time her father was adamant in refusal, as he'd never been before, and it was only Alec Dick's words as they sat in the boat that cajoled him into letting her go. 'John, John, don't they all have till fly the nest as we ourselves once did? And don't I know every single seaman in this port? Let her go. I'll see till it that she comes back safe.'

And so in late June she stood by the rail of the steamer watching the great dome of Ailsa Craig and the Scottish coastline draw nearer, Samuel beside her, a feeling of responsibility settling over her as he tenderly held her hand and talked of his forthcoming travels. This time he was going alone, as Dalton now stayed mostly in Belfast and of Harry there'd been no word since he'd returned to Dublin nearly two months before. The steamer docked beside the waiting train, but they had time to have tea and cakes in a café before departure. What would she like as a present? Perfume from Paris, she called, waving the green scarf as the train chugged away travelling southwards through Scotland and England where he would catch another ship for France.

It was a lonely summer with everyone away. Even Jack had gone, visiting the cattle markets inland to buy a new herd of calves. With Sheila Hawkins she'd become more friendly, the differences in character which marked their childhood ameliorating as womanhood approached. But often she'd return to her old love, the seabirds. Alone walking the shore and rocks she'd watch for the sea-eagle and osprey and gulls, the cormorants with distended gullets as they swallowed their catch whole as they plopped up from the depths, the falcons that nested high up on the cliff face and the flashing nervous sandmartins as they swept with a frightened whirr of wings from clefts and grassy dunes. And she called to them as she'd done so many times before.

There was news from Europe that made her father look very solemn. In a faraway place called Sarajevo some grand royal person had been shot dead: the Archduke Ferdinand. And she thought of Samuel on his travels. A freak summer gale blew up for several days and passed. Sitting in the late evenings with her father, the fire blazing because he always complained of being cold, she would make him his nightcap of hot whiskey as he read the newspapers and talked to her. The archduke's wife had been shot dead too. There was also news from Dublin. Guns had been landed from Germany by private yachts. It was just like the night in Larne in April, but different. This time there was violence and the army had shot and wounded many people. Some were dead. And then she thought of Harry and of standing by the Druid's Altar watching the lights moving up the hillside opposite. Was he all right? No, she didn't hate him and wished he were with them in the farmhouse. Because as she sat gazing into the burning logs another sense was becoming apparent, as though these far-off places were forcing in upon her with a power so disturbing that neither her heart nor mind could resist its intrusion.

The two figures stood on the County Down side of Belfast Lough at a point along one of the rambling walks below Helen's Bay and Crawfordsburn, the woman stout, matronly, greyhaired, the girl slim, blackhaired and blackeyed, who again pointed seaward and repeated her question. 'Warships, Miss Anna Leitry,' the governess said, addressing her ward by her full name as was her custom. 'But I think they'll be leaving us soon.' Lightly the governess stroked the girl's hair, staring into her face, a face of such beauty, she'd always thought, it was like that drawn by one of the great painters. Perhaps it was the eyes, dark, large yet indrawn, unfathomable. 'Come, Miss Anna Leitry, we'll find some buckie roses and then have a drawing lesson before tea.'

Dalton waited outside the study door, his hesitation caused by the vehemence of the voice within. He had just come from Belfast. Not by car, because that was part of Brigade transport and still might be needed. They had been on the point of assembling to again parade fully armed through the streets of the city when the news had been flashed. The Brigade dispersed, he'd immediately gone home to the Hollow, taking the train to Whitehead and then walking the six miles with a long, untiring stride. The voice inside was still shouting. Knocking, he opened the door. 'Father.'

'Aha, Dalton, it's you!'

His father stood beside the desk with David, squirming, firmly grasped by one ear. 'Have you heard about this one?'

Dalton shook his head, taking in the scene and trying to gauge his father's mood.

'Thieving fruit in a market in Belfast! That's what he was doing! A thief, I'm telling you. Why doesn't he steal the apples and pears from his own orchard? And how did he get into Belfast? By stealing a ride on an empty coal waggon and then slipping out through the workshops. The police caught him and then had to bring him back! A respectable man like me all my days and the police bringing my son to the door as a thief! And him only seven years old? If he wants the fare to have a ride on the train why doesn't he ask for the money? We're not reduced to starvation yet!'

There wasn't fear in his younger brother's face, Dalton noticed, but laughter. And his father's temper was that of a querulous old man. 'Father. I have important news.'

'News? What news?'

'War.'

Releasing David, his father slowly turned. 'War?'

'Yes.'

'Take him out of here.'

But David needed no further invitation. Released from his father's grip, he ran through the door with a yell, Dalton closing it quietly behind him.

'War, you say? So Ireland is at civil war!'

'No, father. No. It's not that. It's war in Europe. Germany has invaded Belgium. Civil war in Ireland has passed.'

The voice was quizzical. 'Civil war in Ireland has passed, you say?'

'Yes, father. We are at war in Europe. The government in London has declared war on Germany.'

'I see.' A snorting kind of laughter issued from John Gordon's mouth as he walked to-and-fro in otherwise silence before demanding: 'And you, Dalton? The Ulster Volunteer Force?'

'There's already talk of going to the Front. Should we be needed. There'll be no trouble in Ireland now.'

'I see.' The pacing figure repeated the phrase. And again repeated: 'And civil war in Ireland has passed, you say?' Silence followed before Dalton heard the words: 'You fool!'

Startled, he asked: 'Father?'

The voice was now quiet. 'But no. Perhaps you are not a fool. And I hope you never shall be.'

'I don't understand.'

Dalton watched as, with an abrupt movement, his father went to a cupboard and sent an object spinning across the desk which scattered an ashtray, papers and a vase of flowers, the latter crashing to the floor to splinter in fragments. At the noise Jenny Jackson came running, whom John Gordon peremptorily ordered out.

'What is that?'

Dalton faltered, then trembled, first looking down at the rifle and then at the figure confronting him. Gone was the peevish intemperate man who had been dealing with his younger brother. The face was still that of an old man, heavily lined, sunken-cheeked with drooped eyelids, but the authority in his bearing and stance was unmistakable.

'You know I have never allowed guns into this house. Would you attempt to usurp my position here?'

'Father. I . . . I did not mean that.'

His father now stood by the window looking outwards, head nodding almost imperceptibly. 'No. You did not mean that. Then what did you mean when you brought guns into this house without my knowledge?'

Silence. In the yard outside the hens cackled and came the sound of geese flapping their wings. Ducks quacked while burying their beaks in the mossy banks of a small brook, and from the fields came the neighing and snorting of horse and cow.

'Dalton. My son. My firstborn. So now it is war.'

'Yes, father.'

'No. Not my firstborn. My only living firstborn.' Searching in a drawer John Gordon withdrew an old wallet and set the photograph on the desk. 'This was John. Your elder brother. He died at sea.'

'I've always known, father. But I never asked. Because you never spoke of him.' Dalton paused. 'I did not want to intrude.'

90

For several seconds Dalton felt his father embracing him before they broke apart again.

'Dalton. You have the sensitivity I always felt in myself. But in me it was that of the simpleton. You have also a power—and a power of decision—that I never possessed. Use it well.'

'I shall try, father.'

Dalton wished to say more, but that tiny eternity of intimacy had flown.

'So. You'll be going to the Front. Should you be needed. And no doubt you will be needed. I presume you're giving up your studies at the university?'

'Yes, father.'

'I once asked you if you believed in God. And saw you hesitate. Later you gave up your theological studies to read physics. And now you tell me you're giving up physics to go to war. And now I ask you this. What do you believe about this country?'

'Believe?'

'Yes. Believe. Do you hesitate again?'

Silence.

' "Ulster will fight and Ulster will be right." A warcry dreamed up by an Englishman, Randolph Churchill, so that he could gain a seat in the parliament in London. Right about what? The Union? The Union of 1800 was fraudulent. A trick. London got such a shock at the great rebellion of two years earlier, '98, that the old Irish parliament had to be dissolved in order to bring this country under control. "Home Rule is Rome rule." Another warcry. But what does it mean? Please tell me?' There was a lengthy pause. 'Aha. Again you're quiet. We in Ulster must fight for our civil and religious liberties. Is that it?' Now John Gordon's voice was caustic. 'I see. And I presume the Presbyterian and dissenting Republicans of '98 were fighting in order to put the Pope on a throne here in Ireland. Obviously. That's why they were massacred in their thousands, the leaders like Joy McCracken hanged, and the rest driven overseas. Just like their peasant counterparts in the south. And I also presume industrial agitators like Larkin and Connolly are fighting for a Catholic cause too? Ah yes, I forgot. Civil liberties. I hear that during the carters' strike sons were outbidding fathers for a penny less a day as wages. And should one of them as much as steal a loaf to feed his hungry children he's at the mercy of any old crotchety hanging judge. Where are their civil liberties?'

'I've tried to think about these things.'

'I should hope so. Because I should hope I haven't spawned an idiot who follows any banging drum. Though just at this moment I'm not sure.'

Again Dalton trembled, looking down at the rifle and then at the figure confronting him, a figure he'd never seen before.

'So. There'll be no trouble in Ireland now, you say. You're wrong, Dalton. Very wrong. And if it's to be civil war then it has merely been postponed. But what kind of civil war, God only knows. Because don't equate Catholicism with Nationalism or Protestantism with Unionism or Republicanism with Nationalism as others will do only to confuse. Perhaps we have too many histories here, too many traditions, and have never had sufficient time to work them out. And I hear we have quite a reputation abroad. The fighting Irish, always fighting among themselves. But what of England, France? They had their bloody bloodbaths without the interference of an outside power. And now these bloody bloodbaths are enshrined as wonderful national history with some Corsican bandit called Napoleon who slaughtered half of Europe a great hero and some English puritanical blockhead called Cromwell who slaughtered half of England and Ireland practically God himself.'

Dalton watched as his father slowly sat down at the desk, filling and lighting a pipe, again a silence broken only by the sounds from the yard outside.

'So, Dalton. You are going to war. And when you return—as I'm sure you shall—what storm will you inherit then? I also once told you that if civil war comes it will be brother against brother. Friend against friend. But it might be even worse than that. With a man so divided against himself he won't know which side he's on or which way to go. And there'll be no exit.' John Gordon paused. 'I've lived my days out in peace. For that I'm thankful. Very thankful. And to repeat myself, the farm belongs to Jack. That's his inheritance. May I hope will marry well. She has the beauty and the spirit to deserve it. There'll be a little money for her, of course. As for that David one. A rogue and a wanderer he'll be, I'm sure. As that uncanny man Alec Dick once said. Which leaves you, Dalton.' Again John Gordon paused, slowly puffing his pipe, before kicking the rifle across the floor. 'Is that *your* inheritance, Dalton? Is that the inheritance you have chosen for yourself?'

'If it has to be.'

John Gordon stood up and crossed to the door, his voice quiet as he spoke. 'Then you may keep the gun in this house if you wish. But not in this study. Because now, in this family, you are keeper of the storm. I wish you well.' The door closed softly.

From the window Dalton watched as, a few minutes later, his father emerged from the porch and crossed the yard with faltering, stumbling steps, walking-stick in hand, the collie Shadow at his heels carefully measuring out his master's pace, then disappeared round the side of the barn. Picking up the rifle he stood for a long time motionless before a thread of sunlight drew him to the recess, where he looked up at the large luminous eyes and gnarled horns of the stag's head. In what arctic or subarctic wastes and wildernesses had it lived? But were they wastes, wildernesses? Those regions had been its home. There it had lived, perhaps fought. It was like those questions he'd asked during nights in Belfast when, kneeling on the floor, he'd tried to study the prophets of the Testaments. But his mind had found no rest there. And similarly in the laboratories of the university with mechanical and already disclosed experiments that were worse than boring. Tedious. How unreal they seemed. Tethering the mare to a grassy bank he'd gone alone to the undersea caverns accessible only when the tide was at its fullest ebb, the echoing of dripping seawater like the chant of prayers in his own being. And his father at one other moment of intimacy saying: 'In this practically seagirt place I have enjoyed love and liberty. Fortunate fool that I am.'

But now they were purely private passions, Dalton knew. In his room at the eastern gable wall was a copy of the Bible which fascinated him, yet offered no full belief, and something lately bought, a telescope. On clear nights and nights of broken scudding cloud his gaze would traverse the sky in a kind of oblivion of imagination as though his mind had been on a journey, the logic of which was but infinitesimably understood.

And now there was something else. The rifle in his hands. That too. Every detail of the night of the gun-running stood out clearly in his mind. The seizure of Larne by the UVF into which no one could enter without authorisation. The decoy ship moving up Belfast Lough with a suspicious flashing of lights to be boarded by customs men and police and carrying, of all things, a cargo of coal. The ruse had provided many a joke. The night drive to Fermanagh and Tyrone with McKinzie at his side with signallers marking the route. Perfectly planned and perfectly executed. The feeling had been exhilarating. But would it always be like that? And did his father guess by what small margin civil war had been averted? Patrolling at night, fully armed, with a Nationalist patrol, also now armed, in full view. Orders had been to disarm them if they had tried to intervene. But, Dalton knew, they would have resisted any attempt at such, just as he and his company would have resisted a like threat. Ostensibly both were against the Imperial parliament in London, yet with one single shot civil war would have erupted. And the orders which had gone out only a few weeks previously: the Ulster Volunteer Force must be ready for a *coup d'état* in the north, if necessary.

The pale ribbon of road spun in front of him through the country and hills, the cargo of rifles behind him strapped securely to the seat.

93

McKinzie peered from the window of the passenger seat, scouring hedgerows and banks, a loaded revolver in his hand. And, Dalton thought, there had been a sense of power coursing in his veins, but also a sense of the unknown that was not without dread, as though this mantle of responsibility had been foreordained.

Tears welled in his eyes. 'And so. I am to be keeper of the storm. If so it be. Magnificent beast. God help me.'

PART TWO

I

John Gordon lived longer than he thought he would, dying in February 1915. In the last months of his life it was mostly May who attended to him. He was in his fifty-eighth year. And in that last period before his death his favoured, May noticed, had become David, the child he'd hitherto hardly acknowledged.

Their last excursion had been just before Christmas to Larne where, after buying some presents, they'd sat in a snug of a public house with Alec Dick. She was silent as the men yarned about times past and present, watching the long slim white fingers of her father as he traced patterns in a pool of beer on the table whilst tickling the ears of the collie which lay underneath his chair. Mainly he was the silent one, Alec merry, quipping about all and sundry, alive or dead, and asking her what boys were chasing her now. They spoke also of the war. Briefly. It would be over by Christmas, someone had said, and at this comment from Alec her father had snorted and ordered another whiskey. There was talk too of fraternisation in the trenches at the Front, she heard her father remark, and at this Alec guffawed and swilled his drink in his glass. And during this talk May felt closed out: obviously they were things she did not, could not, understand.

After that he'd taken to his bed, sleeping alone now in a little box room beside her own at the eastern gable wall. She would go to him, even in the night, when she heard those noises which meant he was restless and could not sleep. The bed had been arranged beside the window so that he could look out, the curtains never drawn. Tiptoeing into his room after midnight she would often find him awake, wearing a nightcap and a heavy seaman's pullover Jack had given him as a present, watching the darkened landscape, hands riffling pages of books he never seemed to read. Then she would tread down the oak stairway to the big range, always alight in winter, to make another hot whiskey, sitting on his bed as he sipped it. 'There'll be no fraternisation if the warlords have their way,' he would mumble as she wiped the dribble of spittle from his mouth. And sometimes she

97

would awake to find herself still there, though with blankets covering her and her father still sitting upright watching the land.

And standing beside his grave it was that curious image which pressed in upon her. Of her father sitting upright in the cold damp earth, watching.

He left his bed twice during those last months, for the ceremonial occasions. At dinner on Christmas Day he was at his usual place at table, waiting to greet guests who called in late afternoon. Alec Dick called, as did Dan Hawkins and the farmhands and Granny Hopkins. Her real grandmother had come from Belfast to stay, and sat with him. There were others too whom she didn't know very well, and Samuel. And watching them greet him she understood her father was a man who was loved.

He was there too on Old Year's Night, pushing logs through the top ring of the range until it glowed redhot and little waves of heat shimmered in the lamplight as they lapped across the rambling kitchen. She heard her mother complain. But he ignored her and drank more whiskey than May could ever remember, the dark sometimes amber sometimes clear liquid in the bottles sitting on a little writing desk he'd ordered Joe Jackson to be brought from the study into the kitchen beside the fire. There he sat, fingers nervously playing with spectacles, pipe, glass, pen and paper, rocking to-and-fro in a chair Jack had made, dressed in his best suit and boots. He was waiting, he said to May as she sat on a sofa away from the scorching range, to see who the firstfooter would be, and while they sat together he read to her some poems of Robbie Burns, speaking in a dialect she'd rarely heard him use before.

In the last weeks and days she would remember that, because he would then talk the tongue of the dialect that people around her used and which she knew herself, but somehow not like her father. Because in those last weeks and days he would be talking to David, who in the autumn had run away with a band of tinkers and had again to be brought back by the police. And when they'd brought him back she'd heard her father laughing.

Watching him on those last days she would tell herself she didn't really know her menfolk, because this was her father whom she'd always loved and always thought she knew, and now didn't because he seemed so strange. And there was Samuel whom she knew loved her but whom she did not love. And there was Harry who was so distant and not with them, yet whose very absence set within her a gyre of yearnings and thoughts and dreams that made her feel so much older than fifteen and yet made her also admonish herself for her childishness.

And it was she who saw the firstfooter that Old Year's Night when the ticking of the grandfather clock turned towards a New Year with the hands at seven minutes after midnight and she escaped from the baking oven of the kitchen to the cool night air of the yard outside. As so often in Islandmagee, it was a green Christmas. Earlier she'd noticed the snowdrops and struggling bluebells in the grass of the orchard and on the banks along the lanes, even early primroses that should not show until spring. And then the hoofbeats disturbed her tranquillity.

It was Dalton. She watched as he swung easily from the horse, long legs raised from the saddle. Pausing as he noticed her, she then felt his light seemingly awkward embrace and his lips brush her hair, saw the deliberate tethering of the reins to a post in the yard—a friend's horse from Whitehead, he said, as though wishing to break the silence yet not knowing how to—and then she found herself following him back into the kitchen.

'You.'

The collie, aroused from its somnolent position under its master's chair, barked furiously.

'Quiet.'

It was only then that May saw that he was in full uniform in gleaming boots and brownish tunic and trousers and the equally gleaming broad belt at his waist from which was fixed holster and gun.

'Yes, father. Me.'

She watched her father pour the whiskey with—it seemed to May—a deliberate slowness and solemnity. There were three glasses. Hers was a smallish measure with lots of water, but the men's glasses were full.

'For auld lang syne.'

'For auld lang syne, father.'

Both men raised their glasses and drank, and she followed their gesture, watching.

'The world's last goodnight.'

'If such can be.'

'If such can be.' Her father approached and stood beside Dalton. They were of the same height, May noticed, even though her father was now slightly stooped. And very very thin. 'I've often wondered about that priestly tongue of yours. Just as I've always wondered where you came from. Will it do any good on the battlefield, do you think?'

'That's what I wanted to tell you. We'll be leaving this year. But just when we don't know yet.'

'For the Front?'

'Yes.'

'And Samuel?'

'Of course.'

'Ah . . . Yes.'

A tremor seized May. Secretly she'd been reading of the battles, of so many French and Belgian soldiers dead. And Samuel? Was love an obligation? Not what you wanted to do or be, but what you should do or be? And then she remembered the bullock and the slaughterman.

'Harry?'

'No one has heard from him.'

'Ah . . . Yes.'

An eruption came from outside. 'What the hell, ye bloody oul' git of a peeler!'

Despite the collie's barking, May heard her father laugh. 'That sounds like someone I might well know.'

The door opened to show a police constable and a boy grasped firmly in his hands. David.

'Come in, constable. I presume you're the thirdfooter. With my sons David the second and Dalton the first.'

Embarrassed, the constable looked round. 'Sir . . .'

But it was Dalton who broke the brief silence. 'McKinzie, come in.'

Letting David go, the constable took off his hat and slowly walked in, accepting the proffered glass of whiskey which, May noticed, her father had quickly poured. 'Thank you, sir.'

'A happy New Year.'

'And to all in this house, sir.'

'And what was he doing this time?' Her father paused. 'I mean that one. David.'

'Well, sir. I would hardly believe it. I heard from some firemen in Larne that he was stoking up a locomotive. I went down to the sidings and found him firing an engine.' The constable paused. 'I caught him, sir. In the act, as ye'd say. He told me he wanted to know how it worked.' Again he paused, sipping his glass before speaking again. 'But as I knew the family, sir, I thought it best to bring him back.'

A quizzical expression was on her father's face. 'The family? Don't you mean Dalton?'

'Yes, sir. Lieutenant Gordon.'

'And you'll be going to the Front too?'

'Yes, sir.' The constable's glass slipped from his fingers and shattered on the flags. More embarrassed than before, he stood frozen, and it was Dalton who, with his usual deliberateness that was now casualness, swept the splinters into a dustpan.

'In?'

'The 36th Division, sir.'

'The Ulster Division. The UVF?'

100

Yes, sir.'

'And what about those in it who might be Nationalists?'

'Father!'

'Dalton. This is still my house. Do not forget it.'

'Can I go?' asked David.

'Go?' Her father's voice was abrupt. 'Go where, sir? What Front are you going to?'

David shrugged his shoulders and looked around the assembled company as if seeking either inspiration or understanding. And it was then that May noticed the startling likeness of her two brothers. The longlimbed build she'd noticed before. But there were also the eyes, bluish specks like steel chippings which at moments seemed indeterminate in colour.

'Sit down, boy. Sit down. You'll have a glass of whiskey. So that you'll begin to know how not to abuse it when you're a man. You also, constable. Two fresh glasses, Dalton.'

'I'm sure McKinzie wishes to return home, father.'

'Of course. But in a moment. It seems that my inadvertent remarks caused some embarrassment. You'll forgive me, constable. Not a particularly hospitable act on New Year's morning. But it's said that a man's old age is a return to childhood.'

'Hardly old age, sir. You cannot be much more than a dozen years further on than myself.'

'Age is not years, constable. Age is an erosion of one's sensibilities. Or an erosion of that by which one protects one's sensibilities. Hence the return to childhood. Like a pup, sir. A child or a newborn chick in the yard. Through what eyes do they see this beautiful and terrible world? Through eyes of curiosity, yes. Infinite curiosity. But possibly also through eyes of fear? And what are the eyes of one's second childhood? Eyes of regret? Infinite regret? "I regret nothing" is another saying. And I presume it is supposed to be a courageous saying. But perhaps it really means that one doesn't have the courage to explore and examine one's own past. To see how one has allowed one's sensibilities to be eroded. Indeed, as you might one day experience yourself. Otherwise what is this second childhood? An aged pup that has abdicated from the responsibilities demanded by his reasoning and imagination? I should hope not.'

Though not understanding the conversation, May knew that there was a battle of wills taking place. She watched as her father waved the constable to a chair, the latter slowly sitting down, cap on his knees. Dalton stood by the table, the fresh glasses in his hand as her father slowly poured the whiskey. Silence followed to be interrupted by the entrance of her mother dressed in a flowing black gown with a crocheted white shawl, her jewellery glistening. Going immediately to

101

Dalton she kissed him and then turned to the constable who was standing again, glass quickly emptied, bidding the compliments of the season. Saluting informally, the constable moved to the door, Dalton escorting him with his mother, May saw, holding Dalton's arm. Then the three disappeared into the night, their voices vanishing in the sound of the soft wind that tossed the branches of the trees in the orchard and the crackling of the logs in the range.

'An you, boy. Are ye goin' till be a fool like me?' May heard her father say, as though he hadn't even noticed the others depart. 'But maybe a different kind of fool. One wi' a strengthier will. Stealin' from the markets in Belfast, runnin' away wi' th' oul' tinkers and now tryin' till steal a train. What'll ye be up till nixt?'

And then it seemed that he didn't even notice David leaving, the latter sliding from his chair to run through the door. A motor engine sounded from the top of the loanan. Several minutes later his mother and Dalton returned with further guests; Dan Hawkins, Joe Jackson and Granny Hopkins. After that came Alec Dick with his eldest son Bruce who was now helping him on the ferry. But, though standing to greet them, it was as though her father was hardly aware of their presence.

And then there was the graveside with the hoarfrost making grass and hawthorn glisten in a weak sun that lay above the ridge of inland hills. She didn't think she had any more tears to cry, as she'd cried so much when the body was laid out for last respects, but cry she did. It was Samuel who first laid a comforting arm on her shoulder, and then Dalton. Both were in uniform. The constable was there also, this time in military uniform. Though he seemed as awkward as on that night in New Year, he smiled at May, a soft smile that pursed his lips and made her feel better. Harry was there also, standing alone away from the family group and the clusters of friends and neighbours and other people who had come from Larne and villages inland. And again she thought of how her father was a much-liked man, perhaps much-loved. Had been, she corrected herself whilst watching the hard lumps of frostbound soil break and spatter on the lowered coffin. It was Samuel who had contacted Harry, telephoning an urgent message to the university in Dublin. But why he had come she did not know, because when she'd asked for him the following day she learned that he'd left immediately after the funeral without even attending the traditional meal that followed.

And it was on those days following which seemed to May the truly unbearable, the days treading after the ritual of the body returning to earth. It was the sense of absence, the fracturing of her world, the yawning gap that was a void. An emptiness had appeared which seemingly nothing could fill. And it was Jack who came to her with urgent requests for help with some early lambs that were at the mercy of frost and snow. And grasping the squirming bundles she would look at the lengthening light of pre-spring afternoons and remember the doctor's words: there had been no illness. It was just like a clock that had run down and stopped ticking. A clock that someone had forgotten to wind up. And she remembered that other winter evening when sitting alone in the farm kitchen she'd become aware of a strange silence and only later had she recognised it as being the ceasing of the steady ticking of the grandfather clock.

And then there was another leavetaking. It was in May. The month she'd been called after, her mother had told her, on the insistence of her father. She stood in Belfast watching the soldiers file by, Dalton and Samuel among them. The Division they were part of was on its way to England prior to going to the war in France. The cheering of the assembled crowds lapped across the city to the surrounding hills like the waves lapping round Islandmagee. Then they were gone, the weeks separating the two events vanishing into nothing as she sat on a bollard at the harbour receiving kisses from Samuel and then waving to both him and Dalton as they stood on the deck of the steamer which was carrying them away. And later back at the farmhouse she took her father's spyglass from the study and went to the Gobbins cliffs to scour the sea. But by then the ships were only specks on a virtually empty expanse.

And it was then that she found Shadow who, after his master's death, had whined in the yard and exploded in fury at the innocently hoaking hens so that Jack had had to tie him up and would howl in distant fields at night before finally disappearing. The corpse had already been plucked at by crows and gulls as it lay beside the watermark and it was not pleasant to look at, but on her insistence Jack wrapped it in an old sack and they buried it outside the churchyard walls on a line with its master's grave.

And so in days after she went to Rosinante to talk and tickle its ears and feed it some grass or sugar or buns from the kitchen. Because in the emptiness of those days there was nowhere else to go.

Was this to be the last time he would be in Ballycastle for whatever reason, possibly even death? His own?

Sitting on a wooden bench outside the pub, Harry looked musingly across the smooth sea, the summer sun warm against his face, the genuine feeling of pleasure in his and Niall's greetings marred by a feeling of uncomfortableness, sadness almost. It had been a year of such contradictory feelings. Having just managed to pass his degree examinations he'd remained in Dublin frittering away both time and the little allowance which was left, surprised that time can pass so quickly while one is doing nothing. Yet often restlessness would turn to rancour at his idleness and inability to make a decision of any kind. He was but a shell of a human being: a straw man to be blown this way and that by any breeze that sifted the air, he told himself. The news of John Gordon's death had taken him to Islandmagee where, confronted by the uniformed figures of Dalton and Samuel and questioned about his own intentions by the latter, he'd said nothing. Standing on the periphery of the mourners he'd felt himself a stranger, an outsider, and he'd left as quickly as he could, feeling as though it were an act of running away. It was like that in London too, several weeks later. Young Charles is dead, James had informed him. He fell at the battle of Neuve-Chapelle. And the expression on James's handsome moustached face was one of accusation and open hostility as his eyes lingered on Harry's civilian clothes, saying that though he himself longed for action his regiment had been ordered to stay in Ireland. In London for this second funeral ceremony he'd then walked the streets surprised at the feverish temper the war had created among the populace. But was it not also invigorating? Even, in a way, liberating? Despite the fact that, though the newspapers were full of the war there were very few actual details of what was happening at the Front, except for the casualty lists. The posters glared down at him demanding his services for Kitchener's army. From those same posters the women of the nation pointed and told him to go. And it was on his departure to Dublin when, in answering Valerie who'd enquired if he was going to the war, he'd said yes without thinking. James had then visited him in his digs, smiling and calling his Irish cousin 'brother officer', having received a letter from home about Harry's decision, offering his help and assistance and asking if he had already decided which regiment he'd like to volunteer for. Yes, Harry replied: the 36th Ulster Division with his own fellow countrymen, wondering if his companion's feelings towards him would have been so warm had he known that his decision sprang not from conviction or belief but simply from an indifference to his own fate and future.

'Dreaming, Harry?'

Niall had rejoined him and was sitting opposite, the two glasses between them on an upturned barrel.

'If you could call it that.'

'It's good to see you back.'

'Even if it's only for what might be a last look?'

104

Niall scrutinised the other's face. 'And what does that mean?'

'I've joined the Ulster Volunteers. I'll be following them to the south of England soon. And then to the Front, I suppose.'

'Ah.' Niall's voice was soft, and it was a while before he replied. 'I often wondered about that. And, you know, I didn't think you would.'

'It just seemed the thing to do.' Harry shrugged.

'And while fighting for little Belgium's freedom what about little Ireland's?'

'The Home Rule Bill's been passed, hasn't it?'

'But postponed for the duration of the war. And after the war? No one knows what it's supposed to be or what kind of freedom it will be.'

'Well, I've only enlisted for the duration of the war. So what my thoughts will be after I don't know either.'

Niall smiled thoughtfully, but was silent.

'And you? What will happen here?'

'Harry. I'm no more in touch with the High Command than you are. All I know is that the Nationalist Volunteers were approached and asked what they intended to do. And they simply said they'd protect the shores of Ireland against anyone.' Niall paused. 'And yes. Casement is going to Germany, I heard. You remember we heard him at Ballymoney?'

Harry nodded, momentarily recalling the intense bearded face of the orator on the dais and his passionate words demanding independence for Ireland and freedom from British military occupation. 'Germany? For what?'

'More arms.' Niall's smile was gently mocking. 'After all, weren't you and your friends the Kaiser's friends not so long ago? During the gun-running at Larne?'

'But that would be treason.'

'Big words, Harry. How can you be treasonable to an authority you don't accept? The majority of people here aren't English, never were English, and never shall be English. But they're made to think English by force of arms. If they refuse, where is the treason?' Accepting Harry's silence as a desire not to continue the conversation, Niall stood up and grasped him by the arm. 'Come on. Let's find you a bed for as long as you want to stay. And if you're a soldier home from the wars you'll be welcome then too.'

Yes, thought Harry as, a few days later, he sat in a train as it puffed and whistled through the countryside towards Belfast. Me and my friends the Kaiser's friends. His decision had immediately put him into an opposite camp to that of his childhood friend, Niall. Just as a different decision or no decision at all would have put him into another camp from that of Samuel and Dalton and even James, or would have earned him nothing but the name of coward and the gift of a white feather. Even indecision is a decision. Or is interpreted as such by others.

Through the air outside the speeding train the clowns hurtled as the cannon disintegrated. Harry laughed. Yes. That would have been his real vocation had he had the talent.

II

Dalton stood at the rail of the troopship watching the lights of the English coastline flicker yet more fitfully before plipping out as though sucked under the water which surged around the vessel. The wakes of other ships shone dully against the sky, at times leaving phosphorescent trails that curved out driven by wind and tide. From behind him came a regular stamping of booted feet and the cacophonous clatter of rifles and other equipment being repositioned on the decks amid a steady swirl of talk and laughter. But not all showed the same jollity, he noticed, turning to survey the groups and knots of men. Single figures here and there, some with Bibles in hand, while others were like himself standing by the rail staring at the tossing water and vanishing coastline. And how young so many of them seemed, he thought, mere boys of a bare seventeen with hardly down on their cheeks. Accents of villages and towns of Ulster mingled with those of the cities in such quantity it was as though not one hamlet of the province had failed to represent itself. That was good, he'd heard a superior officer remark. And the High Command thought so too. No other division in the army could be so tightly knit, so brotherly in singularity of purpose and determination. And wasn't it said that it was Kitchener himself who demanded them: who, on seeing them on parade had declared—I want those Ulstermen for the Front?

A lone figure sitting under a lifeboat caught his eye. McKinzie's son Aubrey, a youth with neither the height nor breadth of his father. Nor, thought Dalton, the inward strength. He'd noticed him on the rifle range but more particularly during bayonet practice when the shrieking yelling men, officially allowed obscenities battering the air, came stampeding across the grass to gut their straw and sandfilled targets. Tardier than most of the others, he would arrive at a sandbag to find there was nothing left to bayonet. Turning round again, Dalton gazed at the water. It was that kind who worried him. How would they react under fire? Yes. They were all volunteers. But had

107

they really meant to volunteer for this? The war in France? Because it was obvious in reading the numbers of casualties and the little information trickling back from the front lines that slaughter was taking place of a kind that no one had ever imagined when the UVF had first been formed. And, of course, its forming had been for a different purpose. Yet they had volunteered for this. Or if not this then it was as if the times themselves had fatalistically intervened like some shaping hand to volunteer them for a battle quite different from the one originally envisaged, their intent and design having been eclipsed by others much greater.

And there had been others who, during this year of preparation, had been discarded like rotten apples from a barrel—thieves, drunkards, cowards, each one a menace to any body of armed men in tightknit fraternity. But among them there had been a few who were—what?—astute, astutely playing games? As though they sensed or understood the great gap between their original motives and that which was now unfolding as their future. It hadn't been quite military practice to simply dismiss them back to farms or street-corners as the division was by now part of the army proper, yet in those early days it had retained that kind of separateness. After all, wasn't it but a year ago that they were preparing to confront the British army itself, the army of which they were now part?

A brooding smile drew Dalton's lips taut as he studied the lapping water, as though these thoughts were not without a sense of maleficence.

And during that year spent training in Newtownards in Down and Finner in Donegal and Seaford in England which they'd just left, he had discovered things about himself: that for most men his dominating bearing was sufficient to prompt immediate obedience, that he was rarely inaccurate in his understanding of others. Indeed, his insight seemed at times uncanny, even to himself. And, if he did not openly welcome the war—as he knew others did in a romantic national self-glorification founded on a vacuity of thought—he knew he looked towards it with a feeling of satisfaction and anticipation as though the prospect of battle was a test deliberately acknowledged and sought.

'Is there anything you require, sir?'

Turning, Dalton allowed himself to smile freely. 'Corporal McKinzie?'

'I thought you might require something, sir.'

There was a smile on his companion's face also, Dalton noticed, because of the deliberate acknowledgement of the second stripe he'd received before leaving Seaford. 'No. Nothing. Later you can leave out a clean uniform for mess.'

'Yes, sir.'

Motioning him to stand easy, Dalton watched as he leaned slightly against the rail, though his stance still held a sense of formality. He liked this man whom he knew had almost a fatherly concern for him, though his own feelings he did not permit the other to observe.

'And so, sir. Boulogne and France. We'll be spending Christmas in France. Another Christmas. So quickly.'

Dalton nodded without speaking, the scene coming to mind of the previous New Year in the farm kitchen with his father's irascible yet inquisitorial voice demanding explanations. It had been deliberately provocative, a final stratagem employed as an attempt to understand them both. But particularly himself, Dalton. And it was only after his death that Dalton realised he knew as little about his father as the latter had done about him.

'Shall we be in the lines by Christmas, sir?'

'I doubt it, corporal. There'll be more training before that. Without trench acclimatisation there have been too many losses, I hear. We'll probably have a quiet Christmas at the rear.' Dalton paused. 'Which is something I was thinking about. When we do go into the lines I think I'll find another orderly. You're too valuable an NCO to deal with that.'

'Oh, sir, I can cope with it. I enjoy it. When I'm not on duty with something I get bored.'

'It's not a matter of your coping, McKinzie,' Dalton replied, allowing himself the easier formality of the UVF days. 'It's a question of what's most important.'

'Sir.'

'We'll review it in the lines.'

Now Duncan paused before saying: 'I heard Second-Lieutenant Ogilby asking for you, sir. He was with the second-lieutenant who joined us at Seaford.'

'McKinstry?'

'Yes, sir. He's an Antrim man too, sir, I believe. From Ballycastle?'

'That's right,' Dalton replied, then said: 'I'll see them both later at mess. Though I'll be here should the captain or major require me.' Turning on his heel he heard McKinzie move away, acknowledging his wish to be left alone, though noticing out of his eye that the corporal had gone to his son who still sat alone under the lifeboat.

Boulogne. The harbour showed up through the spray and castellated waves and squally windtorn clouds. From behind him came different sounds as the various companies collected kits and rifles amid the snapping of orders as they prepared for disembarkation, yet still he lingered at the ship's side. Yes. Harry had joined them at Seaford. Though not given to surprises, Dalton had to admit that that had surprised him, even to the extent of making him involuntarily pause at the entrance of the mess when he saw Samuel greeting the newcomer so fulsomely. Yet it was as if he himself had had an encounter with a ghost. And why? He'd recalled the time at Malin Head and Harry's evasiveness at declaring his sentiments. They'd talked about it, Samuel and himself, during the winter they'd spent under canvas in Ulster, at times driving from Strangford in the east to Donegal on liaison duties between the different battalions with Samuel declaring emphatically that Harry would be with them. And he'd been proved right. But were his reasons for thinking so correct?

Because now Dalton doubted Samuel. Not his bravery, that was not in question, but in his ability to judge others and in his powers of endurance. He'd noticed errors and failure in both in the early days of reorganisation when, ill-equipped and untrained for trench warfare, they'd weighted themselves down with makeshift packs during route marches even to the extent of carrying the German rifles they'd earlier smuggled in because the standard British weapon hadn't yet been available in quantity. But there might be a reason for Samuel's omissions. Love. He was in love. With May. At every opportunity he returned to the island, where on several occasions Dalton had witnessed his timid or pathetically clumsy attempts to gain her attention. And she would respond sometimes gently though often with a fiery outburst that was unmistakably a rejection of intrusions on her privacy. But, Dalton mused, love was something he himself had not yet experienced. Indeed, outside the family his knowledge of women in any emotional sphere was nil.

As the ship swung into harbour and the engines began to fade, he looked intently inland where a low rumble sounded that might just be the crackling exchange of heavy guns.

The letters had arrived just before Christmas, one addressed to herself from Samuel, one to her mother from Dalton. During those autumn and early winter mornings she'd eagerly awaited the sight of the postman in the lane only to see him pass by on his bicycle on the road above the Hollow. Some mornings she would go to the roadside itself as though her act would ensure a letter's arrival and then, empty-handed, would shout at the cattle to vent her frustration. And there was the postman on a morning towards noon when she'd either given up or forgotten what she'd been waiting for standing bulkily in the hallway, waterproof dripping with rain, lifting a glass of whiskey her mother had told Jenny to give him. Taking the letter she went to her bedroom, sat for a moment without opening it and then spread the sheets on the little table, recognising the handwriting instantly not without a feeling of disappointment.

They were all well, Dalton, Harry, Samuel himself. They'd already had their first experiences of the trenches and it wasn't at all bad. Not as bad as some people imagined. The weather wasn't good and that was the worst thing of all, being soaking wet all the time. It was just like at home in winter, rain, rain, rain. And mud. But they would be having a quiet and peaceful Christmas as they were billeted in villages well behind the front lines and would be staying there over the New Year. Dalton he saw every day as they were in the same company, though Harry he didn't see all that often. Yet twice already all three had met and gone horse-riding together, galloping across the country and even stopping at a village café for a bottle of wine. And Dalton was teaching him how to shoot better because in the thousands of little lakes and ponds there were plenty of wild duck and other gamebirds. Already he was looking forward to his first leave so that he could see her—not to leave the war, of course, because that must be fought. It was because not a day passed without his thinking about her. After the war perhaps they could . . . Could they become closer? He sent his tenderest regards and love, yes love, to the family, but especially to her, and would be thinking about them at Christmas.

After her first perusal she let the letter fall on the bed. Why had Harry not written? He hadn't even come to say goodbye before he'd left, and her first news of his having joined the army was when Samuel had written to her from England.

She read the letter again. There was also some writing in French and she peered at the unusual script, trying to pick out the meaning of the words, thinking of how he'd tried to teach her a few simple phrases in the months before going to France.

Gentle, faithful, loving Sam. She called him Sam as Harry did and not Samuel as was Dalton's way.

It was her first proposal of marriage. And that was a very serious matter. Though she didn't understand many of the words or phrases, she grasped the general sense of what he had written.

Yes. She would soon be sixteen. In a few weeks, in fact. She was a young woman. Yet in these days of young womanhood and pre-maturity she instinctively knew that in her innermost self she could not, could never, reciprocate these feelings and emotions. Gentle faithful Sam whose obedient responsiveness to her moods reminded her so much of Rosinante whom they'd christened together when she was a child, big soft protuberant eyes shining with pleasure. She thought hard. A name from a great romance, had he not said?

J'aime la Picardie. Vous savez que j'ai vécu ici avant la guerre avec Dalton. Les gens y sont comme chez nous, gentils et amicaux.

    Il y a des centaines de petites collines, des bois et de petits lacs—étangs.

Nous pêchons dans les ruisseaux et les rivières exactement comme en Irlande, comme si la guerre n'existait pas. Nous observons les loutres s'ébattre dans l'eau.

Bientôt, vous aurez seize ans. Vous serez une jeune femme. Je vous aime, May, je vous aime. Voulez-vous m'épouser lorsque la guerre sera finie? J'attendrai le temps qu'il faudra.

Oh, I write this letter in French because—la raison pour laquelle je vous écris cette lettre en français est la crainte de vous effaroucher. Vous êtes mon premier amour et vous serez toujours le seul. Je vous aime, May. Je vous aime.

Quand je vois les oiseaux en liberté dans les marais—les éperviers plongeant, les craintives hirondelles de mer, les hérons majestueux qui s'élèvent avec lenteur—je me crois avec vous à Islandmagee.

Je vous aime, May.

It was her first true letter of love.

That evening she and her mother had a violent quarrel, shrill angry voices battering against the seasonal gale that swept over the Hollow, leaving grumbling echoes in the nooks and crannies of the farmhouse. They were alone, Jack having gone off to see to the northern fences because of the strength of the wind, with David, as usual, someplace no one else knew where. The subject was May's future. Since leaving school the previous year her life had been centred around the farm, though often she would think of the city and the world outside and wonder what place there could be for her in life. Now she regretted the waste of her schooldays and at times felt almost illiterate. Propositions she tentatively put forward—becoming a nurse, going to work in an office in the city—her mother opposed. And when she thought about it, how few these openings seemed to be. A good marriage, her mother declared, was all that was necessary. After all, hadn't she herself lived the life of a lady with all her wants without having spent one single year at school? And wasn't there Samuel who, after the war, would be a college teacher or even a teacher at the university? Couldn't May learn from him? Then she could live in the city if she wanted to and have a place in society. Beauty, her mother also declared, was what a young woman in May's place needed most, and that she had in abundance. Beauty, a firm hand, and shrewdness. And if Samuel didn't take her fancy, weren't there plenty of other men from which she could choose? Perhaps a man like her father with a farm and land who would think himself fortunate in having such a beautiful wife. And as it was the kind of life she'd known since childhood, she'd have no difficulty in settling into it.

Against these dictates and restrictions on her freedom May chaffed, blushing and turning her face away at the mention of Samuel and her mother's laughing understanding of his passion for her, struggling with an angry frustration because now so suddenly life's horizons had foreshortened instead of widening out into new vistas, yet learning for the first time that her mother's life had been one which suited her perfectly and trying to think of herself in such a role. And she also learned for the first time that upon her marriage she would have a little money of her own. Which had been the wish of her father.

Before going to bed she extracted one measure of freedom. After her sixteenth birthday at New Year she could go to stay for a while with her grandmother in Belfast.

After the church service on Christmas Day she talked to Sheila Hawkins who, like herself, had the same rebellious moods when she looked beyond the island to other kinds of life. But though many things were discussed, no decision was made. Later, alone, she gathered some early wildflowers to put on her father's grave and even dug up a primrose root to transplant it to the piece of ground where Shadow lay, thinking that it was nearly a year already since they'd died yet still there was that gap in her existence that nothing had filled.

Gasping, choking, tongue lolling with saliva and mucus spurting from mouth and nostrils, slithering in the damp soil and mud and layers of wet rotting leaves, the great stag was at last run down and turned at bay with one horn ripping the side of an over-eager hound. Several minutes later its last choking breath created bubbles in the blood flowing from nostrils and gashed throat. Slit from end to end its heart was tossed in the air among the savagely barking yelping dogs. Cleaned, gutted, it was roped up to be dragged back behind the hunters.

Fieldglasses in hand, Dalton watched the scene from the edge of a wood. The year had turned with the Division in the rear and the hunt had been organised by another division billeted close to them which would also soon be going into the lines. Officers from the 36th had been invited to join. Dalton had declined the invitation but had followed the hunt from afar. Alone, he would allow his emotions to show, and as the great beast took its death in a desperate yet forlorn bid for life and survival the lines creasing his face were those of a melancholy sadness which belied his youthful years. Still with the fieldglasses held firmly in one hand, the other lightly stroking the neck of the horse as it became restless with the scent in the air, vapoury breath stabbing out, he watched the activity to its last moment. Dusk creeping across the fields still he waited, upright, immobile. From the distance came patches of muttering sound, artillery. A Very light burst out and was gone in a second like a falling star. Half-turning, glasses traversing the terrain, he abruptly stopped. At a further corner of the wood was another figure, also on horseback, also with fieldglasses, watching. In a most unsoldierly fashion his cap dangled from one ear of the horse, the tunic was undone as the figure slouched in the saddle and bent forward across the neck of his mount. Though the face was turned away, Dalton recognised him by his shape. Harry. The face turned. Yes. Adjusting the glasses to maximum advantage Dalton found himself anxiously scrutinising the other's features. Nothing but a kind of still unsmiling thoughtfulness. Dalton waited. And kept waiting. But as the other did not move it was Dalton who left first, carefully steering the slowly walking horse over the thickest covering of leaves for no other reason than that he wished to listen to silence. In the open he turned again, but Harry had merged with trees and night.

'Stand to.'

In the brumous spectral landscape what awaited him? The mist was thick across the marshy land of river and ponds. The grey uniform advancing with rifle and bayonet topped by the squarish helmet.

Again I shit myself. The muck running down the sheughs of my backside and my trousers sticking to me. Afterwards I'll have to find some little place in the trenches where I can wash myself, one hand holding my cock and balls in case some scurrying rat thinks I'm dead. The rats are big and fat here because they've plenty to feed on. And they don't seem to be shitting themselves with fear like me.

'Stand down and clean rifles.'

Dawn. The time of a surprise attack is over. That's what I'm told, anyway. At noon the fog lifts for a while. But it's cold. Very cold. And the wet and rain creeps intil your feet and bones and nearly all day you shiver. The rum ration warms you for a while. But only for a while.

What is there till do all day?

I find a little hole where the duckboards are broken and, squatting like I don't know what, I wash my arse and cock and balls too. And I think of my mother in the glens when I was a kid and giving me that oul' horse medicine, I called it, that would give me the runs and the diarrhoea and sometimes I'd come back from the church on a Sunday with the shit like water running down my legs. It's good for you, she'd say, and you won't have any pimples or spots or sties acause your insides'll be all cleaned out. Clean and fresh. She was right. I didn't have any pimples or spots or sties or any of them oul' things. It was just sometimes the shit ran down my legs like water.

'Stand to.'

At the trench again with my rifle and bayonet and the mist is back

114

thicker than I don't know how till say. I feel the looseness in the back part of me and think I've done it again—shit myself, I mean—and part of me doesn't care. Fer now it's like all my body smells that way. Shit and rum and tobacco and rum and cold and muck. I have a little Bible that I put beside me and in the little whiles when I can let my finger go from the trigger of the rifle my hand runs through the pages.

The day has finished. Where did it go?

A clear single shot and a groany yell that says somebody's dead or hurt bad and there's a feeling ye wished it was you. And it was from a fixed rifle from yer oul' man on the other side I think. It's like out after the rabbits and it isn't like that at all. Yer man in the other trenches sniping straight like some oul' shark ye'd read about wi' big fierce teeth that'd frighten the daylights out of ye if ye tried till think of it.

I'll have till wash myself again. Sometime in the night if I get a chance and feel the clean water round my parts and body. The water isn't clean. Not like in the brooks and burns in the glens where it's so white clear, splashing fresh wi' the lime and oul' min'rals coming out of the rock that's good fer yer health so's ye can drink it straight and if the birds and fish shit in it that does no harm fer yerself.

And out of the mist will yer man come? Come wi' a bayonet that's a bit like mine till slit yer gullet or chest? Him that's standing like me over in his own trench?

Aye, it's nearly night when the surprise attack'll come. That's what they tell me anyway. In the dirty part of the day.

'Stand down. Fix sentries.'

And I find myself a little hole somewheres where I do what I have till do. Then I sleep for a while 'cos I'm not on one of the sentry posts and I hear noises that might be a patrol going intil no-man's-land or a land no man knows I think and that gives me a smile and I'm not shitting anymore, not now anyway and I think what if yer man over there in his trench like me comes in the middle of the night wi' his bayonet and I feel it going intil my ribs and then I must've bin asleepin' because I see lights in the sky that aren't stars but not a one's movin' so it must be safe and quiet still.

'Stand to.'

Morning and I didn't know when it was. And there's me from the glens that should've heard the wee birds call that bring up the day like they were callin' till it wi' their songs and saying day it's time till come up now out of the oul' night.

'Stand down and clean rifles.'

A bit of steel gauze is the best way till clean yer rifle but it's hard to find but most times my da gives me a bit. I'm lucky like that. He's a corporal now. Most times we have till say the army things till each

115

other but in moments he says are ye all right son and I say till him aye da I'm all right even though there's that bubbling in the back part of me that tells me I'm nearly shitting myself again and as though he knows he puts his arm on me and says Aubrey, Aubrey you'll be all right son but I don't know whether till listen till his words or not 'cause a feeling inside me makes me want till say something else I don't know what.

'Stand to.'

It's that order again and I wonder what.

'Stand down. Fix sentries.'

In the lines and I never knew nor even dreamed what it was going to be.

'Stand down. Fix sentries.'

In one hand I hold my balls and cock and feel the oul' water splashing round me and sure's God there's a big fat scamperin' rat wi' what looks like a finger atween its jaws and I thrash out ascared of my own parts and I say FUCK after it.

'Stand to.'

It's like the order has no human voice and just comes up through the duckboards from the water and muck and I'm at the parapet again wi' rifle and bayonet watching willothewisps all tight in the parts of me and wonderin' what till do if yer man comes out of his own trench and thinking atimes it's like a family house if it wasn't fer th' oul' bayonets and guns 'cause yer man over there often calls out till us good morning and how are you today Englishman or Scottishman or Irishman or Welshman and we call back sure isn't it a fine day oul' German man or Bavarian man or Austrian man because just like them we want till know who's in the little place afront of us.

'Stand . . .'

And there's still just the mist and yer man over there maybe gettin' a drop of rum or tryin' till heat his food in th' oul' freezing watery muck in his wee home just like us.

'. . . tand . . . and . . . nd . . . d . . .'

Is it morning?

Or is it night?

III

It had been like that with Aubrey McKinzie since his company had first moved into the lines. The morning and evening ritual of hugging the parapet of the trench with his rifle tightly held and bayonet thrust up was a solemn occasion. It was a quiet time, like a time of prayer. As, indeed, it sometimes was, as on occasions he found himself praying or heard the whispers of others doing so. And it was a time of fearful expectancy too, when his nervousness was so great that his body functioned wrongly. And he wasn't the only one. He knew that without question. Waiting, waiting for the moment when the enemy would lurch out of the rain and mist to strike him down. And when the order came to stand to, the thick air around the trench would shift slightly as though blown by a loud sigh.

The bombardments were also frightening, but somehow not quite as much as standing to, waiting for an attack. You could hear the shells coming and had just enough time to find a corner or a hole to crouch in. Those you didn't hear and were aiming just for you didn't matter. You wouldn't know anything about it. Already he was aware of a sense of fatalism about certain things. Perhaps why it was different waiting for an attack was that you didn't know what you yourself would do if you saw him coming. Would your finger pull the trigger or just freeze when you saw his bayonet? And would you stab up with your bayonet in the right way to kill or get him down? Because this time it won't be sand or straw from slit canvas that'll be tumbling out, but his blood and guts. Or yours.

You had to be careful too of the snipers with their fixed rifles that were always changing position. A pop in the mist and it's the end. Just like a few nights before, when Aubrey saw someone stand up in the trench that bit too high. Pop as the mist parted and folded back again and he was looking down at a figure lying slackly against the side of the trench as though asleep. Except that there was a line of blood and the remains of one eye trickling into an open mouth.

And sometimes Aubrey would talk to him in his own fashion. To

117

him. Because the man over there in his own trench with his rifle and bayonet was simply called 'him'. And he'd say: the clegg comes in summertime wi' a sting on him that'd kill a horse nigh on. Is that you? Or are you like me afeared in the parts of myself wonderin' can I kill just like that. Over there you're standin' like me in the night wi' the lights in the sky that aren't stars. But when ye come and if ye come I hope ye'll see I'm not as green as I'm cabbage lookin'.

The sound of his own voice or the voice that sounded in his head with the mention of things familiar to him in the glens of Antrim was comforting. As, oddly, was the sound of *his* voice at times. The trenches in places being barely fifty yards apart, the sound of an unfamiliar language would drift through the brume as though he were a friend beside you.

'Cushy, mate. Cushy.'

That had been the call through the darkness from an English division they were relieving. A pair of dead horses lay on the road. A dog too, wrapped round a machine-gun it was pulling when hit by a shell. Approaching the lines the heavy guns are louder and closer. He knows the Front's being changed and his howitzers try to catch you as you come in. And one of his blasts catches some. Five dead and the wounded back through the lines. Crawling up to the first line through slobbery muck ankle- knee- or thigh-high like midges stuck in cows' clap. Belly tight to the ground patrolling in no-man's-land and we get one of him with a bayonet through his shoulder and bring him back. Creeping out again like the fat rats looking for God knows what. Greasing your rifle and feet for fear they'll both freeze solid. What if he comes and your two legs are stuck in the ground like tree-stumps and you can't move? I've got trench feet lance-corporal corporal sergeant lieutenant captain, sir. And I've got trench head he says but your medical man doesn't know what it is yet.

Day and night, night and day.

Day when there's nothing much to do except try to get the water and muck out of the trench and before you know it there's more back than before. Or revetting or boarding or shoring up or sandbagging for a bit of comfort and protection. Or watching his lines through a periscope to see what he's doing or even if he's moving.

Night and day.

Night when the patrolling's done and yet another bloody line of barbed wire to be strung out.

Four, five, six, seven, eight days and nights.

Relieved.

And the battalion back through the lines with your incoming mates asking you how it is and you hear somebody say quiet very quiet oul' han' brave soft morning but you notice the two horses still and the dog

118

and an oul' ass now with its two back legs missing come to join them.
And his guns are trying to catch you out again as you go.

All quiet.

It was a time of total confusion. Orders came, were countermanded,
counter-countermanded and came back again hardly different than
before. But now it was too late. Parts of Dublin were burning and
British infantry were closing in on all sides. Fieldguns were being used
also. So he gathered but didn't know what to believe. And in the
outlying country beyond the capital he knew nothing of what was
happening. If anything.

A few days before, on Easter Sunday, the Republic of Ireland had
been declared.

In the week prior to that it had also been a time of total frustration
during which Niall didn't know what to do.

The uprising in the city against British rule by the Dublin
Volunteers was to be followed immediately by similar activity in the
provinces. The military barracks at Enniskillen, Athlone and the
Curragh were to be encircled to prevent troop movements, the
firstnamed by volunteers in the north from Belfast and other areas.
Arriving in Belfast and making contact he found that preparations
had been halted. And there was more than that. The German ship
bringing arms from Germany had been blown up by her own crew in
Queenstown harbour after being intercepted by British warships.
And he also learned that Casement had been arrested in the south-
west after landing from a German submarine. It was he who had
organised the supply of further arms while in Germany and had even
attempted to get Irish prisoners from the war in Europe to return to
their own country and join the struggle.

But quite what was happening in other areas of the country no one
knew. It was rumoured that some towns in the south in Cork and
Wexford and in the south-west in Kerry had been taken by
Republican units and were still in their hands. The only thing to do
was to go to Dublin. Others had already gone and no doubt still others
were making their way from the south and west to join in the main
fighting. But it wouldn't be easy, he was told, because after the
proclamation on Sunday the military had practically sealed off the
north and it would be like that elsewhere with the police and military
in action to cut off Dublin from the rest of the country. Already large
numbers of known Nationalists and Republicans were being seized
and imprisoned.

Yet Niall was surprised how easy it was to get to Dublin, at least the
main part of the journey. He simply took a train. Halted at Newry for
a few hours, he thought his journey had ended there until he saw the

packed lorries of armed troops enter the station yard, with many civilians being ordered off as they clambered on board. Sitting alone in a corner, wearing dungarees and with a knapsack in his lap, no one seemed to notice him. And by the tenor of their conversation he judged that the military authorities themselves were as confused as anyone else as to the extent and state of the conflict. Carefully watching the reflections in the window as the train again clattered through the countryside, he noticed the regimental insignia on some of the soldiers and allowed himself an ironic smile. From a battalion of the Royal Irish Rifles. Harry's regiment. Briefly he thought of Harry and the scant news he gleaned from the newspapers of trench warfare and mused at his own absence of emotion. That touched him not at all, and he wondered how he would feel when they met again. But that was a future no one could tell.

Only once was he disturbed. A cane poked him in the ribs and he looked up at a tall officer standing over him, a revolver casually held in his dangling right hand. Who was he? What was he doing and where was he going? He was a footplateman on the railway, Niall replied, giving a false name, and had been going to the engine-repair yard outside Dublin when all this happened. What a time he'd been having trying to get there! What was happening and had the whole country gone crazy, he asked in turn. It was a simple story he'd rehearsed and he knew he looked the part. And he'd even taken the precaution of obtaining a railway pass before leaving Belfast. But this wasn't asked for, nor was there any information forthcoming. Standing for a few moments scrutinising him, the officer then simply said that they might be in need of him as they'd heard the line was cut outside the city, then turned and passed along the carriage.

The line had been cut. The train slowed down to a walking pace, the carriages jolting and clanging against each other, sending the occupants reeling in their seats or where they stood. Shunting the carriages in reverse, the locomotive hissed on to another track. Then came a few miles of speeding before the train finally stopped altogether.

Now it was late evening. And they were on the outskirts, but where? Watching the soldiers disembark and form into columns with bayonets fixed Niall acknowledged the fact that in his sudden decision he'd forgotten the simple fact that Dublin was for him an unfamiliar city. He'd been a few times before, as a liaison officer from his own battalion in the north. But that was all. Was fixed bayonets a sign that fighting was imminent? Or was it just a precaution by the officers because they knew as little as he did and weren't sure of their surroundings? There was little sign of fighting save for sporadic popping sounds in the distance and the occasional dull boom.

120

The lines of infantry had disappeared among the dusky streets and buildings before the simple expediency of following the railway track came to his mind. And being in the guise of a railwayman there'd be nothing suspicious in his being there if he were stopped and questioned and he wouldn't expect at this juncture a full interrogation. He could walk to the terminus and thus be close to the centre of the city.

Having had little sleep for the past week and fatigue cramping his muscles he lay on an embankment for a few hours, finally arriving in the centre of the city about noon. But now the seeming futility of his mission had to be acknowledged. What was he to do and to whom could he report? At practically every step he was brushing against or being thrust out of the way by British infantry while only in the distance could he detect barricades and concentrations of Irish fighters like himself. And small concentrations they appeared to be, by the sound of the firing. Close to the swirling Liffey he saw a gunboat whizzing shells in the air and heard the answering explosions thucking across the rooftops. In one street a flood of British soldiers rushed forward in a bayonet charge and were halted with a number hurtling or slumping to the ground. But he could not get past them. Evening and night came with a reddening sky that was part of the city burning, bringing out looters too, who were busily dragging every available object from shattered shops and houses. He was a helpless spectator. And a spectator at a sideshow with a few thousand men at most taking on an infinitely greater army. A sideshow that should have been the full tide of a national revolution.

The days followed quickly to their inevitable end. The spectators increased in number as the number of insurgents dwindled. And already he could see them, hands above their heads walking or stumbling or carrying the wounded as they were herded along the streets to the different prisons.

During those few days Niall slept by the river or wherever he thought was a place of safety. Food wasn't difficult to obtain. He simply joined a group of looters and took what he wanted from a littered shop. Only once did he fire a gun. Discovering a dead sniper in an empty house he patiently waited for a passing patrol and discharged a full magazine before fleeing down an already chosen escape route, leaving rifle and body behind and with the exhilaration of seeing at least one soldier fall to the ground with a scream.

It wasn't a time for heroics. That he knew. It wasn't a time to stand his ground one against twenty with no prospect of flight. If there had been a time for heroics it had already gone. It wasn't now. It had vanished among the dust and rubble and dead.

Standing among the crowds of onlookers watching the last of the prisoners being marched through the streets amid jeers and catcalls, anonymity was his. But he had to get back to the north. And there were others in the crowd like himself, watchful, waryeyed. Because now not a county, not a town or village or hardly a street would be without the presence of police or military. Or, worst of all, informers.

' "Not shriving time allowed." Eh?'

'What did you say?'

'I said—"Not shriving time allowed." '

'I didn't know you knew *Hamlet*.'

Harry gave a quick smile. 'You're teaching me to read, Sam, aren't you? What else is there to do in these bloody trenches?'

'I often wonder what you did at the university in Dublin.'

'I often wonder too. But whatever I did I didn't do much reading, I can tell you that.'

Samuel looked over Harry's shoulder at the headlines of the newspaper he was holding. The execution of the rebel leaders in Dublin had begun.

'*C'est la vie.*'

'And what's that supposed to mean? Just because you're liaison officer with the French there's no need to show off your bloody superiority. Tell me in plain words.'

'It's life.'

'Well, if those are plain words I'm beginning to think I don't know English either. Pearse, MacDonagh, Clarke. Shot. All court-martialled and shot.'

'What else did you expect?'

' "Not shriving time allowed"!'

'I said what else did you expect!?'

'Tell me. Those German officers we captured last time in the line. Will they be court-martialled and shot? Just like that. Straight out of hand. Not shriving time allowed?'

'Oh, shut up, Harry! You're beginning to get on my nerves.'

But Harry persisted, asking quietly: 'Or will they be treated as prisoners of war? Like us, Sam. If we're captured. Will we be shot not shriving time allowed or be treated as prisoners of war?'

'I asked you to shut up, Harry.'

Seemingly unaware of the other's febrile intensity, Harry pursued the question, indifferent to yet another harsh reply.

A different voice joined in. 'What's all this about?'

Harry laughed. 'Enter the ghost!'

With relief Samuel turned to the towering figure of Dalton who stood in the doorway. 'We were talking about the execution of the rebel leaders in Dublin.'

122

Dalton nodded as he slowly strolled into the mess. 'Yes. It's a cause for some concern.' He paused. 'No one thought of what effect it might have on some of the soldiers here in the trenches. Many of the men are of a . . . different persuasion.'

'True,' Harry said. 'Of a Nationalist or Republican persuasion.' He also paused for a moment. 'As someone said to me before I left. They're supposed to be fighting for the freedom of little Belgium. A freedom destroyed by a usurping power. But what about the freedom of little Ireland?'

'We don't want it.'

'We, Sam? Who are "we"? And if there are more of their "we" than your "we", what then?'

Stamping his foot in nervous anger Samuel turned to Dalton for support, but the latter remained silent. An orderly appeared with a bundle of fresh newspapers and Harry snatched one and began to leaf through the pages.

'More executions. Plunkett, Daly, O'Hannalan, McBride—Ach! And Connolly. A wounded man in a wheelchair taken out for a final bullet while thousands of prisoners are taken off to fill the gaols and prison-camps in dear old England.'

'That's enough.'

It was Dalton's voice, quietly commanding.

But Harry ignored it. 'And, says General Maxwell—A revolt of this kind could not be dealt with by the velvet gloves method.'

'I have said that that is enough.'

'But I seem to recall another . . . revolt . . . that was dealt with if not with velvet gloves then with something very close.'

'Second-Lieutenant McKinstry. You know we're going back into the lines tonight and probably for a longer time. You're aware than an attack's being planned and there's much work still to be done in preparation. As much of this as possible is to be kept from the men. We can do without any news that might sow doubt in some or sap morale. Just one man's refusal to act could destroy the spirit of a whole platoon. Or more. You know that. And above all we can do without officers who behave in a fashion you're now indulging yourself in.'

Dalton's voice had been deliberately low, all three aware that their conversation had become a subject of curiosity from other fellow officers who were lounging in the mess taking an hour's rest, and Harry allowed his tone to momentarily fall, matching that of his adversary.

'Indulging? Who is indulging in what? It's pure bloody bastardry if you ask me. As for shooting Irishmen in Ireland. We'—here he paused, putting a deliberate emphasis on the word 'we', 'we don't

123

have to do that. We can shoot them here in the trenches of France.'

Dalton's voice was implacable. 'Second-Lieutenant McKinstry. I order you to leave.'

But Harry had already left, quickly walking into the late May evening with the sunset a golden glow on the waters of nearby lakes, waving the newspaper which was still grasped in his hand, his laughter not without mockery. 'Yes, Lieutenant Gordon. We can even shoot ourselves, sir. Not shriving time allowed. Aye. There's the rub!'

IV

It was May. The month she was named after. Seemingly in the blinking of an eye the countryside had burst forth into greens and yellows that tumbled down the hills to the sea. Psshiieee came the piercing whistle of the locomotive which swept past the carriage window, startling a heron in the shallows of the lough-shore and she watched its long slow flight as it climbed the air. Almost cumbrous-looking at first, its long neck and legs outstretched then suggested an arrow with wings. The train turned inland and then Carrickfergus came in sight, the massive keep outlined against the farther shore of County Down. Her father had taken her inside the castle once, a soldier of the garrison showing them around. She'd been in the dungeons where prisoners long ago had been kept in chains and had been repelled by the dank air and damp smell. She'd skipped along the broad parapets with her father anxiously calling to watch she didn't fall onto the rocks or into the sea below. And she'd peered into the gaping mouths of the cannons that pointed down the lough as though still ready to boom out warnings of intruding ships.

Her father had known practically everyone. He'd stood at the great wooden gate quietly talking to an officer and asking permission to visit. She saw his face and figure so clearly that he might as well have been standing in the carriage beside her. And afterwards they'd had tea in Dobbin's Inn with her father talking of the local tales of secret passageways between the castle and the inn and the church of St Nicholas whose spire she could see glinting in the sun. In bed at the farm it had been thrilling and a bit frightening to think of the ghosts that flitted through the passages at night, chains rattling. But then she had been a child.

They were beside the lough again, the town left behind. After passing through Whitehead she would be able to see Islandmagee. Eagerness and anticipation flushed her senses. But after the first few days at home would she be like before? Bored?

Why had her father called her May when she was actually born in

January? Hers was a winter birth with a summer name. Or almost summer. It had been during one of those times when a quizzical exploration of self-identity had been pressing multitudinous questions on her mind that she'd suddenly blurted out the thought to her mother and the latter, in something like an astonished silence, one hand caressing and fiddling with a gold locket that hung to her bosom, finally said that it had been her father's wish, that for him she had come like the flowers in early summer. A flower in summer, her mother had repeated, before opening the locket to let her see the two photographs inside, one of Dalton whom she recognised immediately and the other of an equally young man who looked vaguely like her father though she didn't ask whether it was or not.

Eagerness and anticipation. There would perhaps be more letters waiting for her at home. But from whom?

The train swayed and rattled and whistled in warning before roaring through the tunnel which meant that they were arriving at Whitehead. She felt just like that, swaying, swaying. Swaying with opposing urges: a quick restlessness at this new homecoming and thoughts of what might be waiting for her and a desire to sit still and sift through the past few months and its new experiences.

Yes. She could still see her father so clearly it was as though he were still alive. But already she was learning the fallibility of memory. How often in other things it had failed her, and in its failure came a sense of pain because those things which she *knew* to be there and was reaching out to grasp had already gone forever. It was a capriciousness within herself that would not come within the bounds of will no matter how strongly she willed, and at times the scenes and incidents which did come to mind were such that she did not know whether they were truly true, actually had been, or were only her own fancies.

But such lay in a long-ago past. Now there were the recent weeks since Christmas and Easter to think about.

It had been mid-January before she'd gone to stay with her grandmother in Belfast. Though she'd been there before, the little room had the feeling of strangeness. Early in bed because her grandmother insisted on it, she would softly pace the room before going to sleep, inspecting her clothes in the wardrobe or her jewellery laid out on the bedside table, or simply sitting by the window listening to the night sounds of the city. Magazines she brought from the living-room to leaf through the bright pictures of grand houses and lawns and gardens with ponds, and again thoughts would steal over her of a future life with Sam in perhaps a house like one of these. Often at home her mother would now take the opportunity to allude to such a future, with Sam as a professor at the university. Instinctively shying away from open acknowledgement of this possible life, she would nevertheless allow herself to think about it in secret. And in bed she would caress her own body, her thighs and breasts and shoulders, and in brushing her hair would feel the tingling sensation as its long silkiness strayed across her skin. There were moments like that in the daytime too when a quick feeling thrilled through her, as when the heavy amber pendant suddenly made itself known, bobbing and slipping between her breasts, and in an instant she felt hot and embarrassed as though she'd been caught wearing no clothes.

And at times there were gestures similar yet different because deliberate. On the promenade at Bangor in her new Easter bonnet and her jacket open and her shoulders held upright and straight she was quick to see the eager alert eyes of the young men on her figure. A pleasure, proud yet slightly guilty too. And then the question afterwards: had she been flaunting herself? Only hussies did that.

Her elderly guardian looked frail and sometimes walked stiffly, yet was spritely and clearminded. Her routine was strict. Early to bed, early to rise and her afternoon nap, the only violation of the latter being when they went to the seaside. Together they went shopping in the city, invariably visiting a tea parlour before returning home where her grandmother would have another little something to drink with her tea. For an old lady's afternoon sleep, she would smilingly explain, her face creased in deep lines and her eyes bright like a bird's glittering behind her spectacles. When her grandmother had visitors in late afternoon or early evening, May would go walking along the banks of the Lagan whittling a cane and wondering what it would be like to always live in the city. She didn't mind being alone. In fact, though introduced to girls of her own age, she was often happiest in her own company. With city girls she felt awkward. They seemed to know so much. And one, on seeing her in a moment of high spirits fashion a fishing-rod from a stick, some thread and a bent pin and try to catch a fish as she'd seen Jack and David do and which would have been natural for her to do on the island, actually called her a silly country girl so that May had to restrain a violent urge to slap her across the face but instead simply walked off with the retort that city girls were stupid and knew nothing. But her remark did not diminish a feeling of humiliation.

There was one girl she liked immediately, despite the great difference in their ages, a girl named Anna Leitry. They met during the evening her grandmother had taken May to the opera. Entranced by the gorgeous costumes, the heavy velvetlike drapes of the stage, the scenery and music and singing—not one whit of which she understood—the carved elephants and other figures which seemed to float above them entwined with the private boxes, she found herself confronted during an interval with a very thin, darkhaired girl with luminous green eyes. Though, May learned, she was only nine, Anna was nearly as tall as herself. Her thinness and the slight pallor of her features made the bones of cheek and face appear even more prominent, also suggesting someone older. And when she spoke it was in a quiet careful voice with no hint of childishness. Beside her stood a tall heavily bearded figure in a frock-coat with a broad gold watch-chain across his waistcoat, whom May took to be Anna's father and who was listening, head slightly bowed, to her grandmother. And hovering in the background was a stout woman with greying hair and wearing a black dress who smiled now and then at some comment and agreed but who otherwise said nothing, whom May took to be Anna's mother.

Such were May's first impressions, and it was through this meeting that she had spent Easter at Bangor and at Anna's home in County Down.

The woman was not Anna's mother but her governess. And Anna had never been to school but had been educated privately at home. Though she would soon be going to school. In England, possibly, because of the fighting that had now broken out in Dublin and other parts of Ireland. She liked singing and music and books. And drawing too. Her governess had taught her to draw. And if she, Anna, wasn't very good at drawing, she wasn't very bad either. And when she said this it was with a smile that was shy but which hid something else. Her mother she never mentioned. Nor did she often speak of her father. She liked the idea of soon going to school, but would miss her governess and home. And Dandy too, Dandy being a young Irish setter which made May wonder how it got its name, as it belied being a dandy in any sense, invariably crashing a door open with its paws, plastered from nose to tail with sand, grit and seaweed with the governess or a maid trying to chase it back outside to be cleaned. These details May learned while staying at the house in County Down overlooking Strangford Lough with its flower gardens and small wood and avenue of silver birch and broad brook at the southern periphery where wild duck and water hens would nest. Though the extent of the land could not be more than the farm and fields in Islandmagee, May nevertheless felt herself overawed by her surroundings, and by the house in particular which was so spacious she actually lost herself on a few occasions, yet was so silent. Pictures and tapestries hung in rooms and halls showing portraits and country scenes and battles and in every corner stood delicately carved pieces of furniture, many of which she didn't know the purpose of. In the evenings Anna would play the piano—Dandy, cleaned and washed after his gambol with them at the shore, sprawling beside the log fire. And then the two girls would talk, though it was May who mostly spoke, telling about Islandmagee. No, May had said in a surprised way one evening when asked the question, I haven't many friends. And yet she had, she then thought, and explained how her father had always called her a tomboy and she'd sported with Jack and Samuel and sometimes Dalton and Harry and now David when he could be found. And there had been the farmhands and girls at school. And her father, whom she'd gone everywhere with. And looking into Anna's large green eyes May tried to think of the sheltered life she'd had, a thoughtful response which held a feeling of gratitude because May knew that though her awkwardness and ignorance often betrayed her in these so different circumstances her companion never remarked upon it nor even seemed to notice.

Not that Anna wasn't sportive also. Her shyness and reserve with May gone, she was as agile and high-spirited as the latter herself, particularly when the governess was well out of sight. So it was that on Easter Sunday and Monday they strolled among the throngs of people along the promenade at Bangor, parasols and new bonnets catching the sun, both dressed in tightwaisted laced grey skirts, laced white blouses with short jackets and boots buttoned at the sides. Yet despite the finery they were not averse to clambering into boats for an excursion round Bangor Bay with the breeze and spray assailing their bonnets whilst May pointed out Whitehead on the opposite side of the lough and where the shoreline rounded into Islandmagee. Back on shore they tried to judge who best acted the coquette, making their eyelashes dance flirtatiously at a passing male figure, the assurance of her young companion startling May. Yet it was also as though she had momentarily discovered a sister.

They had heard of the fighting in Dublin but didn't think much about it. It was only when May returned alone to the city to find it full of soldiers that she began to wonder. Asking her grandmother she was simply told that some stupid foolish men had killed a lot of people and would soon be in prison where they should stay for the rest of their lives. They were rebels and no good. If they wanted to fight why didn't they go to France to the trenches where other men were fighting to keep them safe? But during the ensuing days watching the soldiers and police in the streets of Belfast and seeing the pictures of the prisoners being marched through the streets of Dublin she asked herself if it were as simple as her grandmother said. Hadn't she, May, heard her father and Dalton quarrel violently about something like this? Not long before her father died? And from some of the angry phrases she thought that her father didn't believe as Dalton did. Or Samuel. And there was the scene in the kitchen on that Old Year's Night when the policeman had brought David home. It wasn't David whom her father was angry at, but Dalton. And the war they were going to in France.

129

Beside a bank a swan sat on a nest, its mate in the water closeby. Across the narrow strip of Larne Lough lay the island. Leaning through the window of the carriage as the train curved, she could see Larne harbour and the ships clustering the quays. Some ten minutes later she was walking towards the docks when an arm fell on her shoulder.

'Well, Mistress May. Home again?'

'Alec Dick.'

'Alec Dick, is it?' The grizzled, tanned face frowned. 'What are you young ones comin' till? Aren't ye supposed till call yer elders Mister?'

May laughed. 'All right. *Mister* Alec Dick.'

The face laughed into hers. 'Now I hear it that doesn't sound right. Ye'd better go on callin' me Alec Dick the way yer oul' da did. And what a good man he was.'

'Yes,' May said simply as she climbed into the ferryboat. Then, like an explosive spark, thoughts collided in her mind and she demanded: 'Why was there fighting in Dublin?'

'Now what does a young life like your'n want till know about fighting fer?'

'I want to know.'

His eyes first studying her thoughtful face Alec then turned to his son who was sitting in the stern. 'Bruce, younker. I'll take the lass across by herself. Tell any others I'll be back on the half-hour.' So saying and his son nimbly jumping out, he skimmed the boat away from the seawall.

'There were people shot, weren't there? By the military, I mean? There weren't just prisoners.'

'That's true.'

'Why did they fight?'

'Because, May Gordon, they didn't want to belong any more to England across the water. Nor be ruled by them.'

'Will the fighting happen here?'

'Where?'

'Where we live.'

Alec paused. 'I don't know. But I don't think it will. Not now anyway. And that's true also.'

'And who do you want to be ruled by?'

Alec's voice was soft. 'My dear young life. Who rules and who doesn't is none of my worry. Because whoever does—king, no king, or whatever—I'll still be a ferryman.' Changing tack and speaking louder he asked: 'Did you hear about the last trick of that David of yours?'

From staring at the water May quickly looked up: 'David?'

'Aye, David.' Her attention caught, Alec continued quickly: 'He

130

was caught at a horse fair in Ballyclare trading in a horse he didn't have. And he got money for it too!'

Imagination netted by this sally, laughter bubbled from her. The very idea of it! Trading in a horse he didn't have! And he got money for it too! 'And he actually got money for it?'

'About twenty pounds, so I hear. And yer man who bought it thought he'd got a bargain.'

Still she laughed. 'What happened?'

'Ach, when some oul' fella was yarnin' in a pub didn't David sell his horse for him. Without him knowin', of course. And when yer man who bought it tried till take the horse away, him and the owner had the divil's own fight so the police had till be called. And then they found David on the road halfway back till Islandmagee with only ten pounds in his pocket because he'd spent the rest.'

Now Alec's laughter boomed out in unison with her own.

'And what then?'

'Yer ma had to pay the ten pounds back. And David got another hidin'. You could've heard the squeals and yells of him as far as the harbour.' Alec paused. 'And him only . . . What age would he be?'

'Nine.'

'Only nine? Dear God. He'll have us all bought and sold at some country fair before he's ten.'

Skilfully Alec curved the boat to the shore and shipped the oars, handing May on to safe ground and placing her suitcase beside her. Waving the proffered coin aside he said: 'This trip's fer me. You can tell that oul' ma of yours if she wasn't so proud and ladylike I'd marry her. That's if my own wife would let me.'

Hearing her laugh again, Alec sat in the rocking boat watching her walk up the shore, his face creasing into a quizzical frown. 'Child dear, what do you want to know about war for? But you're a strong and proud and haughty one like yer ma. Though that's yet to show.'

She waved to him from the top of the hill and was gone, and only when he heard the shouts coming across the water did he turn and see the group of passengers waiting on the other side and recall his saying that he'd be back on the half-hour. Waving an oar in the air and then splashing both in the water he started to ply, talking to himself: 'Jump in, John Gordon. Jump in, oul' friend. Though you're as light as a feather now wi' no flesh on ye hardly at all I'll still row you across. You asked me to see her well. But she's a curious mind and I'll not tell her lies. And how can the likes of me look after a spirit like that?'

She had kept the letters until bedtime. One was a postcard inside an envelope, a postcard of a town called Albert, in Picardy. A second was from her new friend Anna, saying how much she'd enjoyed their time

131

together and the Easter days spent in Bangor. A third was from Samuel, longer than ever before and as usual partly in French, which she skimmed hastily through except for one sentence which had been partly erased. The censor, she knew, having discussed the subject with her mother on a previous occasion. Soldiers weren't allowed to say anything at all about the war, and even family letters had to be censored. The one remaining had unfamiliar handwriting on it and this she'd deliberately kept to the end. It was from Harry. The first time he'd written. It also was a postcard, of two swans. Disappointment yet gladness. The words were perfunctory, yet held her attention. He thanked her and her mother for past hospitality, said he was in good health and spirits and said also that during a leave period he would try to visit them again in Islandmagee.

Placing the postcard upright on the little night table she read Samuel's letter with greater care, stopping at the partly scored-out sentence. He and Dalton had quarrelled with Harry, and the quarrel—she could pick out the letters, the censor having been lacking in thoroughness—had been about what was happening in Ireland.

Snuffing out the candle she sat on the edge of the bed, the sifting folds of deepening gloom on either side of the window like the edges of a chasm.

Muffle and clip, clip and muffle. Stop. Clip. A muttered oath. Muffled rubbing sound again. Clip. Silence. Clop. Again a muttered oath and a coughing sound that was certainly not human.

Below was a pony, hoofs ungainly bundles of sacking, one of which had loosened and was trailing behind. A hand held it by the halter, another was clasped over its mouth to stop it from neighing while a voice was softly cursing the animal to be quiet. The pony was shying back as the hands of the figure tugged forward in this snuffling, snorting, oath-whispering battle of wills.

Like a bright laughing star in a moment of sadness. David.

Her giggles carried her to bed and sleep.

V

Niall had been expecting them, though earlier than when they actually appeared. At work in the yard repairing a shaft of a cart he saw the uniforms out of the corner of his eye but did not turn round, as though unaware of their presence. Humming softly, shavings fluttering to the ground as he tapered the wood, his attention was seemingly directed totally to the task at hand, though he felt his senses sharpen as questions and answers probed his mind. At the sound of a cough he turned round, face showing surprise.

'Visitors? And at this early hour?' He smiled, knocking the plane against the side of the cart and scattering the heap of shavings with his foot. Redgold in colour, they were blown across the cobblestones towards the others. 'Have you work for me?'

'It would depend what that work is.'

There were three of them. Two policemen in uniform and a third figure who was in plain clothes. Lifting the partly hewn shaft he ran his fingers over the still rough surface in a casual fashion, his mind assessing the details. The policeman who had spoken was a stranger and carried a rifle in the crook of his arm. Obviously one from a barracks in a different district. The second was familiar, a friendly soul who was a native of the village. The third person was also a stranger and stood some little distance away from his two companions.

'Well, I've got a cart, a good horse and a boat. That's if you're thinking of having anything shifted. As well as that I can carpenter and plaster with the best of them. And fix an engine or two. A man of some trades, if not all.'

The policeman who was his near neighbour was about to speak but, Niall noticed, a slight indication from the figure in plain clothes made him pause and it was he himself who had to break the silence again, against his will. 'What brings you here, Billy? Interrupting an honest man in his toil?'

Another slight indication was the signal that the person whom he addressed was given leave to speak.

133

'We were looking for you a while back, Niall. But you couldn't be found.'

'A while back?' Niall tugged thoughtfully at his long locks. 'It must've been a brave while back as I haven't been far for months.'

The second policeman spoke, lowering the rifle and placing the butt on the ground. 'It was during the shooting in Dublin. At Easter.'

Niall's tone was derisive. 'Oh, that.'

'Yes, that. With a handful of rabble whose war was over in a week.'

It was the voice of the third man who had now moved behind him. Turning, Niall saw him standing beside the stable, fingers lightly tracing over a harness which hung on the inside of the open door. He was tall with a reddish fair moustache and thinning hair at his forehead. Dressed in a dark-grey suit broken by a silvery-coloured tie and a pocket handkerchief of the same colour, highly polished shoes, his appearance was immaculate. A trenchcoat was draped from his shoulders, belt casually looped at the back. But it was his voice that interested Niall most. There wasn't just sarcasm in it, even though he had spoken softly, but a kind of spleneticism that suggested a finely controlled savagery. Like the purring hiss of a wildcat. And it was an educated voice and accent which did not readily betray its origins.

'Have you any guns?'

It was the policeman with the rifle who'd asked the question and again Niall was forced to turn. 'A shotgun. Who hasn't one of those?'

'What for?'

Humour was now deliberate in his tone. 'What for? What does anybody have a shotgun for? For a bit of hunting. And to keep any vermin out of the yard.' Nodding towards the back of the stable and barn he used as a workshop, from where the sound of clucking and quacking could be heard, Niall added: 'I keep some fowl at the back and don't want a rat or fox to help himself to a meal.'

'Like the vermin shot in Dublin?'

He couldn't keep turning like this, Niall thought, with the questions coming from different sides. It was an attempt to disorientate him. Hearing the question repeated with a slowly savoured mockery he tossed the plane onto the cart and walked a few paces to lounge against a wall, hands in pockets after lighting a cigarette, his three interrogators now in view. 'If you want to call them that.'

'And what do you call them?'

'Fools. Madmen.'

'I think "vermin" is the better word.'

Niall shrugged his shoulders and sucked on his cigarette. 'Why all the quiz, Billy?'

'We were looking for you in Easter week. On the Saturday. You weren't around. One of us happened to call by.'

134

Happened to call by? Yes. They would have been swift in action in the north. But they had nothing on him. Of that he was certain. Nothing except a name. 'I wasn't around?' Again Niall thoughtfully tugged at his hair. 'No. I wasn't around here. I was in Rathlin. You know I spend half my time taking stuff over in the boat.'

'Can I see the shotgun?'

Going to the workshop Niall fetched it, watching as the figure in plain clothes carefully inspected it, handling it intimately as someone used to weapons.

'And the shells.'

The bandolier was brought and handed over. A cartridge was inserted and the gun snapped closed, the barrel pointing directly at him with his antagonist standing upright several yards away, the trenchcoat fluttering at his calves in the breeze. Niall grinned as though an accomplice to the other's joking gesture, but it was the sudden clicking accuracy of guesswork in his mind that was uppermost. Of course. He should have detected it before. Intelligence. And by his stance and mannerisms Military Intelligence at that.

'What do you think of Casement?'

'Casement?'

'Don't tell me you don't know of that famous man from this part of the world?'

Niall paused. 'Him that was made a Sir by the King?'

'Yes. Sir Roger Casement. Knighted by the monarch of Britain and Ireland.' A slitted colourless smile lengthened the mouth beneath the moustache. 'And now in an English prison for dealing with the Germans.'

'Another fool.'

'Or another one of the vermin to be shot?'

The shotgun made a crashing sound in the confines of the yard, slapping back from the walls. From above the rooftops a passing swooping seagull came tumbling down in a shattered flurry of blood and feathers, one wing practically severed as it hit the ground. The other was still smiling, eyes lingering on the broken form, Niall noticed, controlling the spasm of anger at this outrage of an innocent wild thing. And still the eyes lingered on the carcass before the spent cartridge was ejected and the gun slowly closed and placed carefully against the stable wall.

'Do you know of any of them in the district?'

Niall shook his head. 'I'm not interested in politics, if that's what you're asking. It takes me all my time to make a decent living. In fact, I need more time in the day than there is.'

The other nodded while lifting the partly planed shaft from the

135

cart. 'You seem to have good hands for wood.'

'I do my best. I've been at it since I was a boy.'

'We need all the information we can get.'

'And what information could I get?'

'Anything.' The other paused again, a long pause this time, weighing his words as if in fear of betraying his own secrets. 'You'd be surprised to know how much can be known out of . . . the slightest thing. The slightest detail.'

True, thought Niall, and said nothing.

'Information.'

'And how am I supposed to get it?'

'By listening.'

'I doubt if I'm anywhere long enough to listen for long.'

For the first time Niall found the other's eyes staring into his own, eyes that shifted in colour and penetrative power as light and cloud overhead varied. 'And that I take it is tantamount to saying no?'

Niall watched as he walked to the gate without waiting for an answer.

The enquiry came from the policeman with the rifle. 'Sir?'

The figure stopped to look back, allowing a few moments to elapse before speaking. 'I don't think we've had any success here. That is, if success here is to be had.'

They'd gone as unexpectedly as they'd arrived. The yard was empty save for himself and the ripped body of the seabird whose blood was already congealing in the cool air. Lifting it he tossed it onto the cart and tried to work again, but his thoughts would not settle. The bird in one hand he went down to the shore and tossed it into the water, then got into the boat and began to row, the hard exercise pulling at his muscles and draining away the clotted aggressive anger. Mooring the boat below a cluster of cottages he climbed the shore again and entered one that was a spirit-grocer's, slowly sipping the dark porter and watching the sea.

Yes. They had been fools. Madmen. That's what he'd originally thought.

But now?

Perhaps Pearse had been right. A baptism of blood, a sacrifice, to rekindle an old flame of flickering centuries that had long lain dormant and smouldering. They couldn't have expected to win. Not two thousand or so men against an Imperial army that could have been swiftly brought from all quarters of the globe. That they'd held out for a week was practically a miracle in itself. And if the whole country had risen as intended it would have meant defeat also in open battle. Had the cancelling of such a rising then been a mere muddle as everyone thought? Or had it been an inspiration on the part of a doomed few?

Mere speculation. That could never now be known.

He tried to think of the war in France. Hundreds of thousands of men against opposing hundreds of thousands. But they, Ireland, did not have hundreds of thousands of men and horses and the equivalent in arms and machinery to throw into such a conflict. And so in such a war they must always lose.

He'd fired the rifle and heard the English soldier scream. And had fired again. The rifle lay beside the already dead Irish sniper. And then he'd run away. Run away to fight again another day.

The beginning of the executions had started it. The mood had not crept but swept over the country. Even in the north where the British and their Unionist cohorts felt safest. Those who'd jeered and catcalled when the Irish fighters were led to prisons and deathcells were now eulogising them in ballad and song, were cheering and festooning them with flowers as they were marched onto cattleboats destined for prisoncamps in England. The Easter débâcle had sown seed in the soil of every corner plot in the country.

Niall smiled. If débâcle it had been.

To run away and fight again another day. Hadn't the great O'Neill used such tactics against the English Elizabeth with success? The time when Ireland had come nearest to unity?

Again he tried to think of the war in France, of the marshalled thousands of soldiers in their trenches facing each other, and failed because two faces kept blurring the images. Casement in his cell. And Harry.

Yes. Theirs would be a different kind of war.

Run away to fight again another day. Leaving the enemy dead behind. As many as possible.

Aubrey.

All I know is there's going to be a big push. A big shove. Against him in his trench over there. He knows it too and sometimes he comes over in the night to find out more and there's a bit of a fight in one of the trenches with maybe somebody getting a bullet or a bayonet stab that'll not kill him but'll take him home out of it all and you feel yourself wishing it was you.

Abbeville, Amiens, Albert, Beaumont-Hamel, Beaucourt. I've marched through them all and sometimes back through them and can hardly tell one from the other. Front lines, second lines, behind the lines, it's all work now with buildin' bits of bridges and diggin' pits for the artillery guns that'll pound your man over there to nothin' they tell us so that when we attack it'll all be easy. In the dark the bell men creep out with their telephone wires and we ask them what's happenin' because they can listen in to everythin' even the brass at HQ but they don't tell us anythin'. The tunnellers too disappearin' into the ground like ferrets with their tunnels goin' God knows where and sometimes I laugh when I think of a kangaroo jumpin' out of a hole in the ground instead of the rats. It's wee things like that you make up for yourself so's you can smile at it. When it's quiet and I can hear the splashin' of the wee river, Ancre they call it, and the ponds round it I think I'm just out fishin' for a bit of trout.

Inspection and drill, drill and inspection and it's the gasmask drill that's the worst runnin' with full kit and chokin' for air and your belly heavin' ready to spew your guts out. But they say if the gas comes it'll kill you for sure and you've a chance with the rubbery stuff stuck over your face. When I see my mates it looks like a lot of funny pig faces and I suppose I look like that myself and I think if we came at your man in the night with the masks he'd think the oul' divils had come for him sure and'd be so scared he couldn't shoot. But then he must have the same tricks too.

Your man in front of the firing squad just crumpled up like a pancake and fell kind of sideways. It wasn't one of him. It was one of us. From another battalion. The court martial said he'd tried to desert and so there was nothing but the firing squad for him. A lot of us were marched up to see it happen. I'm glad I wasn't one of the firing party 'cause I don't know whether I'd have pulled the trigger or not. And all of us kept skellyin' at each other out of the corners of our eyes and shufflin' a bit I suppose wonderin' different things. He just stood there with his face a kind of nothing. Because what could he do when there wasn't a snowball's for him? And though I didn't want to I kept wonderin' what it'd be like if it was me. Knowin' this was your very last minute seein' the clouds sailin' across the sky or a patch of grass you'd be sunnin' yourself on. Others on field punishment are luckier even though they have to spend half the day roped half-naked to the wheel of a waggon. You could maybe blind out the minutes passin' even through the pain 'cause you know somebody at sometime'll come to take the ropes off and it'll be over and it'll be forgotten in a week or so.

I'd write all this to somebody at home if I'd somebody to write till. But there's only my ma and young Ned and they wouldn't understand. But then I think that's daft because you're not allowed to say any of those things when you write home.

Sometimes my da comes through the trenches till yarn with me for a minute or two. He yarns with the others too and looks after us. Like Bertie Knox who lives not far from us at home. In Islandmagee. Bertie with his bangalore torpedoes that you're supposed to throw across your man's barbed wire to blow holes in it so's you can get through. Some wit christened him Bunglory Bertie and he swears when we get back home he'll hound us all with his dynamite. But it's

mostly behind the lines me and my da meet and we've even had a beer
at times in a wee French pub in the village 'cept they're not called
pubs here. And havin' a yarn and a glass and it's just like being back
in Glenarm talkin' about the sheep rounds on the hills.

It was after the soldier was shot by the firing squad I said it to him. I
didn't mean to. It just came out by itself so I think it must have been in
my mind all the time. I was on sentry duty lookin' out between the
mist patches and listenin' to the river splashin' when he came down
the trenches checkin' on us. I could feel his hand big and easy on my
arm and see him smilin'. Then he says it'll be soon now son you're
not afraid are you and I says what's the point in bein' afeared? The
attack he was meanin', I knew, and I thought of myself walkin'
across the high ground towards him in the other trench. What's the
point says I 'cause if I don't go on I can't go back either, else I'll have
the firing squad too like him we had to watch the other day. And then
I thought yes that's why we were told to watch it 'cause if we did the
same sure's anythin' we'd get the same. And I says again what's the
point da in being afeared 'cause if I do go on your man over there'll try
till kill me and if I don't go on or try till go back my own'll kill me for
sure.

We stand for a bit saying nothin' and just listenin' and I think
maybe it's because of all the broken bodies I've seen already. Bits of
arms and legs and heads and things lying around like somebody's
smashed up a wee girl's dolls. And the moans comin' from
no-man's-land when you can't get the wounded in and the stink when
they die. Awful, it is. And I wonder if I'll be like that. And then all of a
sudden I don't know why I says I don't believe in you any more. I
don't believe in anythin' you tell me. I'm not fightin' for anythin'. I
don't believe it matters how I die because you've given me no true
reason why I die. All you've given me is a trap. And when I
volunteered I didn't know I was volunteerin' for this and I can't
unvolunteer myself now. I don't even know if it was myself who
volunteered me. And I says again if I go on him over there will kill me
and if I don't go on my own side will kill me.

And then he stands for a long time with his face close to me and I see
his lips movin' as if he were repeatin' my words and he gives me a kiss
on the cheek and I watch him squeezin' back along the trench.

And standin' at the sentry post keepin' a lookout for him in his
own trenches I'm still thinkin' about the same thing and wonderin' if
he's ever thought about anything like that.

No. I can't unvolunteer myself now, can I? And I suppose he's like
that too over in his own trench. He can't unvolunteer himself either.

The attack'll be soon, da says. But hardly this mornin', else we'd
all be crushed tilgether in the trenches waitin'. I didn't mean to hurt

139

him like that. I saw it in his face. He's a good da and not like some who beat or play the master with their sons and we've been more like brothers. When it's over I'll tell him I'm sorry and it was just because of the fear in you when you're waitin'.

But when I come across the high ground with my rifle and bayonet and tin hat I hope your man sees I'm not as cabbage as I'm green-lookin'.

Maybe when he hops out of his house in the ground I'll see he's only a kangaroo.

VI

Zero hour minus sixty.

'The first of July. Eh, sir? It seems we'll have an early Twelfth. But with bigger bonfires. And not forgetting the din.'

A flicker of a smile crossed Dalton's face as he looked down the packed lines of men in the trenches, many of whom were wearing orange sashes which showed as a strip of colour mostly hidden beneath water bottles, ammunition pouches and bandoliers. 'An early Twelfth just as you say, corporal.'

'And just a wee bit like the gun-running in Larne. As one of the men was saying to me,' added Duncan, trying to keep his voice at a normal conversational level despite the thunderous cacophony of sound which was the artillery blasting the enemy trenches in front with every gun that had the range.

'Except that then we were looking out for a different uniform.'

'Except . . .?' Duncan paused, uncertain of his superior's reference.

'See that the stores and ammunition are still being brought up. And see that every platoon commander checks what his men are carrying again. We want as many Stokes mortars and Mills grenades as we can carry. And get them to check the seniority of privates again also. In case they have to take over. We'll need precision, corporal. Precision.'

Precision. Yes. But how, thought Dalton, as the other slipped away and he again turned to train the fieldglasses on the German redoubt on the ridge across open ground, his vision mostly filled with splintered earth and trees as shells exploded without interruption. Yet though the bombardment had continued without respite since before midnight he could still see, during those moments when the air cleared, heavy lines of enemy wire unbroken and uncut. And in other places it was even worse as the bombardment, rather than shattering the wire as it was understood it should have done, had coiled it into even greater tangles so that it was more of an obstacle than before. From Thiepval Wood they would have to attack. And what lay over

141

the ridge where he could not see? More wire and machine-guns grouped at strategic points. From experience before this mass attack he knew that the German machine-gunners were good, very good. From the valley of the river Ancre they would have to press upwards. What? In unison with his thoughts he saw the field-grey uniform of a German soldier appear here and there, as though undaunted by this maelstrom from the skies. It tallied with reports that patrols had brought in during the previous few nights. That in many places the enemy's fortifications had weathered the days and weeks of shelling and were still sound. More than that, from his own intelligence observing weeks of preparation he would know that an attack was imminent and would have put further divisions into the lines. And in less than an hour the Somme battle would begin, at 07.30 hours. Across the valley of the Ancre a white mist shifted slowly in dense folds like a great succubus drawing fragmented soil and vegetation into itself with seemingly malefic impassivity. What was it going to be like for the men?

Sliding back into the trench from his observation post he paused to look down the mass of packed men, many of whom were already fiddling with bayonets awaiting the order to fix. Pushing past them with a casual word of 'good-morning and now we'll have the fight we've been waiting for' and giving an answering smile to those who laughed he reached an elevated position and stopped beside a group of men huddled around Lewis and Vickers machine-guns. 'Second-Lieutenant Ogilby?'

'Lieutenant Gordon?'

Finding a corner they both crouched.

'Well, Samuel. This is it.'

Samuel nodded. 'Good luck, Dalton.'

'And to you. Remember. Bring the machine-guns behind us as quickly as possible. We'll need them. Use the dead as protection if need be. As sandbags. Do you understand?'

'I understand.'

Samuel watched as Dalton with that abrupt manner of old turned without another word and thrust his way back down the trench through the packed ranks of the 11th Rifles, then turned to give an order that the guns be checked yet again.

Again at the observation post to watch the crescendoing curves of fire in a breaking mist that was beginning to show a bright dawn. The men. Use the dead as sandbags, he'd said. Did he really care about the men? Though he had the tangible sense of physical presence in sweat and low voices and muted clinking of metal and nervousness in the rippling air all around him were they not for him—abstractions? In the large circle of the fieldglasses turned towards the enemy Dalton

142

pondered the enigma of self. Himself. And as if reflected by the flaring barrage came a startling display of visual images in the mind of he who had no visual imagination whatsoever except in dreams or nightmares. His father stood, toe kicking the rifle on the floor. Would you attempt to usurp my authority here? In the nakedness of night in the farmhouse the wifely breast of she who bore him. And again his father quoting a poem by Burns: '*On Seeing a Wounded Hare Limp by Me*'. One of the few creatures who refuses to live in captivity, it's said. The shrieking of May as a child witnessing the slaughterman and the bullock and then his arms closing round her in the saddle of the black mare and he being the terrified one as pressing against him was this pulsing throbbing crying life, against his thighs and belly and torso. And then seeking escape with the seawind pushing the mare on across the sands at Brown's Bay. But they did not know his terror, of that he was sure. And now perhaps death? A lingering sensation went coiling through his being. No, no terror, but a peacefulness as though even the tinges of darkness could be savoured, opening to a different continent. At bay the great stag fell, horns slashing, and on seeing the figure in the wood slouched over the horse he turned violently at the touch on his elbow.

'McKinzie!'

'Last briefing, sir. For . . .' About to say 'for junior officers', Duncan hastily corrected himself. 'For officers going over, sir.'

Why had he been thinking about Harry, Dalton wondered, when Harry would be somewhere among the adjoining battalion of the 12th? 'Time?'

'Zero hour minus thirty, sir.'

Zero hour minus thirty.

McKinzie leaned against the side of the trench for a few moments' respite, knowing that his next moments of such would be in a time not of his knowing but maybe God's or the Devil's. One voice stood out above the booming drumming of shellfire, the tiny whispering inside his own head that said he must see his son now. Since that exchange at the sentry-post of a few nights before he'd deliberately avoided a meeting, being both frightening authority and father to every man beneath his rank, cursing them on to greater vigilance, comfortingly yarning about the girls at home, harshly urging them up through the trenches with supplies. But that tiny rift in his mind remained and mostly he was cursing his own weakness, even for a son. Casually elbowing his way down the line, pausing at intervals at a hunkered figure with a small Bible in hand, sensible to every lurch and slither of his own feet, he at last confronted the one he sought as though he were a foe.

143

'Corporal?'

'It's your father, ye wee eejit.' McKinzie tried to give a conspiratorial smile. 'Just thought we'd have a last yarn before the bang.'

'Ye know, da. I was hopin' you'd come. I just wanted till say I was sorry.'

'For what?'

'The other night. For sayin' what I did.'

'That?' McKinzie paused seemingly to think. 'Oh . . . that? Sure you know you've always been free to say and think what you please. I never took the heavy hand to you.'

'But that's just what I was thinking. You're a good da and I shouldn't have said what I did.'

At the back of his eyes McKinzie felt the tears well and inwardly he cursed himself viciously. Of all times, why this one? He who was supposed to show strength?

'So. I'm sorry. I volunteered myself. Maybe it's just I didn't know what I was volunteering for.'

McKinzie grasped him by the arm. 'Enough of that for now. Soon we'll have an oul' pack on our backs and be going over the glens again. 'Member that time trying to fish in the vanishing lake?'

His reward. A smile.

'Ye know, I thought ye were havin' me on. Wi' all yer oul' talk about a lake that disappears and comes back again. When I was a wee lad lyin' in bed I used to think of the fairies or such carryin' the lake away so's nobody could see it and then bringin' it back again. And they didn't even have buckets till do it with. You quare'nd fooled me.'

McKinzie laughed in relief at the boyish amusement on the other's face. 'Just a matter of soil, son. Like a dry river-bed in summer. The soil's too porous for the water to stay when there's none the heavy rain. And when there's the rain both water and fish'll come back.'

Came an explosion that encompassed the sky and drowned the noise of the artillery and reverberated in the ground beneath their feet and both knelt at the side of the trench before Duncan, shielding his eyes, peered over the parapet.

'The Hawthorn Redoubt. The engineers have done it, son. They must have blown up half the German army. The going'll be easy now. We've ten minutes to go. Fix your bayonet.'

'Are ye sure it isn't Bunglory Bertie, da?' said Aubrey, looking round for Bertie Knox who was one of the bombing team. 'He says he'll blow us all up even when we get home.'

'Away or that wi' ye!' McKinzie laughed and began to push down through the men. 'Fix bayonets! Fix bayonets!'

Zero hour minus ten.

In Thiepval Wood behind the trenches Harry was lolling against a tree fiddling with his revolver when the mine exploded. Squinting, he saw a large area of ballooning earth that blotted out the sky turning morning to twilight. Focusing fieldglasses he picked out larger objects: bodies, machine-guns, trench-boards, what seemed to be part of a horse waggon. All around him in the wood men in full battle kit stood quietly, others hunched with eyes half-closed as if in prayer. From the trenches he could see helmets bobbing. When figures began crawling out it would be the signal to attack.

He hadn't slept much during the night but had wandered around the recumbent figures who were trying to get a few hours' rest before the battle began. Some were like himself, unable to sleep, and here and there he paused to listen to bantering conversations which at moments became completely sober. Yes, it was the imminence of possible death that quelled any attempt at prolonged humour. Except for himself, it seemed, for his own feeling was one of amusement. Uniformed, gun in hand ready to kill or be killed, he couldn't take the whole thing seriously. Despite the shelling of the heavy guns in the rear he'd heard a lark singing and had stopped to listen. When had he listened to others? At school, at university. And hadn't it been with the same kind of amused stoicism at the aimlessness of his own life? And here he was now in Picardy in a war involving millions, yet for him it didn't matter whether he was here or not. If he were to die. So? If he were to live. So? The latter might be the worst prospect as he would again be confronted with choices and questions all demanding action, action which he didn't seem to possess. It baffled him, this absence of feeling, had even begun to haunt him. At home too he'd listened to a lark. But where was home? Had home ever been? He was a zombie, an automaton, flesh without spirit, a form wandering through its own night that was an inability to live. 'Good-night, sir,' some soldiers called as he walked among them, feet scuffling among grass and twigs. He knew that they thought he was there to give reassurance, comfort even, and wryly he smiled. Did they but know the truth. They who so much wanted to live and he who did not care. A shadow passing. Merely. Would it always be like that, assuming he survived? Briefly he thought of Niall and Ballycastle, heard the sound of the sea crashing on the shore. Would he return there when the war had ended? Or was that like himself, a place of no substance that could call him back? Other images drifted through his mind and he laughed. Yes, the clowns. Always the clown in a travelling circus whose destination was nowhere.

In the morning sun he walked among the soldiers as they shaved and breakfasted and made the final preparations of kits, before completing his own toilet. It was all so ordinary. And there in front of them beyond the wood figures were crawling out of the trenches, sunlight glinting on helmets and bayonets. Revolver in hand he beckoned: 'Come on then, lads. Let's follow. Let's go for a walk in the sun.'

Zero hour.
Voice of an unknown soldier in Thiepval Wood.

And so we followed him for a walk in the sun, him that had dandered among us through the wood all the night long laughing and wisecracking, a revolver in his hand as if he was going till shoot the sky out and the whole German army into the bargain all by himself. Playing cards we were, a group of us, by the light of a wee torch. Not that we needed it because wi' all the banging and flashing going on it was like daylight sometimes. And he sits down beside us in the middle of a game of poker and says—Did you hear a lark singing? And we all looks at him and then looks at each other and we was all thinking the same thing. Is he crazy or what? This is the real joker in the pack this one for how could you hear a bird singing above this hell of a din your artillery men are making? But we went quiet for a wee minute or two and sure's God there was a bird singing away in the trees somewhere. And then he took a hand and we were playing jokers wild and damn it all didn't he win when he played a joker as an ace for a full house. And then he starts yarning and asking us what we'll do when we get back home. And then we starts talking all at the same time like it was a real relief till talk about that as so it was for we was all secretly thinking of the hour and minute of attack creeping closer and closer like the dead hand of th'oul' divil. A trawlerman says I and I wish I was back at the fishing for there's a shiver up my spine that might be the divil walking over my grave. And when I says that I think of the boat coming back intil port with us a week out or maybe only a few days depending if the catch is good and the wife and children waiting and how long it's been since she and me had a good laughing time in bed. And I can feel we're all thinking that way whether we come from the farms or the docks or the shipyards or the flaxmills. Because as the hour passes seven and the minutes tick by I wonder if I'll see her again and we all get very quiet and just stand around looking at each other the way you see a lot of oul' sheep just standing staring. And up front they're out of the trenches now and across no-man's-land yelling and cheering as if it was a football match with McKinstry after them waving his wee gun in the air. Aye, that's his name, McKinstry, Second-Lieutenant, and not like some of the other officer nobs that'd bawl you out for no reason at all. Not a big man, not a wee man either, about middle size with a strange kind of face that sometimes'd remind you of a girl's. And so we go for a walk in the sun. Or a walk intil hell for where's the choice now? And it might be the last. Because for all their talk of half

146

the German army being blown up or running away already I can only wonder. Your German soldier's a brave good fighting man and won't give up that easy. But then I think as I swing my rifle up and kind of crouch as I go running through and out of the wood that maybe your man McKinstry was right till talk that way. About the bird singing, I mean. Because if I'm till die here this day maybe some other day a wee flower'll be growing or a wee bird'll be singing in the clear air over my grave when the guns are silent.

And within an hour they were in their thousands dead.

Aubrey.

And so I come crawlin' out of the trench and go across the high ground and up the slopes of the hill where we're to take him in the Schwaben Redoubt and I can hear us cheerin' and I wonder if I'm doin' that too because already I can see some of us fallin'. Though a thousand should fall by thy side the minister said before the battle and I says till myself is he with us so that he'll maybe take the chance of fallin' too? And when we come to the wire the big guns have stopped their whizzing and shooting and we can see him come up out of his trenches wi' already the light machine-gunners coming running at us from their end of no-man's-land and the breaks in the wire stacked high wi' the dead and dyin' and half of somebody goes bouncin' back down the slope and as I run over the tops of the bodies somebody's screaming under me. Then we're intil him and I see Bunglory Bertie already at his trench wi' bombs before he starts spinning round and round like he's crazy drunk or doin' a funny dance. And I'm still runnin' and shootin' at him, runnin' and shootin'. And stabbin' too. And I wonder what I'm thinkin' about but there doesn't seem till be anything in my head except bits and pieces of bodies and all the crazy jumpin' runnin' figures and I hear some wit sayin' it's like a Belfast riot on top of Vesuvius and I thinks it's like some daft oul' fair where everybody's drunk out of their minds and then I hear somebody shoutin' we've taken it! we've taken the Schwaben Redoubt! and I see some of us already in his trenches but he's still fightin' like fury and then I see him comin' at me in his different uniform a big German soldier jabbin' and stabbin' wi' his bayonet and I'm doin' the same and go lungin' at him just as he does and there's a kind of surprised look on his face and I wonder why and then it's funny because everything's all misty and swimmin' round and round like the sky too's doin' a dance and I think I'm walking up through the mist of the glens very very slowly because something's trailin' at my feet makin' me slip or through me holdin' me back when . . . stop . . . I . . .

*

Attack was followed by counterattack, and followed by counterattack and the dead and wounded littered the slopes and the woods and choked the gaps in the wire and floated in the river Ancre to form loglike barriers when they became stuck in the weeds. Some, crossing enemy terrain with an unexpected swiftness, were caught by their own artillery fire and destroyed. Harry, regrouping the remnant left under his command, reached German trenches which had already been taken to watch prisoners being filed back. They came out of the ground, some weeping, some laughing, some crazed and dazed with the intensity of the bombardment which on parts of their lines had shattered their senses. Samuel, caught by enfilading machine-gun fire, was driven back with himself and a private as the only survivors. The new line was held all day until new waves of German infantry fought their way back into their trenches and the order came to withdraw.

Duncan.
It was evening when I found my son. We were told to move back because there weren't enough of us left to hold what we'd taken. It was so unexpected. That kind of meeting. Even though I'd been fighting and killing all the day long up the hill from the river. He was lying at the top of a trench, the bayonet through his chest so hard that it came out of his back and his own bayonet still stuck in the big German soldier that he'd ripped from belly to throat. Lying like lovers, I thought, in that moment of quietness when I lay beside them both. Their arms were linked where they'd held onto each other as they fell. And then I wondered what I'd been doing all day because I could hardly remember one clear thing about it so fast had it all gone. And I went through my son's pockets and took a few things. And my hand was already in a pocket of the dead German soldier to take something of his when I thought—No. It seemed wrong somehow. To take something of his. Something personal. Even though he was dead. And it was then I found I was crying when I looked up and saw a revolver sticking into my face and I thought I was dead too until I recognised him. Lieutenant Gordon who'd been driving us like some big silent demon all day. 'It's my son, sir,' I said. 'He's dead. My son. He's dead.' 'There are many sons dead here today. Many. Yours is not the only one. Many,' he repeated, and then said: 'Now get up, soldier, and keep fighting or I shall kill you myself.'
And the moment had gone.
Then I searched among the dead for a gun and some ammunition. My own rifle had been shattered and I'd thrown it away when it was no longer of any use and had been fighting with an empty revolver and

a bayonet. With some bandoliers still full of bullets I loaded up a machine-gun and what was left of us went back down the slopes with the German infantrymen and bombers pushing at us from each and every direction. But we got back to the woods and the rivers and beyond them. Later in the night, in a quiet moment when we were trying to get a bit of rest, a quiet moment, that is, despite the moaning and crying from the slopes with the stretcher-bearers and dogs out trying to find the wounded and bring them in, I went to find him. He was sitting at the edge of the woods with his fieldglasses in his hands watching the sky. He seemed so all by himself and as if he wanted it that way that I felt I shouldn't disturb him but I said: 'It was a moment of weakness, sir. With my son, I mean.'

Slowly he turned to look at me and we were silent for a few minutes, and then he handed me the glasses and pointed to the sky and simply said—'Look.'

I looked at the stars and it was as though I had never seen them before. They were all dancing around the way you'd see fireflies in a bush perhaps, probably because my hands holding the glasses were still shaking a bit. And then he told me again to look and I pointed the glasses at the moon and the bumps and lumps and dark patches he told me were mountains and craters and deserts, and I hadn't seen anything like that before either, or even thought about it.

I gave him back the glasses and said: 'What was it like today, sir?'

'Oh that,' he answered, as if the day hadn't meant anything very much. 'It was like the face of a dead planet.'

'I don't understand, sir,' I said.

We went quiet again for a while and then he turned to look at me and smiled. I'd never seen him smile before. And it was a strange smile, a smile that had no humour in it. Nor was there the opposite of humour, whatever that is. Just a deep kind of calmness. And then he said: 'I often watch the stars. In that vast immensity I find a sense of peace.'

I didn't understand that either. It was too deep for me. But I knew he didn't want to be disturbed any longer and wished to be alone so I went away alone too to try to find a sense of peace for myself.

On the second and third day of the battle thick folds of a heatwave hung over the slopes and fields and ponds and the land lay shimmering in sweat and blood and on the fourth day a thunderstorm turned it to a mire of mud and the broken remains of men and animals and equipment. Being relieved and returning to different sections of the line Duncan found that the village of Beaumont-Hamel had disappeared in a heap of littered fragments. The trees too had gone. And on some quiet nights a pale waning moon would throw

149

pitchblends of light across the blackened stumps and it was as though they had been petrified into stone, and then he thought he had a glimpse of what Dalton might have meant. And sometimes too he heard a cuckoo call from a distant tree that had not yet fallen. Returning again to a line section he and the others stumbled over horses and mules and dying dogs that some battalions were using to carry ammunition pouches to the front. And as the nights passed the thought and vision of his son became far off in his mind as if he had indeed found a sense of peace, but it was more the peace found in utter fatigue.

And so the Battle of the Somme continued through the August and September sun to the October and November rains and frost when the land became a quicksand of slime that sucked men in waistdeep and at times pulled them in altogether so that they choked and drowned. And in dry weeks dustclouds floated carrying the stench of rotting bodies. And when November came troops returning to the front trenches found that there was no one to relieve any more. Only corpses floating in stagnant water or held sitting stiffly upright by the frostbound mud. And it was during these last days that Harry was wounded by machine-gun fire in the left shoulder, but managed to crawl back to his own line and was taken to a field hospital at the rear and later sent to a convalescent hospital in England. And as the year ended, the darkened windows of homes throughout Ulster and the similar rituals of homes in the other provinces and countries of Europe told the same story. Mourning has come to our house for the Somme's million and more wounded and dead.

VII

She was seventeen. Yes. She was in her eighteenth year. And that sense of womanhood which had for so long hovered in abeyance now at times threatened to engulf her in full flood.

The regular seasonal flow of farmlife had enclosed her within a warm safe cocoon, or so it now seemed. Times and hours of anxiety were forgotten, or would come at moments with a dim flickering memory which occasionally brought with it a slight tremor. Year had followed year with the white snows of winter or the hawthorn abloom with its own whiteness that glistened in the green hedgerows amongst the frail red and pink bucky roses, the budding flowers of Maytime and the balmy September days with a chill in the evening air heralding the approaching winter and its storms. In those years she had been a child. Now she was a woman. But it puzzled her. All the strength of her body and mind and desires still not fully understood groped towards something, a future perhaps, which she could not perceive, and often she would sit quietly beside her father's grave and try to think, a blade of grass between her teeth, as if something would come to tell her what she wanted to know.

Her visits to Belfast became less. Her grandmother, bright and kindly still, soon bored her and restlessness drove her back to the island to listen to Alec Dick's banter as he rowed her across in the ferry or do the rounds of the farm with Jack. While engaged in the latter she would at times play skittishly just like a child again and then would suddenly stop as that precarious balance of her nature would force her into this new realm of being. Sometimes at night she would sit naked in front of her bedroom mirror, the lamp casting flickering shadows of her own shape on the walls, exploring her own sex and feeling the sensation of anticipation and excitement in a kind of dreamy wonderment.

In the autumn her friend Anna had gone to a private school in England. They'd spent the last few days together flirting with the boys along the promenade at Bangor. Where May was fully formed,

151

Anna's body was still spindly, that of a child. It was her face with the serious questioning green eyes framed in flowing dark hair, the way she spoke and her knowledge of so many things that made her seem so much older. It was the strictness of her upbringing, the loneliness, being an only child, which had made her that way, she'd intimated to May, and she envied May's bright, carefree, fiery tomboy way of dealing with things. And in turn May admitted she envied her companion's knowledge and how she could read and study where her own butterfly mind could never settle on anything for any length of time. During the last night she'd spent at Anna's home, while undressing for bed as they shared the same bedroom, Anna had reached out and touched her breasts, had stroked and kissed them for a few moments, while May had sat stiffly in frightened fascination. But in the morning they did not speak of it.

Christmas brought sorrow and not joy. From the war in Europe came a steady stream of the names of the dead at the Somme and the towns and villages mourned. And that to May seemed to be her first real anxiety, her first real dread in her new experience of being a woman, an adult, as she waited for news from the Front. An anxiety no less than her mother's as the latter paced the house in a shrill fulminating anger as she waited for news of Dalton. And then the news came. Dalton and Samuel were well, had survived the battle, but Harry had been wounded—how badly she did not know—and was in a hospital in the south of England.

And the New Year brought a series of homecomings.

First down the lane of the Hollow Farm came a tall man with a broad face and thick moustache whom May did not at first recognise. He brought letters from both Dalton and Samuel. They too would be home on leave soon. Only when she watched him talking to her mother did she remember. He was the policeman who'd brought David home one New Year's Eve when her father had begun to argue with him. And later she'd seen him again standing beside Dalton at her father's funeral. He sat in the kitchen drinking tea and then a glass of whiskey, before leaving to cross to the mainland to his home at Glenarm.

Samuel's letter said the usual things. It was about herself, herself and Islandmagee, about their times together. And about Rosinante. The donkey they'd christened together. Was Rosinante all right too? And, in bed that night, reading the letter yet again, the wind brought a loud braying from across the fields as if in answer. But there was something else. He'd decided, Samuel said, to go to Paris for a few days before coming home, and would bring her a present from there.

Je t'aime, May. Je t'aime, May. La guerre est trop longue et je voudrais être auprès de toi à Islandmagee.

152

And at this she felt a little anxious, a little frightened, a little ashamed.

But there was not one word from Harry.

How stupid she'd been, she thought. She hadn't even asked Mr McKinzie what was uppermost in her mind. How badly had Harry been wounded and what hospital was he in?

Dalton arrived soon after. It was February. He had been promoted to the rank of captain. He was even more silent than before, if that were possible. To May he said little, but kissed her and gave her a hug, which she couldn't remember him having done before. And to her questions about Harry he readily answered. Harry had been wounded in the left shoulder but was otherwise all right. He too had leave due to him and could take it when his wounds were sufficiently healed. And he gave her the address of the hospital which was in Sussex, south of London.

Dalton stayed a fortnight, during which he either went riding the black mare around the island or along the sands at Brown's Bay or took their mother out to dinner in hotels in Whitehead, in Belfast, in Larne. Only once was she invited to accompany them, and she sat quietly at table, timidly even, daunted by her mother's flow of conversation as she sat with her jewellery sparkling in the lamplight with the powerful handsome brooding figure in officer's uniform—to whom everyone, May noticed in a quizzical fashion, immediately gave way—silently listening. And on returning to the farmhouse she saw their embrace before retiring to bed. And then he was gone as though he had never been, so infrequently had she seen him.

But while he was there May wrote a brief note to Harry, saying that she had heard he'd been wounded and asking if he would like to come and spend some of his leave in the peace of Islandmagee because she knew he didn't have a home anymore in Ballycastle. And then in a state not unlike that of intoxication she posted it before her heart failed her and she tore it up and threw it away.

Samuel sat in Notre-Dame Cathedral in Paris. It was his second day in the city, and his time had been spent wandering along the banks of the Seine and the quays where for hours he'd browsed among the booksellers' wares. Sometimes he just sat gazing blankly at the flowing river. Two things were uppermost in his mind: the war and May. The experience of the trenches, instead of hardening him, had already torn his sensitive inner nature to shreds. He dreaded the thought of returning, to the point of considering declaring himself a conscientious objector, but quailed at the thought of the trouble which would ensue. He, already something of a veteran, would not be allowed to leave military service in the middle of a war that easily.

Besides, what would others think? Dalton, Harry, other people at home, May? Would he be handed the white feather of cowardice? And May. He dreaded returning home also. He was in love, and knew he must declare his love, declare this passion that breathed inside him. And to herself, her physical presence, instead of merely writing letters which only partly showed his feelings. But what did he know of this young woman whom he'd loved since she was a girl? What did he know of women in general? Nothing at all. He'd listened to the coarse talk of some of the men, talk about the brothels behind the lines, had heard others talk of their wives in various different ways and moods, had even heard Harry making the occasional flippant remark about the girls he'd known in Dublin. Dalton was different, for Dalton women seemingly didn't exist. What was love? What were these feelings of sensual longing and desire, of sexual passion? In his thoughts and feelings it was all so ambiguous, was all such an enigma.

And here he was in France, in Paris, his boyhood dreams realised but not in the way he'd anticipated. And if she accepted him would he bring her to France when the war had ended, a war that now, when he thought of it, made him visibly tremble?

In his fantasies of their being together he had given her those things he loved.

Before leaving the next day he bought presents of perfumes and jewellery, then caught a train to Calais and a steamer and train again to Waterloo and another train through the length of England to Scotland for a steamer to the glens, the world slipping by outside the window barely noticed.

Duncan sat with the letter in his hands. It had arrived that morning, and bore a local postmark, which had surprised him. He'd been expecting such a letter, his call back to the trenches. But the contents weren't quite as he'd thought they would be. He was to return to a military base in England to train recruits and then go with them to the front lines. The letter also stated that he'd been promoted to the rank of sergeant and gave the date on which he was to arrive at base. It was signed by Captain Gordon of the 11th Irish Rifles.

Consulting a calendar on the wall he saw that he had a week's grace. Sergeant McKinzie. Yes, he felt certain that his promotion had been the work of Captain Gordon. But had he deserved it? Or was it merely that dead men's shoes had to be filled, so many dead men's?

The big cottage was warm and comfortable, yet held a feeling of emptiness. His wife Martha had already received the news of Aubrey's death before he arrived, so it had been an awkward homecoming. He didn't give any details but merely said that Aubrey had gone missing like so many others. For the first week he had

154

wandered among the hills with the sheep or sat in the pub listening to the local tongue he knew so well, or played with his remaining son by the fire, or slept, and slept. He wasn't even sure if he could remember the details about Aubrey himself. It was just a dull ache somewhere at the back of his head.

White snowflecks danced and swirled beyond the windowpane in the darkness of early evening. He could hear Martha moving about upstairs as she put young Ned to bed. During his leave they had only managed to arouse each other in a half-feeling fashion. But now it happened. Sitting by the fire with a glass of whiskey they awoke to each other with a painful hunger and then the week had gone and he was whistling down the lane with Martha waving to him from the window.

Sam, Sam, gentle Sam, it's not you I want.

So the voice whispered inside her but the words found no utterance.

And now they lay in a little copse, her breasts and body feeling the lingering touch of his fingers, her fingers wet with his own dewy silky moisture which had come when he panted and cried out.

For ten days he'd pursued her and then said in a hesitant tremulous way that he loved her and wanted her to marry him. And again responsibility was pressing in upon her. What was she to do with this soldier who was to return to the war and might like so many others not come back, a man she loved much in the way she loved her pet donkey? What was *her* responsibility, the responsibility of being a woman, which she now was?

And when fumbling, he'd finally tried to make love to her and she'd brought him to a sexual climax, her feeling was that same kind of frightened fascination as when Anna had touched her in bed.

He sat beside her, silent, motionless, leaning back against the windbreak of the copse, half-asleep, as her own thoughts drifted with the drifting snow. What had been that dream of her girlhood when she'd wandered beside the lilyponds in Masserene that her father had confused with Shane's Castle?

Her coat wrapped tightly round her against the wind she waved to him from the harbour wall at Larne as the steamer eased away from the quay and he began his journey back to the trenches.

There had been several visitors to the hospital to see Harry. First had come his mother and stepfather, and then Valerie who had now qualified in medicine and was a practising doctor. With this woman he liked so well the encounter amused him and they innocently flirted as she examined his wounds. Dalton arrived, which surprised him, spoke of his new post at a training camp and mentioned that the family hoped he would visit them in Islandmagee. And when Harry congratulated him on his new rank he merely shook his head as if it were of no particular concern.

A few days before he was to be discharged from the hospital James arrived with his friend Christopher. Sitting on the lawn in the early April sunshine a hand descended on his shoulder and he turned round.

'Well, my Irish cousin. A hero home from the wars.'

Harry laughed. 'I'm not sure what a hero is supposed to be. Or mean.'

'How badly were you wounded?'

Harry shrugged. 'Ach, enough to put me into a hospital for a few months. I ran at the wrong end of a machine-gun.'

'Well, I think that is what I would call a hero.'

'Or maybe it's just that I've no sense of direction.'

James's mirth echoed Harry's. 'That might be one way to put it. But I should be inclined to think it wouldn't be a full explanation.'

'And I suppose you'll be going to the Front soon?'

James slowly shook his head. 'No. Though I've tried to be sent there. The regiment has been ordered to India.' He paused. 'The only action I've seen was in Ireland.'

Harry nodded. 'Ah, yes. In Dublin.'

Christopher gave a whinnying laugh. 'If you could call that petty little farce action. It was begun and over in less than a week. Still, I suppose, it was a diversion from hunting. Merely a different kind of game.' Standing up, he looked around. 'I'm thirsty. Is there anywhere one can find a drink?'

'There's a lounge at the end of the building,' answered Harry, indicating. 'On the ground floor.'

Both were silent as they watched him cross the lawn and disappear, then James suddenly asked, 'What do you think of our friend?'

'Think? How can I think anything when I know nothing about him?' Pausing, Harry asked: 'He's in Intelligence, isn't he?'

'Yes. And what I heard of his actions during Easter week . . . well, left a lot to be desired. Perhaps I've no longer the same opinion about our . . . colonial . . . mmm . . . Ascendancy friend?'

'And what do you think of what happened in Dublin?'

'That perhaps things weren't quite right. Aren't.'

'Do you mean the executions?' asked Harry, suddenly remembering that there were thousands of prisoners from Dublin and other parts of Ireland still in English gaols. 'There was talk against the executions from some of the men in the trenches.'

'Yes,' James said slowly. 'That was one thing. They put up a fair fight and could have been dealt with more honourably. But perhaps

156

my opinions are changing on other things also.'

Harry glanced at the thoughtful face of his companion, the puckered frown indicating that beliefs long held, beliefs stamped upon his personality since birth, were fracturing, even if only slightly. For a moment he measured himself against the other, he who seemingly had been born with no beliefs whatsoever and had drifted into a war which he felt did not particularly concern him and would no doubt drift out again in the same fashion should he survive. And James, a life of firmly implanted beliefs and goals to be achieved, a life of comfortable ease yet also of strict duty which had protected him from the morass of experience and indecisiveness and possible choice which lay beyond the frontiers of accepted thought and codes of conduct. Yet now a tiny worm of doubt had begun to gnaw. Which was the better kind of existence, his or James's? Deliberately breaking both their trains of thought, he quickly asked: 'When are you leaving? For India, I mean?'

'We're being shipped out within a month.' James paused. 'There's trouble there too. With this fellow called Gandhi.'

'Yes, I've heard of him. And he's already seen the inside of a prison, hasn't he?'

'Yes.' James stood up. 'And now I must leave you. Here comes our friend Christopher.' Waiting for a few moments he put his hand gently on Harry's shoulder. 'And remember, my Irish cousin, don't run at the wrong end of any more machine-guns. I'm inclined to believe that such an action is rather detrimental to one's health.'

Harry grinned. 'I'll try not to. Good luck.'

'Good luck.'

Going to his tiny room in the hospital Harry sat on the bed and tried to think. On the day after tomorrow he was to be released but, after convalescing in hospital, still had three weeks' leave due to him. Where would he go? The following day was spent in a half-hearted attempt to pack and trying not to think. Leaving the following day, he went to his mother's home in Highgate and then spent the next four days wandering around London, usually ending up in a music hall or at a lighthearted play where he could laugh easily and openly with a closed mind. Once his strolling feet brought him to Westminster Abbey. But the interior, with its silence and lifeless banners and dangling flags which seemed a confusion of sepulchre and sanctuary, repelled him. As did the draped pathetic figure on the cross, for him a symbol not of hope but of hopelessness, and he found himself shaking his head as if in disagreement as he left. Crossing to Dublin on the packetboat he spent another four days walking around the city, strolling by the side of the Liffey, visiting Trinity, the pub above which he once had rooms, the theatres. He stood among the ruins of the Post Office and other buildings which had been the result of Easter week, and in the pro-cathedrals where once again he simply shook his head at the hanging symbol. It was when, sitting in his hotel room idly going through the contents of his wallet, May's short letter of invitation dropped out. Reading it, Dalton's words also sounded in his thoughts and, on impulse, he quickly packed and crossed the city and took a train north for Belfast and Islandmagee.

VIII

Good God. Sweet seventeen. And has she ever been kissed?

I didn't know it was him.

What brought me here?

I was only told a visitor had come and . . .

Is this beauty . . .?

I thought it might be . . . might be . . .

And more than beauty? More than . . .?

Thought it might be Samuel back or Dalton back . . .

What is more than beauty?

Or might even be . . .

Life?

Someone I didn't know . . .

And what is that?

Who it might be . . .

Life, I mean.

Someone I didn't know who . . .

I didn't even think it would be her when I heard the footsteps.

Just a visitor I wasn't expecting yet . . .

Or was I . . .?

Was I hoping it would be him?

Senses and thoughts in a tumbling whirl they simply looked at each other, aware of an increasing panicky embarrassment.

'May.'

'Harry.'

He stood up, a book in one hand, the other resting on the study desk. 'I wasn't expecting it to be you.'

'I didn't know it was you.' Her face was flushing so hot that she wanted to turn and run yet hoped it didn't show like that. 'No one told me it was you. I was only told we had a visitor. And I came to see who it was.'

Never before had he felt so awkward, yet tried to appear nonchalant. 'I received your letter. Thank you for the invitation.'

'We knew you'd been wounded and were in hospital. So we thought you might like to come here. Now that you have no one left at Ballycastle. For some peace, perhaps.'

'It was a lovely thought.'

'It wasn't mine really.'

'No?'

Again she felt herself blushing. And was it that he looked very disappointed when she'd said that? 'Well, I suppose it was really. I suggested it to Mammy and she agreed.'

'Then it *was* a lovely thought.'

They stood looking at each other, uncertain.

'What were you doing?' May asked.

'Reading. That's what I do in the trenches when there's nothing else to be done. Read. Those years at the university I threw away. I did nothing. Or next to nothing. But in the trenches it was Sam who started to teach me how to read. And what to read.'

'Yes. Samuel.'

'He's already been here, I suppose?'

'Yes. He stayed for nearly two weeks.'

'And I'm sure he enjoyed his stay?'

'I think so. I hope he did.' For a third time May blushed violently, scenes of herself with Samuel flashing through her mind, of walking around the farm together, of saying good-night on the stairs before going to bed, of sitting in the little copse and her hand streaked with the moisture of his body.

Harry nodded and, not knowing what to say, said nothing.

'He looked so frail. So terribly frail.' May paused, a vision in her mind of Samuel slowly walking up the gangplank of the steamer making his long way back to the front lines, a feeling of pity and tenderness seeping through her. 'I don't think he should have been allowed to go back to the war.'

'True. I don't think it's doing him any good.' Harry paused. 'But, then, that is true for a lot of others also.'

'Of course. It's silly of me. I shouldn't be talking about it.' Walking to the window and looking out, May felt his hand on her shoulder.

'Thanks, May. It was a very lovely thought.'

'You'll be sleeping in Dalton's room.'

'Yes. I know that. I've already put my things up there.'

'What would you like to do now?'

Looking out also, towards the orchard, he felt the pressure of her shoulder against him, the warmth of her body. 'Oh, it's nearly evening. Let's just go for a walk across the fields. Then tomorrow we could go down to the shore for a picnic or go across to Larne or take the horses out for a trot.'

160

The next few days passed in a dreamy serenity for both, the weather balmy with the faintest ruffle of breeze from seaward and the sun catching the tints of budding flowers. They stood by the Druid's Altar where they had once met unexpectedly, looking inland with their hands caressing the ancient stone that other hands eons before had erected. On horseback they trotted to various parts of the island, sometimes pensive and silent, sometimes gay and bantering. On the ferry to Larne, Alec Dick joked with this other soldier home from the wars and slyly teased May, saying that she'd have half the army to visit her before it was all over, whilst quietly musing on the absence of her usually highspirited nature. From Jack they borrowed a boat and, with Harry rowing, went round the lobster pots, May pulling them up and, when there was a catch, laughing and squealing when trying to get the lobsters from the pots into a sack. Fastening the boat near the rocking stone at Brown's Bay they lay in the sun and then decided to go for a swim. The water was cold, exhilaratingly cold as they splashed closeby the shore, playing like children as they scooped water into each other's faces. Lying in a little fissure again she became mesmerised by the pale scars on his back which curved from the upper arm down across the shoulder, and was unaware that she was lightly stroking them.

'How did it happen?'

His voice was quiet. 'Oh, nothing very much.'

'Tell me. Please tell me.'

'It was in November. During the last days of the battle. We were out on a patrol in no-man's-land. Six of us. But we were surprised by two German patrols. And of course the shooting started. But I managed to get back to my own lines.'

'And the others?'

'All dead.'

An immense feeling of fear and dread caused her to choke on the sandwich she was eating and sting her eyes with tears. 'You were lucky.'

'I suppose you could say that.'

'You sound as though it didn't matter.'

He shrugged. 'I sometimes wonder.'

'Why?'

'I don't know why.'

'You're so strange, Harry,' she heard herself say. 'One moment you're like lightning with your temper and joking. And the next you're so distant, just as if you didn't care about anything.'

He turned to her and smiled. 'May, May, don't ask these questions.'

Lying quiet for a while she asked: 'What do you think of Dalton?'

161

Harry laughed. 'Well, if you say *my* nature's strange—heavens, I've nothing on him. I don't know what goes on inside him.'

'Yes. Even though he's my brother I feel about him the same way.'

'He visited me in hospital. That surprised me. And told me that the family wanted me to visit here.'

May was intrigued. 'It would surprise me too. He's not usually like that. Making invitations and things, I mean.'

'All I know is that he's the most powerful man I've ever met. The most powerful personality. Some of the things he did in the trenches it would have taken ten men to do. I even heard he threatened to shoot one of his own men on the spot if he didn't get up and keep on fighting.'

'Tell me some of the things.'

'May, May, they're not for you to hear about. Besides, I've no wish to talk about them.'

Again came the feeling of fear. 'Of course not. How silly of me. You're home on leave and want to talk about other things.'

His voice was barely a whisper. 'Home, did you say?'

She blushed. 'Well, you're here.' Jumping up she folded the towels and packed the remains of the picnic in a bag. 'Let's go back. By the time we get to the Hollow it'll be time for dinner. And we'll stop and see Rosinante on the way.'

'Rosinante?'

'My pet donkey when I was a child. And it's still a pet. I thought I told you about it before. It was Samuel who named him that when he first came here.'

'Ah yes, Sam.'

Standing, he took her gently in his arms and kissed her, feeling a disturbing flow of emotion welling up inside him. And when they broke apart again she busied herself with refolding the towels to hide the fact that she was trembling.

They returned to the farmhouse without speaking, the silence broken only by the heehawing of Rosinante in both greeting and leavetaking. In bed she could not sleep properly, and at times found herself standing naked in front of the wardrobe mirror remembering that she'd done this before with a kind of guilty laughter. But now it was with a different emotion, a wondering seriousness, and she quietly danced and made her body sway and it was exhilarating like when she'd splashed among the wavelets at the shore. Several times she peeped out of her room along the slightly curved landing to see a light shining in the tiny window inset above the door of the far bedroom where Harry was, and knew that he wasn't sleeping either. Perplexed, she would sit in front of the mirror again trying to think. Was he just reading? Or was he . . . what?

162

For the next few days they were both very subdued in each other's company, and then Harry went off to Belfast for a day, leaving her feeling angry because she'd not been invited to go with him. But he returned in high spirits to tell her that there was a show on in town which he wanted to see, an operetta called *Naughty Marietta*. It should be good fun and they would enjoy themselves. They could go to the early performance so that it wouldn't be too late when they returned to the island. And yes, she said, yes, that would be great fun, and spent all the next day in trying to decide what to wear, eventually choosing a white blouse with ruffs at the collar and wrists, a buckled, pleated green skirt and buttoned black boots. Long jet earrings brushed against her hair and a silver bracelet her grandmother had given her slipped up and down her left wrist. A dark cloak casually hanging from her shoulders, she stood in the study waiting, trying not to think of how she felt as she looked up at the great stag's head hanging in the recess while fiddling with a gold locket on a slender chain which rested on her bare throat and then saw him appear in the doorway to pause for a long moment to stare before they went out to where Jack was waiting with the trap to take them to the station at Whitehead.

'Parakeets, parakeets, very cheap I'm selling . . .'
'Figs, oranges, come and buy—Come and buy your posies—Don't pass by—Make haste while you may . . .'
'There are two different Mariettas in me—one is good—so sweet—so discreet—She'd never say one word amiss—But the other Marietta dat's also me—Has a temper so warm it's torrid—So you see, when I'm good I'm very good indeed—But when I'm bad I'm horrid—But naughty Marietta broke every rule—Though it's true when I'm good I'm very good indeed—I confess when I'm bad I'm shocking . . .'
Harry's laughing whisper fell against her ear. 'Make haste while you may, naughty May.'
Entranced she sat, the figures on stage in front of her swaying and singing in voluptuous costumery, colours caught by slivers of light to be carried across the Opera House and reflected in the carved figures above her as the music swelled through the audience. The city and outside world did not exist, were closed away, Great Victoria Street and the Great Northern Railway and the buildings curving to both sea and hills lay in a different dimension. There was only this, the unfolding story in song and orchestration. A New Orleans of the eighteenth century opened to her gaze, as to her senses did the passions of mistress and slave-girl, pirate and adventurer and runaway Contessa and the market girls with their wares and their

163

male counterparts. Excitement, fun, but with things that could be potentially otherwise than humour. That her body and imagination told her. There was only this, sitting beside Harry in a whirl of laughing sound that made her skin tingle beneath her clothing with little electrical shocks, to the extent that she imagined she could hear the crackling.

'But naughty Marietta broke every rule—Though it's true when I'm good I'm very good indeed—I confess when I'm bad I'm shocking . . .'

In the intervals among the thronging audience at the bar Harry sang the song softly in her ear and she found herself laughing uproariously, a little hysterically even, and in some other fashion also. And back watching the costumed dancing figures she felt herself aroused to an almost fear of excited longing.

'You and I—Here's my hand—We're friends you see—You promise you'll never make love at me?—Solemnly swear we'll never, never speak of love—never, never speak of love—I'd never want a kiss from you—we'll face what e'er befall us—but never, never speak of love! . . .'

'But the other Marietta dat's also me—Has a temper so warm it's torrid—So you see when I'm good I'm very very good—But when I'm bad I'm horrid . . .'

Laughing, laughing, laughing, the glass of wine in her hand sparkling in brilliant colours.

'Yes, Marietta, something has happened to me . . . And is *still* happening to me . . . And I'm hoping it happens to someone else too . . .'

'Adventurers and heroes have stridden every age—in history books their doughty deeds loom large on every page—From Caesar to Columbus, from Rob Roy to Captain Kidd—They've done things I'd like to do, but somehow never did . . .'

'To arms has lost its charms, my blood's no longer stirred—a rippling stream's soft music seems so much to be preferred . . .'

And then the runaway Contessa who had been posing as a casket-girl and her captain and the finale and '*The Dream Melody*' again . . .

> '*Ah! Sweet mystery of life, at last I've found thee,*
> *Ah! I know at last the secret of it all,*
> *All the longing, seeking, striving, waiting, yearning,*
> *The burning hopes, the joy and idle tears that fall!*
> *For 'tis love, and love alone, the world is seeking,*
> *And 'tis love, and love alone, that can repay,*
> *'Tis the answer, 'tis the end and all the living,*
> *For it is love alone that rules for aye!*'

164

They were quiet on the return journey, sitting opposite one another and staring through the window across the darkened landscape as the train puffed and whistled along the railway track to Larne, as though the febrile nervous tension which the operetta had unleashed between them had been drained. It was only when the train was running along the shore to the approaching lights of Larne and Larne harbour that Harry suddenly burst out laughing and began singing—'Parakeets, parakeets, I'm selling, very cheap I'm selling, Oh when I'm good I'm very very good but when I'm bad I'm horrid'—to a startled audience of homegoing travellers who then, on seeing a young man in military uniform obviously just home from the trenches, joined in the humour. He kept on singing as they crossed to the island in Alec Dick's ferry, the latter's banter unavailing in catching May's attention, and it was only when they jumped out on the other shore that his voice was heard.

'Parakeets ye're selling, are ye? So that's what ye do at the Front and ye'd tell the likes of us at home ye're fightin'? Well ye can bring me a couple back so's I can send them round the island till squawk in the ears of them that doesn't pay the ferryman.'

Harry laughed. 'You'll hear them squawking in a few weeks' time. I'll give them special orders where to come to.'

Watching them chase each other along the shore as he swung the boat round, Alec said softly: 'Well, I think somebody's found something the night. Or maybe a pair has found something. Jump in, John Gordon. He's a good lad. I've watched him come and go. Didn't I tell ye all them years ago when young John was lost and you sayin' ye'd niver have another and May was born and after her comes along that rogue David one. Out of the oul' darkness.'

'Ah! Sweet mystery of life, at last I've found thee,
    Ah! I know at last the secret of it all,'
Heehawheehawheehawheehawheehaw . . .
'All the longing, seeking, striving, waiting, yearning,
    The burning hopes, the joy and idle tears that fall!'
Heehawheehawheehawheehawheehaw . . .
Sitting on a bank May was convulsed with laughter as Harry, arms outstretched as if in embrace, directed his voice at the longeared bellowing figure in front of him. 'You silly old fool. You're singing to the donkey. Rosinante.'

'For 'tis love, and love alone, the world is seeking,
    And 'tis love, and love alone, that can repay,'
Heehawheehawheehawheehawheehaw . . .
' 'Tis the answer, 'tis the end and all the living,
    For it is love alone that rules for aye!'

Heehawheehawheehawheehaw . . .

Impulsively she ran to him and kissed him on the lips, pushing the pulpy substance of petals from an early flower which she had been chewing into his mouth, and then ran. Chasing each other, running, hiding behind hedgerows, they crossed the fields and she felt her body, heart, crying out as though with tears, her imagination peopling the moonlit terrain with erotic dancing figures. So this was it. But what was it? Reaching the Gobbins she fell panting on the grass hearing the low rumbling of the sea in the subterranean caverns beneath, feeling his body as he lay beside her. They were silent then for a little while as they watched the smooth swell of the waves.

'May, May. I want you. I need you.'

Her blouse was undone, her breasts a pale glow as she felt the night air tingling her skin. Pushing him away she ran again, the breeze on her nakedness exhilarating. Yet still she was afraid.

'May. May.'

Caught, she felt his firm maleness pressing against her.

'No, Harry, no.'

'No?' He broke away, his tone soft, quizzical, painful in defeat.

'No,' she heard herself say again, but it was a voice of indecision as she stood with her breasts heaving as though forgetful that they were still uncovered.

Abruptly he turned and picked up his cap where it lay on the ground, now a note of savagery in his words. 'Then I'll not force you. If you don't want me as I want you, then I'm damned if I'll try. I too have my pride. I'll take no woman who doesn't want me.'

And it was with fear that she watched as he, triumphant, turned and walked away. 'Harry.'

'Well?'

'Must it be so?'

In the dusky light he shook his head. 'No. It doesn't must be so. If that's what you wish.'

'That's what I wish.'

'Go to hell, then.'

'And where's that?'

'Many places. At this moment the absence of you, perhaps.'

With a deliberate tantalising gesture she dropped cloak and blouse to the ground, the little gold locket gleaming against her flesh. 'And perhaps at this moment it's the absence of you.'

Puzzled, he stood looking at her. 'Yes?'

And now she was the triumphant one. Like a cat playing with a fieldmouse there was a moment of deliberate pleasure in watching his emotional torment. And then, as he again turned away, her senses swirling with desire, she pulled him to the grass, tongue searching his

166

mouth, breasts pressing against his throat and chest, fingers seeking his body.

Later, and so much later it seemed, they lay side by side, all passion spent, and she felt the tears trickling down her skin.

'Why are you crying?'

'Because it was so beautiful.' He paused. 'And perhaps I've seen too many other things. Too too many other things.'

'I understand,' she said, thinking of what he'd told her and of the others dead in his patrol and of how he had struggled back to safety, though knew that she did not really understand because the intensity of the experience was beyond the grasp of her imagination. In a short while she heard him quietly breathing in sleep. 'Kiiiyaaa kiiiyaaa scceeheeee, my love,' she called softly to the seawind, 'sleep, sleep, my darling, sleep. Sceeeheee kiiiyaaa.'

A few light flakes of moisture brushed her face as she lay looking upwards where clouds crossed the moon and she pulled the cloak tightly around them both, the lingering sensation within her bringing a sense of fulfilment. Yes, it were as though she had been like that. A dry early summerland needing the slaking of rain. And then she too slept and there were only the whisperings of the creatures of the night and the soft rippling lapping sound of the sea, the eternal sea.

IX

Just over a week later Harry left to return to France, and several days
after that she received her first letter of love and affection from him,
postmarked London. He was leaving to cross the Channel that
evening to rejoin his regiment. In bed she put the letter under her
pillow but found she could not sleep, and then kept rolling her
shoulders so she could hear the rustling of the paper which seemed as
though some secret voice were whispering.

After the second time they had made love she'd said no. No, Harry.
Wait now. Wait. And he'd simply acquiesced and they spent the
remaining days rambling around the island or trotting on horseback
or, when the weather was bad, sitting in the study playing cards. If
her mother guessed May's passion she made no comment, but simply
left them alone. Occasionally, seeking male company, Harry would
do the farmrounds with Jack or go for a drink with him and other local
people in the little pub at Millbay. At these times she was glad to be
alone, glad not to feel his presence and the disturbing desire of his
which drifted in the air around her and was for her a tangible thing.
She needed these hours of privacy in which to think of this new
experience of womanhood which had come to her.

And when he had gone there was too, too much time to think in.
Insomnia brought a raw aching nerve as she sat heavyeyed and
sluggish by her bedroom window, the dusky twilit nights of mid-
summer alive with the harsh cries of corncrakes. At times, in a kind of
abandonment, she helped Jack on the farm and he, curiosity aroused
at her feverish desperate activity, would ask why. But, upon receiving
no answer, soon quietly worked with her as he would a mare in foal.

During these months the same question would come again and
again. Now with her men at the war, Harry, Samuel, Dalton, what
could she do to help? She, who had had a boyish tomboy life of
comfort and freedom, who knew more about farming and fishing and
things like that than most other people, but who was, in any formal
schooling sense, ignorant, uneducated. And at moments, as she'd

experienced similar moments with Anna, she regretted the easy carefree days of her childhood when she could do what she pleased. On a visit to her grandmother in Belfast, an answer came. Women and girls were going to work in the munitions factories, as the government was urging. With so many men at the war an hitherto unthought of thing was happening, their womenfolk were filling the empty places at work. Expecting an argument with her mother concerning her decision, May prepared her answers. But, surprisingly, none came, and by late autumn she had found lodgings and was working in a munitions factory in Birmingham.

Time passed more quickly then and she eagerly looked forward to the regular homegoings and sitting in the ferry-boat watching the island approach with Alec Dick bantering her about her war effort and saying she'd probably driven dozens of Englishmen crazy already with her fiery temper. And laughing into this grizzled face she'd known since she was a child she began to understand that the affection they held for each other was also a form of love. Her body and emotions still maturing in their demands and desire to give, twice she experienced a further sexual encounter. But in the aftermath she felt unsatisfied. Guilty also, particularly the second time when, on going upstairs to her room, she thought she saw a form on the landing which was Harry. And so strong was her feeling that she stood for a moment in shock, as though it were indeed an apparition.

Autumn and winter and Christmas again passed when, visiting cottages on the island to listen to stories old and new, she would sit in a half-amused half-serious fashion having her palm or teacup read or, experimenting, would stand at the door having her fortune told by a passing tinker woman. Walking in country fields outside Birmingham, or on the island, she measured the time by watching for the first snowdrops or bluebells or daffodils. And at home she would watch for migrant birds also, sitting close by the shore to see which would arrive first over the Gobbins cliffs. But early that year, 1918, brought something else that she had long since feared and dreaded.

Another great battle had begun at the Somme.

Duncan.

The battle of Cambrai ended the old year with the tanks in action in force and then the blizzards came and we were snowbound in various little villages. It was a godsend that, being hemmed in by drifts so that we couldn't move. Back to the Somme we were going, a word that will ever bring a clawing feeling to my heart. There weren't many of the original ones left. Reorganised and re-reorganised the old Division had gone and many of the accents now were from men of other parts of Ireland, and English and Scots ones too. Sitting in the warmth of a village café watching the large burling snowflakes cover all the land beneath white blankets I thought of all those I knew and the thousands I didn't know who were simply gaps left behind and who were now sunk under the snow and earth with their remains perhaps never to be found and with nothing to mark their fall. Aubrey was such a one. And when I think that I light my pipe in a kind of distracted fashion and feel the comforting warmth of the bowl seep into my hands and take a letter from my pocket which I've read so many times I'm sure the print will start to disappear. It's all crumpled and the edges are torn now. It's from my wife saying we have a daughter and that is comforting too.

And then the thaws come and we move up to take position astride the Canal de la Somme and the Canal de St Quentin and the river Somme itself facing the German front-line trenches with weeks spent sending patrols and raiding parties into no-man's-land. We can hear him too out in no-man's-land and sometimes we meet and sometimes we pass each other unaware. And then in early March his bombardments begin with every night the tempo and weight of shell increasing and we lie in the redoubts, Boadicea, Racecourse, Jeanne d'Arc, with our eardrums crashing and roaring seeing the night sky being split into pieces. For those who are looking, that is, for many have their heads and faces stuck in the ground as if they were trying to chew or claw their way down to some place of safety like some ferret or badger. And then he's on top of us coming out of nowhere and as the redoubts fall one by one I know that something has gone wrong somewhere.

It was a real peasouper, that morning. You could hardly see the length of yourself. And before the big guns have stopped firing he's already into our trenches and fighting with everything he has. And as the mist breaks in patches I can see the German infantrymen everywhere. Long lines of them, attacking from the front, from the flanks, and in the rear. They're more than a mile behind us, I'm sure, with their machine-gun platoons covering the ground at speed and appearing from every angle. Then the orders come to fall back. Not that we needed orders for that as we were already falling back under the sheer weight of numbers. The mist lifting again we can see even his transport columns behind us and as we manage to rout one completely that gives us some hope. But it doesn't last long because up front we can see groups of prisoners being moved back to the enemy rear. And so our retreat begins, through Seraucourt, Ollezy, Berlancourt, Bussy, Avricourt, Andechy and dozens of other meaningless names and places as we fight hour after hour day and night with whatever we have left, mile after mile after mile with our lines vanishing like grass before a scythe. Crossing the shell-craters

170

towards Arvilliers I find myself slapping my own face and hitting my chest with my fist to try to block out the numbness and tiredness while shouting and kicking at the crawling survivors to keep going. And it's there I see Lieutenant McKinstry go down, spinning like a Catherine-wheel on the edge of a crater before falling over the rim. But there's no time now for the wounded. We can't evacuate them. No one can. Except perhaps for the enemy infantrymen who might show them mercy and then might not. Just as I've seen some of their wounded shown no mercy and killed and some of our own killed by their mates because that was more merciful than leaving them as they were.

And then came the first real lull and I sleep a little and am then awake thinking we must have been fighting for about four or five days and maybe covered about forty or fifty miles when suddenly Lieutenant Ogilby is staring into my face asking if I've seen McKinstry. His eyes are all bloodshot probably like my own but there's a really strange expression on his face and he's shaking all over so violently his head's jerking from side to side. I tell him I saw McKinstry fall into a shellhole just about three hundred yards back and before I can stop him he's slithering back across the pitted fields. And then my attention's taken up because somebody says there's a German patrol seen on our left flank and I wonder how they got there with all the bombing and blowing up of pontoons and bridges during our retreat. But that's a stupid way of thinking. I know that. Because during the retreat we didn't know half the time where we were or what direction we were taking. But then I think that even stupid thinking is good thinking at times because it keeps your mind active and you need that when the fighting isn't finished. I'm about to shoot when I hear a voice calling. It's seven of our own men coming in from a different quarter. When they crawl in to join us the senior private tells me they're all that's left out of a few hundred. The rest are either dead or prisoners. And as I look round the little group of thirty or so I think that this is all that's left out of a few thousand.

And it's then that Captain Gordon is squatting beside me asking if I've seen Ogilby and McKinstry and I tell him and say also that I think Lieutenant Ogilby has cracked, has broken. And he looks at me silently and then nods and I'm beginning to go out across the craters when his hand stays me and I hear him say: 'No, sergeant. You're the only senior NCO we have left. You stay. You're in charge. We'll still have to move back, I think.'

And then I see him simply stand up and walk out through the craters without taking any cover whatsoever.

It was in his side, that's all he knew, his left side. Drifting between

171

sanity, clarity, hysteria, delirium, hallucination, unconsciousness and consciousness, all he knew was that it was in his side. Several times he put his hand to the place, and brought it up again close to his eyes to examine the flecks and traces of blood before his eyes could not see any more.

And then his hands were scrabbling at the soil where he could find moisture to make a child's mudcake and he was laughing at the longforgotten activity. A child's mudcake! And this he pressed to his side like a bread poultice to stay his seeping life. And he stopped laughing too, or tried to stop, because he knew that that only put pressure on his system, which forced the blood out.

And as he lay some slender silvery cord held him as he drifted through hysteria, delirium, hallucination, unconsciousness.

And when he was conscious again he put cupped palms to his cock to salve his cracked lips and throat with his own piss. Truly now a clown.

He was rocking gently rocking in a rowing-boat with the old man his grandfather plying the oars and laughing as he reminisced about the antics of the clowns and he laughed too, mind enclosing the crater in a bunting-fluttering marquee where the clowns trundled on the cannon and rode through the air on coloured arrows at the command of the ringmaster's cracking whip. On the banks of the Lagan he sat, studious yet comic face reflecting back as the surface was broken by the tossing pebbles, while across the fields and gently flowing water came the deepthroated roar of laughing spectators.

Conscious again, attempting to crawl to the crater lip, it seemed that the mud and blood of others which caked his side and stopped the wound seeping also held him fast to the earth and would not let him move.

And time was in reverse again. No, there was no one single time but a multiplicity whose dimensions lay like parallel lines yet which intersected so that he could effortlessly pass from one to the other to join those whom he could but faintly recognise and of whom he anxiously asked—Where am I? Where am I? Where is this place? Country? City?

'Harry.'

The voice came from a long way off and he tried to open eyelids that were stuck together.

'Harry.'

'Yes?'

'It's Sam. Samuel.'

'Sam? Samuel?'

'Yes, Sam. You love her, don't you? And she loves you.'

'Love her?'

172

Watching the recumbent figure, kneeling beside him, sensitive fingers gently exploring the wound in his side, it was that which was foremost in Samuel's mind, a thought which blotted out the shellhole littered with human remains and brought to mind the lush fields of Antrim rippling in the sea-breezes.

Feebly Harry rubbed his eyelids and forced them open with his fingers. 'Samuel. It *is* you. Go back. Go back. You can't save me now.'

'You do, don't you?' And in Samuel's mind there was a last faint spark which threatened to flare into such intensity that it would explode inside his head.

In front of his eyes knotted veins stood out on the other's temples as he felt hands as weak as his own trying to drag him. 'Go back, Sam. Go back. Leave me here.'

'Leave you here? No, no, no no . . .'

'Lieutenant Ogilby!'

Harry looked up to where Dalton now crouched beside them. 'Tell him to go back.'

'Go back, Lieutenant Ogilby. I'll bring him in. There's only an NCO in charge. You're needed.'

Slowly Samuel stood up but otherwise did not move. 'Needed? I'm needed? Where? What for?'

Ignoring him, Dalton's hands ran expertly over Harry's body before pulling him into a sitting position. 'How bad is it, Harry?'

'Bad. But the bleeding's stopped.'

But even the effort of sitting was too much and he lost consciousness again, being brought back to life by a cacophonous medley which he at first thought was gunfire until the sounds differentiated into piteous brayings and chokings and whimperings and screamings. A fourth figure came lurching down the side of the shellhole, its own intestines wrapped round its hindlegs and tripping it up. A mule. Sticking out from the shattered remains of the rump was the torn canvas patch of an ammunition pouch. And as Dalton lifted his revolver to fire, Harry saw Samuel wrap his arms round the animal's neck and both slither to the ground.

'Rosinante! No, Dalton, no! No!'

Drifting into delirium and hallucination Harry laughed uproariously as visions of this macabre comedy broke and reformed, and then he drifted back again still laughing. 'Remember, Dalton? That time at Malin Head? The three of us? With you watching the stars? And me talking about Swift's philosopher who was so intent at gazing at the stars that he walked into a ditch? Some bloody ditch this one is that we've walked into.'

As Dalton again tried to take aim Samuel covered the mule's head with his body and again screamed—'No! no!'

173

And again Harry laughed and drifted into unconsciousness and again was brought back, this time by the gunshot that thwacked above his head, to see the mule's nostrils and mouth flare with blood and mucus. After a few spasms it lay still.

'Lieutenant Ogilby!'

But Samuel didn't answer. Slowly standing up he first saluted, then embraced the carcass and began trying to stick things on its chest and shoulders; a human hand, parts of a dead rat, the remains of someone's head and face, pieces of a tunic with buttons still gleaming, anything he could find amongst the debris of flesh.

'Lieutenant Ogilby! What are you doing?'

'Pinning on its war medals, sir.'

Laughter threatened a further time but, feeling blood begin to seep again, Harry choked it back with eyes intent on the soiled and tearstricken face.

The voice was soft. 'What do you think, Harry?'

'You know as well as I do, Dalton. He's broken. The poor bastard's gone mad. Totally mad.' He paused, looking up at the first flush of oncoming day and listening to the silence that seemed so loud. Only in the distance could he hear what he took to be gunfire. 'Hopefully it'll only be temporary. Take him back.'

'I'll take you both. Can you bend?'

'I think the wound's opened again but we could try plastering and tying it up.'

'All right. I'll take you over my shoulder. Samuel's quiet now. I think he'll just come with us if I tell him to.'

Pulling Harry to the top of the crater, Dalton draped him over one shoulder and, holding Samuel by the arm, began to walk back the way he had come. A few scattered German soldiers saw him approach but, on noting his burden and seeing him walking behind a babbling idiot, simply filed on in a different direction and left him alone.

Duncan.

I watched him come in with Ogilby walking in front of him the way you would push a child on in front of you and the other one, McKinstry, over his shoulder that I at first took to be dead. But there was still some faint breathing in him so we dressed the wound and made up a stretcher and then we started pulling back to Hangest-en-Santerre where we were to stop. And then we saw them. Relieving troops. I recognised them as the French Alpine Chasseurs by their dark-blue uniforms. They sped past us in motorised columns and those of us who could cheer cheered and those who could only croak croaked because some were on their hands and knees and I had to kick

174

them to get them walking again, with Ogilby stumbling in front talking in French. I didn't understand what he was saying and kept looking at Captain Gordon who only once turned towards me and simply shook his head. Amiens, now a shell of a town and the roads thick with refugees with their carts and barrows piled high with belongings. Then boarding the train and sleep, sleep, sleep. The air is thick with the smell of snoring mudcaked sweaty bodies and I open the window as the train lurches and clanks into motion towards the Normandy coast where we're to reorganise yet again. I pull my pipe from my pocket and see that the stem has snapped and then open my shirt and find a skelf sticking into my skin. I smile. My only wound. But I fill the bowl and light up and suck in the tobacco smoke even though it burns my lips as I watch the afternoon fading and dusk swallowing up the fields. Then I walk through the carriage to have a look at the sleeping men and say to Captain Gordon at the other end—Sleep, sir. I shall watch. But he simply shakes his head and answers—No, sergeant. You sleep. I shall watch in the night.

So I return to my place and sit and think because I can't sleep. Of McKinstry being sent back a second time to a hospital in England, that's if he's still alive. Of Lieutenant Ogilby here sitting with bulging vacant eyes, muttering in another language. I pass my hands in front of his eyes but he gives no sign of even seeing them. He too will have to be sent back. I try to talk to him but get no response from that either. What is his wound, I wonder? His sleep? My only wound, did I say, the splinter from my pipe sticking into my body? No. That's wrong. The wounds are in my mind, in my memory. But as I sit in this train rocking across the dark land I think that those I'll have to learn to blot out because the day will come when I won't have the will or courage to remember. And so I take the letter from my pocket again and try to think of this new child my daughter.

Sam, gentle Sam, Lieutenant Sam, Samuel Ogilby, now Shellshock Sam—what are you trying to say? *Je suis maintenant à recherche de ma ville natale—mon pays—mon île bien aimée. Connaissez-vous la route? Où est le bateau à vapeur pour Waterloo—pour Antrim? Connaissez-vous mon île—mon amour—ma vie? Montrez-moi le chemin.*

Sam, Sam, be at peace.
Montrez-moi le chemin.
Be at peace.
Soyez en paix?
Yes.
Où-est-ce?

175

X

Remember.

In Belfast the crowd pressed in against the bulk of the City Hall and its lawns from all four sides of Donegall Square, some laughing and cheering, some openly weeping, some sober, some drunk, some dancing whilst others stood in frowning stupefaction as though not knowing what had happened or was happening. On the southern fringe spilling into Linenhall Street stood May, coat tightly pulled against the blustery wind sweeping down from Divis and the Cave Hill. Remember.

What would she not remember of the past five months, a time which had brought her experiences of searing intensity and those of a seeming lethargic forgetfulness until she realised that it was her own will that was causing the latter, her own will that was deadening the images in her mind, fudging the edges so that all that remained was a grey blankness? And then her emotions were dulled also, bringing temporary respite from the tremors of her being. It was like a deliberate exercise in self-discipline. And now why the opposite fear that she had in fact forgotten some detail of immense importance?

Abruptly she broke from the surging assembly and began walking slowly towards Malone, mentally recording the date. November 11th, 1918. Armistice Day. The generally held belief of the end of the war being imminent had brought her a few days previously from Islandmagee to stay with her grandmother, so that she could be in the city for the celebrations. It was a duty. Head held high and hair flowing, it was as though the wind itself was charged with emotion like some fretful yet mischievous child, and she found herself alternately laughing and crying. When had it been, and what had she forgotten? If anything?

May. That had been the month, the month of her own naming, when she'd received a letter from her mother telling her that Harry had been wounded a second time. And in the same battle Samuel had

176

been wounded also. Leaving the munitions factory and returning to the boarding-house, she'd lifted the letter from the hall table gleefully, as her mother didn't write often. An hour later she found herself sitting on her bed staring at her reflection in the mirror without being able to recall what she had been thinking other than that she'd decided to return to the island. The letter lay on the floor. She didn't read it again but slipped it into a bulky notecase amongst others.

June and July passed, during which time she immersed herself in the routine of the farm alongside Jack, her mood febrile and tense, which at moments caused her to snap at him for no good reason. But he, as on a previous occasion, made no remonstrance and simply worked beside her, quietly humming to himself or talking to the farm animals. The farmhands, who would often quip with this fine big girl about country matters in a rough yet good-humoured fashion, now left her alone, whether because they too perceived her mood or because Jack had told them to she did not know. At times, watching her brother out of the corner of her eye, she marvelled at the innate sense of grace within that squat ungainly-seeming form with the merry eyes for whom the privacy of another's being was sacrosanct, and though she often felt like impulsively hugging him as she'd done in bygone years she found her natural instincts fettered. Nor did Alec Dick's cajoling make her respond, on those few occasions when she and her mother took the ferry to Larne, and she would snap at him also so that he too left her alone. It was her mother who insisted on such trips. Ostensibly they were for shopping, but the real reason was so that May could be trapped for a few hours and forced to listen to continual questions and suggestions about her future, about her feelings, about Samuel, even though neither of them knew anything of the extent of his wounds, or of Harry's. And often in the evenings, seeking solitude, she would sit in Granny Hopkins' cottage thinking of childhood and stories of the lamp being lit in the window as a guide for the sailors tossing on the stormwaves. It was then that she allowed her thoughts and feelings to drift among the many and varied impressions created by the menfolk around her, males and opposites and somehow not opposites who by their very physical presence were creating her or forcing her to create herself by delving among the multilayered facets of her own hopes and desires, though not yet fully understood. In contrast to childhood she felt herself to be a prisoner and her mood would become one of baffled sullen resentment. Yet, as though in an act of contrition, one morning as they crossed the fields she threw her arms round Jack with her old impulsive demonstration of affection and was greeted with the words: 'Well, May, it's still a warm world when you get a hug like that. I was beginning to think you'd left us for good.'

177

August came bringing the harvest moon and with it came Harry. It was Jack who told her he'd arrived. Rushing down the lane and through the orchard she stood in the porch to regain her breath before entering. He sat by the range talking to her mother. And how frail he seemed, as if the first strong wind from the sea would blow him away. The dark line of the moustache accentuated the sallowness of his features. As she crossed the room she watched him awkwardly stand up. Hardly taller than herself, he now seemed much smaller, the uniform hanging from him as if draped from pegs.

'It's nice to see you again, May.'

Sullen anger. How she hated him, this stranger who had caused her so much bafflement, torment, sleeplessness. And a stranger he was, that she understood and was grateful for the knowledge. Taking the proffered hand in her own, and how slim and almost fleshless it felt, it seemed that she was towering over him. Suddenly conscious of the scene, of her own physical form in full maturity with her broad shoulders and swelling breasts in rude vigorous health contrasting with his wounded diminutive body, she blushed violently. 'It's good to see you've recovered.'

'Not quite.'

'But you will here,' May heard her mother say. 'That's why you've come. With plenty of good food and good sea air you'll soon be your old self.'

'Thank you, Mrs Gordon. It's very kind of you to allow me to convalesce here.'

'Nonsense. You're almost one of the family. And the sooner you start eating the better.'

How slow and awkward even his voice seemed. And how glad she was that her mother, who was now busily striding towards the kitchen, had been with them so that she did not have to meet him this first time alone. 'And Samuel? How is he?'

'Physically . . .'

As he paused she repeated the word. 'Physically?'

'He's in good health, it seems. But his mind . . . Shellshock, you know. But we hope it's only temporary.'

'Yes,' she said, echoing him. 'Only temporary.' And as they fell silent again she felt relief at the familiar sounds from the kitchen.

That first afternoon they had walked over the fields. Feeding Rosinante she saw him staring at the animal, at herself, in a way she couldn't name. Almostly rude it was, as though in this simple act he found something aggravating. Walking on he turned at the sound of braying and, with a wistful smile, said: 'Ah, sweet mystery, May.' Reaching out she felt her hand brush his, but he didn't respond. Was his state also only temporary? What scars had this second wounding left and would his old volatile impulsive nature return? During the night her restlessness caused her to roam the house, several times pausing outside his door. Once she heard a long moan and what sounded like a stifled scream. Involuntarily opening the door, she stood on the threshold watching the pale features and shock of dark hair on the pillow and the slim feminine-looking hand lying on the quilt. Moonlight glowed softly in the room. He moved, his lips opening and closing soundlessly, and she answered. 'My love, my love. Is it you? Can it be you? Tell me what love is. I do not know.'

September approached and in the last days of summer they went swimming. He'd regained his strength and his body was sound again. By the shore they made love, hesitantly, fumblingly, an act which both found unsatisfying even though each wanted more. Examining the fresh wounds in his side she suddenly heard him say that he was returning to his company, was returning to the war. Why, she had asked, when he really didn't have to? Not yet, anyway? Because he would finish what he'd begun. For no other reason than that. And she'd been surprised to find that she was glad, though whether because she'd sensed in him again that wilful stubbornness, determination which attracted her, or that his leaving would give her respite from questions which troubled her, she could not decide. And in the weeks following his going she'd reverted to her former indrawn mood.

And now suddenly the war had ended. Leaving Belfast and the celebrations she returned to the farm, eyes fixed on the scudding waters of the lough as the train whistled along the track. Soon they would all be coming home. Soon Harry would be coming home. She knew he would come back to the island and would not stay in London as she once had thought, and this time she wouldn't be able to avoid answering both her own questions and his. He would press himself upon her, she knew that also. And in any decision he took he would show that stubbornness in carrying it through. Briefly she thought of a different future for herself, an independent future away from home in perhaps a nursing career. That was within her reach and abilities. But was it what she wanted? And when she thought of that she pictured Sam who was still in a hospital in England. He would be coming home soon too.

A letter from Harry was waiting for her. She waited until after the evening meal and retired to her room to read it there. He'd rejoined the Division in time to take part in the last battle, at a place called Coutrai. They would be spending Christmas on the Belgian border, and he expected to be discharged from the army early in the New

Year. He'd already decided on his future. After a short spell in London he'd return to Ireland and try to find work either in journalism or publishing. That was what really interested him now. His degree would qualify him and the past years of reading in the trenches stood him in good stead. Could he stay at the farm until he found a position and a place for himself? And the most important thing of all, would she marry him in the summer, by which time he hoped to be established?

The following day she told her mother of his request to stay for a short period, which was granted, but did not speak of anything else.

Came Christmas again and another New Year and it was her nineteenth birthday. As now, how often had she sat up to hear the twelve o'clock pealing of bells and shrieking of whistles and to welcome the firstfooter, saying it's my new birthday, another new birthday. But the fluctuating moods which had been with her since Harry's sojourn at the farm stayed with her, and the seasonal merriment surrounding her touched her little. Others were subdued too, commenting gloomily on the results of the recent election in which the Republican party of Sinn Fein had taken most of the seats in the country. Only in the counties of the north-east was there a concentration of the Unionist-minded, stout as before in their allegiance to the Imperial parliament in London and Empire. Yes, the war in Europe, which had taken such a toll of the population, had ended. But what now? Though forced into a minority position in Ireland, those who looked to Britain for cultural identity refused to admit it, and from their political leaders and the leaders of the Orange Order came the same warlike statements as a few years earlier.

Warlike. Was one war to end only for another to begin? And hadn't it been said that the war in France would solve the trouble in Ireland? She'd heard it from Harry's lips, and from other people's, but Harry had said it with an odd mocking smile as though he didn't believe it. He'd mentioned Russia also, where revolution was taking place, saying that he and Dalton and Samuel had talked about it in the trenches. Briefly she tried to think of Russia—though she couldn't even picture that country in her mind—and Ireland blanketed by a war like that of France, but failed. Nevertheless she experienced a feeling of foreboding that was not unlike a premonition. And then she chided herself for being silly, wasn't this way of thinking simply because she didn't know what to say to Harry or how to answer her own questions? And anyway, what could an uneducated person like herself know about such things?

Two events heightened her spirits. One was a long letter from Anna describing her life at the private school in England. It was mostly one of dull routine except for outings to cathedrals, great houses and museums in and around London. But that suited her, as there was nothing more she liked to do than reading. She had also been allowed to go horse-riding, and now she could do that perfectly well. Perhaps she and May could go riding together when she returned to Ireland? But before that she would be going to the Continent, to France or Switzerland, to another school. But a lot of her letter, May noticed, was about their own few occasions spent together, and she wondered why Anna seemed so close to her, they whose lives were so different. Because not once did May notice a similar solitariness in herself, she who had grown up in the company of men.

The second was with David, now practically six feet tall though not yet thirteen. It occurred at dinner on New Year's Day when he announced that he was going to run away to sea. And, after a lengthy wrangle with his mother, the latter declared that where she was concerned he couldn't run away far enough because she was tired trying to thrash some sense into him for stealing ponies and horses, so he might as well try stealing a fishing boat and no doubt the sailors would drown him on the spot. Taking this as a sign of permission, he packed and left two days later with May accompanying him to Larne where she saw him off on a trawler, thinking that, compared to either Jack or Dalton, it was David who had that streak of wildness she sensed in herself.

And then came a homecoming. Samuel.

Learning that he had been transferred to a hospital in Belfast, she went to visit him. Though forewarned by Harry and knowing his wounds, she did not expect to find the vacant spectral face which greeted her. Sitting on the chair opposite him she didn't understand a word of his gushing speech though she knew it was in French, and gradually understood also that he had no idea of who she was. And walking in the grounds with him she noticed he already had the gait of an old, old man. On a third visit she learned that he was to be discharged. There was little hope of his returning to sanity. Gentle, showing no trace of violence, physically in good health, the only thing to be done was to return him to his family, especially as he was daily attempting to leave the hospital and was often to be found wandering the lawns or the fields and roads beyond the perimeter. But even they did not keep him, either abandoning him out of their own grief and shock or deciding that it was better to let him go as he willed rather than make him a prisoner. And as the months passed May sometimes heard of him, a shuffling tramplike figure who so unceasingly walked the streets of the city and the surrounding villages that he was looked upon as a kind of moving monument who created within those he approached a superstitious reverence, giving him bread and water

181

and milk when asked and feeding the mangy donkey or dog which at times were his companions. And May would think of the figure she'd once known, Samuel with his timid caresses and their feeding Rosinante together, of a figure whose future was to be a prisoner like a bird in a cage, and of the figure now.

Dalton arrived, but not for long. He brought with him the man she'd seen twice before and who'd gone with him to the war and who now seemed almost like an uncle. Duncan McKinzie. Both were going into the police. Duncan to rejoin the Royal Irish Constabulary and be stationed initially in Larne as before, with Dalton going to Dublin to train at Phoenix Park. Of Dalton May saw little, but could hear long whispered conversations between him and her mother in the locked study. And then he was gone.

But gone where? Hadn't the Republicans already declared an Irish Republic and threatened to seize Dublin and begin another war should what they ask not be given?

Now there was only Harry to return. But May had other suitors. Once, walking back to the farm with Bertie Knox, she had given herself to him in a wild eagerness to sate her own passions, and another time to Alec Dick's son, Bruce. She lay on the grass, breasts and belly heavy with male weight. Was she then a whore? Or was it loneliness, the loneliness of her own flesh and spirit with their demands? And then the feeling of guilt and fear of pregnancy which almost drove her to say Yes to another's marriage proposal.

Ah, sweet mystery of life at last I've found thee—

In the darkness of a spring night his song coming across the fields. Mystery.

Ah! I know at last the secret of it all—

In the darkness of a spring night the old donkey braying marking someone afoot.

All the longing, seeking, striving, yearning—

Rosinante heehawing through the clear air. And the figure of Samuel walking the city's streets on a spring night.

The burning hopes, the joy and idle tears that fall—

In the clear air of a spring night the darkness of her own tumultuous confusion.

For 'tis love, and love alone, the world is seeking—

Once there was so much time. And now there is no time at all.

For it is love alone that rules for aye!

At the study window she watched him enter the yard and waved, then waited for the door to open.

'May.'

'I heard you singing. And Rosinante braying.'

182

'Sure isn't it nearly as good a singer as me. Or maybe I'm nearly as good a singer as it.'

The same Harry. Robust, quick, laughingeyed. The Harry she'd known on the Gobbins cliffs. The same she'd drawn to herself to lose in his mercurial passion. What weight had then been on her breasts? None but her own wanting.

'Well, May?'

Confession.

'Well?'

'I've had a proposal from someone else. And have made love to someone else.'

'Oh?'

And in the silence she asked: have I lost the dream I'm looking for, if I knew what it was?

Contemptuously he said: 'To be wooed and won in a day? Do you not think better of yourself than that?'

'I wasn't won.'

'Oh? What then?'

'Tell me what you think.'

'That doesn't matter.'

'I didn't think it did.'

Harry nodded. 'Well, May?'

'Yes.'

The marriage was arranged for August, the reception being held in the old inn of Dobbin's in Carrickfergus. By that time Harry had acquired himself a job as a reporter with a newspaper in Larne. They talked of the honeymoon and decided to spend it in a cottage in Donegal close to the Atlantic. She'd thought of Samuel's idea, of going abroad to France, to Paris perhaps. But no, for all of them the war was much too close. In Donegal, alone together to learn and discover, there would be peace. Time. Passion.

And in a hired car they left Carrickfergus where the miles of breezeblown fuchsia and hawthorn and honeysuckle were like confetti.

Sam, Sam, Don Samuel, Shellshock Sam as they call you now, shuffling, shuffling, stick in hand, sightless, an idiot babbling, a bag of buns and a milk-bottle draped from the bit of rope at your waist, some other mangy cur at your feet and licking your hand because it has at last found a friend: *Savez-vous ce qui passe en Irlande? Mon Dieu, que la guerre est longue . . .*

PART THREE

I

'Heaven.'

'Yes.'

'How strange to find it here.'

'Here? Perhaps *here* is ourselves. Wherever it might be. A place in a different sense.'

She looked at him. 'Yes. You once put it as the opposite. As absence.'

'Hell.'

'That was the first time we made love.'

Turning, he encircled her waist with his arm. 'I'm the sea and you're the land. I girdle the earth.'

Again they bathed between each other's thighs, lips tasting the tang and salty sweetness of their different essences. Her tongue exploring the sensitive tissue of his maleness in drowsy langour, she felt the flexing of his muscles and heard his soft cries which anticipated the hot spurting emission she sought, her own body in rhythmic motion as his own seeking flooded her senses in a surging glow and carried her to oblivious flight. She was truly a wild bird. Wings outstretched, she soared and glided over the promontory where her calls echoed against land and sea. Even more drowsily she lay back and then eagerly reached out to take his weight, saying cover me cover me, and opened to his penetration as she pulled him against her.

Time possessed no time. The cottage lay behind them, gable end towards the ocean. She knew it was built that way because of the gales that would rage in from the Atlantic. But how long had they been there? A year, a week, a moment? As long as the earth, the sea? And if not in this form, in some other? Because it seemed like that. And because now it seemed she possessed a knowledge that could not be spoken, could not even be thought. Adrift on each other's tides the fragmentary thoughts and voices which welled up like flotsam gave the same lulling sound as that of the waves near where they lay. Dance

187

for me, May, he'd coaxed, and at first she'd been shy. But tonight she would dance for him again. With the flames of the peat fire tingling her skin she would sway bare-breasted across the flagged floor while watching his mute adoration, then swiftly thrust her breasts into his mouth wanting the warm wetness of his lips' pull at her nipples. It was the way I first really saw you, May, that first time in Islandmagee. And it was an image I carried with me back to the trenches, an image I shall carry always.

Yes. That first time in Islandmagee. The music and dancing on the stage in the Opera House bringing desire that was unruly and clamorous, unwanted yet wanted. And his singing on the train. Parakeets. Parakeets I'm selling and the other passengers laughing. And then, with her blouse on the grass, the feeling of delight in taunting him and listening to the hard anger in his voice before going to him.

Rousing herself, she looked at his body, slim yet muscular, tanning now with the sun and wind. The scars were fading, though traces would always remain. Across his chest was a patch of fine dark hair which narrowed to a thin line running to his navel and beyond. How beautiful he looked as he lay sleeping, one hand shading his eyes, the fine girlish features turned slightly away from her. With a little laugh she kissed his thighs and then took him as before, her fingers stroking his chest, watching along the length of his body and feeling him stiffen against her tongue until he suddenly broke from slumber in climax and fell back panting, and then she was on top of him pushing his own saltiness into his mouth so that they were joined in that too.

'May, May, my darling May. You're my dream. My beautiful dream.'

She laughed. 'That took you by surprise, didn't it?'

'And I hope it will many times again.'

She pouted in a deliberately childlike fashion. 'Old greedy belly. You always want too much.'

And she felt like a child as she ran across the beach to the shallows where she danced and swayed while kicking the wavelets into spume which glistened prismatically in the sun, eager for his attention. Washing in the sea she then ran with arms outstretched feeling the drying breeze against her nakedness, running with the old innocence of childhood when she had imitated the seabirds, an innocence which this new experience had seemed to heighten rather than diminish. Returning to where he lay she took the proffered glass of wine and drank deeply and they sat in silence as afternoon lengthened into evening, thick towels wrapped round them against the chill in the air, watching the antics of the birds and seals who were their only companions in the broad and lengthy bay. It was a landscape meant for loneliness, she thought, and yet she didn't feel at all lonely. Even life on the island seemed too tumultuous, too busy, too filled with others, compared to the quietude of this land which enfolded her and within which she wished to remain undisturbed. Yes, this was love and within her its probings were deep, bringing to her ever newer feelings and realisations. The wine was warm and stimulating inside her, like the way the firelight would soon be on her flesh. Softly she smiled, thinking of those times in girlhood when she'd sat on her bed watching her own changing form in the mirror, asking questions. And now in the cottage she could watch her own reflection again, fully shaped, but with another as audience. Him. And there was no shame.

'A penny for them, May.'

'I was just thinking about when I was a girl. Of watching myself in the mirror and wondering about love. Of who would love me.'

Despite herself she blushed and laughed, and felt his lips pressing against her breasts.

'Many would, May. Given the chance.'

'But then it seemed to be shameful somehow.'

Noticing her musing expression, Harry asked: 'And now?'

'It seems so innocent.'

He nodded. 'And so it should be. There's nothing that a man and woman can do in love that can be wrong. Our teachings, May, aren't always right. And sometimes we have to unlearn what we learned.'

She paused to think of his words, sensing that for him they held a deeper significance than what she understood, only then realising just how long they had sat in silence watching the sky gain a deeper hue. 'And you? What were you thinking about?'

'About the walking tour I was on before the war. With Dalton and Samuel. We came to this part of Donegal.'

Piqued, she asked: 'And not about me?'

Laughing, he rested his hand between her thighs and stroked her hair. 'Of course. How could I not?'

Yet apart from the tenderness of his touch and the world it held, that other world brushed against them both, and she shivered. 'Yes. I remember you going. Leaving the Hollow with your rucksacks. And you wouldn't let me go with you.'

'You were too wild, May. We were afraid you'd jump over a cliff or something.'

'That's what my father used to call me. "My wee wild thing." '

'At least he knew that part of you,' Harry teased, before adding: 'But there's so much life in you, May. It spills from you like the wheat flung at harvesting.'

Another image of leavetaking came to her mind. Dalton and Samuel on the deck of the steamer at Larne, of Harry going alone, all three in uniform. Pursing her lips, she said: 'Poor Samuel.'

His voice was very soft. 'He was in love with you, wasn't he?'

'Was he?'

'Didn't you know?'

In the gathering dusk a figure shambled along the beach a few yards away, and came an unsettling feeling not unlike pain. 'Tell me what you know.'

'He told me he did. Or as much as told me.'

'Oh? When?'

'When he came out to save me. To bring me in. That second time I was wounded.'

'Oh? It was Samuel who saved you? You didn't tell me that before.'

'I didn't want to. I didn't see the point. And particularly as it wasn't Sam who saved me at all. He came out to try. But in the end it was Dalton who saved us both.' He paused. 'And also because I knew he loved you. And wondered . . .'

'Wondered?'

'If you would have chosen him. Did he propose to you too?'

'In a way.'

'And?'

'No, Harry. I wouldn't have said yes. I didn't feel for him in this sense or anything like it. And wouldn't have done even if he had come back.'

Had come back? But hadn't he come back? Gentle Sam. The way she talked it was as though he were dead. The way they were both thinking it was as though he were dead. As in a sense he was. Seeing that he was about to speak again she said firmly: 'No, Harry. It's not of our doing.'

Surprised at the conviction in her voice, he looked into her eyes and fleetingly saw something of Dalton's nature. Yes. She was right. It was not of their doing. Yet for him the thought didn't entirely assuage a feeling of guilt.

'I was wondering more what's going to happen now that a Republic has been declared in the south.'

Jumping up he pulled her to her feet and held her tightly. 'No, May, no. Not that either. If war's going to come to Ireland it'll come soon enough. Fire, food and bed for us. And no talk of anything other than those.'

And so the ritual continued and continued in a time without end or beginning either, passionately, wantonly, somnolently, the musk scent of the night which was the land and their own bodies and the brisk breezes from the bay and the ocean beyond and the beasts from land and sea secret sharers in a marriage feast. Hours and days passed in discovering the sensuality of the other in mind and imagination, flesh and spirit. Fatigue would come in dreamless slumber with the cords that held them to new realms of intoxication, thrusting, intaking, seeking a whole.

What could be innocence and experience? Experience and innocence? Could such a marriage be possible? Be?

What?

And so their dreamful minds slumbered on the edges of being. Or attempting to be.

Ceremony. What else?

Of the quick and the dead. Of?

Those vestiges which are both and neither. Themselves.

'Love! You startled me.'

She rose over him, attempting a new awakening.

'May.'

'What?'

'I was dreaming of Picardy.'

'In my heart you shall always be. Now and the beyont.' Deliberately she had used the colloquial pronunciation in a gesture of their own intimacy and nativity, and suddenly paused. Hadn't the big man's son, Duncan's, Dalton's friend, died by a bayonet? Who had told her that? Remember. But how much had been forgotten already?

'Perhaps I shall take you there.'

'Where?'

'Picardy.'

'Perhaps it will be too painful,' she said, then added: 'For both of us.'

And in the ensuing silence they shared a phantom as it passed their gaze, shuffling, stumbling, head bent, seeking, searching, perhaps seeing. Perhaps.

Sam, Sam.

Je suis à la recherche de ma ville natale—mon pays—mon île bien aimée—mon amour . . .

'Is it to be war then, Harry?'

'I asked you not to speak of that.'

'Why not?'

'Because . . .' Looking towards the sea, he fell silent. He had nothing to say. The clowns. The coloured arrows sticking to them as they spun through the air. The shellhole and Sam and Dalton and the mule lumbering to its demented end. How could one tell that story? Pinning on its war medals, sir. A severed hand, a tin of bully beef, the

191

stock of a shattered rifle, part of a human head. Someone's dreams and hopes in anticipation of love and joy. That, now, never can be.

'Why don't you want to talk about it?'

'May. May. No.'

'Hasn't war already started? With all the shooting in the south, I mean? A war that the war in Europe—in France—was supposed to stop?'

Surprised, he looked at her. 'Who told you that?'

'I used to hear father and Dalton argue about it.'

Again he was surprised. 'Oh?'

'Yes.'

Another afternoon on the Atlantic shore, another cloister of obsessive intimacy in their lovemaking which made them as one, truly androgenous, other words to jar them apart in separateness, anxiety, a fear not shared.

'And what did your father believe?'

'That the war in Europe would have nothing to do with what was happening here.'

'And what else?'

'That he didn't want to see Ireland divided. It would only create more trouble.' Watching the sea crash over the rocks and the gulls glide through the foam, she waited. 'I used to hear them argue half the night in the study. They didn't know I was listening.'

'And what does Dalton believe?'

'Does anyone know? Or does anyone know what kind of person he is? I don't. And I'm his sister.'

Startled, Harry looked at her. Experience, wisdom. A kind of finality of knowing, a probing of layers of being not yet within consciousness was part of her grasping. Another scene came to mind, that night at the Front when he'd challenged both Samuel and Dalton on the executions of the leaders of the Dublin rebellion. Dalton— then Lieutenant—Gordon could have charged him. It was within his right to do so. But he didn't. And James gone to India where there was more trouble with that fellow Gandhi. James sitting with him in the military hospital in England, intimating that his onetime companion, who laughed like a hyena, was no longer a companion. What questions were being asked of himself by others, what questions were being asked of himself by himself: Must he always remain the clown? Fodder for other people's decisions? His only decision had been in joining the Ulster Division at the Front. But even that now seemed not to have been a decision, but to have been caught in the sway and flow of things decided upon outside himself. Another thought, memory. Niall. Niall McNeill. The one childhood friend whom he knew must be in an opposite camp, Nationalist and Republican.

192

Would he have the courage to return to Ballycastle, to greet a childhood comrade? Against whose beliefs he must have fought?

The clown. Perhaps his only true decision ... Perhaps ...? Undoubtedly his own true decision was in wanting May. Needing her. Kneading. Was that his only attempt at courage? Don't run at the wrong end of a machine-gun, James had said, and thought of him as a hero. My Irish cousin.

Kneading May. What beauty lies in love. May.

Still watching the sweep of the birds across the oceanic bay and the darkheaded sporting seals and the showery back of a large fish that sometimes rose to the surface, she turned to the wistful smile she'd been studying at length. 'A penny for them, Harry.'

'That's what I said to you a moment ago.'

'A moment ago?' Outrightly she laughed. 'That was yesterday.'

'Yesterday?' Wistfulness, frowning, then attempting to concentrate before all merged in a chameleonic spume and he laughed, seizing her again in playfulness. 'May, May. How long is yesterday? How long is love?'

II

Sitting on a bollard idling away half an hour with a flask of whiskey in his pocket, to an onlooker apparently daydreaming while scratching his beard, Alec Dick was thinking about the couple who were standing, seemingly in argument, at the entrance to the harbour. Eyes missing nothing, he'd noticed their appearance at the gates some fifteen minutes before. Suddenly grinning, he looked down to where the boat bobbed in the water and at the lanky tousle-haired figure who was partially hidden beneath a piece of tarpaulin. 'Well, if the police don't get you this time, here comes yer big sister.'

The figure peered upwards. 'To hell with her.'

'And what if she tells Dalton?'

'To hell with him too.'

Alec tried to hide a grin. 'That's a quare thing till say about yer own family. I'm sure yer oul' da would be turnin' in his grave if he could hear yer words. Him that made yous all.'

'I didn't ask him to, did I? And I didn't ask what him and ma were up to either.'

Still quietly grinning, Alec sighed and shook his head. 'Dear Lord and lack the day when skitterin' youngsters have no respect fer their elders who begot them.' Receiving no response, Alec sat watching the couple who stood in the same place while musing on the figure in the boat, who was David Gordon, the latter's latest escapade having been to trick some fish merchant in Scotland into parting with money for a catch that didn't exist and then flee before the police could stop him at the ferry in Stranraer. So David had told him and, knowing the truth of his exploits of old, Alec did not doubt him. A rogue he was, Alec mused, but there was much more than that to his character. There was a precocious intelligence allied to a sense of total independence and a rare kind of honesty which made him in Alec's mind like some Robin Hood figure. There was a scepticism too which outweighed his boyish years. There'd be few who would be able to outwit the same David Gordon, thought Alec, whilst acknowledging him as one of his own favourites.

The couple approached, May being the first to speak. 'Will you ferry us over, Alec?'

'I wondered when ye were goin' till come. It looked like ye were goin' till stand there all the night long. Was it divorce ye were talkin' about already?'

'No,' May said, then paused: 'About leaving the island.'

Noticing the sadness in her voice Alec ushered them down the steps and climbed into the boat, pushing off from the quay when they were seated. 'Well, there'd be no harm in seein' other parts of the country, I'm sure. The island'll always be here when ye want to come back.' Stopping to look into the faces of Harry and May and try to gauge their moods, he turned to pull the tarpaulin off the recumbent form. 'And here's a relation of yours that'll be leavin' fer some other place if the police gets their hands on him.'

Seeing David's blunt chin and blue eyes appear in front of her, May laughed. 'And what have you been up to this time, Davy?'

Quick to her changing mood, Alec related the story while David churned the water with one hand and chuckled to himself.

'The rapscallion of the family. The black sheep,' May said, adopting the terms Harry had used when she'd recounted the tales which had grown around the youngest of the family.

'Aye,' responded Alec, 'and if he doesn't mend his ways he might even end up on one of those.' And again he was quick to see that Harry, who had laughed with May about David, reverted to his former sombreness.

The ship lay towards the centre of Larne Lough like a cell buoyed on water, the bars on deck and heavy steel mesh sinking below the surface clearly discernible.

David's gaze followed the pointing finger, mind perplexed by the contours of a ship whose kind he'd never seen before. 'What is it?'

'There's the man that can tell ye,' Alec said, nodding towards Harry. 'Doesn't he write about all the things that's now happenin' in the country?'

As David again asked, Harry replied: 'A prison ship. It was brought round from Belfast Lough a few weeks ago.'

'I'll not be on one of those!' David exclaimed so emphatically that Harry was forced to smile. But it was a smile, Alec noticed, which had no humour in it.

Harry nodded. 'No. I shouldn't think you would be. It's not meant to be for . . .' Not wishing to say 'thief' or 'your kind' or use any other such term, he stopped short. Anyway, he thought, while still gazing at the object which had all the appearance of a floating cage rather than a ship, everyone including himself looked upon David's exploits as those engendered by adolescent truculence and high-spiritedness and without criminal intent.

'Who's it for, then?' David asked.

'Other kinds of prisoners,' Harry said quietly. 'Political prisoners.'

Alec peered at the face which was again gazing up the lough, one hand shadowing the sun from the eyes, then at May. It had been a good match. The two of them truly made a pair. He'd often felt that during the past year when they'd been living in the Hollow Farm since their return from Donegal, ferrying Harry across to Larne to the newspaper office with May sometimes accompanying him. Harry, seemingly slight of frame yet as steely as a newly forged blade and quicksilvered in temper, had drawn May out into her full bloom of young womanhood. Obviously each had found a deep response in the other. Wishing to change the subject, he turned to May. 'And no sign of a firstborn yet, May McKinstry? With you youngsters all the time to make one in.'

'Don't we want time to ourselves first, ferryman?'

As exuberant as ever, Alec thought, grinning to himself, then found the conversation being brought back to its previous subject by Harry's quiet though insistent voice.

'And what do you think, ferryman?'

May was now frowning and staring at the lapping water. Had there already been some kind of breach? 'Think? Of what?'

'Of that ship.'

'That it must be a sour country when ye have till have the likes of that 'cause the gaols are so full. For political prisoners, as you say. Though to others for criminals.'

'Oh? Is to be a Nationalist or a Republican to be a criminal?'

Alec shook his head. 'I only listen to what other men say.' He paused. 'But tell me, reporter, you that scour the country fer till get news. What d'ye think of all these troubles? If wi' fair judgement they're till be called.'

If with fair judgement they are to be called. Turning the phrase over in his mind, Harry replied softly: 'You'll have to read the newspapers, ferryman. Like you, I too only listen to what other men say.'

Sculling the boat into the other shore, Alec jumped out and grasped his passengers' arms each in turn before claiming the fare, watching as they walked up the shore. The three figures paused then broke apart, with May and her brother taking the route towards the farmhouse and Harry continuing alone. 'Aye,' Alec thought, keeping his eyes on the solitary rambling figure, 'I'm sure ye do listen to what other men say. But not only that. Ye do yer own thinkin' too and maybe nobody knows what way ye think yet.'

He'd wanted to be alone when leaving the newspaper office that afternoon. May had come to meet him, and had noticed the annoyance on his face. Why, she'd asked, only to receive the answer that he didn't need her to escort him every day. As if she did, she'd retorted, and hadn't he been so glad to find her waiting for him through many of those days in winter and spring? Remonstrating against the other, spiteful, arguing over nothing, they were like children. Yet there was a deeper root that each was vaguely aware of, and lay in the state which the country was now in. Over the past several months she had commented often on his brooding solemnity, had resented his attempts at talking politically, while he in turn had called her silences on the subject despicable. That was not fair to either of them he knew, and knew that she knew. It was as though they were in the grip of some invidious cancer from outside themselves. Which caused them some nights to lie in bed angry and apart.

Soon they would be leaving Islandmagee to go to Newry which lay almost half-way to Dublin. The editor of his newspaper, the *East Ulster Times*, had said it would be a good vantage point to see what was really happening in the midland counties and those south to Dublin. He knew Dublin well, which was to his every advantage. And besides, if the country did find itself partitioned as was now mooted, he didn't want to find himself on the wrong side of the border, did he?

Harry assented immediately, knowing that he wanted to leave Larne and its environs in order to judge for himself what was taking place elsewhere. And what *was* taking place? Really taking place?

What do you think of all these troubles? If with fair judgement they are to be called.

The words of the ferryman resounded in his mind like a constant loud echoing which demanded to be answered. Above Brown's Bay he walked along a narrow path almost overgrown with blackberry bushes, striking them with a stick to make his way, pausing at times to look out to sea and its drapery of cerulean sky. Out there lay England, an England he had fought for and nearly died for. Like so many others. But now so many others, other Irishmen, had sworn a different allegiance. Not to King and country, but to a Republic.

On leaving the ferry he'd told May that he had an important article to write for tomorrow and so needed to be alone. That was the cause of his present mood. He needed time alone to think in. She nodded and accepted, though in her look there was a shadow of doubt. And he had stood there watching the two figures of her and David until, towards the top of the other hillside, she'd turned to wave.

Troubles? If with fair judgement . . . Was it not a euphemism for war? A war England refused to acknowledge as being a war?

Looking down across the seagrained sand of the bay, he sought which path to take. What is to be my decision, my part to play, my future, my destiny?

197

Was he always to be the clown? The servant of the wills of others and not his own? Was he always to do nothing but skip and jump and leap in the sawdust at the crack of the ringmasters' whips?

In thought May came towards him and he embraced her. It was a year now since they had left that honeymoon sanctuary in Donegal to return to live on the farm and for him to take up his work again on the newspaper. No, May, no, he'd said then, when she'd tried to ask if there was to be war in Ireland. He'd wanted to push it away, to avoid thinking about it, and for a year it had been gnawing his mind and spirit to the quick.

Two years before, practically eighty per cent of the people of Ireland had voted for independence, for an independent Republic. Their wish denied them by the Imperial parliament in London, the country had then been flooded with police and troops so that their desire could be quelled by savagery if necessary. And it *was* necessary. More and more irregular bands of troops, some of them made up of men returned from the trenches, leftovers from another war and who were now little more than a mercenary army, combated a people who only wished to have their own political will. From the hills and other stretches of the country the guerrilla flying columns emerged to fight and retreat, and in revenge villages were burnt and pillaged.

Ghosts rose up before him. Casement. Hanged in London as a traitor. A traitor to whom or what? The leaders of the Dublin uprising which he had learned of in the trenches. Shot by firing squads as traitors. Traitors to whom or what?

The prison ship now lying in Larne Lough. That was no ghost. Certainly not yet.

And India. The massacre in Amritsar of a year before after which the Indian leader Gandhi had declared that the British must leave, must get out, as they had already shown themselves incapable of governing a country against its will. And now more news from India where soldiers of the Connaught Rangers had refused to obey orders, had mutinied, on hearing of what was happening in Ireland. What was to be their future, their destiny? Another firing squad?

Little Belgium overrun by the Kaiser's armies. Democracy, liberty, the freedom of small nations: all must be protected! The grand phrases issuing from London and the ghoulish ceremony of the Somme.

Now at the shore Harry kneeled, smiling as he ran the stick over the rivelled yellow surface. Had he thought that before, talked of that before? He couldn't remember. Perhaps it was that night in the tent wth Sam and Dalton.

The grand phrases. Cracks appearing in the fabric of a vast empire which was supposed to last to the millenium and beyond, cracks

198

which were to be pasted over by blood if necessary. And that meant if one could not vote one's way out, did one have to fight one's way out? Democracy. The grand phrases.

India. James was there. Briefly Harry thought of their last meeting when he was in hospital in London and his companion's slight note of dissent at what had happened in Dublin, as though an old mould was showing its first fractures.

The seagrained sand. Slowly Harry's stick sifted among its marks, probing, tracing. What was to be his destiny?

'Harry.'

Startled, he looked quickly up as horse and rider loomed over him in the dusk. Oblivious to anything but his own thoughts he hadn't heard the muffled sound of hoofbeats or noticed day fading.

'I didn't mean to disturb you.'

On the back of the snorting, sweating mare the tall figure in the uniform of a District Inspector of the Royal Irish Constabulary sat erect. Dalton.

Rising to a standing position Harry massaged the stiffness from his kneejoints. 'That's all right. It's just that I was away in a world of my own. Thinking.'

Dalton nodded. 'It was May who asked me to look out for you when I decided to go riding. She expected you back earlier.'

'As I told her. I have an important article to write and needed to be alone to try and think how to work it out.'

Again Dalton nodded. 'She mentioned it.'

Looking landward where the dusk was thickening Harry adopted an apologetic tone. 'Though I must admit I didn't expect to be out this long. But then, often thinking doesn't take account of the passing time.'

The arm was partly outstretched. 'Jump up. You can ride behind me. Dinner will be ready soon and you're expected.'

Pausing, Harry slowly shook his head. 'No thanks, Dalton. Sitting here for so long has made my legs stiff and riding won't help. I'll go at a fast walk back.' Smiling, he added: 'Like other days, eh? A hard route march.'

'I'll see you at dinner, then.'

Abruptly horse and rider wheeled and broke into a canter across the sands.

'See you at dinner.'

Everyone else was already seated at the dinner table by the time Harry arrived. There were six in all: May, her mother, Dalton, Jack, David and another figure in the uniform of a police sergeant who was familiar yet whom he didn't recognise until introduced: Duncan

McKinzie. It was only then that he remembered him as being Dalton's sergeant in the trenches. It was a special occasion as Dalton and Sergeant McKinzie had arrived unexpectedly on leave from the south, his mother-in-law told him, though of course he couldn't have known that as she hadn't known herself until they appeared in mid-afternoon. Apologising for his lateness, Harry quickly washed and changed before rejoining the company.

The meal passed with pleasantries: Elizabeth, dressed in a long gown and glittering with jewellery, saying how good it was to have the whole family together and pitting one against the other about their different occupations, Jack, squat and bald and humorous, telling comic stories of the farm and island, May, wearing a green blouse and a flowing buckled skirt, responding with tales of her childhood and how Jack would frighten her by sending lobsters scuttling at her. Uncharacteristically, or so it seemed to Harry, Dalton joined in also with stories of earlier years. Duncan spoke of the glens, thanking Mrs Gordon for her hospitality in allowing him to stay overnight before travelling on in the morning to his home in Glenarm. There he would spend the days wandering over the hills, where he had a small flock of sheep, with his son Ned and his small daughter in his arms, who'd been born while he was in the trenches with Captain Gordon. Then, face flushing red at this conversational blunder, he lapsed into silence and stared at his plate until rescued by Elizabeth who related how Sergeant McKinzie, just before the war and when her husband had been alive, had brought David home because he was trying to steal a train in Larne.

Silent himself, Harry watched the assembled group. It was like a conspiracy, he thought. Nothing was to be said about the present circumstances, troubles, war. Nothing *must* be said. Forced to speak of his and May's imminent departure from the island, he merely said that his newspaper wished him to be based in Newry so that he could have more access to what was happening in the south, but after that he intended to buy a house in Belfast where he hoped to obtain a position with one of the larger newspapers or even with a publishing firm. I might even, he said in an attempt at jollity, run into Sam, and then cursed himself at his own *faux pas*.

'Ah, yes,' May said. 'Samuel.'

A shadow fell across the laden table.

'You might think I'm a quare fool what with things called stealing and whatever. But I'll be a fool till nobody. Yous go on about your wars and heroes but I'll go about my own business.'

All gaped at the gangling figure now standing beside them.

'David!' Elizabeth remonstrated.

'I'm too big fer ye till thrash me now, ma. And who's the one in here that'll do it for you?'

200

Inwardly Harry laughed, and laughed loudly. That this gangling boy should throw down the gauntlet to all and sundry. The fool. Fool? The circus clown. Himself. But unlike a fool unable to choose. To declare himself. Eyes quickly flitting from one face to another he paused at Dalton's; Dalton who was staring with a quizzical expression at the face above him, and in whose features Harry saw both these brothers who were so alike, and yet not. And in those few moments he saw another intimacy, that of mother and son. Elizabeth bending forward to grasp Dalton's arm.

On the heels of David followed Jack, his excuse for leavetaking yet another task on the farm urgently needing attention. The rest of the meal passed in silence and then Elizabeth left, though not before requesting Dalton to walk with her in the loanan before retiring. The night was warm and the September moon bright and high. Elbows on the table and chin cupped in palms, Harry watched Dalton escort his mother to the door and then sit down again.

Silence. With May restive under Harry's mocking eyes.

'And what is your article about, Harry?'

Irked as he was before about what he deemed a conspiracy of silence, Harry found himself now even more irked over what could be a confrontation. 'About if Ireland is divided. If partition comes.'

'And what do you think?'

'You tell me, Dalton, what you think. After all, you are the one who is fighting in this theatre of . . . Of the troubles.'

'Sergeant?' asked Dalton.

'I'm not a thinking man, sir.'

Quivering now like a tempered blade Harry laughed sardonically, adopting the other's formal mode of expression. 'Then what happens, sergeant, if one day you find yourself in a position in which you have to think?'

'I wouldn't know, sir.'

'Tell me what, then, sergeant . . . As we are all . . . shall I say, old comrades? This mutiny in the Punjab with the Connaught Rangers. What will happen to them?'

Uncomfortably Duncan moved in his chair, broad forehead gleaming. But it was Dalton who answered.

'The firing squad for some, I'm sure.'

Harry nodded philosophically, but with eyes still full of mockery. 'And what about the Curragh mutiny just before the war? I don't believe there were any firing squads there. Tell me the difference.'

And in Dalton's slowly pursing smile Harry saw something that was more terrible than mere mockery, whatever it was.

'Why, Harry. You tell me. You're a thinking man, aren't you?'

'I'm merely a journalist. I only listen to what other men say. Like now.'

201

Still the pursing ambivalent smile. 'Is that all?'

'And if we are divided. Partitioned. The country, I mean. Where will you go, Dalton?'

'Why. Here to the north. Sergeant?'

'Here to the north, sir.'

'And where will you go, Harry?'

'Come, come, come. Can't we have a family meal without all this?'

They all turned towards the voice. 'May.'

'You shouldn't have done that, Harry.'

'Done what?'

'Provoke them.'

'I didn't provoke, May. I simply asked questions. Of them. Of myself.'

Sitting on the edge of the bed in her nightdress, she asked: 'And you, Harry? As Dalton said. Where will you go?' Gaining no reply, May continued: 'And in what do you believe?'

'I don't know. If you wish me to be truthful.'

'Harry, Harry.'

'Come here.'

From their bedroom window they watched where, in the far loanan, Dalton and his mother walked.

May trembled. 'You two sometimes frighten me, Harry. You're almost as strange as he is.'

'Almost?'

'Perhaps just as.' Shivering again, she said: 'Dinner was awful, wasn't it?'

'Oh. One of those celebrations that celebrate nothing but differences. In the wrong way.' Pausing to watch the couple outside turn back to the farmhouse, he added: 'But I must admit I admire your David. I don't think there'll ever be an army that'll get him.'

'No more talk of that. Bed, my love, bed.'

And with May asleep Harry still lay awake, watching the drifting latesummer cloud through the uncurtained window. There was an origin to which he must return, another person to whom he must now talk. Ballycastle, and Niall. Niall McNeill.

III

Before Harry could travel north he found himself going south again, to Dublin, this being at the instigation of his editor who wanted him to report on the return of MacSwiney's body to Ireland. The train broke from the towns and countryside to run alongside the Irish Sea prior to arriving at its destination. Idly listening to the muffled whistling of the locomotive and watching the pluming gulls on the aniline water, he looked down at the pile of English newspapers beside him which he'd bought before boarding. His mood was one of lassitude, lethargy. Sleeplessness stalked his nights when he lay with eyes open foraging among his past, images flitting about the room from shadow to shadow. The Dublin of his carefree university days. Ballycastle. His first impressions of Islandmagee. May. Their first lovemaking after the evening at the Opera House in Belfast. *Ah sweet mystery* . . . Lying in a shellhole trying to gauge how long it would take to die. The bearded, dirty, stumbling form of a onetime comrade-in-arms, Samuel. *Parakeets, I'm selling, parakeets.* And why not? A profession as good as any other. In some ways, perhaps, he was as numbed as Sam. Again his eyes took in the gulls, dipping, beaks rooting among feathers, fathoming themselves. As he was in the anfractuous paths of his own experience. And from this lethargy would come a bitterness of self, a mood of self-destructiveness centring on his incapacity to decide. He'd gone to another war loyal to no one and nothing, merely allowing himself to be swept willynilly by the tide. Was now to be the same?

As dawn gently slipped into their bedroom in the Hollow Farm he heard the bed creak as loudly as a ticking clock and felt her warm body turn into him in that half-sleep of veiled yet awakening desire, her lips seeking his flesh: Harry, Harry, come to me, come.

And if a decision were made it could only be *for* this country he lived in, not *against*. What then of this love? What of the future? A future more important than his own, May's? And then he would wish that he'd never known this joy that gave so much delight, that was for him

203

so fulfilling, that was as necessary to his being as food and air and water.

And in a daemonic moment he would curse it because it made his divided will and spirit even more divided.

And in early morning with the first shredded light the choir would come: thrushes, sparrows, jenny wrens, the chortle of the magpies and the cawing of crows. But, Harry, I am a seabird, she would say. Listen. And in the intersected lines of sleep and non-sleep he would see the edges of seacliffs, tumbling. *Kiiiyaaa kiiiyaaa, my love, scceeeheee* . . .

In a dream, in winged ascending. Come.

The newspaper was in his hands. Terence MacSwiney, Lord Mayor of Cork, arrested in early August as being a Republican sympathiser. Refusing to plead in a British court as he did not recognise its authority and then taken to Brixton prison in England, he engaged on a hunger strike which was to lead to his death eighty-seven days later. There were photographs of the funeral procession going through the streets of London with some members of the British public saluting as though MacSwiney's act had jolted their senses. In the prison in Cork similar deaths had taken place.

More decisions, more choices, sacrifice. And his own?

Arriving in early evening he went to the hotel in the city centre where he'd already reserved a room, then went walking. No, it wasn't the Dublin of his university days but resembled more a city in siege. Armoured cars and soldiers blocked many intersections or filed slowly along the main thoroughfares. Twice he was stopped and questioned, but on showing his Press credentials and explaining his mission was otherwise not troubled. In the night there was the same insomnia and rather than go to bed he sat in the darkened room watching the flittering shadows, asking, asking, and in the early hours listened to the distant popping sounds which he knew to be gunfire.

And if I choose that, what of May?

His report of the procession and the various incidents accompanying it telephoned back to the newspaper, he lingered a few days longer. Strolling through the streets carefully taking in every detail, it felt at times that a decision had been reached. And then night would come and the darkened hotel room and the disembodied figures that appeared at his bedside. From twilight and dusk, scenes of battle emerged also to be woven around the popping sound of guns, and he would shudder. Not that again. Because though now he knew where his sympathies lay he also acknowledged within himself a deep reluctance ever to lift a gun again. Old moulds, patterns, were breaking apart. But to reveal what?

'Harry!'

204

Startled, one hand shielding his eyes against the strong morning sunlight, he saw the tall uniformed figure swiftly approach him from across the street.

'Harry!'

The broad handsome face was smiling, and a friendly hand descended on his shoulder.

'James!'

'For a moment I thought you didn't recognise me, my Irish cousin.'

Harry laughed apologetically, if a little nervously. 'Oh, it's just that I was so engrossed in my own thoughts. Writing my next piece.'

'Yes, I heard that you were now a man of letters.'

'Hardly that. Being in Grub Street is more like it. But journalism is something I enjoy. And who knows what might happen later.'

'It must be rather different from being in the army.'

'I sometimes wonder,' Harry said, watching a tender full of soldiers pass by, 'when I'm reporting on a situation like this.' He paused. 'But I thought you were in India.'

'I was until a month ago. We were ordered to return to Ireland.'

'And what's it like there?'

'At times like what it is here.' Now James paused, before abruptly grasping Harry's arm. 'But don't let's stand here in the street. There's an hotel along here we use. It's a safe place.'

The lounge was quite full even though it was only mid-morning, most of the occupants being in uniform though with a fair sprinkling of others in civilian clothes. Beginning to feel uncomfortable as he sat down, Harry ordered a coffee and a whiskey with it, casually glancing around the room. We? A safe place? Yes. The others not in uniform would be in military intelligence or one of the police special branches. Across the city would be other places like this, exclusively reserved for army personnel and trusted guests where no bullet or bomb would suddenly burst from window or doorway. For them also it was a state of siege. Inwardly Harry smiled. A trusted guest? Perhaps not.

Briefly introduced to a few of James's acquaintances, Harry heard his stepbrother mention his war experiences in the trenches with pride and pleasure, and his discomfort grew. What a gulf now lay between himself and these men at whose side he had once fought. As they moved away he stared at their gleaming uniforms and belted holsters and insignia. Had he really worn those once? How far off it was. Those spectral shapes that came in the night did not wear uniforms.

'. . . I spent some time in London, of course, when coming back from India. They said they rarely heard from you now and only knew you'd got married and become a journalist.' James smiled. 'Have you deserted us, Harry?'

How that innocent remark agitated him, Harry thought. And how distant London also seemed, as though it no longer had any significance in his life or future. It was nearly two years now since he was last there, and seldom did it intrude on his thoughts.

'At least you might have brought your wife to visit us,' your mother said. They were all anxious to see her.'

Harry nodded. 'Yes. I feel a bit guilty about that. But it was simply a question of circumstances: Time, you know. Trying to establish myself in this new profession and having to travel all over the country.'

'I understand, of course.'

'Particularly as things here are in such a state of turmoil.'

'Yes,' James answered, and lapsed into silence.

How devoid of meaning were his words, thought Harry. Without substance even in the act of speaking them. Conventional excuses uttered without conviction. Sipping his whiskey in the ensuing silence and again glancing around the uniformed assembly he wondered also about his relationship with James. Apart from the initial *bonhomie* and pleasure at their unexpected meeting there seemed to be nothing that bound them together, and he found himself wondering if it had always been like this. He recalled the incident on Hampstead Heath when he had first met his new family, with James coming out to meet him after Valerie had questioned him about the possibility of war in Ireland. Between then and now lay an aeon of shattered flesh in Europe, and in its wake came that conflict long delayed here at home. The James of that period had been assured of everything, certain. And then the cracks had appeared after the Easter week executions and prior to his departure for India. And now? Was it that as Harry was gaining in assurance, in conviction, James's beliefs were fracturing further? It was difficult to judge as the latter was seemingly intent on avoiding any talk of Ireland or even India and spoke mainly of family affairs, and Harry was content to follow his lead. Another incident came to mind. That night when James, breaking towards him abruptly from the fog, had laughed quietly and said—Don't be alarmed, I'm not exactly a highwayman. A highwayman. In a way that was how he felt. Like an intruder in another's camp.

'James.'

As James stood up to greet the newcomer Harry noticed that there was no smile of pleasure or welcome on his face, but rather a stiffness which barely concealed an emotion quite different.

'Christopher.'

'I was told I might find you here. I enquired in the mess.'

'I thought you'd left Dublin.'

'Oh, no. Just travelling around the country.' He paused and smiled faintly, a smile that to Harry, noticing the slightly curled lips and protruding teeth, resembled a snarl. 'Hunting game.'

Yes, Harry recalled, Christopher Campbell, the military intelligence officer who had come with James to the hospital and whose conduct James had expressed doubts about. There was no need to ask what kind of game he'd been hunting. Or how he hunted it.

'A reporter now, mmm?'

'Yes.'

'Well, with your war experience it should make your new occupation here much easier.'

The eyes, Harry saw, had narrowed, and the indrawn features had lost their handsome looks, to be replaced by a composed mask hinting of malevolence. 'I'm not so sure about that.'

'No?' The other paused. 'Why? Is this situation any different?'

'In many ways. First of all, it's not a European war. And second, it's a war involving quite different tactics.'

'Oh?' The voice was heavy with sarcasm. 'You say it's a war. When everyone knows—as the government has repeatedly stated both at home and abroad—that it's merely a policing operation against a band of criminals attempting to usurp authority.'

How many times had the same tired phrases echoed down the centuries, Harry thought, while furious with himself at the gaffe he'd made. 'I merely meant it in the loosest sense. There are enough guns being shot off to make it sound like that anyway.'

'Firstly, you're quite right. It's not a European war. But simply lawless acts against the legitimacy of Britain and the British Empire. By a lot of Catholic malefactors who'd be better off in Rome. As for different tactics. Quite right. Like the tactics of MacSwiney. It's a pity they don't all do as he did. It would save us the trouble of shooting or hanging them.' The speaker paused and grinned, teeth bared more. 'Though I must admit it can be good sport.'

Hanging them. The youth swung at the end of the creaking rope. Kevin Barry, hanged as a Republican activist a few days previously. For the majority of the people now another martyr as impotent British officials ordered further executions. It was an incident he didn't want to think about yet which comprised another spectre lurking in the shadows of his room. The boy had had the courage to choose his future, his destiny. What had been in his mind when he'd walked on to the gibbet, felt the noose slip over his hooded face? Stick in hand, another figure knelt on the seagrained sands of the bobbing shore. What imprints lay there? Past. Present. Future. Present? Present was, is, an impossibility. To live in the present is to live in a future that is already past.

The voice was imperious. 'Well, and what do you think?'

207

'Christopher,' James remonstrated, 'we were relaxing and talking of other things.'

'Why, allow me to disturb you, my dear James. It's not often I've the opportunity to speak to the Press. Perhaps our friend here can acquaint me with the thoughts of politicians and ministers.'

Deliberately changing mood, Harry laughed openly, boyishly, mockingly, and was pleased to note the chagrin on the face of his interrogator. Obviously it was a tactic he wasn't accustomed to. 'You've made a grave error if you think I have access to those exalted circles. I'm still junior staff on the newspaper and merely report on events I'm assigned to.' Pausing to sip his drink and light a cigarette, Harry laughed again. 'But. What do I think? I think it's pretty obvious that many people in this country don't agree with the ideas of either you or your government. After all, the government-in-exile, as it were . . . this provisional government that's been set up is making nonsense of your attempts at administering the country.'

'You almost sound like one of them.'

Harry blew a smoke ring. 'A newsman's first criterion is objectivity. Have you never heard that said before?' Pausing to blow another, he added: 'I hear there are similar difficulties in other parts of the Empire. India, for example.'

The smile turned to a sneer. 'They will soon end in this part when we get Collins.'

Collins. Rumoured Chief of Intelligence and army on the Republican side and already a legend. And, though it was thought he had his headquarters in the city, as elusive as the proverbial Pimpernel. 'That's *if* you get him.'

'We soon shall.'

'But,' Harry continued, 'if you really want to know what I think. I think it won't be guns or bullets that will stop this. What is needed are new ideas. New ways of thinking. New political concepts. For example, why can't there be a republic within a monarchy or an empire with power equally shared? Old political forms don't last for ever. Can't. And if new ones aren't devised the old ones just burst at the seams.'

The broken, highpitched laugh was more reminiscent of a jackal or its cousin the hyena, Harry thought.

'We don't need intellectuals.'

'We?'

Again the hyena sound. 'Yes. We.'

Harry watched as the other stood up, first offering his hand to James and then turning towards him to give a slight nod. 'Until we meet again, newsman. Or should it be intellectual?'

'Not a particularly pleasant chat, I would have thought,' said

James in an embarrassed tone. 'Sorry about that.'

Placing one hand on James's arm in an attempt to ease his discomfort as he called to a passing waiter for another drink, Harry smiled. 'Think nothing of it. By now I'm well used to that kind of thing. If anything it's the essence of the newspaper business.' Paying for the whiskey, he continued: 'I didn't mean to mention India, though. I— '

But James interrupted. 'Harry. Thinking men have to consider many things. Now let's talk about something else.'

On the instructions of his editor Harry spent a further fortnight in Dublin, during that period meeting James twice. There was a pleasant intimacy in their dinner conversations which, seemingly by silent mutual agreement, involved every topic they could think of other than the course of events in Ireland and elsewhere. In his hotel room at night there was the same sleeplessness, the same sounds of gunfire, the same spectres moving, questioning. On one occasion he saw Christopher who stood at a corner talking to others, shoulder holster in view under an open jacket, and who greeted him with that slight mocking bow from across the street. On board a Sunday train travelling north he read the first reports of what he had just missed: in the early hours fourteen British officers had been shot dead. Now knowledgeable of the undercurrents of such happenings, he instinctively understood. The spy network whose design was to track and kill Collins had themselves been outwitted and destroyed. Their orders had been countermanded in a way they'd obviously not anticipated.

The reflection in the window of the speeding carriage was one he barely recognised because the smile was so harsh and grim. Himself. And there was another. One with malevolent eyes and a hyena laugh. Had he been one of the fourteen?

And there was something else. An emotion he'd never known before and one he did not wish to recognise. Hatred.

IV

'Vairmey-oh a rooin' oh,
Vairmey-oh a rooin' ee,
Vairmey-oh ro-oh-ho,
Sad am I without thee.

When I'm lonely dear white hart,
Black the night or wild the sea,
By love's light my foot finds
The old pathway to thee.

Vairmey-oh a rooin' oh . . .'

Standing on a rock with legs firmly apart for balance as he wrestled with the mooring ropes of a large rowing boat, the tall form was framed in the sunset of a January afternoon. Reddish slivers lay across the water from the fiery ball slipping among the western clouds, and at times streaks of light would catch the locks below the tassled knitted cap and the bearded face and gleam a russet brown. In a mood not unlike a trance Harry watched the controlled yet seemingly careless movements as the singer repeated the refrain. Now so often living in the cities and towns it was a sight he'd almost forgotten, a man so completely in harmony with his environment that he was truly but an extension of it, or it of him. Two huge sacks were swung on to the rocks and then the boat drifted out on a pulley to swing gently in the middle of the narrow channel. A heavy cleat was fastened to the rock face on the other side, Harry noticed, to take the pulley cord. The refrain finished, he found himself involuntarily joining in with another verse.

'Thou'rt the music of my heart,
Thou'rt my joy, oh cruich Machree,
Moon of guidance by night
Strength and light thou'rt to me . . .'

210

'Harry!'

'Niall!'

The figure bounded over the rocks, face beaming with simple enjoyment and pleasure, and he found himself embraced.

'Harry. Harry. Harry McKinstry.'

'Niall. Niall McNeill.' Tears momentarily pricked his eyes. It was like embracing the brother he never had.

'It's been a long time, Harry. Longer than before.'

'Too long.'

They stood silently for a few moments, the pressure of each other's hands and arms a sufficient statement.

'I'll just get these sacks and we'll take them up to the yard. And then what about a good stout?'

Harry nodded, not wishing to speak, and again he saw Niall outlined against the sky as he turned back towards the boat. Isled, the latter stood, yet for Harry the picture didn't convey a sense of isolation but rather a peacefulness brought about by a merging of all the elements.

The contents of the sacks made a slapping, croaking sound, which made Niall laugh. 'Netted a good few the day. And there'll be a good few pound in my pocket come the morrow.'

Looking down at the glinting fish scales, Harry said, 'I didn't know you had a boat here. I went to the harbour looking for you and it was only by chance I walked this way.'

'Sure I've wee bits of boats everywhere. With the sea running that wee channel's a better spot to have a boat than many other places.' Niall paused to squint into his friend's face. 'Besides, it's no bad thing to have boats here and there. There's too many pairs of eyes about, Harry. 'Specially when you're doing something that many would think not quite legal.'

Going through the village Harry saw the pinpricks of light from the old family home. Raindrops spattered against his face as the sky clouded over and he thought of himself in boyhood hurrying towards the door to escape from the cold wet winds. Inside, a fire of turf and logs would be blazing and beside it his mother would sit crocheting. Knocking at the small study he would find his father at the desk writing out his sermons in a neat scholarly hand. Across the years of battle and the idleness of youth the figures came to meet him. The funeral hearse wound through the village streets towards the cemetery and then he was sitting in the study in another's place looking down at the familiar handwriting in an unfamiliar script. It was strange then, and more so now. Until that moment he hadn't known that his father had been as learned in the native Irish language as he was in English. He'd wondered about that before, but now there

211

was an urgency in his probing the recesses of memory. What would his father have thought in times such as these? Have done? On which side would his sympathies have lain? And, though again ruefully acknowledging how little he knew of the man from whose loins he came, his guess seemed to be instinctively correct. Ireland's.

'A change of plan, Harry,' Niall was saying. 'We'll go straight to the pub otherwise we'll be soaked to the skin.'

The rain was hissing among the cobbles and he felt his feet slithering on the glair. So engrossed had he been that he hadn't noticed the downpour which lanced slantwise across his vision. The sacks dumped in a dry corner beside the outer door, Harry stood by the fire feeling the heat seeping through his damp clothing and watching the beads of rain streaming across the window.

Niall placed the pints on the scrubbed wooden bench. 'You seem very quiet all of a sudden.'

Wryly Harry smiled. 'And that's just the way I feel.'

'And what brings you here?'

'The past, perhaps. Nostalgia. Or that's all I can think of for the moment.'

Niall paused to drink and gaze searchingly into his friend's face before speaking. 'Well, tell me all your news. It must be four or five years since we last met.'

Relating the events of his recent past, Harry didn't notice himself being studied by the other's thoughtful, steady look. He spoke slowly, as though telling the story to himself as much as to his companion, so that it was some time before he had finished.

'And how are the wounds now?'

'All right. Occasionally they twinge a little when I get overtired.'

'And no bairns yet?'

Harry tried to answer Niall's grin. 'Not yet. Perhaps soon. May would like that.' He paused. 'But I'm not too happy about starting a family with the country in this state.'

'Children come in war and peace, Harry. And with all that in the trenches it seems we need a new generation.'

'You're one to talk and you not even married yet.'

'Ach, that'll come in its time. And wars won't stop me from starting a family.'

A lull followed, the flames from the crackling logs reddening their faces. Niall's broad hand was stroking the stubble on his chin as he drew on a longstemmed pipe. There was a sense of solidity about him, Harry thought as he glanced several times at his features and physique. Despite his own much greater experience he felt frail by comparison.

'And what was Dublin like?'

'An armed camp.'

Niall nodded. 'Like it might be here soon.'

'What do you mean?' Harry asked, though knowing quite well what the other meant.

'Partition.'

As Niall fell silent again Harry gazed into the fire, mind creating various images from the glowing ashes of logs and peat. So. The subject had come up, the subject he both wanted to discuss and was afraid of discussing because of the decision to which it might lead him. The threat of partition hung in the air like an unexploded bomb. Here in the north-east allegiance would remain as before, to Britain and Empire. But not for all. No matter where the border was drawn there would be large sections of the population who held fundamentally different views. What was to be their future? To be forced into a new statelet by arms and always looked upon as forming some kind of fifth column, or to choose exile from their homes in another part of the country or abroad? In the towns and cities of the north the pogroms against those of a Nationalist or Republican persuasion had begun in the burning of houses and streets and men being driven from or denied entry to places of work. The guns were going off too, and in the dawn after the nightly curfews the dead would be found. Despite the blazing fire Harry shivered as scenes recently witnessed came to mind. Catholics mainly, because those who were both Protestant and Nationalist were becoming too afraid to speak or act. And then came retaliation with the hideous leering lunatic spectre of sectarianism walking among the populace like some death's head with a scythe.

'Are you active, Niall?'

Impassively Niall sat. Though spoken softly the question reverberated in the air between them. 'People don't ask questions like that, Harry.'

'I must ask.'

'Are you a friend?'

Even childhood friends did not escape from this clawing sickness of suspicion, thought Harry, still watching the shapes in the fire. 'Do you doubt me?'

'You were soldiering in British wars.'

'European.'

'Yes. That's true.' Cautiously Niall looked around the otherwise empty bar. 'I was visited a few years back. Just after the rising in Dublin.'

'By whom?'

'Military Intelligence.'

In Harry's mind the hyena laugh sounded and then a face appeared. 'For what reason?'

213

'I was to be recruited, it seems. As an informer.'

'Do you wish me to doubt you too?'

'Doubt me?'

'That you accepted.'

Slowly Niall shook his head. 'I know you don't, Harry.' He paused. 'Do you think the Unionists have a case?'

'A reasonable one. They wish to belong to something much bigger than this little island. And there's the problem of the Church.'

'To live in a country but not be of it. Isn't that their problem? As for the Church, the Protestant churches are as much involved in politics as the Roman. You know that as well as I.' Again Niall paused. 'Have you killed many men?'

'Many . . .?'

'In the trenches, I mean.'

He was lying back there in the shellhole watching the stars and the occasional bursting shell while carrying the piss to his lips and caking his bleeding side with mud. Laughing. The clown. Then Sam again looming over him and Dalton and the mule's head breaking as it slithered and somersaulted as if chewing its own entrails. Would these images never leave him? 'Too many. But in that kind of war you don't know whom you kill.'

'I can understand. Massed armies and all that.' Sipping from his glass, Niall cast another glance around the still empty bar. 'And in this one you do. Sometimes only too well. It's a different kind of war, Harry.'

Yes, he thought, it is, as this is the voice of a man who has already known what this kind of war is like. 'And you?' he asked. 'How many?' And them he grimaced at these ridiculous questions. It was as though they were boys again, playing at cowboys and Indians and counting the number of Injun dead.

'The first was a British soldier in Dublin. It could well have been you, Harry.'

Surprised, he asked: 'In '16?'

'Yes. Oh, I wasn't part of it. Some of us were supposed to go down but then we were ordered not to. I just happened to go down to see what was going on and found a rifle and hit a British uniform. Some of your boys were there. The Ulster Division.'

'Yes. I heard about it at the Front.'

Niall leaned towards him. 'And so, Harry. Who are you? Now, I mean. I don't know who you are any longer. Where your own best friend might turn out to be both betrayer and executioner. And that's a kind of war you haven't fought in. Or perhaps you have?'

The words fell ominously against his ears but he refused to comment simply because there was no way to counter them. 'And you expect to beat an Empire?'

'Those questions are not for me. But I would doubt it. Force them into a position where they have to yield most of what we want? After all, it's not only a war of arms, and many places in the world have sympathy for our cause. America. Europe. We've given the world a lot in our own way. And England can't be allowed to sit here and dictate for ever.' Niall grinned. 'I like the English. In many ways they're so godlordly stupid. An eternity of rule and power is no more theirs than it is anyone else's. Like rats and mice Empires come and go.'

'Alexander died, Alexander was buried, Alexander returneth to dust; the dust is earth; of earth we make loam; and why of that loam whereto he was converted might they not stop a beer barrel? Imperious Ceasar, dead and turned to clay, Might stop a hole to keep the wind away. O, that that earth which kept the world in awe should patch a wall t'expel the winter's flaw!'

'And what's that?'

Harry laughed, the incongruity uppermost in his mind. 'Oh, I'm just quoting an Englishman.'

'Well, you're the university man. And as I said, I like the English fine enough. But when they're playing with guns I like them particularly when they're where they belong. In England. And you, Harry?'

The question was left lying there on the scrubbed bench like a card that had to be played as Niall walked round the bar to rouse the elderly landlady where she was sleeping in the kitchen, with Harry now staring at the whorls and scoremarks on the white wood. And me? When his companion returned and sat down he simply looked at him and said—'Yes.'

A slow smile curved Niall's mouth. 'I've often thought you would come. In fact, I knew you would. And you wouldn't be the first of the British Army to come over to us. Didn't Childers the Englishman even run guns in for us?'

'I heard about that.'

'And speaking of guns. There's more in those fishsacks than fish. Pistols. Wrapped and oiled. Modern German.'

'No.'

'No?'

'No gun. I've had enough of that. The question you asked me before. I've killed too many already.'

'Good. That's just the way we'd want you.'

We? Harry thought, suddenly acknowledging that it was a different Niall who was now speaking. 'For what?'

'Intelligence. A journalist. A newsman. What better cover? Or liaison officer if you want to call it that. We even read British Army manuals, you know. But, Harry, you'll be totally on your own. And if you get caught up in trouble there'll be no help.'

Turning to the fire a last time, he stared into the burling drifting ash that flaked across the hearth and danced in the chimney. And so, the decision. But did it make the clown any less lonely?

Niall was standing. 'We'll go up to the yard where we can talk more freely. And sure I'll read all your words in the papers when you interview Griffiths or De Valera or Lloyd George. Or even your very man Michael Collins himself.'

And now I am the enemy. In the months following as the winter evenings lengthened and spring came sending the yellow-headed daffodils sporting before the gusty March and April breezes, that thought often came to mind. In the day, in the night. In the day travelling the country, a country truly at war, he would watch out for the various military and police uniforms and say to himself—And now I am the enemy, your enemy. In the night too, in those endless hotel and boarding-house rooms where he stayed, that thought would be among the thickening number of spectres whose visitations would not cease. Spectres of possible unities, of conflicting traditions: And now I am the enemy.

Sometimes, melancholy descending to cramp his otherwise high-spirited nature, he would say—Perhaps an enemy even to myself. For even now, though committed, I am still essentially the clown. And this would come when, in a railway carriage, soldiers and police passed slowly by, checking the occupants. Noting their ready guns he would inwardly smile. Who but a clown goes naked in war?

As Niall had said: what better cover? He was alone, known only to a few. A telephone call would come, a note slipped into his pocket, these being from contacts whom he rarely saw twice, ostensibly contacts for his work on the newspaper. In hotel lounges and public bars he collected the packets and passed them on, unaware of their contents. Occasionally there would be a note congratulating him on his work and simply signed by an initial.

And there was May. Now living in Newry, he would return home as often as possible but mostly to sit gazing moodily into the fire. Curfew being the nightly ritual, he would at times sit by the window watching the dark silent street, deliberately avoiding her questions. He did not want her to know. Could not allow her to know. Because now, were not Dalton, her own brother—her whole family—his enemies? And what would his own wife be if she but knew?

It's a different kind of war, Harry. Those had been Niall's words. In bed enveloped by her musky warmth yet failing to respond to her tenderness and passionate needs he would say—Yes, it's a different

216

kind of war when it separates a man from his wife. His love.

There was something else too. His work of reporting the military and civil conflict had begun to pall. Sickened by events, caught by those conflicting loyalties within him, the words gelled in his mind before they reached paper. He wanted a new mode to write in, a new conception through which to spill onto those blank pages that love and rage which welled from his experience.

In mid-week he returned one afternoon to find the towering figure of Dalton standing in the kitchen, one elbow on the mantelpiece. He'd come to talk of what Harry already knew about. Partition. Ireland was to be divided. The Royal Irish Constabulary would be disbanded and the remnants taken into the Royal Ulster Constabulary. No, Harry thought, how can you call it the Royal Ulster Constabulary when all you can hold is two-thirds of Ulster and perhaps even less? Is this what can be called a victory?

And restlessly awake at night he would ask: And in those two-thirds will you be my gaoler one day? Even executioner? Brother?

And then came June with the country truly divided and Harry reporting on the speech made by King George at the opening of the Parliament for the six north-eastern counties. Harry also went to London to watch a coffin being lowered into the ground, sadness carving furrows on his face. On Hampstead Heath he said a last farewell to a city to which he knew he would never return, another ghost approaching out of a foggy sunlight to draw on a cigarette and chuckle whilst saying—Harry, I'm not exactly a highwayman.

Some five days previously James had been shot dead in a gunbattle on the outskirts of Dublin.

Brother, am I culpable?

V

And, Sam, kingly you leave in your regalia, paraphernalia, or whatever it is to be called, in your new uniform of dungarees with buttons bright like badges, even medals maybe, which some workman gave you because you were found lying practically naked in some timberyard. Outside the gates, on the edges of crowds of stamping spectators, you gaze wonderingly up the sloping lawns towards this new Parliament, towards this towering gleaming structure etched against the sky, which seemingly with a flourish of trumpets is brought into being. What war now, you try to think, or what great ceremony, all the while scratching a snattery beard. Thoughts come and go, images, if you can call them that, as you stand with furrowed brow and face: Notre-Dame and a shattered hand, a mulish grin and a heehawing field. A love? Perhaps a dream? And then you remember, if remembering it can be called. The old cur is still at your feet, that's if it's the same one out of the hundreds now that have followed you. Pulling your badges off, you stick them into the cur's filthy fur, not without difficulty, Sam, and then pause, kneeling on the ground, intensely concentrating because somewhere in some other life you begin to wonder if you'd done just that. With now the old hound prancing and licking your shaggy face because it's playing a game with its master. And then you pause with welters of bone and flesh and skin all around you. But for you this isn't thinking, Sam: it's just that you're still stuck in it so far you can't see beyond it.

On you go, Sam, on you go. Around you the forces of law and order herd you away. Despots are always good at law and order and make that and efficiency their warcries. And so you go shuffling down from the east of the city to whatever other corner you're to find a warm comfortable hole come nightfall.

Lieutenant Sam, Don Samuel, Sam Ogilby, Shellshock Sam, forever drawn on with determined though shuffling steps because you're young still and as you weather summers and winters alike outadoors you're becoming as hoary and hard as a nut. Shoulder your

218

Vickers machine-gun, Sam, and follow that cacophonous sound which rends mind and eardrums still though whether in terror or delight you still cannot tell. *Heehawheehawheehaw* . . . Good God, Sam! What's that oul' sound ye heareth? A braying bloody ass? Can we never get away from it? Jesus Christ, Sam: sacrilege, sacrilege! All ye need now, Sam, is a few mouldy figs and bits of broken bread and maybe even some wine and not water and ye might be king of some land somewheres. Sure fer the good political divines ye can only be an exile in spirit or dung. Or piss come till that.

'What did you say, Ned?'
　'I was only askin', da. But you weren't listenin'.'
　'Asking me what?'
　' 'Bout Aubrey.'
　'Aye. Your brother Aubrey.' Surveying the landscape below, an old pain came to Duncan's heart. 'He died a good soldier.'
　'Ye were with him, weren't ye?'
　'To the end,' said Duncan, and this second lie lay like a canker in his being as when he had told Martha that Aubrey had simply gone missing. 'The end.'
　'And did ye get the one who shot 'im? The German soldier, I mean. Didn't ye get him, da?'
　Bending his head over the little fire in the hut, McKinzie said: 'I didn't have to. Aubrey got him first.'
　'Where was that, da?'
　'At a place in Picardy. A little village maybe like the one we live in.'
　'And the name, da?'
　First warming his hands by the flames, he looked through the low window which had a view up the glen. 'What's in a name, son? Listen. Don't you hear them oul' sheep baaing away? Isn't it autumn and do we know when the first snow'll be ontil us? We have till go up the glen and look to them.'
　'And Aubrey, da?'
　Fiercely and bitterly the sergeant lashed out. 'Don't ask! What mind have you for asking these things?' And, in chagrin, he smiled and said: 'Son, let's damp the fire and go and see to the sheep.' Then, feeling their shoulders touch as they walked through the door of the hut, he added: 'Perhaps we'll talk about that some other time. But not now, Ned.'
　Outside the hut they parted, Ned going to the upper fields to bring the sheep down to new pasture. Embracing him, McKinzie watched the figure out of sight with the collie in front and practically hidden by the grass. On his son's head was the cap of a police reservist, proudly worn, though he himself was in plain clothes. Sitting on a boulder he looked down towards the village nestling between glens and sea trying

219

to pick out his own home. Low cloud drifted from the north threatening mist and rain. He hadn't meant to be so abrupt and it was only natural that Ned should ask about Aubrey without knowing that all McKinzie wished to do was to forget. But forgetfulness often wasn't easy, even if strongly willed, and the image of a body on a lip of a trench would loom in his mind with unwished-for clarity. Nursing his daughter by the fire in the big farm cottage he would feel a hand on his shoulder and look into the face of Martha, his wife, knowing she understood the thoughts he was trying to keep at bay and in that gesture of tenderness saying it was a shared pain. Then he would feel a smile creasing his face as he tickled this warm bundle in his arms, the daughter who'd been born when he'd returned to the Front. Naomi. And a feeling of peace would be his.

Shivering slightly and pulling his coat around him he lit a pipe and looked up the glen. Though he could hear the sound of the sheep and the occasional bark of the dog, they were not yet in view. His gaze returning to the village below, he again became immersed in his thoughts. For him it had been a relatively peaceful year, the most peaceful since the Great War had started. Twelve months had passed since the division of the country. Returning north, he'd spent the time attending to his old duties in his home county of Antrim, which were mostly of a civil nature, a welcome change from the nearly two years which he had spent in the south fighting the forces of a fledgling Republic. That's if it could be called a Republic, Duncan mused, trying to get the past year into perspective, a year which had seen a treaty signed by the leaders of the new Irish government in Dublin and Lloyd George's government in London. From this had come the return of Irish prisoners still held in English gaols and the evacuation of British troops from the twenty-six counties. Being one of the last of the old police force to leave the south he'd watched them hand over the garrisons to men who but a few months before had been their enemies. Towards the end, the conflict just seemed to stumble to a standstill with rumours so rife that one wasn't quite sure if the fighting was still going on or not. Where he was concerned it had finished some months previously, as his responsibilities lay in co-operating with the police force coming into being in the new State as the Treaty was being implemented. It was like that for him too, he'd thought wryly more than once as power changed hands and he stood joking with men who up until that time were more intent on shooting him than laughing with him. And often he would think of the Armistice in Europe and the lines of German soldiers surrendering their weapons when he and others of the British contingents were taking over their bases, but in his thinking there was confusion rather than any strict line of comparison.

It had been a strange war. With Inspector Gordon he had moved between various barracks in the south, alert night and day to sudden attack whether in the streets of a village or town where gunfire could erupt from any corner or on the lonely roads of undulating countryside where an innocently passing farm lorry might turn out to be part of a Flying Column and a dozen rifles would appear to shred the silence of a drowsy summer afternoon. Used as he was to the trenches, even at the end he felt he hadn't quite accustomed himself to this new kind of warfare. For all the terrible strain of the war in Europe with the intensity of bombardments and massed attacks, there'd been periods of rest and recreation behind the lines with the enemy so far away they might never have existed. But this was a different kind of strain that constantly sucked strength from the nerve-ends as he moved amongst and around an enemy he couldn't even see but was always lying in wait, and he sometimes thought that this might be one reason why soldiers would run amok and burn and kill. They too could not accustom themselves to a conflict in which they rarely saw the enemy yet who would appear and disappear in a matter of moments, leaving several of their comrades dead and wounded.

In his mind the night skies were lit up with flames. Villages. Farms. The great houses of a ruling class which no longer ruled. Close to the still smouldering ashes of one he stood watching the onetime occupants gather the few remains of what they had owned and pile them onto a lorry. The Inspector stood with them talking. They were leaving for England. Ireland was no longer their country, had no further use for them, now offered them nothing but death or beggarment. In the towering ruins that were left he tried to visualise what their life had been like, and failed, yet knew he was witnessing a fall and exit of human proportions resembling that of the ashes of their home. Because what would they find in England?

And watching them made him think about himself, his own position. Because the war which raged across the land rejected him also, his family, his beliefs. To be British is not to be Irish. But in his allegiance to the Crown and England he was an outcast from the majority who were gradually taking control of most of the country and who had already turned their backs on him and his kind. It was an allegiance he'd never thought deeply about before, it was just there as part of himself and his past. And though a Presbyterian by faith he understood that the cries of Protestantism and Catholicism and Home Rule being Rome Rule were far from being the whole truth, though the intricately knotted strands of politics and all the rest that lay deep in the land and burst out in hatred and vengeance defied his powers of analysis and he began to feel a stranger.

221

Yes. It had been a strange kind of war. And still was. It was not a Republic which had come into being but a Free State in a divided country now in the throes of civil war. A Free State still tied to England by the treaty, a civil war between those who would accept the contents of the treaty and those who would not. Yet again division, with men who were once comrades now enemies. But it was no longer his fight. Within the borders of the northern six counties there was safety. The Free State had accepted the border and would not interfere in northern matters, while any Republicans still active would soon be imprisoned, as many already were. Civil war would pass by outside.

'Da.'

Still preoccupied, Duncan looked up. 'Yes, son?'

'I've been standing here fer ages watchin' ye.'

Returning his son's smile he stood up, taking the unlit pipe from his mouth and rubbing the stiffness from his knees. 'Sure you were watching an old man dreaming of the past. When me and your mother first used to walk here.' He paused to savour the thought of his wife and the prospect of home. 'And I suppose that's what you've been doing instead of seeing to the sheep. Chasing the lassies up the glens. You're a brave one at that game I've heard tell.'

The expression on the boy's face was mildly boasting. 'I know one or two that'll walk out wi' me.'

Duncan's smile changed to a frown as the other's coat fell open and he saw the gunbelt and holster. 'I asked you not to bring the gun with you. We'll hardly be in any trouble in these hills.' Then, noticing his son's disappointment his own face softened. 'You'll make a good policeman. But only wear the gun on duty. There'll be riots and shooting enough in Belfast and the like at times. But hardly here.'

Half-listening to his son's talk as they went down the slopes, he again thought of his wife and home. That had been his greatest pleasure since coming back from the south, simple domestic routine and one which years of war had interrupted. Lifting the latch he went straight to the fireside where his wife sat darning, kissed her, then knelt beside his daughter who was playing with coloured wooden blocks, thoughts of the oncoming festive season beginning to fill his mind. 'It's less than six weeks to Christmas, Martha. And what will Santa bring this bairn on Christmas Day? When she's with her father warm by the fire. On Christmas Day in the morning.'

As the police launch bobbed on the tide Alec Dick recognised the tall figure who emerged from the car on the quayside and made down the steps. 'Well, Inspector Gordon, and who would ye be takin' over this time?'

'No one. It's just a routine visit.'

'Visit, ye say? Sooner you than me. I wouldn't like to visit that in any capacity,' Alec replied, nodding towards the prison ship in the centre of the lough.

'I don't expect you ever will.'

'Aye. I'll be visitin' hell more like. And maybe you along wi' me.' Spitting a long stream of brown juice from the plug he was chewing and watching it curve into the water, he grinned as the other turned away. 'And I might even have to row ye over there one of these days, Inspector Gordon. Or perhaps ye'll row yer own sour self.'

On board the prison ship Dalton began his inspection. Based in Belfast, his authority extended over the northern part of the city and through Antrim. Once a week he made the prison ship part of his tour, and he would also be there if more prisoners were to be brought on board, always choosing the midday exercise period as now it was.

Amidships he sat with his back stiffly against a bulkhead, a small table in front of him, the breeze flipping the pages of a sheaf of documents which contained a list of prisoners and personal inform- ation about each one. Seemingly intent on these and flanked by two warders armed with rifles, he carefully noted the figures who filed around the after rail. Thick steel mesh was lashed to the ship's sides to prevent escape, and beyond this lay the inland shore of Larne Lough. Turning his head to starboard he looked towards Islandmagee, the mesh again giving the impression of a wire cage. Satisfied, he climbed the superstructure to where more armed warders stood and looked fore-and-aft the length of the ship, the figures walking, shuffling past. Treatyites and anti-Treatyites, and had they been free and over the border they would have been engaged in combat as the civil war in the south grew an uglier face day by day. But here, though incarcerated, there was at least some measure of safety. The irony did not escape him. Some of the guards, he knew, deliberately fostered strife by giving misleading reports of what was happening in the war in the south. It was a kind of vengeance to be let loose so that they could take some individual who retaliated to the punishment cell to indulge in a sadistic pleasure. In this he did not and would not intervene unless it went beyond certain bounds, as he'd intimated to those under him. But these bounds must be kept. Must. It was an outlet, he knew, this vengeance, springing from fear and a sense of betrayal now that most of Ireland was cut off from them. And to the gunrunners of ten years before, England and its ways were foreign, despite the Great War. Another irony which again did not escape him.

Steadily he watched the tall hunched eaglefaced figure who stood and walked as much apart from the others as circumstances would

223

allow, his fellow inmates leaving him room as though instinctively divining his separateness. Dalton had noticed him before. When the whistles went to mark the end of the exercise period he went below and stood in the galley as the prisoners filed in for food, deliberately ladling some of the thick practically unpalatable stew onto a tin plate and eating it so that they could see him doing so.

His tour of the ship ended, he stood as the gangplank was lowered to the waiting launch, the documents in his hand opened to show a photograph. O'Donnell. An anti-Treatyite Republican and hill farmer from Tyrone. Captured in Londonderry and brought some months before to the *Argenta*. 'This one,' he said to the sergeant in charge: 'Watch him. Carefully. Very carefully.'

Still chewing the plug, Alec Dick stared at each tracing ripple of the lough surface. Had he seen aright? Had the dusky water opened to show a fin? Concentration disturbed by the return of the motor launch, and again he grinned at the tall figure who briskly strode up the steps. 'Finished yer inspection have ye, Inspector Gordon? Aye, ye might yit be rowin' yersel' 'cross. An' sure's there's no pockets in a shroud there's niver the motorboat in hell.'

VI

Pregnant clouds. It was a phrase she had read in a book and now the two words were repeated over and over in her mind in accompaniment to the dull clacking of the wheels of the train which was carrying her home to the island. It was in one of the many books which Harry had brought home for her, because now not only did she love reading but also was trying to make up for all those lapses in her childhood schooling. During evenings of curfew when Harry was away she would sit reading in the kitchen with curtains drawn, a lamp at her elbow. Worlds were there opening out to her to speak of things within herself. And there were the letters from Anna which at times she took out to peruse, trying to think of a life which was so different from her own. A photograph was in one showing a tall dark-haired girl. There was still that look of seeming older than she was, May thought, calculating the difference in their ages. Anna would be fifteen or sixteen while she would soon be twenty-three. Should they ever meet again what would they share, she wondered, more aware of what separated them yet drawn to the memory of a reserved singular nature. There was that in herself also, a pride or singularity which she found becoming more pronounced as she grew older. It was almost an aloofness from others. Like Dalton. Yes, there was part of Dalton's nature in her. And then she thought of Dalton and Harry and quickly put the thought aside to return to her secret.

Pregnant clouds. Why not the pregnant sky or pregnant earth? Across the land the boisterous scudding shapes rained down, bringing succour to the soil. Smiling at her own reflection in the window she quickly crossed herself inside her coat so that the other passengers could not see. Evenings when he arrived unexpectedly she would play at being startled and angry to hide the desire sparked by this wished-for homecoming. But soon passion would come bursting out and afterwards she would like listening to his regular breathing, the glow from lamp or fire splashing across his features. Invariably it was then that her mind drifted among the threads of the past as she thought of their lovemaking in Donegal and at the Gobbins, of this new life which had opened to her, of times before that playing with Rosinante in the fields and going with her father in the trap through the country. And yes, of that time in girlhood when she'd climbed the big stone wall covered with lichen and moss to wander alone through the beautiful gardens. She'd danced around the lilypond also with the huge dog slowly gliding through distant trees ignoring her trespassing. She'd felt like a princess then in her new green blouse and buckled kilt. But what had she been thinking about, in that dancing reverie with the lilies at her feet flowering from glistening leaves of water? Was it of this passion and joy?

Ah, sweet mystery, May . . . And the silly fool singing to the donkey and it braying the better.

Giggling, she was a child indeed as she again examined her reflection in the windowpane and again crossed herself beneath her coat while looking down the lineaments of her body.

'Tickets, madam!'

Startled and frowning she looked into the smiling face of the ticket-collector as she fumbled in her purse.

'Dreaming of a white Christmas?' he said jocularly. Then, noticing her bulging form, added: 'Or of more personal family matters?'

Blushing, she accepted the punched ticket and turned back to the window. Did her pregnancy already show all that much? Was it there for all to see and no longer a secret? And still Harry didn't know, having been away from home for most of the past month.

With a last piercing whistle the train rolled to a standstill. Belfast. Walking through the city she paused several times at the gaily decorated shops. A group of carol-singers stood beneath the brilliantly lit Christmas tree in front of the City Hall and she stopped to press coins into the collecting-box. The child would be born here, in Belfast. The child. A quiver pricked her spine. It was the first time she'd thought of it as a person. Before this moment it had no definite shape, had been something without name. All she'd been aware of had been her body's strange new experience. But now as she walked she found herself staring in fascination at the children in the streets.

On board the train taking her to Whitehead she looked up at the Cave Hill and the lines of houses spread below. Where would they live? Harry was moving to a job on another newspaper and they would buy a house in the city. It would be so different from living on the island or even in the small town of Newry, that she understood. Though knowing Belfast since a girl, the ritual of daily living within its confines of roads and buildings was a prospect she found unsettling. Dalton was already living there, his reason being that work on the police force demanded that he should. But he too would be returning to the family home for Christmas. That was also something new, the family breaking apart to go their separate ways. Dalton and Harry. Again the thought came and this time she could not avoid it. The civil war that was still sweeping across most of the country spilled over the northern border in riots and shooting. And hadn't she accidentally discovered some papers which Harry had put away and which made it seem that he was in sympathy with the Republicans? Perhaps even more than that? Dalton and Harry on opposite sides? Yet weren't they now brothers? The thought tortured her, yet the more she tried to forget it the more it persisted, bringing with it a sense of fear even stronger than that she'd known in another war.

Jack was at the station to meet her with the trap and she hugged him impulsively. Faithful Jack. Within a few days she was fully in tune with the pre-Christmas activities of cooking, preparing, decorating, arranging presents and visiting elderly acquaintances. The December weather being mild she would stroll during late afternoon to the cliffs to renew her reverie and feel the quickening pulse of life inside her. Fingers lightly resting on her abdomen she watched the seabirds cresting furrows on the face of the sea as they winged gyrelike and she called to them as she'd called of old: *scceeeheee kiiiyaaa kiiiyaaa*. It was here that first time with Harry, wasn't it? And what had he said when she'd provoked him with her nakedness? *Perhaps hell is the absence of you.* And patiently waiting as dusk claimed land and water she would wonder what new life was stirring in those depths, awakening, hastening to birth.

Harry. It's our first child. Come to me.

'Maybe I'll be a fool by profession, May. Wudne' now that be a good way till be?'

And she laughed at this other of her menfolk, this gypsy brother whom she'd yet to know.

'But what's happening, David?'

'Maybe it's that I'm full stupid. Didne' not have a we'en o' jars wi' that oul' ferryman Alec Dick. Pave the way till hell that 'un wud. An' not only fer himsel'.' David hiccoughed and then vomited. 'That's if ye can ha' steppin' stones on the water. But I'll tell ye this. Wi' them oul' bits o' sticks he plies he'd not a bad oarsman.'

'But David,' she said. 'The prisoners?'

'Them that's 'scaped? Damn the prisoners they are now. Have a titter o' bloody wit, woman.'

Gently she held his arm as he bent over in his drunken sickness, this boy of barely sixteen. It was like that with herself in the mornings. Nausea. But for different reasons. Listening to him talk on she was

227

surprised at his command of dialect in its various forms. And it was a language as pure in feeling and sense as any she'd heard. In her early days that was something her mother had insisted on, that she learned to speak properly. But later on comparing the talk of the people with her own way of speaking she wondered at her mother's wisdom.

David hiccoughed again. 'And Dalton's away intil the hills.'

'What for?'

'Till try an' ferret them out. What the hell else?'

'Who?'

'The ones that took McKinzie an' done his son in. Thems that 'scaped from the *Argenta*.'

She stiffened as another and different sickness invaded her senses, carrying with it a kind of hysteria. 'What are you talking about?'

Wiping his mouth with a handkerchief and pointing to where tiny spots of light showed up on the mainland and further down the island, David turned to her, his way of speaking more like her own. 'Don't you see them still searching? Two got away free. And Dalton's out looking for them 'cause they captured his oul' sergeant from the war and killed his son.' David hiccoughed and vomited again and again wiped his mouth. 'I wudne' have liked till be them on board that crabpot of a bastard jail. But I'd like it even less if that bastard Dalton got a houl' o' me.'

'On Christmas Day?'

'Any oul' day fer a drop o' the spirit.'

She wouldn't be getting any further sense from David, thought May, seeing him tilt a bottle to his lips. Fleetingly she smiled at his waywardness, thoughts coming of those times she'd heard whispers of her mother's misdemeanours because this black sheep was so unlike the others. A gay girl in her day was Elizabeth Gordon. But such thinking could not override that other feeling. Of Dalton returning to the farm to talk of Sergeant McKinzie's disappearance and his son with him and the two Republicans who had escaped from the ship in Larne Lough. That night, and days and nights succeeding, she'd seen policemen scour the surrounding countryside. And then the news came that they had found the body of his son half-buried somewhere in the glens. But it was Harry she didn't want to think about; Harry who during these days had avoided their company and even slipped from her embrace to wander off alone, his face lined and brooding.

Why?

Soft flurries of snow broke and melted on the windows of the police barracks in the northern part of the city. In an inner office sat Dalton, elbows on the desk, chin cupped in palms, staring at the sheets of paper in front of him on which he had meticulously written down every detail. It was now Boxing Day and the escape had taken place four days previously. The prison ship had been plunged into darkness as the electricity system had fused. There had been no alarm among the warders and police on board simply because there'd been a rising tide and with an old ship creaking at her moorings something like this had not been an unforeseen occurrence. It wasn't until a rollcall several hours later when repairs had been made that they discovered two prisoners were missing. One was Tidg O'Donnell, and the other a boy, Arthur McLaverty.

Immediately on hearing the news he'd gone to Larne and crossed in the police launch to make an inspection. Loose bolts had been found which fastened the mesh to the ship's rail, and with the aid of a good swimmer they had discovered the method and route of escape. But to which landfall, to which side of the lough? He'd stood aft, the ship swinging, trying to calculate. To the island or to the mainland? To the island would be foolish as it could easily be sealed off and they would be trapped. But perhaps that very foolishness was part of the plan so that their pursuers would try to hunt them elsewhere. There were enough corners and caves on the island where a determined man could hide for a lengthy period. Food? But then, O'Donnell being a farmer from the mountains of Tyrone he would know how to live off the land in the bitterest of weathers. Though the boy might be a problem.

To the mainland then. But where? Known as an unswerving Republican and anti-Treatyite, where would O'Donnell be going? What would he think of doing? With the northern border sealed off by police and troops and the majority of Nationalists and Republicans imprisoned he would hardly think of fighting a war in the six counties by himself. And to cross the border? But in the civil war still being fought in the south the Provisional Government of the Free State which had accepted the treaty with London was winning, the Republicans were being defeated daily.

Pacing the room, Dalton thought of those times he had seen his adversary on board the prison ship, the tall stooped frame with eaglelike smouldering features. Determined and ruthless and devout in his cause.

So. He would cross the border to fight for the Republic even if it were being defeated and dying. But where would he cross? And what of the boy? But the boy's thinking eluded Dalton's analysis.

And what of McKinzie? Because on Christmas Eve the body of his son had been found partly buried in the hills above Glenarm, having been garroted and stripped of clothing and possessions. Yes, they would need fresh clothing having swum the icy waters of the lough, and for a man and a boy in hostile territory two prisoners was one too

229

many. That had been O'Donnell's doing, with the savage intensity of the hunted and losing. That Dalton knew from his experiences both in the trenches and the southern Irish war.

Again he returned to the desk to peruse further details. Before the discovery of the body he'd questioned the ferryman Alec Dick, knowing that if anything had been seen in the lough of an unusual nature he would have been the one to see it. But all the ferryman had said was that he'd thought he'd seen a dolphin. That observation, if a true observation it had been, could not be fitted in. Then upon impulse, on Christmas morning, he'd left the family ceremony and preparations for dinner to hurry to Larne to order a tender and police guard to take him to O'Donnell's home in Tyrone, arriving there in the dusk of afternoon. Would this man have risked travelling west *and* stopping at his own home before crossing the border, something which the police wouldn't think of? Foresight and cunning lay there. But that was precisely what he would rely upon most.

And so on Christmas Day Dalton had been sitting in the farmhouse in Tyrone with the big woman, O'Donnell's wife, bustling around the kitchen range with the smell of roasting chicken wafting in the air and a young boy silently glaring at him from a corner while the constables with him had minutely inspected the surrounds and outbuildings to the furious snarling of a sheepdog. She'd spoken little, her comments either caustic or sad. No, she hadn't seen her husband or even heard tell of his escape and what was this business violating a woman's home at Christmas? There could be more than that, he'd intimated, with a woman on a Christmas Day mourning a dead son. But this remark had brought from her no response and he'd asked: And the other children? Where are they? With the sheep, she'd replied. Don't we have to keep them from roaming too far?

Question and answer, casual remarks, the talk had been all so normal, the ordinary talk of a small farming household which he knew intimately. Staring at his desk he again searched his memory for details. The steaming pudding, the oven with one chicken, the small pile of old newspapers, the boy silent in the corner, the barking snarling sheepdog, the line of books on the shelf and the book sitting on one corner of the mantelpiece, the woman who'd taken his presence as an inevitable intrusion yet who'd offered him something to eat, the constable entering rifle in hand to tell him that nothing was to be found.

But there was some detail which bothered him, excited his curiosity, held some information which he should know. But he could not think what it was.

And where now was McKinzie, his old sergeant?

'Inspector?'

'Lieutenant?'

'Working even over Christmas, I see.'

Casually lighting a cigarette Dalton simply looked at the figure in the doorway without speaking, then turned his eyes back to the work in front of him, the other's manner of entering his office without formality being something he detested.

'I hear one of your men is missing.'

Seemingly intent on his own ruminations, Dalton ignored him. Christopher Campbell, a member of Military Intelligence who had worked with the Special Branch police in the southern war and who, after the partition of the country, had moved north in a similar role. An Ulsterman though how different, thought Dalton, inwardly amused and glad of this diversion which was really a battle of wills. The sense of inborn superiority in the other's nonchalant stance was something which he found at best belittling and comic.

A match flamed in the partly open doorway. 'I hear one of your men is missing.'

'And have you found him?'

'No.'

'Then why repeat yourself on a matter with which I am more intimately connected than you?'

'I only came for information.'

Peremptorily Dalton tossed the papers the length of the desk. 'There are all the details I have. Though when it comes to information, I would have expected that of you.' Rising and going to the window, the baleful leer on the other's face did not pass his notice. 'And in future when you enter my office unbidden I suggest you close the door behind you. Either way.'

'I was only trying to assist, inspector.'

'I'm not without my own intelligence resources.'

'The sergeant was close to you, inspector? In the trenches, I'm speaking of. And in the south.'

'Are you interrogating me, lieutenant?'

Poring over the pages the other's voice was sibilant with hissing venom. 'Merely enquiring. Often we don't know the . . . inclinations . . . of those closest to us.'

'Certain inclinations I do most certainly know. Which you may not. And in the trenches I have seen the sergeant display inclinations, as you put it, which few men could. And that includes both of us.'

The leer was yet more baleful. 'Of course, you know I wasn't in the Great War.'

'That I know full well.'

'If I have information, inspector, I'll let you know immediately.'

'Do so, lieutenant. If you don't find the sergeant I most certainly

231

shall. Please close the door behind you when you go.' Waiting until his visitor was practically in the corridor, Dalton added: 'And should you find this Tidg O'Donnell alive, I suggest you have others with you.'

'Sergeant?'

'I'm broken, sir. That's my last son dead too.'

Dalton's voice was soft. 'But, sergeant, just now you were talking of your daughter.'

'Daughter, sir? Do I have a daughter? Do I have really one child left?'

'Have you not just been talking about her?'

'Yes, sir. But you see . . .'

When the sergeant's voice failed, Dalton asked: 'And you were going to where?'

'Ballyshannon, sir.'

Visualising the long arduous trek across Ulster from east to west, Dalton said: 'That was some march, sergeant. But past experience stood you in good stead.'

'That's what I thought of, sir. About the trenches. And about Aubrey being dead. And now Ned too.'

Carefully Dalton watched the seamed gaunt face with bulging eyes that seeped tears, but said nothing. It had been late on New Year's Day when a message had come from the border that an RUC sergeant taken as a hostage by two Republicans was alive, and orders were immediately given to bring him to a hospital in Belfast. The two Republicans had been shot dead.

'I'd the chance to kill one of his sons. But I didn't take it. I threw the gun away.'

Intrigued, Dalton asked: 'Why?'

'I don't rightly know. Maybe it was because my own two sons were dead and I didn't want to kill some other man's. And there was the boy that was with us. We were both trying to protect him by then. We didn't want him with us anymore.'

'We?' Dalton asked softly.

'That was the strange bit. It wasn't like we were enemies any more, me and O'Donnell. We were just trying to live off the land and survive while he got to the border. And then I was to bring the boy back with me to safety. I didn't even hate O'Donnell then for killing Ned. I just wanted to bring the boy back. He didn't know what he was doing or what he believed in. He was like one of my own sons then.' Duncan rested his face in his hands. 'I was to bring him back and get him on a ship. He was a seaman. But then he ran on ahead of us and into the guns of the Free Staters.'

232

'And when did you have the chance to kill O'Donnell's son?'

'In O'Donnell's home. The wee farmhouse. It was on Christmas Day. The boy had to be brought in because he was nigh dying of the fever. We raided the farmhouse that day too. The police I mean. But O'Donnell and the boy were hiding in the hills behind, with me tied up. It was later that evening when I got the gun from him. After the police had gone.'

Thoughts of himself sitting in O'Donnell's cottage came to Dalton's mind. So he had failed. O'Donnell had been there. And there was still that one detail which had suggested another's presence and which still eluded him.

'And my daughter, sir?' asked Duncan, reverting to a former thought.

'Is alive, sergeant. Alive and well.'

'It's just that I didn't think of her during that time. Like I couldn't allow myself to think I'd one child left.'

Dalton stood up. 'I'll see that you are transferred to a hospital in Larne to be near her.'

'It's not a hospital I need, sir.'

'Then that you are taken home.'

'And the wife?'

'She's well and waiting for you. And she knows about Edward. After all, she's a soldier's and policeman's wife both.'

A smile trickled through tears. 'That she is, sir.'

'And when you return.' Dalton paused. 'Perhaps another position?'

'Maybe, sir. I might be too old for the beat now.'

Dalton lightly rested his hand on the other's shoulder. 'You've done well, sergeant. More than well.'

On leaving the hospital Dalton had already made his decision. He must return to O'Donnell's home. Ordering a police car he arrived at the mountain farm in Tyrone early the following morning and took the same chair in which he'd sat some days previously, with eyes constantly alert as the big woman who was O'Donnell's widow moved about her tasks, though slower in step than before. A heavy black shawl was draped across her shoulders.

Nodding to the young girl by the fire, Dalton asked: 'And where was this one on Christmas Day when I came?'

'With her father.'

'Why?'

'How could a young one like that have any sense? He thought she'd tell you he was here.'

'And when we'd gone?'

'I sent the dog up with a note tied to him that it was safe to come down.'

233

'If you yourself had told me, your husband might still be alive.'

'No, inspector. You're wrong. He'd have fought you to the last.'

'Even when he knew the Republic was losing the civil war?'

'Even when that.' The big woman turned towards him. 'He was a good man, inspector. He would believe in the Republic even if he and it died. He was an Ulsterman and didn't want to leave here. But he didn't want to live under your rule.'

'My rule?'

'English rule.'

'Ah, yes. I understand.'

'Anyway, would you have expected me to betray him?'

'Betray him? No.'

It was then that the book on the mantelpiece caught Dalton's eye. It had been there the last time also. Rising and lifting it, he read the title: *Leaves From a Prison Diary* by Michael Davitt.

'He was reading that here,' she said. 'And joked with me that after the prison ship he could write his own.'

So this had been the clue, thought Dalton, that detail which had eluded him. Satisfied, he turned towards the door. There was nothing more he wanted.

'And the sergeant, inspector?'

'Well. And home with his wife and daughter.'

The big woman nodded. 'I've thought about him too. About him and his wife and the son that was killed. Tidg liked the sergeant. He was a good man too.'

In the doorway Dalton paused. 'I have given orders that the body of your husband is to be brought back to you.'

'That's what I said to him when I last saw him. When he was leaving for Ballyshannon. And when they bring you home to me dead what am I to do then?' Her face reddened by firelight, she was silent for some moments. 'And now all I can do is bury him.'

Without haste Dalton wrote in a notebook and tore the page out to leave on the table. 'If you ever need me, please write to me here. As he himself said, he was an Ulsterman, and, as has been said before, there are few angels and few devils. Most of us live in the murk in between.'

Weeping, she said: 'Me and the children will live.' Then, impulsively, she thrust a sprig of holly into his hand. 'But God bless you, inspector.'

On the stony narrow track outside, Dalton stopped and looked at the recumbent form of his driver, head lolling against the door and a revolver slack in his hands. It was a constable whom he'd chosen more for his mechanical and driving skills than his ability at police duties. Quietly opening the door of the car and taking the gun he hit him across the shoulder and then pressed the revolver against his head. 'Constable Sherrin?'

234

Shoulder aching and vision practically obscured, it was some minutes before the constable replied. 'Inspector Gordon?'

'Asleep on duty?'

'But . . .'

'You may fail yourself, Sherrin. But you shall not fail me.' Tossing the gun on the front seat Dalton climbed into the back. 'To Belfast.'

Starting the engine, Sherrin tried to think. 'I didn't mean— '

'This time there won't be any disciplinary charges. And for your failure you'll be my regular driver in future. But I shall not tolerate other failures.' Waiting until the car had moved away, he added: 'We need a better car than this, Sherrin. Find it.'

'Sir?'

'Constable?'

'What kind of car?'

'Am I to instruct you in your own business? I should doubt it.' Loosening his own revolver from its holster he placed it on the seat beside him and, with eyes partly closed, watched ethereal wisps spume from valleys and sheeptracked hillsides. 'Speed, Sherrin, speed. One day we might have to chase devils.'

'I don't understand, sir.'

'You are not expected to.'

VII

May's first child was born in the early summer of that year of 1923. It was a boy. Harry could not be with her. The final defeat of the Republican forces in the southern civil war taking place, he'd been instructed by his editor to spend the time in Dublin to report on the circumstances of the cease-fire. Used as she was to his absences, nevertheless it irked that he was not beside her at the birth of their son. They had already talked of Christian names, Harry insisting on James while she wished to call him Harry, and so he was christened Henry James, which soon simply became Jim. Nearly four years later she bore a daughter who was named Elizabeth Adaline Ruth. The years spanning the birth of her two children were for her a period of peace and contentment, albeit years of change during which she accustomed herself to life in the city whilst Islandmagee, though often in her mind and sometimes visited, began to recede into the past.

They had found a house which they liked in the northern part of the city and were in the process of buying it. It was a large terraced house, somewhat overlarge May thought at first, with three bedrooms and a spacious attic and cellar. At first she thought the cobblestoned street outside narrow and constricting but, as city life began to dim the vistas of fields and sea in her mind, she gradually found it bright and airy as in idle hours she stood in the shadow of the half-door to watch the children playing. Her nature now reserved, she was looked upon by those around her as being a pleasant person but not a particularly neighbourly one. This suited May, as she did not like the spontaneous visiting, which was the custom of some, and preferred to find acquaintances and friends among those of a more retiring nature like herself. One such person was Mary Clurey, who had come to her as midwife to both her children. Watching this tall, powerfully built woman from Donegal with deft quick hands as she bent over her tasks May would ponder about the other's background, her thoughts also on the honeymoon spent with Harry on those Atlantic shores. There were days, she recalled, when she'd seen a woman like this standing alone among the headlands effortlessly holding a large wicker basket of turf or seaweed, an aura of strength and remoteness about her like the region itself. Invited to visit, Mary would talk of the children and of Donegal and jokingly read May's teacup or her palm which made the latter think of the tinker women who would call at the farmhouse in her girlhood. Her attitude towards such things was not one of disbelief or outright scepticism, imbued by the lore of land and seafolk as she was, and often she would marvel at the images her companion conjured up from clusters of tealeaves and of the accuracy of some of the pronouncements when she teasingly asked of their truth. Soon you'll go on a journey, Mary said one day, with her almost masculine frame bent over the fire and teacup in hand, and it will also be a journey into the past. But listen, daughter, it won't always be like this for you. And then she laughed at all this foolishness, though May noticed that her eyes were grave and did not match her humour.

And there was a journey in the summer of 1929. To Donegal. In those six years since the birth of Jim they hadn't travelled far as all their money had been taken up with furnishing the home and providing for the children. At times the thought of not having an occupation and being uneducated still annoyed and she would suggest finding some kind of job, however menial, but Harry objected. The home and the children were quite enough to have to cope with, and besides, his salary was better now. It did not give them everything, but it was sufficient. True, she admitted. Theirs was a life of reasonable comfort compared to many others at a time when unemployment was the principal subject of discussion and some newspapers were predicting economic disaster.

So that summer holiday was spent in the same part of Donegal where they'd gone after the wedding ceremony. It was their first true holiday as in previous years the most they had enjoyed was the odd day-excursion to a seaside or country town on the outskirts of Belfast. And, as Mary had said, it was also to be a journey into the past. Here their honeymoon was renewed with an intensity that would burst forth in a frenzy of need and desire. Not that it had ever been lost, May mused while watching the children sporting in the shallow seapools, but simply postponed by the ordinary day-to-day rituals of work and home. Their feeling for each other had not lessened, but had merely been damped down by necessary tasks and commitments, the way a fire is damped down when its full blaze is not required. Not that they had been years of constant dullness. With Harry's working life in the city and his salary increasing, one evening a week had been taken up with entertaining themselves at a music hall or theatre or at one of the picture houses then springing up. They even had the experience of enjoying another production of *Naughty Marietta* when it was again put on in the city and that evening, all shyness now gone, had re-enacted their first coming together. But Rosinante was dead now. A letter had come from Jack in Islandmagee to say that her old pet was dead. But on some nights she thought she could still hear it braying to her across the fields.

And one afternoon months later she opened the door to find an old tramp asking for bread and water, at his heels a mongrel as shaggy and unkempt as himself..Standing stockstill, unnerved, she managed to enquire: Sam, Sam, Samuel, can it be you? But in those vacant eyes there was no response, so she gave him things to eat and drink and watched as he walked out of sight.

Those years had also been years of marriages. First it had been Jack, and she'd stood in the Islandmagee church noting the couple with amusement because of Jack's shy fumbling in such formal circumstances, while the tall young woman at his side hesitantly tried to offer reassurance. Later in the farmhouse where the reception was held—Jack having steadfastly refused to enter an hotel for any further do's or damn's or blessings—she instinctively recognised the feelings which drew them together and was as warm towards her sister-in-law as she had always been with this brother she'd once named Monkey Gordon. To her amazement, the second marriage had been Dalton's, of whom she had seen little since living in the city, even though he had bought a house not far from her on the sloping hills at Ballysillan. An invitation card had arrived and again, with Harry, she'd participated in a wedding ceremony. Looking at the slim ethereal figure which contrasted so sharply with Dalton's massive bulk she could but wonder what had brought them together, particularly as she had never envisaged Dalton even thinking of a woman and marriage. Lucy, her name was. In the months after the wedding May, knowing that police duties often caused Dalton to be away from home and remindful of her own loneliness when Harry had been in similar circumstances, visited her frequently. But communication between them amounted to little. Sitting in the immaculately kept living-room which was more a reflection of Dalton's nature than his wife's, she continued to wonder at this relationship in which any sign of natural feeling was so obviously lacking, with her companion moving listlessly around her and in her sighing voice asking the maid to serve afternoon tea. It was as though Dalton had found an injured bird and installed it in a gilded cage, May reflected, involuntarily comparing her sister-in-law's domestic life to her own. And the thought occurred to her again when Lucy died within six months of her marriage and May stood in the cemetery beside Dalton, the latter showing no trace of emotion. Obviously it had been merely out of pity for another that he'd married, yet pity was something he'd not revealed before. And perhaps there was more than that, she thought as, the formalities over, she heard him say that he would not be attending the traditional meal but requesting the others to return to the house: his marriage had simply been a duty and now, having been terminated in this fashion, was not only no longer of any significance but a social obligation that need not be embarked upon again.

David was the last to marry. Spending a weekend in Islandmagee with the children, May heard the story from Jack, of how David had appeared one day to borrow enough money for a wedding-ring, of how some months after he'd again appeared to borrow enough money to redeem it from the pawnshop and returned a third time to ask if he pawned the ring once more would it be enough to pay for a divorce and if it wasn't would Jack lend him the rest. He was at his wits' end trying to be respectable and walking the streets like a tailor's dummy, he'd said. Accepting a further amount he'd returned two days later to say he'd discovered that the money wasn't enough for a divorce and in putting in on the horses to get what he required he'd lost it all, but this time he went away empty-handed. 'And it'll be your turn next, I'm sure,' was Jack's parting remark as the trap came smartly to a halt at Whitehead station and he helped her and the children into a carriage. And it was true. A fortnight later David arrived to expound on his tale of woe but only succeeded in making both of them laugh. The wedding had occurred during a lengthy drinking spree and he'd just the faintest recollection of being in some wee country church where he thought he was doing best man. A few days later he woke up in astonishment to find that he was a husband. But more to the point was that she was determinedly set on turning him into an upright and honest citizen, as she put it. And so had begun a life of purgatory during which time he'd been every kind of clerk from banking to warehousing to finally one in a steamship company, when he'd been so driven to distraction by the sight of dusty walls and mouldy bits of paper that he'd been ready to become a stowaway on the next boat to anywhere. Not that she wasn't a decent sort, David concluded. She was so decent that if he didn't bother to go to work for a day he wasn't allowed into the house to have dinner until he'd written a note of apology to his employer.

May arranging one of the large attics as a bedroom, David became installed as part of the family. She was pleased at this for several reasons. As the years passed into the early 'thirties the political and religious sectarianism still simmering in the city and coupled now with greater poverty and unemployment would explode in riots and gun-battles, and having another man in the house made her feel more secure. It amused her to watch him playing with the children, so much did he seem like a child himself. And he was company for Harry who, from the gregarious person she'd known in the early years of her marriage and before, had become more and more solitary and so rarely brought a friend or fellow journalist home. The natural friendship she'd noticed between the two men in Islandmagee remained. But this was also a time when Harry was again away from home for lengthy spells, with the majority of the north-eastern counties still firm in their allegiance to Britain warily watching developments in the southern Free State as the old Republican leader of the civil war days, De Valera, was seen gradually coming into power. With Harry away on one of his journalistic missions it was good to feel the presence of David in the house.

But was it solely his occupation as reporter which took Harry away so frequently? Those thoughts which she'd had of his own possible political involvement in the years of civil war and after were roused. Only once had he stated his beliefs fully when he'd been deriding Unionism and the Free State: a Republic both politically and economically independent was the only solution. And again when questioned about involvement he'd merely shaken his head and said he'd seen enough guns firing in Europe. But still May's doubts remained and at night when she could hear shooting in the city she would wonder where he was and what he was doing and feel a bitterness welling in her heart for a country that could so divide wife and husband.

Twice she went to see David's wife, driven by pangs of conscience which to her were as genuine as they were absurd: genuine in that she did feel a sense of guilt in harbouring a runaway husband and absurd because it was of the husband's own choosing and anyway wasn't he her brother? David's description of his wife, for all his sarcasm, was accurate; a strong-willed woman whose narrowness in her view of life would have been crippling to any man of a free-going nature. Nor did she seem to be aware that it was her own intolerance that had caused her husband to leave her, an intolerance which, hardened by the feeling of betrayal, would now not even hear the subject of divorce mentioned. To which David, on hearing the news, had emphatically stated: 'I must be the only man in Belfast who's married for life to a woman I'll never see and her hardly a stone's throw away! Because from this day on my eyes are shut to the sight of her!'

And there was another hand which stretched from the past to touch the fibres of May's being, in the shape of a person who had always been a mystery to her and would continue to be so. Sitting in a lounge one winter afternoon with David an oddly familiar figure attracted her gaze until she heard herself exclaim: 'Anna. Anna Leitry.'

The young woman turned slightly, then turned away again.

240

Persisting, May said: 'It is Anna Leitry, isn't it?'

'May Gordon.'

'McKinstry. I'm married now. I wrote and told you. Though that was some years ago.'

'Of course. I had forgotten.'

'We seem to have lost touch.'

'Yes.'

'I've often thought about you.'

May noticed the other's expression change as she smiled, but it was a smile without warmth. Her mannerisms and accent were as she'd known them in earlier years; refined, deliberate. Swiftly calculating, she judged that Anna was now in her mid-twenties. And that element of adolescent awkwardness had gone, as had the thin girlish lines of her body to show a young woman of startling beauty. But something was wrong. The contrast between her looks and voice and the mocking brittle smile told of it. And the threadbare clothing too certainly did not fit the picture May would have expected. There were her companions also, two coarse-looking men and a woman of the same cast. Had this really been her friend in those days when they had walked along Bangor seafront sporting their new bonnets, thought May, at the same time recalling the big house with the long sloping lawns. Becoming embarrassed, she hastily wrote her address on a piece of paper and thrust it into Anna's hand, saying that she really must call and see her, ignoring David's questions as they left.

It was some months later when Anna first visited May. Domestic routine had changed yet again with David's leaving. Not that David had actually said he was leaving. It was just that his sojourns in the house became infrequent to the point that she knew he'd one day vanish. That was his way. And she knew perfectly well that in whatever fashion he obtained his money it was barely within the law. 'To be a bit of a buccaneer is the only way to live,' he would say; and it amused her to contrast him with Dalton. Harry was still often absent, the year 1932 having seen De Valera gain control in the southern Free State, an event which made rumours rife in the north as to the future when the Republicans who were defeated ten years earlier in battle could now win at the elections. And there were the children: Jim, an unruly boy of nine who thought it great fun to be on the streets during the frequently imposed curfews and Ruth, now five and already displaying an independent nature. It was one evening when she was standing at the door watching a file of soldiers pass by and wondering where Jim was that she saw a tall figure in a cape approach and greet her. Anna.

Through that autumn and winter they often sat by the fireside,

241

May talking of the days they'd spent together. Of herself Anna said little other than that she had been married and separated and now preferred to be alone. The family home had been sold and her father lived in a much smaller house in the south side of the city. Fleetingly May thought of the tall bewhiskered man in Victorian dress who would brusquely thrust a silver crown into their hands without a word, the governess who clucked around Miss Anna like a mother hen. And now here was the product, a girl who in outward appearances lived on her wits and was seemingly a set of contradictions. There was something sphinxlike about her, enigmatic. She spoke pleasantly enough, of her schooldays in England and France, of reading that was still her favourite pastime, but there was a remoteness about her which May found uncomfortable. Gone was the acquaintanceship of girlhood to the extent that May at times felt her visits to be a strain, and though she tried to talk of Anna's present circumstances, the subject was avoided. Perhaps these visits to her own ordinary domesticity served as a respite from a life which May did not care to speculate about.

It was on one such evening that another, unexpected, visitor called. Anna had arrived earlier to sit mostly in silence save for the occasional mocking remark about her own past. Her clothing was more down-at-heel than usual, though even this she wore with a kind of majesty. May, acting motherly which was quite contrary to her own desires and wondering how to suggest that her companion might like to try on some costumes and dresses she now never wore, was interrupted by a knock at the door. It was Dalton. With both relief and surprise she ushered him into the large kitchen and, after introductions, said: 'Well, Dalton. It's not often you come this way.'

'I didn't know you had company. And I don't want to intrude.'

'My brother,' said May in a joking manner, 'would call a visit once a year an intrusion. Sit down, Dalton. I was about to make some tea for Anna and myself. Or there's some whiskey in the cabinet if you wish.'

'A small whiskey, if you please.'

'And how small is small?' asked May, again jokingly. 'A more abstemious man, Anna, you're unlikely to meet.'

Pouring a good measure and reaching the glass across, May then began preparing tea in the scullery while listening to the perfunctory remarks passing between her guests. Dalton sat upright in a chair, dressed in uniform, greatcoat hanging open showing a broad gunbelt and the black butt of a revolver. She'd seen him so rarely in civilian clothes, May realised, becoming intrigued by the way Anna's gaze never seemed to leave him. But then another thought came to mind; the reason for his visit. 'And is this a social call, Dalton?'

242

'To tell the truth, I came to see if Harry was here.'

Harry? Why Harry? Dalton had never come to see him before, thought May, feeling that twinge of alarm and fear she'd known before. They were two such different men, their lives quite apart. 'My husband and brother were old comrades,' she said to Anna as she handed her tea and biscuits. 'In the war. Though that seems so long ago now.'

'Is he here?'

'Here? No. And God knows where he is. I sometimes wonder if I have a husband at all,' May replied quite truthfully, thinking of how lonely the house had been in recent months. 'It's almost as bad as that time during the war in the south.'

'It's that I wanted to see him about.'

'Oh? What?'

'Just to ask him what he thinks will happen in the south. Now that this new government has taken over, things are bound to change. De Valera's election speeches were on breaking all ties with Britain. In fact, on dismembering the Treaty. The removal of the oath to the British Crown. Things like that.'

'So he intends the Free State to become a Republic?' asked Anna.

Dalton's eyes flickered as he looked at her. 'Yes. I believe that's the ultimate aim.'

'And here in the north?' said May.

'One of the things he means to do is to release all IRA prisoners. The last government had to set up a military tribunal to have a lot of them interned. They were causing trouble. Now their release could mean another upsurge in the north. Another IRA campaign.'

'Is it never going to end,' May sighed. 'Sometimes I think the civil war has never stopped.' Pausing, she added: 'I can see why you'd like to talk to Harry. He's forever interviewing some politician or other. Though he tells me little about it.'

Dalton nodded, taking a sip of the whiskey which had been barely touched. 'I always read his articles and they're usually accurate.'

'And what do you think will happen in Europe? In Germany, I mean,' asked Anna. 'It would seem that Herr Hitler doesn't particularly like the Treaty of Versailles.'

'That we will have to wait and see,' Dalton said, seemingly reluctant to continue the conversation, though forced to do so by Anna's further remarks.

Leaning back in her chair and half-listening to the others' comments as they spoke of Europe, May felt herself become confused again. It was like a scene from the past with herself as a child and those around her talking of oncoming war. And there was Anna now speaking knowledgeably of the politics of Europe with Dalton's broad handsome face leaning towards her, the so-knowledgeable Anna who in girlhood had unwittingly made her feel foolish and uneducated. And that she still felt herself to be. The open fields and shores of Islandmagee came to mind to touch with all the force of a strong seawind. That was where she belonged and should not have left for the city with its divisions and violence. But her love for Harry had overridden all other considerations and still did. Harry. Yes. Still that niggling nagging fear. Why had Dalton really come?

Anna began to take her leave, Dalton also. She would not walk across the city alone at this late hour, Dalton insisted. He would accompany her.

And still that gnawing inside her as May sat staring into the fire in the now silent house. What if her fears of Harry were justified? Was Dalton to be his gaoler? Or worse?

VIII

Pacing the bedroom quietly yet restlessly Anna paused at a window, pulling the curtains back slightly to look towards the point where she thought she had heard gunfire. But the broad street outside was deserted. In the dark sky a pale sickle of moon drifted between cloudbanks. Waiting, the heavy silence outside was an almost palpable thing before being broken by a whining she'd learned to associate with armoured tenders and which grated viciously on her senses. She clenched her teeth as the sound seemed to travel over her body. It passed slowly below like some great insect, obscene, nameless.

The figure in bed stirred. 'Oh, love. You're not up again, are you?'

'Go back to sleep.'

A light shone dimly to show the shabby interior of the room and the dilapidated furniture. Still standing by the window Anna closed her eyes.

'What was it?'

'The usual. Someone shooting.'

The girl in bed laughed. Blonde and pretty, her voice was hard and coarse. 'It wouldn't be a night for working. Too many peelers.'

'Put out the light and go back to sleep.'

'Aren't you coming to bed?'

'Perhaps later.'

With the room again in darkness Anna drew up a chair and, wrapping the thin dressing-gown round her more tightly, sat down with her feet tucked beneath her. She would watch dawn break and perhaps sleep for a few hours in the morning. It was a time to think. She was a night creature and had always been so. Years ago in the big house in County Down nights had been spent like this, thinking, reading, and in the dormitories of the schools where she had boarded. She smiled as she compared her past abodes to her present one which consisted of two rooms in a rundown hotel specialising in accom-modation for lady artistes on tour, though the area in which it was

245

situated, convenient to both railway station and docks, also suggested professions of a more dubious nature. The girls and women with whom she associated assumed her to be one of themselves, though one who worked privately in town and hence wasn't to be on the streets. But they assumed wrongly. She would socialise with men, allow them to spend money freely on her, would even take the contents of their wallets when thoroughly drunk, but that was all. What fascinated her most was listening to their intimate secrets of wives, mistresses, businesses. It had been over a year since she'd embarked upon this kind of life, just after her husband had gone abroad. She hadn't drifted into it but had chosen deliberately out of a kind of daring. Or perhaps as a kind of penance, she sometimes thought. But now it was time to leave it, the sordidness of her surroundings having become unbearable.

Or perhaps it was that nihilistic streak in her nature combined with an active mind and imagination which caused her to seek out other areas of experience, those edges of one's being which desired intensity and excitement in other forms. As the girl on the bed moved and the faint light caught her blonde hair, Anna smiled. There was that also, the ambivalence of her sexual inclinations which had only truly been revealed to her during her marriage. In her schooldays there'd been the fleeting romances while she was passionately identifying herself with her literary heroines, Miss Hesketh in Dickens' *Little Dorrit*, or the Albertine of Proust or her own namesake in *Anna Karenina*. And there was a certain parallel between then and now in the dormitory of sleeping girls and their adolescent affairs and the young women in such a place as this often turning to one another for affection.

Her marriage. Returning from London and abroad she had participated in the social life of her class with its endless club activities and gatherings both genteel and extravagant, but was soon bored by it all. She'd known the post-war gaiety of London and what she found at home bore only a pale resemblance, no doubt due, she thought, to the problems of the newly created border and the determination of Unionists to maintain control of the north-east. She had probably married out of boredom, she afterwards thought, finding herself in a society which was strange to her but quite in what way she could not determine, knowing only that she recoiled against the restrictiveness of class and the religious hypocrisy which was everywhere apparent. From her own experiences she had intimations of a changing world whose ripples had failed to reach this part of Ireland.

She'd been thinking of returning to England when she'd accepted the proposal of marriage. Her husband, like herself having inherited a considerable sum on coming of age, had believed himself to be a financial genius. He'd also been an inveterate gambler. Soon they

246

were penniless and when he'd taken to physically assaulting her she had left him. Not that she was afraid of him, but rather afraid of what her own anger would lead her to do should she retaliate. She'd then gone to her father and explained the matter in quite matter-of-fact tones. On hearing her tale, he in turn had gone to his son-in-law to throw a leather bag of guineas at him and tell him to leave the city if not the country. Anna had not seen her husband since, nor did she expect to.

She both liked and loved her father. Perhaps because she knew exactly what he was and could see something of herself in him. He was both an excellent businessman with concerns in such things as flax, saddlers and shipping, and a philanderer and spender of bacchanalian disposition. And though now it was the early 'thirties he still strode through the city in his Victorian frock-coat of the late 'nineties. After the incident with her husband he'd said to her with a malicious grin: 'You and me are a pair. Always remember. Listen to anyone you like. But go your own way and take what you want. Learn that, my girl. And when you learn that come back to me and I'll set you up in business.'

And that was precisely what Anna now intended to do. Having spent the past year living on what little money she'd hidden from her husband and surviving on her wits, her life was now about to change dramatically.

Dawn traced fingers of light across the sky and still she meditated. Her marriage was salutary in its way in that it made her realise that she didn't want marriage of any kind. It would not allow her the freedom her nature demanded. It was comfortable to sit with May in her home, but that vicarious element of family domesticity was all she required. May. It was her always curious mind as to the lives and motives of others which had caused her to accept May's invitation. And, after the early visits, she felt the old warmth between them developing anew. Gifted also with an excellent memory, she easily recalled that time in the bedroom of the house in County Down when she had made advances. If May but knew. But what was taboo to others was to her simply the ever-shifting penumbra of one's sensual being desiring exploration. If one's imaginative being was always seeking, why should not one's physical being do likewise?

Dalton. He intrigued her. Sombre, handsome, and with the suggestion of turbulence lying beneath that still surface, a ruthlessness. His eyes had probed her own, attempting to penetrate. And when her gaze had matched his own she thought she'd found a smile in that interior—wry, sardonic, yet amused. There was violence too, but controlled. It had thrilled her to find what she could only describe as a fellowship of feeling. At her request he'd stopped the police car

247

close to where she roomed and had it not been for the other girls and the proprietor she'd have asked him to stop outside the hotel. His features had been composed as he wished her a curt goodnight. A week later a letter had arrived inviting her to dinner at his house in Ballysillan. She had guessed correctly. He was as intrigued as she. And the house was as she thought it would be, meticulous in its order, from the carefully arranged furniture to the large telescope sitting in the bay window and swivelled towards the sky. On the walls were watercolours mostly of sea and landscape, on a table a neat pile of scientific magazines mainly on astronomy. As he opened a drawer she saw a pistol in a holster, quite different from the gun he wore while in uniform. Here was a mind like her own, thought Anna, one not content to remain within ordinary bounds of experience.

The meal, already prepared by a woman he engaged for such household purposes, was pleasant, the conversation casual. On a further visit to May she had offhandedly asked about him. But May had little to say other than that no one knew anything of Dalton except for the outward facts of his life, that he had been in the trenches, was now a District Inspector in the police, had been married for a short time and was a widower. Though why he had married she could never understand as it was obvious he was a bachelor through and through.

Business. It was to be in *haute couture*. She had all the necessary qualifications. She would need premises in the centre of the city and from her clientele could glean most of what was taking place in the city's life. Completing her toilet she then dressed, looking totally out of place in the shabby room in clothes purchased a few days previously. Kissing the blonde hair lightly, she left some money on the table and closed the door. Dalton would be waiting for her as arranged. She'd asked him to be with her when she went to see her father, a gesture she thought not unlike intimacy and reciprocating his own invitation into a jealously guarded privacy.

The early morning was bright and clear. November, decorations in streets and windows heralded another Christmas. Anna smiled. The prodigal daughter was, in a way, returning home.

Thoughts as myriad as the hail rattling tinnily on the roof of the bus assailed Harry's mind. What was the reason for Niall's summons to Ballycastle? Why had May again queried his political beliefs and wanted to know everything he was doing when away on newspaper work? When that kind of questioning had been so long dormant? Why had Dalton called to see him, he who had never called before? They'd never had anything really in common except for the experience of the war in France and the end of that had been the end of any companionship between them. For years he'd rarely ever thought of Dalton, and those times he did it was simply with a feeling of respect and gratitude, because of France. Apart from that he was a policeman of high rank, something other.

As the bus bounced along the pitted road Harry shivered in the cold clamminess, grinned, shivered again, grinned again. What was the shiver? Was it the devil walking over his grave?

Soberly he stared at the sodden fields streaked green and white and brown. What were his own feelings? That was the most difficult thing of all to decide.

Images of home came to mind, the bright kitchen with the brass fender gleaming, his son Jim now a boisterous well-made lad forever getting into some scrape or other. Not unlike himself when young. Ruth, still crawling and tumbling around the floor. Jim had brought a pup home and it was bedded in a wicker basket in a corner of the kitchen, that's when it wasn't scampering under everyone's feet and getting in the way. Shadow, it was called. May's name for it. That had been the name of the collie her father had owned in Islandmagee. So many yesterdays that were both far and yet near. *Heehawhee-hawheehaw*. The time I sang to the old donkey with the wine of wanting her in my senses. *Ah sweet mystery of life at last I've found thee . . .* And it was she who took me in the nightscented air with her breasts bare as we rolled in the grass and the sea surging in the caverns below. *Heehawheehawheehaw*.

But what of those I may have sent to their deaths who can know nothing of such things now?

He tried to wrench his mind from both past and home, but failed. The images kept coming. The parlour where he liked to lounge in a quiet hour, or where he would work with the door locked against the invasion of children and pup. More and more his thoughts were turning away from the morass of political divisions and the squabbling bitterness involved. He'd persuaded his editor to allow him space for a weekly review section in which he dealt with plays and books of a local nature. That was the way to go, his wish of some years before to move into publishing or even to attempt writing a book himself becoming paramount. And the book? Perhaps a novel. He was tired of analysing, dissecting. A comic novel, maybe. That impish part of his nature with one eye always on the look-out for the ludicrous would enjoy such work.

May. Her warmth enfolded him. Comfort and more. Their life together passed from phase to phase yet always in the depths lay that passion to be sparked off anew. Only recently they'd spoken of enlarging the family. A daughter like you he'd said, a son like you she'd said: he smiled. But there was always that dark area between

249

them: his other occupation as a courier in the Republican struggle and her suspicions of his somehow being involved politically. At moments when tempted to talk of it he'd held back, knowing that it could only cause more harm than good.

And that was the decision which now faced him. Niall's summons could only mean one thing, that the Republican movement was again to become active in the north as in the south. De Valera's decision in Dublin to release political prisoners whom the earlier Cosgrave government had incarcerated would be a sign to move. During the past few years activity had been practically nil. But now? Was it again to be nights listening to gunfire, the weekly list of the dead and wounded, of himself wondering about his own share in it all? He'd known what it was like to face gunfire, rifles, machine-guns, bombardments from howitzers. In joining the Republican movement he'd chosen not to use a gun, and the decision had seemed right at the time. But had it been right, and was it right now? The intelligence papers and reports he passed on doubtlessly meant death for some and yet he lay in secret, unknown to them and without fear of retaliation. Yes. At times he felt cowardly. Risk had been there, of course, risk of the sudden arresting hand on his shoulder. But he'd been good at the work, never meeting in the same place twice, rarely—at his own instigation—encountering the same person twice. The occasional letter or telephone call was ostensibly about newspaper work, carefully coded. Yet he knew a few like himself, that was inevitable. If caught, would he betray them?

As the bus swayed he bumped his head against the window and blinked. What had Dalton really called to see him about?

Yes. He wanted to leave the movement, wanted out. And there were deeper reasons for this. Rather than moving towards a Republic with room for all beliefs, the southern Free State seemed to be solidifying into a hierarchy of middle-class interests and the dictates of a repressive Catholic Church. And this had its mirror image in the north: a zealous religious Orangeism allied to middle-class Unionism and remnants of the feudal Anglo-Irish on their estates. In essence there was little to choose between them. Both wished to dominate, oppress, and regard each other from their bastions with wilful ignorance.

Alighting from the bus he stood uncertainly, in one hand a small travelling bag, coat gathered against burling windblown sleet. Ballycastle, his home town, but there was no feeling of nearness here. He'd been too long away. Quickly going through the cobbled streets to the small pub at the shore he saw Niall waiting for him, the broad smile and welcoming grasp on his arm bringing some of the old intimacy, but not all.

250

James. Why should he think of James?

'Niall.'

'Harry.'

An old intimacy? What intimacy? These islands. How beautiful. How sad.

'I was waiting for you.'

'That I knew.'

But.

In a way. All ghosts. Shall I be also?

'You don't look your usual self.'

Gnomish, he snarled and grinned. 'True. I've only been trailing round about four wars.'

And then silence for the night. He lay as he so often lay before in other strange places. Yes, he was an outsider now. Like himself, Niall had married and they'd returned to the latter's home where a room had been prepared for him. The evening's conversation had revolved around ordinary matters: home, family, Harry's career and Niall's new fishing smack. In bed listening to the wind pitching higher he carefully sifted his reasons for leaving the movement. They would be put simply, bluntly. He was sure of his decision now.

Breakfasting early, they went to the workyard where there would be privacy. Niall outlined future activity as he fed the stabled horse. It was as Harry expected. Plans were being made for a possible campaign on the border and inside the northern territory. The Republic could not be achieved until partition had ended. Besides, hadn't the border proved to be at best a makeshift thing with counties like Fermanagh and Tyrone held at the point of a gun inside a territory they didn't want and never had wanted to belong to? The northern six-county state was not merely insecure. Through its own falsity it would one day just collapse.

Harry listened in silence as his activities as courier like before were sketched out, then said: 'No, Niall.'

'No?'

'No. Not again.'

'Why?'

Quietly Harry stated his own beliefs, his present way of thinking, adding truthfully that he'd seen enough active service in various ways. He now wished to be nothing other than a civilian and to pursue his own interests.

'Yes. You're quite a veteran.' Niall smiled wanly. 'But you're a good man to lose. Are you fixed in this?'

'Adamant.'

'Sometimes it isn't so easy to quit just like that.'

'Is that a threat, Niall?'

Niall shook his head. 'No, Harry. There'd never be any threat to you.' He paused. 'There could be an important job coming up. Soon. Would you do it for me? Just one more job, Harry. And then finish.'

Stroking the mare which had ambled into the yard Harry sighed and remained quiet for a while. 'I'll do it for you, Niall. Just one more job. And then finish.'

Niall placed his arm affectionately round Harry's shoulder. 'I knew you would. But tell me, what d'you think of these goings-on in Germany and this Hitler fella?'

'It's hard to say yet. But he's certainly out for power.'

'I just thought we might get some help from that quarter if necessary. Like last time.'

Curtly Harry said, 'You forget, Niall. I'm practically retired.'

'Aye. I forgot.' Leading the horse back to the stable Niall asked: 'I suppose you'll be leaving early?'

'On the noon bus.'

'Then I'll forget about a morning's work. Let's have a few jars before you go.'

Leaving the yard neither noticed the car sitting half-hidden by a corner, or the figure which stepped out to follow them. It was when they were sitting by the fire in the pub, glasses in hand, that Harry heard himself being addressed.

'Well, intellectual. And what are you doing in these parts?'

Surprised, Harry looked up. Prominent features, sallow, a leering curve to the mouth. A slouch hat, brim sideways, a long trench coat, hands in pockets.

'Don't you remember? With James in Dublin?'

Harry sought for a name. 'Campbell? Christopher Campbell?'

'Yes. We last met in Dublin.'

Harry frowned. 'That was about ten years ago.'

'That's right. Just before your brother James was murdered by the rebels.'

'Your brother, Harry?' asked Niall quietly.

'My stepbrother. After my mother married again and went to England. Remember?'

Niall nodded, guarded eyes watching the newcomer. 'Ah, yes.'

Calling for another round Campbell sat down. 'It's rarely I buy rebels a drink. But then, occasions can change.'

'What do you mean by rebels?' asked Harry, his skin tingling at both the intrusion and veiled accusation.

Elbows on the table, Campbell waited until the drinks were placed in front of them, his fingertips rubbing together slightly as he looked into each face. 'Merely a figure of speech. It might have gone out of custom in the south, but not here. And as I remarked, I

252

wouldn't have expected to find you in these parts. Who would you be interviewing now?'

'No one,' Harry said, measuring the other's casual tone. 'I'm here because this is the town of my birth. And Niall my oldest friend. Childhood friend.'

'I see. Sentimental reasons only.'

'It's comfortable to have them. And to know one's birth,' replied Harry, recalling a mocking phrase which James had made about the colonial, and was gratified to see the other's eyes flicker as he stood up to finish his drink, his tone in reply openly contemptuous.

'Until our next meeting, intellectual.'

'If there is one.'

'I'm sure there shall be.'

Watching him as he left the pub Niall said: 'I didn't know you knew that one, Harry.'

'I met him first in London,' said Harry thoughtfully. 'During the war. And then in the south before partition. He's in Military Intelligence, I believe. Or was.'

'Probably still is. It was he who gave me the grilling just after the rising in 'sixteen. When I'd got back from Dublin.'

'Oh?'

'I mentioned it to you. Wanted me to become informer. Though I'm sure he knows nothing about me.'

'I wouldn't be so sure of that.'

Niall paused. 'And James. Your late stepbrother. One of the reasons for leaving us, Harry?'

'One among many.'

Standing up, Harry stumbled slightly as his foot caught the leg of a stool and, reaching out for balance, withdrew his hand with an exclamation. A bright drop of blood welled from one finger.

'Merry Christmas,' Niall said as he pushed the thick holly branch massed with berries upright again.

'Merry Christmas.'

But it wasn't merriment he felt, thought Harry, as the bus swung out of the village and again he stared at the snowstreaked fields and a car which passed slowly and then went on at speed with a figure in a slouch hat driving. Through the air the body hurtled, propelled by a coloured arrow. The circus. Even in adulthood with May the solemn hares too in mystic ritual by the Druid's Altar. At what ceremony was I a guest? Love. He smiled sadly.

Clown.

IX

'I remember my young days, for younger I've been,
I remember my young days by the Mutton Burn stream,
It's not marked on the world's map and nowhere to be seen,
That wee river in Ulster—the Mutton Burn stream.

Sure it flows under bridges, takes many a turn,
Sure it turns round the millwheel that grinds the folk's corn,
And it wimples through meadows and keeps the land clean,
Belfast Lough it soon reaches—this Mutton Burn stream.'

A bright warm morning in January. A freak day that belonged more
to spring than mid-winter. Patches of ice had already melted and the
frost had gone from the grass and hedgerows.

'Sure the ducks like to swim in it from morning till e'en,
Whiles they dirty the water sure they makes theirselves clean,
Och! I've seen them a-diving till their tails were scarce seen,
Woddlin' down in the bottom of the Mutton Burn stream.'

As the gay clear voice came lilting through the air David Gordon
groaned, turned over, groaned again, then tried to sit up. Failing, he
lay back again, pulling his hat across his face to shade his eyes from
the blinding glare of the sun.

'Now the ladies from Carry I oftimes have seen
Taking down their fine washing to the Mutton Burn stream,
And no powder nor soap used, a wee dunt makes them clean,
It has great cleansing powers this Mutton Burn stream.'

Could a man not even get peace when trying to have a sleep in an
open field? It was worse than the baaing of a lot of oul' sheep.

Searching his pockets, one hand produced a whiskey flask. Miracle of miracles. It still held a good few mouthfuls. Tilting it, he spluttered as he swallowed. Sighing, he closed his eyes again.

'And it cures all diseases though chronic they've been
It will red you of fatness or cure you of lean,
Sure the jaundies itself now, weak heart or strong spleen,
All give way to the power of the Mutton Burn stream.'

It wasn't the jaundies or a weak heart he wanted to be cured of, David thought, as the words began to penetrate his foggy brain. Not even strong spleen, though that might be a possibility. Poverty was what he wanted to be cured of. Poverty. At this thought he began to rummage through his pockets again, but not one coin was to be found. Not even as much as a farthing. There was only one thing for it. Another deep sigh and another gulp of whiskey.

'Once a-partying at nighttime, when I'd not be seen,
And they aye give good parties that live round the stream,
Coming home in the morntime, all gay and serene,
Sure I slipped and fell in that Mutton Burn stream.'

And whoever was singing that's where someone should throw her, he thought, right to the bottom of that Mutton Burn stream. Some duck she'd be then with her tail wiggling like a tadpole's. Pushing his hat away he watched fleecy clouds drifting overhead. What day, month or year was it? Somewhere in the distant past he vaguely remembered going on a Christmas binge. Or had it been one at New Year? Yes, that was it. He'd been in a poker school that had begun in Belfast and somehow finished up in Carrickfergus. And he'd been about to take the pot with a pile of aces when some bastard had snatched it out of his hand with a straight run. Damn! And not one miserable farthing had he left.

'Sure the ducks like to swim in it, from morning till e'en,
Whiles they dirty the water sure they makes theirselves clean—'

'What about ye, Missus? Some duck you are. Dirtyin' the clean water wi' that oul' washin' of yours.'

Startled, she turned and stared at the tousle-haired face which had appeared from the long grass.

'But come to think of it. You can wash mine while ye're at it. They're soakin' wet as it is.' So saying, he took off jacket, shirt and trousers and threw them towards her and, as she turned away,

laughed. 'It's all right, Missus. I'm not in my birthday suit, ye know.
I'll not astound yer modesty.'

'You fair frighted me.'

'And I'd like till fright ye more. Ye'd make some man a quare wife.'
Chewing a blade of grass David grinned as she turned round again. It
was true. A strapping bigboned lass with glinting black eyes and a
mass of black hair and barely eighteen. She might just be the kind of
woman that would let a man be himself. 'Well? What about my
washin'?'

'And who's the one'd want the likes of you and yer washin'? I'll get
my brothers till hound ye.'

Fiery too, thought David, still grinning. 'Get twenty of them. The
more the merrier as the sayin' is.'

But this last comment was followed by an oath as he saw her
quickly snatch up his clothes and hurl them into the middle of the
river where they began to drift downstream. Wading in the icy water
he retrieved them and made back to the bank only to glimpse her
vanish behind a copse, a tub of washing clutched to her hips.
Shivering, he shook the last few drops from the whiskey flask, glad of
the sun's weak rays seeping through his underclothing. If the morning
had started badly, it was now even worse. Not only was he poverty-
stricken, but it seemed sure he would die of pneumonia. At least his
hat was dry, he thought as he fingered it, wondering if that was a good
omen. But no. From behind the copse she appeared again, though this
time with a group of seven men. Quickly he thought, noticing the lines
of smoke curling in the air some distance away. So that was it. A tinker
girl, and a tinkers' camp. And if she didn't have twenty brothers she
certainly had enough to give him a rough time. It wasn't pneumonia
he was going to die of. What he needed now was some of those hard
men from the city he'd been spending the last year carousing with and
getting to know, like Tiger Joe and Stormy Weather or that runt Long
John who was so wee he'd have your shins battered in before your own
fist could find where he was.

They came menacingly on, discarding jackets and making no secret
of their intentions. Retreating back into the stream he put two into the
water before a blow flung him to the opposite bank. Fighting on, his
only pleasure now lay in each time his own punches met their mark.
Inevitable. Lying on the grass with his head ringing and more aches
than he wanted to know about, he felt himself being pulled into a
sitting position. They stood around him talking in a language he
didn't understand. Romany perhaps, he thought, blinking and
noticing three rubbing weals on their faces. What now? The girl was
among them, at her side an elderly man who was staring down at him
while searching in the voluminous pockets of an ancient hunting

jacket. But it wasn't a knife that was brought out, as David was inclined to think. Gulping from the proffered bottle he felt the liquid rip at his throat and push tears from stinging eyeballs. Poteen. Not the best but even the worst would have been the best at a moment like this.

He must have fallen asleep, or become unconscious. The sun was already well down and dusk bringing the long winter evening and night. He was naked underneath a blanket and beside him was the circle of a glowing fire whose heat filtered through him. Spotting the poteen bottle and reaching for it he groaned as from his ribs and jaw and seemingly a hundred other places came stabs and throbs. As he sipped slowly he heard the grass rustle and she was sitting a few feet away.

'You are well?'

'As well as if I'd been keelhauled or dragged along by a stampede of horses.'

'My brothers think you fought well.'

'Are they all your brothers?'

'Four.'

'Four's enough.'

'Where do you come from?'

Trying to ease his limbs he groaned again. 'I'm like the man in the song. God knows where. I'm comin' from God knows where and goin' till God knows where.'

'You will eat with us?'

'As I've no money and nothing to eat and nowhere to go I might as well, mightn't I?'

As she raked the ash he looked round the encampment where other fires glowed. He could see six caravans and about a dozen tethered horses. Having encountered groups of the travelling people before, he judged there to be around thirty here. Several yards away a woman hummed a lullaby as she turned strips of meat on a grill, the smell making him feel ravenous. A dog came sniffing at him and he sent it scampering away with a clip on the ear. Wherever he'd arrived it all seemed very peaceful.

'You want me as a wife for you?'

Tempted to laugh he became sober instead. That's what he'd said to her that morning. Was that what the fight had been all about? Some kind of initiation? By the fire she looked even more handsome. And he knew something of her people. She'd be good to him and fight for him too and would never try to turn him into some performing monkey because of some jackass of a neighbour or preacher.

'You have a wife?'

'No. Not one I'd ever want anyway.' A horse neighed and he looked

257

towards where they grazed. 'And what would yer brothers give me as a dowry?'

'What d'you want?'

'If there was a fine-looking mare among that bunch I'd take that.' She nodded.

He paused, thinking. Why the hell not? It's a long oul' road that's no turning and maybe this turning was the one for him. 'What do they call ye?'

'Norah.'

'A good strong name. But I'll tell ye this, Norah. A man can't walk round the country naked. The peelers'd have him behind bars in a twinklin'. And he can't get married naked either. Though if him and his woman want till lie naked after that's their business.'

Watching her go he lay ruminating. Why the hell not indeed? You couldn't tell the kind of woman you married until you married her. He'd discovered that before, hadn't he? The same went for the woman. But when you could just call it a bad deal and walk out why live in misery as so many did?

'They're your own.'

In a neat pile beside him lay his clothes, a brightly coloured kerchief on top. She stood waiting.

'Whatever else, Norah, I try to be an honest man in my own way. And I've seen many's the fancy goodlivin' one that's worse than a rogue. Tonight I haven't a penny to my name. Not a farthing. And nowhere to take you till. Last week I had a hundred pounds and lost it all at the cards. But next week or the one after I'll have another hundred and it won't all go on poker. And I won't be stayin' here. I'll be goin' my own way and always will though I'll never stop you coming back to see yer people when you want. There's my proposal.'

'We eat now,' was all she said as he watched her walk towards a caravan larger than the others where already the sound of merriment had begun.

It was a riotous night. He drank and danced as he'd never done before, hands clapping him on, the patriarch beaming as he waved a longstemmed pipe in the air. His head was held as a redhot needle pierced his ear. Drifting on sleep he felt hair brush his face and quick gentle fingers knead his bruises. In the morning he heard singing coming from the stream but it was noon before he stumbled out into the sunshine where the fresh crisp air began to clear the fumes from his brain. Shaving in the cracked mirror he saw the hoop earring in his left ear as a gleaming circle of gold and in his hand a gold sovereign found underneath his pillow. Mesmerised, he stroked the piebald mare tethered outside the caravan window, his own choice, Norah told him, of the night before.

Dusk of evening had again come when they went down the long loanan together with David leading the horse, reins draped over his shoulder, and Norah cloaked against the night breeze on its back, her belongings in a bag strapped behind her. 'Bare yer beautiful breasts till the moon and stars, my love. Yesterday I had nothing. Today I have the wife I want, a gold sovereign, a gold earring in my ear and a fine strappin' horse as lively as any liltin' tune. Wouldn't that bate any of the oul' millionaires that ever was!'

'Once a-partyin' at nighttime, when I'd not be seen,
And they aye give good parties that live round the stream,
Comin' home in the morntime, all gay and serene,
Sure I slipped and fell in that Mutton Burn stream.'

Dalton studied the file a third time, storing essential details in memory. Going to a room further down the corridor he returned the papers to their original place, relocking the drawer and door with a skeleton key. Back in his own office he sat at his desk drinking whiskey and chain-smoking. From other parts of the police barracks he could hear voices of the on-duty staff and the clacking of radio equipment, but knew he wouldn't be disturbed. It was still dark and looking at the clock on the wall he judged it to be another two hours before light. Opening a window to dispel the fumes he put on gunbelt and greatcoat and made his way to the entrance of the building, declining a lift offered by the sergeant at the desk but leaving a curt message that Sherrin was to meet him at Ballysillan with his own car at ten o'clock sharp. Walking through the drab working-class areas he listened to the ring of his own footsteps on the pavements and felt the gelid air on his face. So, these streets were to know bloodshed another time. From doors and alleyways gunfire would spurt, as in years previously. He'd been expecting a new Republican campaign, and the bitter retaliation it would undoubtedly unleash. Crossing the Antrim Road he saw the dark mass of the Cave Hill as a smudge in the darkness, the avenues here having a more genteel and respectable air. Like those on the south of the city where Anna now lived. Malone. There'd be that too, the talks and discussions in which he was expected to participate about how to ferret out the enemy within. The enemy within, when many of those who talked of such were more intent on keeping the enemy there, in adding to ferment, because that was the surest way to safeguard power and privilege. He knew he was trusted by them, trusted absolutely, was known to be one of the finest and most disciplined officers in the Force. War experiences and bearing marked him for easy promotion. In those functions among

259

political and social dignitaries he stood apart, simply listening. In conferences he assimilated the facts and made his case with both ease and command and in the fewest possible words. But it was not all that his nature demanded. It was this. Alone in the dark streets or country with a gun at his belt. Perhaps he'd never left the Somme. Or was carrying it with him, in a way.

The night before the war in France had begun with his father hurling the rifle across the study. Dalton. You have the sensitivity I always felt in myself. But in me it was that of the simpleton. You have also a power of decision that I never possessed. Use it well.

Yes. He'd left the Church, left physics. He'd no beliefs like that. War was what had drawn him, finding in this that same cold exhilaration as when he studied the night sky. Through darkness he peered, seeking what lay hidden there. Or was he actively seeking it in the nihilistic streak of spirit his father had once briefly mentioned also? Sombrely he smiled.

He stopped. On his left side lay the high bank of the Waterworks enclosed by railings. A figure sat on a bench, ragged, tattered, shoulders hunched and head slouched forward. An old tramp, nothing to alarm him. He walked on.

Reaching the house he bathed in cold water and, wrapping a dressing-gown around him, lay down on a couch. A smokey-coloured cat appeared to curl up in the armchair opposite, a present from Anna. To make the place seem more lived-in, she'd said. He was to meet her that morning when they would visit her father to settle financial affairs. She wanted him to be with her. Later he would make a tour of the police barracks in south Antrim and call in to sit with McKinzie for a short while, who was retired now. In the cottage the two photographs on the wall, one son dead at the Somme and another on a County Antrim hillside.

In the study at Islandmagee hung the stag's head. He watched as the stag died in throaty spumes of blood and through the trees on the far side of the wood saw Harry, also watching. Their horses turned away. That had been before the first battle. Harry. He had long known of his sympathies and of his work. But now others knew and his arrest was imminent. Campbell. There was nothing he could do. There was nothing he would do.

Dressing in civilian clothes he carefully locked the revolver in the bureau and slipped the pistol into his pocket, waiting for the sound of the car in the driveway.

And yet.

And what, Harry? Shall this cloak of our dreams cover us? Pain?

260

Yet?

Cratered earth, sky, limbs. Wading in the water. The prison ship. O'Donnell. The boy. Duncan. Duncan's boy. When I told him to fight on, soldier, or I shall kill you. In those vast fastnesses. See.

From dark minefields, darkened doorways. Darkness. I shot the mule because there was too much pain. Myself also.

On Malin Head Harry's swift philosopher in a starry ditch. Laughing in the shellhole we were. A black hole.

Anna?

Sam, gentle Sam, Don Samuel? Rosinante? *Mon Dieu, que la guerre est longue!*

Yet.

X

Harry's arrest was executed simply. So was his torture. Then he died. In all it took no more than three weeks. Whatever that space of time is. Or might mean.

Leaving the newspaper offices a hand fell on his shoulder, the packet taken from his grasp. A slouch hat led him to the back seat of a car where a malevolent smile greeted him. 'Well, intellectual? We meet again. As I said we would.'

May, May, have I betrayed even our love, our future?

Looking out over the cliffs the sea wild in the wild grass we lay calling kiiiyaaa kiiiyaaa scheeeheee my love and you're a wee wild thing May the wildest wee thing iver I seen my father saying smiling his face sad too for the men at the war and you're a wild stubborn woman but sure I love you in his arms wild like the seabirds sweet mystery before he went away too foouuuuuuffff the autumn wind blowing mystery aye mystery it is too all of it dreaming where is my dream the dream of my girlhood peace of my old age sweet memory cruck crick unsteady old bones by the fire rocking.

A task. I believed. Now not shriving time allowed.

Aye, aye, my beloved dream. Peace. And now again intimations of mortality. Of love's end and time with only memory to warm me.

In a small room a pool of light, a table, a pen, paper, typewriter, a man. The city his birth, its hills, streets, alleyways, darkness, this city at war, city of fear, despair, death sudden and slow, laughter, love, ordinariness. Reality. Speak, voices, speak.

Heehawheehawheehaw . . .

What is that? Words upon a page, laborious and slow. Listen, a tale. Laboriously, words upon a page. That only. A man, a room. A pool of light. Breaking. Speak, voices. Broken words upon a page.

You're away again, Sam. This time to the hill at Carnmoney where sit upright the stone tablets of the dead. Nearly springtime now, Sam. I can see you go, the pair of you, the donkey patiently bearing your sack, coming this time from a travelling circus visiting the city with you now wearing a false nose thieved from one of the clowns. A good raid that, Sam, with the roars and shouts and booming of cannon and bellowing of animals drawing you thither as to a magnet. No, not quite the Somme now, Sam, but still, a place where good spoils are to be had, with you wearing not only your false nose but also a bowler hat and coloured waistcoat and in your hand a cane. And your ass? Yes, a feathered Alpine cap for it sitting jauntily between long ears. A real fighter in the mountains maybe it is. Away again, Sam, munching a chunk of mouldy bread with your mount trailing a string of early buttercups and daisies, your cane lancing only the air, away never stopping, always on and on, looking, still searching, Sam, searching—*Nous sommes à la recherche de notre ville natale . . . de notre pays natal . . .*

Ceremony, perchance.

Heehawheehawheehaw . . .

Reality.

Dalton! D. . .A. . .L. . .T. . .O. . .N!

A face turned to where darkness grins, a broken face.

Heehawheehawheehaw. . .

263

XI

Dalton knew of Harry's arrest and interrogation. And he waited. Over a week passed and May came to him, asking, pleading, demanding. At first she thought Harry had gone away on some urgent work for the newspaper, not having time to tell her. But now she knew the truth. That he was in prison. She did not ask why.

A visit was arranged. In a small room they faced each other, a policeman standing silently just inside the door. There was another person sitting in a corner dressed in civilian clothes, a hat shading his face as he slouched in the chair staring at his toecaps. She ignored them both.

'Why, Harry?'

'Because I believed. In a country at peace. For those who live in it. For those who will live in it. Our children, May.'

'And this was the way to do it?'

'So I was told by those who created the war in Europe. And in this I didn't carry a gun.'

A voice from the corner. 'Others carried the guns. It was you who carried the orders.'

In Harry's quick smile there was a glimmer of that youthful volatile merriment she knew so well which even the bruised features failed to hide. 'Oh to be rid of self-righteous serpents. St Patrick didn't do his job well enough, obviously.'

'What can I do?' she asked.

'There's nothing to be done.'

'Nothing?'

'Take care of the children. And remember our love. But don't spend all the rest of your days alone.'

'God bless you, Harry.'

'And you, May.'

She waited until he was led away before leaving herself and crossing the courtyard of the prison and going out through a small door set in the tall broad gateway. Pausing outside she turned to look

264

at the blank iron and wood, thinking. In her passion the bright air seemed to fill all her senses. No, there was nothing to be done. His eyes had been fixed elsewhere, the expression on his face that of an already dying man.

Night and day were one, broken only by that pool of light when again they came for him. Wearily he faced the glare, his one conscious effort now trying to trace this new level of disintegration. Invisible silver cords held him in some realm of space, multitudinous beings threatening to supplant that which had been him. A foetus now, turning in the brine of impending birth or death.

Light whiplashed across his eyes, shattering his sight.

Yes. Him.

Another him. Another betrayal.

We have killed him.

Yes.

And another betrayal.

He is dead too.

That was what he had always feared most, he thought when thought would come and he clutched at threads to grope his way back to that which might be him, might have been him. Whom now have I betrayed? Over the cratered ground of his past he crawled and would say to the slouch hat—I have been here before, lying in that suppurating slime which is all that's left of life. You live there. I do not.

Hunger he chose as a weapon, accelerating his end. And intensity, as though the little energy that remained must be forced to consume itself in a final swift paroxysm. Clarity came, absolute. He lay in his own excrement, the hair on his face matted with it. In the clanging cell doorway a tall figure stood.

'Dalton.'

'Harry.'

'I was thinking of the shellhole.'

'I heard you call.'

'How many did I betray?'

'Enough.'

It was a different voice, a different face. It grinned down at him. He offered names.

'Yes.'

'Where is he?'

'We shot him.'

Another name.

'Yes. We killed him too.'

'Then kill me too. Have you no pity?'

265

'Pity's for the weak. Didn't the trenches teach you that?'

'Is that where you died? And having died destroy in order to believe again?'

Which voice, he thought, which face? Because it wasn't Campbell who'd been at the trenches, but Dalton. The two faces merged again to show Dalton's only. What had been his thought? That it was Campbell who was some dead thing that had adopted the guise of the living?

'I couldn't save you this time, Harry.'

'I know that.'

The figure turned to go.

'Tell me. Who betrayed *me*? Were you my Judas, Dalton?'

'Harry. If Judas were not, Christ were an impossibility. Is it that both are necessary?'

'Your fight is not of men.'

Two mornings later Harry died in his cell with the guards who found him wondering why he was smiling.

In the parlour the open coffin rested on two pedestals. The house was silent and the blinds drawn. The children were staying with a neighbour for the night. In the early morning others would come to join her. She was alone. That was her wish.

She busied herself with tidying the room and arranging the flowers, ordinary household tasks. Upstairs she remade the beds, plumping pillows into shape, and then polished some silver pieces in the kitchen which had been wedding presents. Evening came, the time of his homecoming when she would listen for the sound of his footsteps in the street outside or the welcoming cries of the children as they ran to greet him. In the parlour once more she lit the fire, the kindling crackling and sparking. Sitting down she poked the coals as they burst into flame, all the while talking naturally, normally as she occasionally glanced at his face. What she said she did not know. Meaning was unimportant because, impossible to find, it could not be expressed. There was only sound which eddied back in wavelets from the walls of the room. Had she been trying to imitate his voice, she asked in one astounded moment, or had she really heard the echo of Harry's voice from the coffin? She paused to kiss him, kiss features that still held the marks of that last ebb of a broken spirit, and then started up because this was no living bed where she could embrace. Anger was hers, and bitterness, and a savage grief whose mutability threatened to rupture the umbilical cord of self and she would again pause to ask — who am I? For those gleaming threads leading down into that misty sea of non-self held her to multiple forms.

266

And so she danced. She was Marietta, Contessa, casket-girl, flower-girl. And, nimble-fingered, she put flowers around his head and body. Don't you remember, Harry? Remember the time you first tried to make love to me? I knew you would. In the Opera House I knew it. It burled in the air around us and made my breasts burn with their own heat. On the train to Larne singing. I knew it then too. Parakeets. Parakeets, I'm selling. I can still hear your voice. With the whole train laughing too. A wounded soldier home from the war. Yes. Home in the hope of love.

The candle at his head flickered and quietly she sat watching it. Home to what, Harry? What war is this that broke you? And the war between ourselves, between you as a man and I as a woman? What of that? The nights and days I lay or sat in silence wondering where you were, knowing what you were doing, sat or lay in silence listening to silence and the silence of my own grieving. And now a last silence for us. Our dream, Harry. Sweet mystery. Ah sweet mystery now I've lost thee. The old donkey was better at singing than you and now it's dead too. What have you done to me? What have you given me? The children too. I hate you. God how my heart hates you.

Kiiiyaaa kiiiyaaa scceeeheee scceeeheee I called pushing my breath and the wet warm flowers from my mouth into yours standing with my blouse on the grass and my breasts bare pushing too at your tunic and my thighs finding yours no Harry I took you yes it was me who took you not you me with that wildness scceeeheee kiiiyaaa and the spray on the rocks below leaping to us talking to us out of mystery sweet and bitter and though I hate you I want you now just as then and yes I'll dance for you like the birds winging dancing high on squally winds watching my love watch you who have no longer eyes to watch with see me dance as I call for the firmness of your body and spirit in mine find me come to me come scceeeheee kiiiyaaa kiiiyaaa . . .

And in the street outside neighbouring doors opened and people stood and stared at the house with the blinds drawn as they shook their heads in wonder, listening the while to the strange cries calling from eaves and sills and rooftops as though all the seabirds of the loughshore and the islands and windpitted cliffs had come to join in a ceremony of grief.

As she walked in a garden. It was the same. The same as she had always known it. Through the avenues of trees she gaily walked, solemnly walked, the tall heads above her crowned in sunlight whispering as they bowed to her presence. By the lilypond she knelt watching her own reflection in the gently rippling water, the buckled pleated skirt around her legs and against her skin the cool moistness of granite slabs. How peaceful. An eternity of peace. With one finger she spun a huge lily seeing the circular form of flower and leaves trace a kaleidoscope of colour in the air. The great hound appeared. Like a guardian it came to look at her, and then padded silently away to stand motionless between the tall trees. Yes. The Celtic cross would be further on, standing serenely, massively, in its own bower. She knew that. She had been here before. On tiptoe, arms outstretched, lightly she skipped along the path as though winging on air, the breeze dipping flowers a mosaic at her feet. And there it stood, arms thrust out from the intricately patterned circle. She knelt again, gazing upwards, its column aslant on the clouds making her feel dizzy. From an adjoining grove he came in greeting, slim, muscular, with that mass of dark shining hair she had so often patterned across her body as he slept. And his voice. Hearing his voice in the farmhouse as through the orchard she went running running running it is you . . .

'May.'
  'Harry?'
  'May.'
The hand was on her shoulder. She was lying face downwards on the floor with her knees and cheek against the coolness of the brass fender. A tiny glow of ash was all that remained of the fire, and the candle at the head of the coffin had gone out.
  'May.'
  'Dalton.'
  'It will soon be light. And others will be coming to sit the vigil with you.'
  'Yes.'
Weakly she stood and brushed her dress as Dalton lit candles which had been set previously at various corners of the room.
  'I was worried about you.'
She stared into the broad, handsome, inscrutable face, seeking for what she didn't know. 'Before you came . . . I was dreaming. If dream it was because it was so real. If it had not been for that . . . Do you remember when I was a girl? When you took me to . . .' She stopped suddenly. No. That was sacred. Sacred to herself and him. 'Dalton. Whatever Harry did he didn't deserve such a death as that.'
  'Tea, May.'
It was Anna, holding out cup and saucer.
  'I heard and came to be with you.'
Yes. It was right that Anna should be here. The woman she had befriended had come to befriend her. Numbness, exhaustion. Like an

automaton she awaited the morning light. Another figure stood in front of her, huge hands brushing her face. Mary Clurey, she who had brought their children into the world and whose soothing touch now held some mysterious balm. And another voice in the hall, David's. Tousle-haired, sad yet with a mischievous smile not quite over-shadowed by all the solemnity, pouring whiskey into her teacup from a bottle. 'Take this from the black sheep, May. You'll be in need of it before the day's out.' And with that entranced sense ebbing she heard the first birds begin to sing.

She was glad of the exhaustion, the numbness. All she had to do was to perform the ritualistic gestures. In the cemetery she found herself thinking of her father's funeral with Harry standing away from the family in a different part of the group. But that kind of thinking was too much of a strain and so she began to count the people around her. There were the children, Jim and Ruth. Anna, and there was Mary Clurey, Jack from the farm in Islandmagee with his wife Anne, and David with his tinker girl Norah, and faces she recognised to have been Harry's fellow journalists. And there was Dalton. No. Surprised, she studied the mourners. Where was Dalton? A yet different face intrigued her. Closeby stood a stranger, bowed shoulders enfolded by a homespun jacket, his face carrying that flush which came she knew from constant exposure to the seawinds. She reached out to touch his arm.

'Who are you?'

'Niall. I was an old friend of your husband. A childhood friend.'

She paused, wondering. 'Strange. He never mentioned you to me.'

'No.'

The thump and patter of earth upon wood. Last flowers from her hand plummetting into the gash as the gravediggers wielded their spades. She turned to the stranger again, in whose eyes she had seen tears. But he had gone.

'Home, May.'

Where was Dalton?

It was David's arms around her, earring glittering. 'Home, May. And we'll wake him well.'

Smiling wistfully, she nodded in agreement.

Afternoon was wearing into evening by the time the last of the mourners had departed, during which time the tall figure who stood outside the cemetery and partially hidden by a knot of trees remained motionless, simply watching as the gravediggers paused in their labour to loll on the grass, swilling beer as they exchanged ribald comments and speculations about the newly deceased. With the first raindrops they hastily completed their task and, cleaning spades with pieces of slate and slinging canvas sacks across shoulders, they too left. The air sifted slowly, humid, clammy, under a sultry sky. With the rain beating heavily he saw the sexton emerge from his cottage closeby the main entrance and, first surveying the walled enclosure, clang the gate shut and chain it. Still waiting, impervious to the elements, he watched the light in the cottage move from room to room before climbing over the wall and treading an irregular path through the gravestones.

There it was, the freshly turned earth seemingly gleaming. A wind thrust down from the hills to the east, and ceased again as the lowbellied sky pressed closer. In the lough below, lights flickered as a ship made seawards. Kneeling, oblivious to the mud and soil on his clothing, he bowed and pressed his forehead against the damp earth.

'Harry.'

Leaning back, one hand searched in a weighted pocket, withdrawing the revolver to stare at it as it too became wet and gleaming.

'Harry. You knew I could not save you this time. It was not within our power.'

It was his own way of leavetaking. He could not have been amongst the others, amongst those gestures which attempted to still anguish rather than allow its heightened savour. He'd understood May's lonely consummation of her grief and now this was his.

'Harry,' he said again, slipping the gun back into the pocket of his heavy overcoat, both hands now kneading the dark soil as though he were an animal digging into sanctuary. 'Harry.'

Laughter burst from the grave, braying. It stood there, a few feet away, the clown. From the matted beard a red nose stuck out. Bowler hat askew, cane in one hand, it was half-draped across a donkey which was heehawing furiously. In a wondering terror that had never before been his Dalton seized the apparition only to find solid flesh. The hat fell, as did nose and cane, and now in the tramp's features he sought to recognise. And did.

'Samuel. Samuel Ogilby.'

The other said nothing through laughing spittle dribbling.

'Yes, Samuel. Don't you remember that last time? The three of us. And what did he say? "Remember that time on Malin Head? Swift's philosopher? And what bloody ditch is this?" '

And what bloody ditch is this, thought Dalton, turning to the donkey to try to quieten it. No intestines hampered its feet now and there would be no gunshot. And what did rationality make of coincidence or chance but a logical impossibility which was always possible.

'And what would yous two be doin' here, eh? Dessicratin' the graves of them that's dearly beloved and departed? Graverobbers, are

270

yous? Git away till fuckin' hell's gates or I'll have the polis ontil yous both!'

Dalton turned. It was the gravekeeper, the sexton, a spade held high in one hand and holding a snarling bitch. Behind him the lights of the cottage shone in full.

'Didn't I tell yous till git till hell away or by God I'll brain both of yous! What's this? Some kind of oul' divil's rites ye read about in the papers? Them that's paid their respects till their dearly one have gone. An' I won't have them people under there snatched up by the likes of yous or molested wi'! For the last time git away till fuck or I'll have this oul' bitch ontil yous as well!'

Walking quickly along the path, leading Samuel and donkey, Dalton left the graveyard. Stopping in the middle of the road he looked back to where the sexton, still brandishing spade and snarling dog, again clanged the gate shut. Then he made towards the Shore Road to walk to Islandmagee.

Away yet another time, Sam, I can see you go, and now you've lost your clown's nose and your bowler and your cane that were all good spoils but your oul' ass is still with you as you make for the hills or God knows where. Not even graveyard or gravekeeper wants the likes of you, Sam.

Nous sommes à la recherche . . . Ach, Sam, Sam, Lieutenant Sam, Don Samuel, Shellshock Sam the Crazy Man the kids shout at you as you go by . . .

Slàinte . . .

XII

In the dusky water he saw the form. 'Aye, John. An' one fer you too.'
But no. It was not the Christmas Eve of 1899, but now. Blearyeyed, to
him the form looked the same.

'Ferrying?'

' 'Cross till what place?'

'To the island.'

'An' what oul' island would ye be looking fer, Inspector Gordon?'

'Just across there.'

'My whiskey's good, ye know. It's not contraband I'm drinking nor
ferrying.'

'I hope not.'

'Have ye a search warrent on ye? It's the best of oul' spirit I have.
But maybe not fer the likes of you.'

'It's not quite what I'm looking for.'

Ceasing his banter Alec Dick cupped one hand over the side of the
boat and splashed some water across his eyelids, feeling the whiskey-
enforced drowsiness clearing. On the lough surface the shadow
rippled, cast there by the moon. Turning, he stared at his would-be
passenger, at the shoes and overcoat to which mud and grass still
clung, the face and hands which were streaked black. Rarely had he
seen the other in civilian clothes, and never had he seen him like this.
'Well, as I've often ferried yer father I s'pose I'll ferry you too, Dalton
Gordon. But I'll tell ye what. I'm an old man now an' feeling it. This
time it's you that can ferry me.'

The boat rocked as the other stepped in and took the oars while he
changed places, the beamy craft being immediately pushed out from
the harbour wall. Twice Alec tried to engage his companion in talk
but gave up to watch the fierce methodical strokes as the oars were
plied and the set countenance which stared fixedly at the sky. Gravel
grating harshly, they arrived on the other shore. A coin was thrust
into his hand in silence and he was left to again watch as the other
strode up the slope and vanished over the lip of a hill.

'Well, Dalton Gordon. There was a time when I said that the day'll come when I'll see ye row yerself 'cross. An' that day's now. It's not what I'm looking fer, did ye say? Whativer it is ye're looking fer—or whativer person ye're looking fer which maybe's the more likely—I wouldn't like till be the one that has till meet wi' ye. Fer wi' that face on ye ye'd put the fear of God intil hell itself.'

Only now did he break his stride and at moments stop. On the long walk from the outskirts of the city to Larne he had forced his pace so that his shoes cracked and his feet began to bleed and cake with mud and glair. Now when he paused he could feel the pain seep through his ankles and calves and thighs. In the moondrenched landscape he noted every line and silhouette with a familiarity which had never left him even after long absence. Pausing at the Druid's Altar he looked towards the mainland where the glens stood against the stars. The stars, an old passion. The Plough, the Milky Way. Here the stars were myriad. Anna, a passion he'd never expected forcing aside the shield of self. Once in the lough below, the iron ladders of a prison ship rang with his own booted feet. May on the kitchen floor unconscious.

It was not yet midnight, a time when he knew that Jack would be doing the last round of the farm before bed. Approaching down the lane to the Hollow he saw him closing a gate against some cattle, the dog at his heel turning to bark at this new presence in the night. He felt his intensity begin to subside as the stocky figure placed a hand on his arm and a warm smile greeted him, the dog being shushed to silence.

'Dalton. It's good to see you. You're a rare one at home.'

'It may not be the visit you expect, Jack.'

'Oh?'

'I want to be in the farmhouse alone.'

'For how long?'

'Three days at most. I'll be gone again on the third evening.'

Jack stood musing and scratching his chin.

'And I want no questions.'

Beneath the bald crown the shrewd eyes glinted. 'I wasn't going to ask any, Dalton. I was just thinking.' He paused. 'Well, after today's affair. Harry's funeral, I mean, everyone's a bit upside down.'

'Who's with May?'

'Good company and enough of it. There's David and Norah. And that woman friend Anna. And another big woman who was midwife to her children, so she told me. We're only back a few hours ago. Anne and me.'

'And May herself?'

'As well as can be. But this other thing you mention. Those two women, Anne and our mother, have been ontil me for months to take them to town. And you know how I hate leaving the farm to stay in cities and hotels. But they're due their likings just as much as I am.'

'I don't want them to know I'm here. Mother especially.'

'They won't know. We'll be gone by the afternoon. I'll tell them it's a surprise that we're off till Belfast or Dublin for a week and with May's trouble and them wanting to go for months past they'll say yes without as much as thinking. I'll see the hands first thing in the morning and tell them the house isn't to be disturbed only that you might be down for a day or so. Just in case they catch sight of you and think somebody's in there that shouldn't be.'

'Thanks, Jack.'

'No thanks, brother. It was your home as well as mine and now it seems you're more'n need of it than me. But what'll you do the night?'

'I'll sleep in the barn.'

'Fair enough. I'll go back in. Anne'll still be up and I'll get her to start thinking about packing.'

Through a chink in the barn he could see the orchard and behind that the farmhouse where lights shone. He waited, standing motion-less, until they went out, then settled into a pile of straw, feet and calves steadily throbbing. A horse snuffled in a stabled corner acknowledging his presence. He sat with eyes open staring into the darkness. Night sounds came and went and then came the sounds of the farmyard fowl heralding morning. It was from this place that, years ago when he was a boy, he'd heard the lamentations of his father and his mind probed the space between then and now. He had come to refurbish in himself what he might.

Jack appeared and led the horse out, saying that in an hour they'd be gone. He listened to the clattering and swishing of trap and harness, watched as the luggage was secured and the women climbed in, absorbed in the tall form of his mother. Then the horse strained up the path towards the road.

All afternoon he prowled through the farmhouse going from room to room, sitting for a while in each. Only then did he bathe and change, the hot water gradually easing away the dried blood. In the evening he sat in the study drinking steadily, a pistol and whiskey bottles sitting on the desk. In here his father had sent the rifle spinning. You inherit the storm. Sleepless yet alert he again paced the house, pausing at various windows to gaze across the landscape over which the moon traversed its brilliant passage. On the sloping hills were dotted white blobs of sheep, cattle slowly lumbered in lower fields. In the orchard a ring of hares sat, so still it were as though they had been fixed to the earth. From object to object his gaze slowly moved. It would be his last time. This was a farewell. The boyhood home to which he had never really belonged now served him as a momentary retreat. In silence he had come to it from the womb, in silence he would go. The past lay not here, but was ever present in his own being.

His own being. Anna. He had not expected to meet her, had not expected that fierce yet tranquil sensuality within himself to be reciprocated by another. Yet she had come, giving as he gave, asking nothing, finding what they sought. Alone, he smiled.

Only once did he leave the farmhouse. Saddling a horse he cantered down to the shore at Brown's Bay, barely acknowledging those who greeted him in passing. Filled with a savage energy as in years before he spurred the animal back and forth across the sands and then dried it down. Pausing, his vision sharp, he noted the exact place where he had come upon Harry that evening when he'd gone out to look for him, noted the startled expression on the other's face as though he, Dalton, had irrupted into his thoughts to plumb their secrets. Intuitively he had understood Harry's inclinations even from the time of the argument at the Front about the Dublin executions, but had done and said nothing. There are many many different sides in war.

He would leave in the morning, the third day of his visit. Wrapped in a cloak of impenetrable self he sat gazing towards the stag's head which hung in the recess until the large eyes shone forth with the first streaks of the lightening sky. That would be his, would be the only thing he would take with him. In what arctic wastes had it once fought, had he not asked himself? 'And so, father, I was to inherit the storm. I did not understand you then. And no, Harry. Whatever you did you didn't deserve such a death as that.'

PART FOUR

I

The Riley tourer was waved down at the police roadblock on the Queen's Bridge but, the driver being immediately recognised by the officer in charge, was signalled to continue. As her companion accelerated Anna looked down to where the broad stretch of the Lagan began to open out to Belfast Lough and the sea. Clusters of ships lay alongside, the seamen and dockers diminutive from her vantage point, while other vessels were manoeuvring into the shipping lanes. Soon they were driving eastwards out of the city, passing narrow cramped streets where men lounged and women haggled outside the numerous pubs and pawnshops. They stared at the car as it went by and in return Anna eyed the women, lumpy, slovenly dressed, with little trace of sympathy. At a corner a youth deliberately stepped out in front of the vehicle causing the driver to brake hard and exclaim—'Stupid little bastard!' Amused at this pathetic act of rebellion on the boy's part, Anna became thoughtful again as puffs of smoke drifted across the lough followed by dull booming sounds. Obviously the riots in the western part of the city were continuing. Adjusting her scarf she noticed that the district had changed to one of a more residential air and soon the spacious avenue leading to Stormont showed on the left with the Parliament building itself serene and grand as it stood high on a hillside.

'Not too cold?'

'Not at all.' Anna wound the window down a little further, feeling the warm autumn air fan her face. 'It's good to get away from the dust of the city for a while.'

Her companion nodded. 'I agree. You were born in County Down, you told me?'

'Like yourself, yes. And I spent most of my childhood and girlhood here. But I return to it without nostalgia.'

'You're a strange woman.'

'Oh?'

'For one thing, I don't understand why you don't marry. It can't be for lack of opportunity.'

'Simply because I like my independence. And I've money, or enough money, to enjoy it.'

'In such a provincial city?'

'Oh? So you classify yourself as a provincial?' Anna asked, and watched him frown.

'You know what I mean.'

'No. I don't know what you mean. No more than I know what other people mean when they say I should know what they mean. Provincial? Is London less provincial? Paris?'

'But there's a different feeling, isn't there? Of being in a wider world. Of being closer to the hub of things. Of having more opportunities, scope.'

'Perhaps for the very few. But for most people it's probably an illusion. I'd rather live without illusions. Or, if I indulge in some, recognise them for what they are. As for the very few. When I think of them I picture a little coterie at court making terribly important decisions which no one's interested in because no one can change them. Which for me would be very boring.'

'That makes democracy sound like the life of a salon.'

'And what else is it but that? For many people democracy's simply various degrees of despair. Would you call those streets we've driven through *democracy*?'

'So you're a Socialist?'

'Any convenient label can stifle an argument. Can't you think of something better?'

'They're free to do whatever they want.'

'Like doing what we're doing now? Driving their touring cars to their estates in the country?' The incongruity of the picture created by her words made her laugh, and again she saw him frown. 'After all, think of that boy who stepped off the pavement in front of us.'

'I could easily have knocked the stupid fool down.'

'Obviously he did it deliberately. Didn't you notice the hatred on his face?'

His voice was heavy with irony. 'A martyr.'

'Just a protest. A protest which says that we're in this car because of birth and inheritance and he isn't because he hasn't inherited anything. And if there's anything intrinsically superior about any of us it has yet to be proved. Intuitively that boy understood even if he couldn't think in those terms.'

'Do you usually romanticise the working class?'

'Good heavens, no. I leave that to the middle-class intellectuals who write about them. As a class I despise them only a little less than I despise other classes.' Anna paused. 'But let's leave this provincial talk aside and play at being metropolitans. Now that Hitler's in power in Germany do you think another European war is inevitable? After all, it seems that the drums have started up already. And what about India? If it does manage to break away and become independent do you think the Empire will collapse? Or what will happen in dear old Ulster now that rioting has started yet again?' The mockery in her voice was having its effect, she thought, noticing the other's face lose its urbane look and become sullen and sneering. Chameleonic, her own expression changed as she pointed ahead to where a sign protruded from a clump of trees. 'There's a pub. Shall we try it?'

Once the car was parked at the side of the low whitewashed building she allowed him to take her hand as she got out and walked in front of him, aware that he was watching her movements and deliberately emphasising her loping masculine gait, the sway of her body. In the dim darkbeamed interior a few farmworkers sat at the bar. Choosing a seat close to the fire, she leaned back with one hand thrust into the pocket of her open coat while the other toyed with a slender silver chain which lay against her tight silk blouse. Another chain, holding a heavy locket, fell to her waist. He was at the bar ordering drinks and sandwiches and again she was fully conscious that he was covertly watching her. Christopher Campbell. She'd met him nearly two years ago, though since then had only been in his company about a dozen times, and always with others. One of those times Dalton had been there also, and immediately she'd sensed a latent antagonism between these two men who were nominally in much the same profession. Certainly Christopher showed it if Dalton didn't. And this was the first time she'd accepted one of Christopher's many invitations, this one being to visit his family home.

'It seems we'll have to wait until they've baked the bread.'

Anna smiled. 'Oh, I doubt if it's as bad as that.' She paused. 'But do you think there'll be another war in Europe? Dalton thinks so. Though it doesn't seem to perturb him much. But then, nothing ever does.'

'Dalton?'

'District Inspector Gordon.'

'Ah, yes. Inspector Gordon.'

His lips were thin and tight, Anna noticed, and his mouth curved downwards at the corners. But analysis of his mood evaded her.

'No doubt he could judge the situation best.'

'Because he fought in the trenches in France? Perhaps you're right.' Musing, she moistened her upper lip with the tip of her tongue. 'I don't believe you were in the war in Europe. Only here in Ireland?'

'Something like that.'

He didn't like the way the conversation was going, she knew, watching him as he went to the bar a second time. In playing with him she found more than amusement. There was the thrill of danger. That was what had at first fascinated her yet made her keep her distance. Dalton. With Dalton she could truthfully say she felt awe. Since becoming lovers he had unleashed within her emotions she'd never known she possessed. And it was all so natural. And in Dalton there was a depth leading to what region she could neither name nor imagine. With this man it was there also, but was somehow less. With him she would ultimately feel only fear, a sinister fear.

'And how were your visits to the various metropolises?'

'Interesting.' Biting into her sandwich she pouted. 'It amuses me to chatter as I did in the car. Being able to travel when and where I please undoubtedly makes this provincial place more than tolerable.'

'Though at times one needs to be careful of what one chatters about. I'm sure you're much too good a businesswoman not to know that.'

'You're right, of course. Fashion is like any other business and one must be shrewd. Chatter is kept for the inconsequentials.'

She thought she'd shown ignorance of his covert threat but when his eyes suddenly gleamed at her last remark she found herself unsure of her own judgement and how he had interpreted her words. He was an interrogator in the best manner, or worst. Allowing him to guide the conversation she talked of her recent trips abroad, not failing to notice the note of triumph as though he felt he had indeed made her bow to his will.

They continued the drive, taking the road that hugged the east side of Strangford Lough where nests of islands broke the surface like backs of whales. Turning deeper into the Ards peninsula the sea could be seen on the other side, a dark band stitched to a white sky which swept against the bluish range of the Mourne mountains. Woodsmoke drifted in the air from smouldering mounds of brush and grass and leaves that sealed the fate of another summer. Another summer. As conversation had lapsed she allowed her thoughts to wander. It was now 1936. She was in her thirtieth year. Dalton came to mind again and the house he owned on the heights at Ballysillan overlooking the city, each corner of which she now knew intimately. When had it begun? It was she who had initiated the relationship, not expecting to find an indomitable engulfing passion. Had she had the gift of foresight would she have started it at all? Yes. Because rather than lessening her independence it strengthened it. Had it been there in the early months? She'd tried to give herself to him because he'd helped her, seeing in him only a lonely man whose work was everything to him. And then enveloping them both had come that intensity. But when had *then* been? Fragmentary scenes curled with the woodsmoke. Had it been after May's first husband had died? She recalled May remarking on Dalton's absence. And neither had seen him for several months afterwards though, of course, May knew nothing of what lay between them. Or if she suspected she didn't say, as May's judgement of her brother's bachelor nature seemed fixed. May's first husband whose death seemingly held traces of mystery. A sudden violently debilitating illness originating from wounds received years before at the Somme. There was nothing strange about that. Thousands of men had returned from the trenches to die in a like manner. One could still see them, cripples, the shellshocked, begging, wandering through a hopeless existence towards an equally hopeless end. A political correspondent of sound repute and a blossoming writer, some of the obituaries had said. And yet where had she heard the rumour that his political activities . . . Glancing quickly at her companion she again turned her head to study the fields, baffled. May. May who had married a second time but whom she now rarely saw. Their paths in life had parted another time.

'We're here.'

The double gates were open when they arrived and sped along the drive lined with lime trees and clumps of fuchsia, behind which were small woods. From the gatelodge Anna noticed a plume of smoke, and at one window an elderly woman with white hair. Curving round the side of a broad lawn the car stopped, its tyres scraping loudly on the gravel. A long, lean man dressed in shabby tweeds was descending the steps. As she got out Anna saw the neat rows of shrubs, a blob of light some distance away which was an ornamental lake, the profusion of ivy clinging to the front wall of the main building. Yet for all its apparent neatness at first glance, a second took in the suggestion of decay with the stealthily encroaching vegetation that showed in tufts of wiry grass among the gravel and trailing branches of shrub that gave an irregular line to the borders. A stillness reigned, seemingly held there by the solid though distant face of the mountains. In that moment's pause she watched a large hare cross the lawn, poising motionless with long ears directed toward the wood whence came a crack like a muffled pistol shot followed by a soft flopping sound, obviously a rotten branch finally succumbing to the weight of time. Somehow it suited, she thought, watching as the hare continued its passage, unperturbed by the human figures not far away.

'It's good to see you, sir. I've set the fire in the big room.'

'You needn't have bothered, Lylly. We shan't be staying long. Only an hour or so.'

'Even so, sir, it's good to see you.' Turning, he raised his hat. 'And the lady. I thought it might take the chill out of the air. There's little heat now the year's on the turn.'

His face, Anna noted, was etched not so much by hard work as by boredom brought about by knowledge of an empty life. In the sunlight filtering through the trees his was a gaunt figure, thinfaced, the largejointed fingers awkwardly toying with a heavy bunch of keys on an iron ring. 'That was kind of you. The house is bound to be chilly with it standing empty.'

Responding to the pleasantness in her voice he tilted his head slightly but spoke to his master. 'Shall you be eating, sir? When we knew you were coming Mrs Lylly got some things in. Some fine lobster straight off a boat at Portaferry this morning. And I've got some game hanging . . .'

Christopher turned away to look at the mountains. 'I don't think so, Lylly. We'll be dining on the way back to town.' Pausing, he looked towards Anna. 'Or perhaps, if . . .'

A whitehaired face at the window came to her mind, the thought of a useless existence. 'Not too much. A little lobster? One can't really refuse fresh lobster.' Smiling, she noticed a slight ripple of emotion pass across the servant's face before he again lifted his hat to her and walked quickly down the drive.

The house, really a fortified manor in original conception, still raised a few conical turrets and battlements towards the sky. Many of the rooms were shut off completely, the few remaining furnishings in others adding a spectral touch. In several places there were signs of work having been started in reshaping the interior and then abandoned. And at one side of the ground floor a new wing, date of construction uncertain, had been left half-finished. Now the only part which showed signs of habitation was the great drawing room leading from between the double staircase and a few adjoining rooms which seemed to be studies and bedrooms. From the upper storeys the view commanded the lough and undulating countryside with neat fields enclosing farmbuildings, cottages and cattle. In the basement she found yet another library, a snooker room, a children's playroom where toys were stacked in corners and a rocking-horse with one leg missing sat in the centre in melancholy isolation. There was a gunroom with trophies and glassfronted cases and yet another which housed fishing tackle and a small dinghy.

Putting her hand on another door handle Anna paused, then turned back the way she had come. Lifting a racquet from a corner and looking out towards a tennis court and what might have been a croquet pitch, she said: 'There's so much of it.'

Her companion did not reply but stood looking at her intently, and she turned away wondering why he had brought her here.

Silently they entered the drawing-room where logs hissed and crackled in the enormous grate but hadn't yet dispelled the damp

284

damp air which was a common property of the whole. Accepting a drink, she continued to walk round inspecting the pictures: family portraits, scenes of war and military campaigns stretching back centuries, exotic Eastern temples and dawns breaking over farflung lands. In one corner above a writing-bureau a line of faded photographs told of the demise of two gigantic crocodiles surrounded by natives and men in bush hats, the natives having jammed open the jaws of the reptiles.

'Well?'

Eyes slitted, back to the fire with a whiskey tumbler clasped in one hand, he stood watching her. She turned to face him, glimpsing a likeness showing in many of the portraits but which was now without vigour, bland. If there was anything to be detected in that face it seemed to be a nondescript cruelty which could at moments be tangible, reaching out to make her feel cold yet clammy. 'Well?' She sipped her drink, suddenly anxious as to why he had invited her here. 'What is the stock response?'

'I'm not asking for that. Besides, as no one sees the place there isn't one.'

'Then I'm honoured,' Anna said, disturbed by this anxiety which was not usual to her nature. 'The family?'

'London. Some abroad. What's left of them.' He turned to look into the fire, a long thin scar showing on his throat where the silk cravat had slipped. 'But you haven't answered my question.'

'Because I truthfully don't know how to. Except that perhaps it certainly captures history.'

'Ah, yes. History.'

She was relieved by the entrance of the Lyllys bearing trays and a wine bucket. Yes, history. Dust and damp and the limp bedraggled banners of a once glorious future now a nest for spiders and other creatures of the dark. The pink flesh of the lobster among the greens of the salad gleaming brightly from the silver. The wine was poured, more logs from a wicker basket in a side recess of the chimney tossed onto the fire, and they were alone again.

Shredding the flesh, he asked: 'And you?'

'Surely with your intelligence you already know.' As he kept looking at her without comment, she continued: 'Oh, my father was one of the nineteenth-century *nouveaux riches* who had a great appetite for everything. Particularly women. Probably vulgar by some standards, certainly shrewd by any. Strongwilled, determined. And on my mother's side there was probably more than a touch of the Ascendency. But she died when I was very young.'

'Like his daughter?'

'The vulgarity?' she laughed quickly, trying to break his gaze.

285

'No. Strongwilled with a great appetite.'

'How was the war?' she asked, sipping the champagne. 'Or rather. Your war, as any war seems quite different depending on the individual concerned.'

'I enjoyed it. And still do. Tell me, what do you think of Inspector Gordon?'

'Think? Nothing. It's difficult to know what to think of such a man.'

'You seem to have few answers.'

Which is quite unlike me, Anna thought, knowing that she had failed to break the hypnotic stare. 'Only chatter. As I told you.'

'Your feelings, then.'

'Fear, perhaps.'

Resting his arm lightly on her shoulder and toying with the long silver chain, he asked: 'Fear?'

'In terms of respect, I mean.'

His lips rested lightly on hers, then more fully. Her blouse was open, his fingers caressing the silk of her underclothing. Unaroused, she saw the dull sheen of her breasts in the gathering dusk of the room, his drawn lips bending towards them, the grey ash tumbling from the fire into the spacious hearth. The strong dark colouring of her nipple held her gaze momentarily, bringing a slight tremor of emotion. Pushing him away she stood up, arranging her clothing.

'No?'

She shook her head. 'No.'

Contrary feelings swayed her, one triumphant, the other simply a desire to run. The former won, though didn't quite obliterate the latter as she watched him stand in the centre of the huge room which, in the greyish light, made almost a shadow of his presence. Slipping her coat over her shoulders she walked to the window. It was raining now, a murky evening that heightened the damp cold of the house. She shivered. 'Shall we go?'

On the way out she asked him to stop at the gatelodge where she thanked the Lyllys. Pausing at the double gates she looked back but now the house was featureless, showing only a brooding mass constantly slipping through the heavy veil of mist and rain, nameless and alien. Tyres swishing on the rainsoaked roadway, she talked lightly of her business travels, feeling herself become more buoyant in mood. Approaching the city he turned down a narrow lane leading to an inn. Over dinner she increasingly closed him out, sensing her will return as though it had been forced into abeyance and making no attempt to conceal that her attention was more drawn to a slim auburn-haired girl at a table in the opposite corner.

II

The tall stooping whitehaired figure stood hesitantly in the doorway. 'I don't mean to disturb you, sir . . .'

'Please come in, sergeant.'

'It's just that . . . Well sir, as you're so kind to call in and see me when you're along the Antrim coast I thought that this time I'm in town I'd make a courtesy call.'

'Come in, sergeant. And do sit down.'

'Thank you, sir.' Gently closing the door Duncan McKinzie crossed the room and sat down, hat nervously held in his lap, looking almost reverently into the face of the man behind the desk who, unlike himself, apparently hadn't aged a day in all the years he'd known him. Even though the other was younger, he thought, the face should show some lines of middle age. But there were none.

'And what brings you into the city, sergeant?'

'My daughter, sir. She's hoping to go to the university. To be a doctor. That's all she's ever wanted to do since she was a wee girl. And we've scrimped and saved to get her the education.' Duncan paused, at once both bashful and proud. 'She was born just before that last retreat from the Somme. In 1918. Don't you remember, sir?'

'I remember it well.'

'We were certainly hammered then, sir. But it wasn't the first time.' Fumbling in his pocket, he asked: 'D'you mind if I have a pipe, sir?'

'Of course not.'

'A fine strapping young woman she is now, sir. And nearly as tall as the last lad, Ned, used to be.'

'I am very pleased for you, sergeant.'

'I knew you would be, sir. That's why I thought I'd call in. It must be years since I've been in the city. I always thought there was some strong feeling between us, sir. If you don't mind my saying so. That had nothing to do with rank.'

'You were the best sergeant I ever had. I could not have expected a better one.'

Face flushed. Duncan pulled on his pipe. 'Thank you, sir.'

'And your retirement? Are you still enjoying it?'

'Yes. It was a good thing I retired when I did. And it was at your suggestion, sir. These years for me have been ones of peace. Watching the wee girl grow up and tending the sheep that I've a good hand at. It was your doing. Thank you, sir.'

Dalton waited, saying nothing.

'But not peace for the land with more riots and shootings and whatever. Catholic and Protestant. Protestant and Catholic. And I sometimes wonder whether it's anything to do with the churches at all. Not that some of them in the churches and lodges aren't involved. And now I hear the city's under curfew.'

'Parts of it, sergeant. Not all.'

Again Dalton waited as the other lapsed into silence and puffed smoke into the air. Obviously he wished to talk.

'Did you ever hear anything else about Lieutenant Ogilby, sir?'

'He never recovered.'

'I remember wondering that at the time. On the train that took us to Belgium.'

And again there was a pause.

'And Lieutenant McKinstry died, sir?'

'Yes, sergeant. Of old wounds.'

'Aye. Of old wounds. He got fairly knocked about. I used to read his writings in the papers. Even though I sometimes didn't understand quite what he was saying.'

'He was a good man.'

'That's what I thought too. And there's somebody been asking about him. And about yourself, sir.' Looking at the stern composed features and gaining no response, Duncan continued: 'At first I thought he was a stranger. It happened when I was down in Glenarm for a pint one evening. McKinstry's name came up in conversation. And yours too, sir. But there was something familiar about him. And then I remembered who he was.'

'Who?'

'Intelligence, sir. Though I don't know his name.'

'What did he want?'

'I don't rightly know, sir. He was just asking about this and that. I thought he was just doing his usual job because these troubles had started up again, and then McKinstry's name and your name came up just because he happened to fall into talk with me. We were talking about the war, sir. About what it was like in the trenches. It's a thing I don't talk about at all and it surprised even myself. But then he had such a way with him like he'd even get a stone to talk. And then another name came up.'

288

'What name?'

'A Niall McNeill, sir. Whoever he might be.'

'Not one that I know myself, sergeant.'

'Yes. And then I remembered who he was. He was the Intelligence man from the army who came to see me after I was brought back from Ballyshannon that time when the civil war in the south was on.'

Dalton nodded. 'Yes. I know him.'

'I just thought you might have liked the information, sir,' McKinzie said, his voice again hesitant.

'As I said. You were the best sergeant I ever had. And as we both know of old, any information can be valuable.' Dalton paused. 'And as you no doubt deduced correctly, it has more to do with these recent riots in the city.'

'D'you think they'll come to anything? Get worse, I mean?'

'I shouldn't think so. They'll pass over. Like many others. And if it is the Republican movement you're thinking of, I do not think there can be any threat. De Valera in the south has proscribed the IRA as illegal and imprisoned the Chief of Staff. They have enough to think about across the border.'

'What do you think of De Valera, sir?'

'What do you think, sergeant?'

Penetrating the quietness of the room came sounds from the barrack yard. It could not be. In all the years of their comradeship at arms this was the first time that Inspector Gordon had asked him what he thought. About political things, that was. About things that were happening outside the field. And it was because they were old comrades, because they'd known so much. His heart warmed, despite old wounds and old tears. If only he were young again he would follow this man anywhere. As he had done before. 'I don't know what to think. And you, sir?'

'That he is an astute man. Neither the fool nor evil man some are inclined to think. But with others I may have to speak differently.'

'I understand, sir.'

Rising, Dalton paced the room to stop and stare at a blank wall. 'The name was Niall McNeill?'

'Yes.'

'As for De Valera again. He is too much interested in trying to break ties with the Crown and thinking of what will happen to the Free State in another European war.'

'Germany again, sir?'

But there was no reply.

'Do you believe in evil, sir?'

'It is one possibility among others. But from where it comes often one does not know.' Dalton turned. 'And we are a small country, sergeant. Divided or not.'

The authority in the other's voice was of that old unmistakability heard in mud and slime, and he stood up. 'I must go now, sir.'

'Where, sergeant?'

'Home.'

'I shall drive you. Or rather, my driver shall. We have to test out a new car.'

Confused, McKinzie paused. 'That was a funny feeling I had about him, sir. When we were talking. That his home doesn't lie here.'

'Where are you meeting your daughter?'

'Outside the university, sir. After her interview.'

Crossing the barrack yard he was proud and young even though the reflection in the windows was whitehaired and stumbling. Aubrey, Ned, O my sons that I have outlived you. Low, with a long wheelbase, the black limousine sat in front of them.

'Sherrin!'

'Sir.' An oily face appeared from under the back axle and then Sherrin stood up.

Dalton introduced. 'Sergeant McKinzie. Constable Sherrin.'

'Ex-sergeant,' McKinzie said softly, smiling at the young man's consternation as he scrambled for his peaked hat. 'Maybe I'm old now, but I think I used to know a car with a shape like that. What is it?'

'Citroën, sergeant. French. With her engine well tuned and those wheels on her she'll hold the ground till anything.'

Duncan smiled at the enthusiasm in the young man's voice. 'I'm sure she will, constable.'

With Dalton and Duncan in the rear seat the car crossed the city, collected the girl outside the university, then retraced the route, travelling northward through Larne to McKinzie's home on the Antrim coast. Though listening to the conversation between father and daughter and commenting when appropriate, Dalton was thinking about other matters. Yes, he knew the person McKinzie had been talking about. Christopher Campbell. And Campbell wasn't being too intelligent, he thought, recalling how Anna had mentioned that she had been questioned about the same subject. Himself. But as with the sergeant he had made it appear that he considered the affair of no importance. She had shuddered when speaking of Campbell and pulled a wry face, the first time he'd known her to be perplexed by another's personality. And yes, he also knew who Niall McNeill was even though he'd disavowed it to McKinzie. But the true core of the Republican movement was of little importance now that it had been defeated yet again on both sides of the border. Perhaps it would emerge in another generation, but that was for the future. The riots which were occurring in various parts of the city were by the mindless who, trapped inside their own fears and frustrations, were willing accomplices of power-seekers, petty or otherwise. But Campbell was of quite a different kind, and liked to have trouble within which to work. And his activities were becoming known to others, as recently he'd heard comments even from Sherrin who was more cut out to be a chauffeur than a policeman. With deliberate concentration he brought every detail of Harry's tortured features to mind and felt his body flex then relax again as the image was dismissed.

The road was running parallel to the sea now and as he looked across the billowy surface his decision had been reached. A message must be taken to McNeill. But by whom? He could not involve either Sherrin or McKinzie or any other member of the Force, nor was there any petty informer he would trust with this. Several names were considered and discarded. Drawn by McKinzie's words he nodded and agreed as the former spoke of the days preceding their leaving for the war in France. He was standing in the study, arrested by the face of authority which had replaced the tremulous features of an old man. What should he have said when asked about his beliefs? In good and evil, father, and not in the questionable morality of war and politics. But had his father not already known?

Duncan laughed heartily, the merry eyes of his daughter turned towards him. 'And there he was, dear. Nearly charged with stealing a train.'

Dalton looked at him. 'Who?'

'David. Your brother David as a boy. Don't you remember, sir?'

What might have been a smile fleetingly curved Dalton's mouth. Of course. 'Yes, sergeant. I remember.'

Indicating where Sherrin should stop, Duncan said: 'I suppose you won't come in, sir, even though I'd like you to?'

'There isn't time, sergeant. I have other business.'

'I understand, sir. And thank you for the drive home.'

Watching the two figures walk up the lane towards the farmhouse, Sherrin asked: 'Where now, sir?'

'To the barracks in Larne. I shall only be a few minutes. And then back to the city. But stop at Greencastle before we reach town. And on the way back take the car over the narrow roads in the hills. I have still to see what it can do and if you know your business.'

'Sir.'

Some thirty minutes later Dalton was again seated in the rear, a sealed envelope in his pocket, as the car sped along hilly pitted roads with Sherrin taking the most difficult bends and corners with ease and skill. Arriving at Greencastle on the northern outskirts of the city the car dropped from speed to a smooth stop.

'Well, sir?'

'Quite good, Sherrin. But I suggest more practice. Wait here.'

Enquiring of Norah as to David's whereabouts he walked towards the shore, passing huddled cottages and small boats lying on patches of sand and spiky grass, and approached a group of men sitting on a broad seawall.

'Jesus fuck, it's the peelers!' exclaimed one, a tiny figure by the name of Long John.

'So what the hell are you getting excited about?' asked David, looking towards the uniformed figure without at first recognising who it was. 'There's no law in the country that says a man can't have a game of cards with his friends, is there?'

'David.'

'Oh, it's you.' Seeing Dalton turn and walk away, David paused for a moment before slipping off the wall and following. Falling into step, he said: 'Next time you come calling why don't you arrive in full dress uniform with a squad at your heels. Then you'll frighten everybody so much they'll jump intil the lough and drown themselves.'

'Are you working?'

'Working? How can a man work when all you hear about is unemployment? But yes. I found a few jobs and walked out of each one. I wasn't born to be anybody's factory donkey or foureyed penpusher. But you've hardly come here to ask me about work.' Feeling something being pushed into his hand David opened the ten-pound note and stared at it. 'Nor did you come to give me this either. You're hardly likely to wander round the countryside handing out tenners to the public.'

Alone now on the shore, shingle crackling underfoot, Dalton stopped and held out the envelope. 'You will go to Ballycastle. This evening if there's a bus or train available. If not, then first thing in the morning. Find a man called Niall McNeill. Remember the name. Niall McNeill. It's a small place so you won't have any problem. Give him this. Then return here and forget all about it. All right?'

David slipped the envelope into his pocket. 'For you, yes. But for any ordinary peeler I wouldn't.'

'Good.'

'And I've been offered another job. Selling motor cars. But I've a feeling something shady might be going on. So if I'm nabbed you can say a good word for me to the magistrate.' As Dalton was already walking away, he called: 'But I don't suppose you would. You're so bloody straight you're a pair of parallel lines all by your bloody self.'

Returning to the company David was greeted inquisitively by Long

292

John. 'Who the fuck was that?'

'Who the hell do you think? A long-lost brother come till tell me about a skeleton in the family cupboard that'll be the talk of the whole of Ireland including Greencockle if it manages to rattle its way out into public. So you keep your fuckin' snout out of them oul' skeletons' private affairs.'

III

She was pregnant again. In the short winter days she would often sit
dreamily by the fire, conscious only of her body and moods changing
with the new life being formed inside her. Then the bells chimed and
tolled, ushering in yet another year. 1937. When spring came she
escaped from the confines of the city and walked heavy and weighted
on the lower slopes of the Cave Hill, through the bluebell woods and
the clusters of crocuses and wild primroses. The trees were leafing to
life too and the birds already spying out nesting-places. This time,
would it be a boy or a girl? This time. This time, it was the same and
yet new. It was an experience she had already known and yet it was
always new. But there was another reason apart from the physical act
of childbearing. This child was by a different man. It was not Harry's
child but that of her second husband, Patrick.

He had come down the street knocking on doors asking where he
might find lodgings. So unlike the other one. A big man, soft-spoken
and, she was later to learn, so very gentle. Shyly he stood in the
doorway dressed in a dark suit and winter overcoat with beads of rain
shining on his high crown. A hat was held in one hand and in the other
a small suitcase containing his working clothes and a few other
belongings. Invited in he sat awkwardly by the fire, the cup and
saucer looking so tiny in his large strong hands. He was a labourer on
a building-site. He liked that as it meant he was working out of doors
most of the time. He didn't like to be shut in. Like herself he had been
brought up in the country, a place in the glens of Antrim. Reluctant to
send him out into the rainy night, she arranged a spare bedroom. A
week passed and he was still in the house and only then did it seem she
began to think. Payment from lodgings would mean that the constant
worry about money would be relieved. Since Harry's death she had
gone to work in menial tasks, cleaning in the houses of the more
prosperous and occasionally in a hospital which helped to eke out the
small sum she received from an investment Harry had made while a
journalist. Returning from such in moods of pride and shame, her

thoughts often turned to the days of her girlhood, days of freedom yet wasted days, when everything was in abundance and penury did not and could not exist. If only she had had the foresight to develop whatever talents she possessed. But what could she do now, a woman approaching middle age with children and in such an economic clime that even able-bodied men couldn't find decent employment. Only Dalton understood both her circumstances and her pride, and neither mentioned the sums he discreetly left on the mantelpiece when he called. Perhaps Jack did also as she was regularly invited to Islandmagee, the letters arriving each month from his wife Anne.

Islandmagee. She went there for the children's sake, she told herself, and as time went on found this to be true. It became a penance for her almost, the sights, sounds, the scents and smells of land and sea, the memories, the warm domestic scene of the farmhouse mirroring that from which she had been sundered. But there were the children to think of, who loved it all, and so she went for their sakes. And there were other practical reasons, to get away from the violence of the streets which she loathed and which would erupt without reason. Then she would sit by the fire during periods of curfew, worrying about Jim who in his daredevil merriment liked nothing better than to explain how he'd slipped through the darkened cor doned streets without the soldiers or police even knowing he was there.

Jim. How like Harry in temperament—quick, highspirited, and so difficult to chastise because he never took it seriously. And now as she walked through the bluebell woods her firstborn was leaving her. He was going to sea as a captain's 'tiger'. And she'd laughed at his audacity when he explained how he had obtained the job, simply by finding a captain at the docks and talking him into taking him to sea as his personal cabin-boy. He'd be running all over the ship doing every kind of job, Jim had explained, and would see the whole world. And when he came back he'd know everything there was to know about a ship and might one day be a captain himself. Yes, he'd inherited that gift of Harry's also, the ability to charm a bird from the proverbial bush. Even though having decided to let him go, she'd nevertheless asked Patrick's advice, who agreed. For a boy the sea seemed a better prospect than anything to be found in the streets of the city.

Sitting on a knoll to ease her swollen figure she watched the ships in the lough making for harbour or for the open ocean. Soon he would be leaving her and soon another would come to her, perhaps also a boy. After Harry's death she had withdrawn even further into the small family circle of herself and the two children. Her visitors were few but welcome: Mary Clurey who called regularly; Anna who called seldom; David who would call every day for a week and then disappear for months; Dalton. Of the neighbours only one couple had she become in any way intimate with, the Hopkins. But they had left the city having inherited a small farm in Antrim not far from Lough Neagh.

When she had first agreed to Patrick lodging with her she had found herself irritated by his presence, as it seemed to her he was both there and not there, so quiet was his manner. In summer evenings he'd go walking with her or go rambling by himself in the hills above the city. In winter he'd sit engrossed in reading. It was what he'd done during the dark nights in the glens, he said, when growing up with an elderly grandmother. In this one aspect regarding books he and Harry were alike, she thought, yet in all others so different. But in these matters of intimacy neither questioned the other, she as to his parents, he as to her late husband. It was sufficient to know that they were dead.

One habit of his at first irked and then amused her. Promptly on the half hour before closing time he would leave the house for his one pint of Guinness and noggin of whiskey and would return with some little presents for her and the children: chocolates, or flowers, or shellfish from the boys with heavy baskets who shouted their wares through streets and public houses, cockles, winkles, crab, lobster, oysters. The children loved him for that and on hearing his footfall would rush to the landing to see what he'd brought them. And later May discovered that they simply loved him for himself. In a way he was not unlike a child and it also amused her to watch this big ungainly man on the kitchen floor playing at whatever the children wished to play at. On sunny days he would be in the playground with Ruth or kicking a football with Jim, on wintry days fashioning a toboggan and waiting for snow so that he could play at being the reindeer. Unknown to her, her second wooing had begun.

The first proposal came after he'd been in the house for nearly a year and, surprised, she rejected it without thinking. When he quietly persisted she laughed at him. Alone, she admitted to herself that the subject alarmed her because it threatened to awaken feelings and desires she would like to believe had gone for ever. But of course they had not. She was still a young woman just entering her thirty-fifth year and there was that other prospect which lay before her, one which comprised little but loneliness. And, in the circumscribed life which had partly been forced upon her and partly chosen, could she ever expect another suitor to appear? Discussing it with him she pointed out, where he was concerned, the drawbacks: that he was nearly six years her junior, that he would have to take care of another man's children, even that perhaps her first marriage had marred her and she didn't know if she could love him the way he would want her to, and that in a place where both knew how religious differences could cause so much wrong and heartbreak they had to acknowledge they were of separate faiths. But, he replied, there were only two things that needed considering in all this. One concerned the children and she could see that they already loved him like a father. The second concerned herself and her love and for that he would wait.

Marrying one bright frosty morning in a little chapel of his own choosing, they returned to the house as if nothing had happened. She cooked a light meal while he poured drinks for them both and then returned to work for the afternoon at the building site. And it was months later before she came to him in the marital bed, during which time he quietly waited and offered no word of remonstrance.

And now it was another self and another family. The thick, muscular arms of Mary Clurey held the child out, saying that it was another boy. He was perfect in every detail, she said, except for one thing. The lip is crooked. But that's little wrong, dear.

Smiling as the child was placed on the pillow beside her, May kissed the strangely shaped mouth. 'His name is to be Colm. It is Patrick's wish. I believe in Irish it means "*the dove*".'

War. Again war. Just after Colm's second birthday she read the headlines in the newspapers and the Prime Minister's speech. There was again war in Europe. Britain had declared war on Germany. Germany which was devouring other people's countries one by one.

War once more. She'd heard it talked of, rumoured. But she didn't want to listen, tried to push the thoughts away. She had known it all before. And having known it all before she, a woman in her fortieth year, should be prepared. But she wasn't. The tremors in her being spread back across the years and confused her. Nightly she talked to Patrick who tried to console her and failed. It would come to her door, she said, as it had done before. She was adamant in this. And she was right.

She received a telegram saying that Jim's ship had been torpedoed in the mouth of the Thames, but that Jim was all right. Reading about the incident together, Patrick pointed out that it had been a lucky chance by a German submarine which happened to be in the right position, that there was little loss of life. But still she refused to take comfort from his words, going to a bureau to take from it all his carefully kept postcards and letters and turning them over and over in her hand. On one was a signature: Neville Chamberlain. That was when Jim had become a steward on passenger liners.

Her fears increased when he returned home to say that he'd left the Merchant Navy and had already enlisted in the army, in the Royal

Iniskilling Fusiliers. She pleaded, argued, saying that he wasn't yet of age. True, he had faked his age, not yet being quite eighteen. But she could plead with the army authorities who had him now and wouldn't be prepared to let him go.

Months of lull. But a lull before what? From the bollards at Larne harbour I watched them go: Dalton, Harry, Samuel. Gentle Samuel who had christened Rosinante, my pet.

Dunkirk. The British Army had been driven out of France and into the sea, to be machine-gunned and bombed in the waves where even the smallest fishing craft were trying to drag survivors from the bloody waters. Frowning and even more quiet, Patrick paced the kitchen. Returning one afternoon he told her that he'd enlisted in Jim's regiment. Again she pleaded, but to no avail. Kissing her he said: 'Can I allow the stepson I love to go to war and not think of following him? What kind of father would you have me be, May? And what kind of man when I say—I love you!?'

Events, as before, carried her along as though she were no more than a twig caught in a river in flood. Patrick returned in uniform, as did Jim, and both were gone again. France had fallen as it had not done in the previous war, and from the airfields of Europe thousands of planes droned over the sea to begin the bombing of the cities. A blackout was ordered and strictly enforced. Adjusting the curtains and heavy blankets which covered the windows she would return to the fire nursing an old loneliness whose lineaments were both rage and fear, the night enfolding her being in the web and warp of time where the past glowed indistinctly as the loom of the future.

IV

For most of the afternoon Niall paced the cobbled yard, the heavy gate securely bolted from the inside. When the storm came up and the rain hissed round his feet he retreated into the workshed to pace that before sitting beside a brazier. Poker in hand he stirred the ash and glowing coke, aware of his own nervousness and brooding on what the evening was to bring. He knew he would go to the rendezvous, but did not know for what purpose. When had they first come into contact? In this same yard nearly twenty-five years ago just after the rising in Dublin, when he was asked to be an informer. Infrequently after that, and then several times before Harry died. Latterly, several times again even to the point of being approached at the shore while working at the boat or being stopped in one of the streets of the village.

What did he want? Information? But information about what? For all practical purposes the Republican movement on both sides of the border did not exist. Some had believed that now another European war had begun Germany would again come to their aid. But there was little hope of that. Talk of submarines at sea with agents on board didn't amount to much. Germany had other things to think about. If Britain fell things would be different, totally different. If it did. But then—the old adage. Better the devil you know than the devil you don't. Under the German imperial eagle who was to say that Ireland would be in a better state?

What information was there to give when there was so little that could be done? A few fanatics might try to raid a bank or an arms depot, but that could hardly be called political or military strategy. Particularly when there was no longer a central command. The few bombs planted in England at the outbreak of the war had been acts of stupidity; the only thing gained being acts of internment both north and south of the border with De Valera in Dublin determinedly guarding the Free State's neutrality at whatever cost to old comrades. All over Ireland the prisons were again holding Republicans.

So, what then? Was it nothing more than to settle an old score

299

because he, Niall, had outwitted him in the past? That such occurrences took place on both sides was no secret. Hence not long ago Admiral Somerville in the south answered a knock on the door to be shot dead. And for what reason? Perhaps for no other than he was an admiral fighting in the British Navy when many of his neighbours were fighting the British for their freedom.

Still nervously poking ash and coke, he felt the years burden him. He was old and tired beyond his days. Tired and old and filled with broken hopes and dreams of a Republic rising phoenixlike from the ashes of the General Post Office that Easter Day in 1916 which he and all of them could hand on to their children and children's children in a land free at last of English dominance. But the Republic had been defeated, thwarted, fragmented, with the pieces thrown to the winds.

Old, weary. And now, was he being lured into a trap?

Across the village lay home and fire and wife and children. There he wanted to go, but could not.

Yes. He was afraid.

Crossing the shed, he withdrew a damp crumpled letter from a hiding-place and read it even though he knew the simple message by heart. *Campbell killed Harry McKinstry. He will kill you also.* Beneath the words was a telephone number. He'd received it over three years ago from a tall tinker-looking fellow with an earring in his ear who'd simply put it in his hand and walked away. It wasn't a good thing to know that a killer was somewhere behind him, and he'd even had nightmares about it. Painstakingly he'd gone through the telephone book to find that the number wasn't listed. He'd then tried to get information from an operator, but had rung off when questioned.

Yes, he would go. For Harry's sake if for no other. Holding the letter he read it again. In it lay hope and perhaps only in it. From another hiding-place he took out a revolver and, checking the chamber, slipped it and the letter into his pocket. Standing on the cobbles outside he looked at the sky which was now clear save for the odd ragged band of black cloud speeding across moon and stars. The wind was still high but it invariably was on this part of the coast. He loved it beating against his face. Sea and storm wind was part of his home.

Squeezing into a private niche in a pub, he lifted the telephone and dialled.

'Yes?'

'Niall McNeill.'

Silence.

'He's here. Campbell is here.'

Silence.

And suddenly he wanted to put the receiver down and run. What if

300

it had been Campbell who'd sent the letter? As a trick, a joke? As another turn of the screw? But when the voice sounded on the other end he knew it was not Campbell's. It was too authoritative, emphatic, solid.

'Be precise.'

'I'm to meet him tonight.'

'Where?'

'After the third crossroads out of the village on the main road. There's a fairy-mound thereabouts shaded by some hawthorn.' Niall tried to bring humour into his voice, which didn't come. 'Old superstitions, you know.'

'Will you go?'

'Yes. For Harry's sake if for nothing else.'

'At what time?'

'Between ten and eleven.'

'Good.'

But now Niall wanted to talk further, as if he were kneeling in a confessional. 'I said for Harry's sake if for nothing else. I want you to understand something. It was me who partly killed Harry. Yes, me. He wanted out. He wanted to leave the movement. But I persuaded him to do that one last job. That one last mission to carry some papers. Even though Campbell had seen us and had even sat down to talk to us together. And had baited Harry. I knew Campbell had guessed. But I waited. I was too sure, you see. I wanted to bait Campbell. To do it my way. When what I should have done was to stop Harry—let him go—and give the job to somebody else.'

'I understand.'

'I said I was partly to blame. Partly?' From his belly Niall gave a despairing laugh. 'No. Not partly. It was I who was Harry's real executioner.'

'I said I understand. I shall not repeat myself again.'

'Who are you?'

'No one you know. Nor is it of any concern to you.'

'How did Harry die?' An innocent gull dying in a bloody instant. There was a slight pause before the other replied.

'Slowly. By torture.'

Niall paused also and shuddered. 'I'll be carrying a revolver.'

'You'll need one.'

As the telephone clicked and went silent Niall stared at it for a few minutes before replacing the receiver. Calling for a hot whiskey he sat by the fire, watching as the letter flamed and writhed into ash. Whatever the evening's outcome, he had no use for it now.

As Sherrin turned into the driveway of the darkened house he saw the tall figure of his superior approach from the shadows.

'I came as soon as I got your call, sir. They had to knock me up from the barracks.'

'It wasn't quite soon enough. We have time to catch up on.'

Waiting until Dalton was seated in the rear he began reversing the Citroën into the road. 'Where to, sir?'

'Ballycastle.'

'How fast, sir?'

'Do you have a memory, Sherrin?'

There was an odd tone in the super's voice, Sherrin thought, quickly slipping through the gears as the car gathered speed northwards out of the city. Yes, the super. Because now there was only one super to Sherrin. 'I think I have a memory, sir.'

'Then do you remember the time when I said that one day we might have to chase devils?'

Frowning, puzzled, one hand on the steering-wheel while the other either scratched his chin or flicked the gear-lever, Sherrin tried to think. 'I don't remember, sir.'

'Then how fast would you have to go to chase devils?'

Still frowning, Sherrin said: 'Very fast I'd think, sir.'

'Then please go very fast.'

'And how fast is that, sir?'

'As I also said then, Sherrin. Am I to instruct you in your own business?'

'I hope not, sir.'

'And I equally hope not.' Watching the roadway for several minutes, Dalton added: 'Use full headlights if you wish. Ignore the blackout.'

'Sir.'

'And I'm pleased to see that you have been practising.'

'Thank you, sir.'

Reclining in the seat Dalton watched the swiftly passing countryside, one hand at times tracing the butt of the revolver protruding from the holster, eyes noting details and landmarks for no other reason than that this was an habitual exercise. There was nothing to think of other than to gauge his own feelings and sense of anticipation. The car was rolling slowly now, headlights dimmed. It stopped. Sherrin, a small torch in hand, was peering at an Ordnance Survey map.

'We're about a mile from the crossroads, sir.'

'Good. Drive there and stop.'

It was better that way, Dalton thought, as the car moved off again. The sound of the engine would carry a long way and would alert him. He didn't want to come on him silently. If he already held suspicions, that would only heighten them.

'A car, sir. Over there under the trees. A Riley tourer.'

'Good. Wait for me here.'

'Good luck, sir.'

Outside the car Dalton stretched his limbs, the winter cape, fastened at the throat and open, falling to his calves. On the edge of the field beyond the trees lay a large mound. Opening his pocket-watch, he consulted it. Five minutes past ten. Campbell had arrived. But McNeill? Large drops of rain occasionally spattered against him, driven by a high wind, but the sky was mostly clear with the moon well up. Stepping over the sheugh separating field from roadway he paused in shadow to look down the sloping terrain. Yes. Towards the bottom right-hand corner a squatting figure was silhouetted against the gnarled branches of hawthorn, an object on the ground beside it. But what? Or whom? It was an old trick to deliberately confuse the time of meeting. With a measured walk he approached.

The figure stood up. 'Well. If it isn't Inspector Gordon.'

Merely nodding, Dalton looked at the body on the ground. 'And who is that?'

A slight high-pitched laugh sounded in the air. 'Was that, I think you mean. Someone called Niall McNeill.'

'I see.'

'You were on to him too, I gather?'

'Yes.'

'But then I thought you might be.' The other paused. 'And know of all the associations. Including the past.'

'Yes. I know of all the associations.'

Again the laugh. 'He thought he would trick me. By arriving before I did. But what he didn't know was that I knew that's what he'd do and so was here waiting for him.'

Kneeling beside the recumbent form, Dalton stared at the hideously mangled features and genitals, at the bullet wounds designed to cause pain but not to kill. 'What did you get from him?'

'I might share it with you later, inspector. But not a lot, I think. After all, we both know there isn't much going on. Some of them might think they'll manage to do what they failed to do in the first war. But what it makes for us is sport, Inspector. Great sport.'

'I am much more interested in the information.'

There was deliberate mockery in the voice. 'A good policeman, I see. You'll get it, inspector. But only when I have sifted through it. I have it all in my mind. But as I told you, I don't think there'll be much of worth. Though certainly enough to lead us to more sport.'

The lips were curled, Dalton noticed, the teeth gleaming in the moonlight as the other again squatted beside the corpse. But there was something else that he had noticed earlier, the gun that was

303

casually held in the right hand. Quietly he said: 'That is not a service pistol, captain.'

'Why no, it isn't. It's one of my own.'

'It is not a common make.'

'Common enough, inspector. That's if you happen to be in the region where it's made. A Mauser. I had it brought to me from Germany before hostilities were declared. It's used by the Gestapo.' Smiling, Campbell opened his hand to look at it. 'A good piece. I've already used quite a few but there should still be seven bullets in the magazine.'

'May I see it?'

Taking it in his palm Dalton tested the texture and balance and slowly stood up, barrel pointing downwards.

'What are you doing?'

Silence.

Fear was now piercing the words. 'What are you doing?'

Silence.

'Inspector?'

The first bullet grazed the left temple to cut away part of the ear. The second bullet grazed the right temple to cut away part of that ear. Dalton watched as the other slowly stood up.

'Who are you?'

He fired again, the third bullet glancing along the left cheekbone, deigning not to kill but to pain and disorientate consciousness. The fourth bullet furrowed the right cheekbone likewise.

And now death struggled with being and articulate sound. 'Who . . . are . . . you?'

Dalton fired again, slowly, choosing his mark, watching the other writhe among the many possible shattered selves of an infinitesimal eternity. And the other, shedding all, could but watch the massive shoulders with arms crossed that grazed the clouds until darkness invaded his eyes.

Quickly Dalton adjusted the bodies, placing the Mauser in McNeill's palm, the corpse being not yet cold. From McNeill's pocket he took a revolver which hadn't been used, put it in the other palm, and fired one shot into Campbell's body. Satisfied, he took off his gloves, sniffed them, and put them in his pocket.

'I heard gunshots, sir.'

'I believe you did, Sherrin.'

'Can I ask what happened, sir?'

'You can, Sherrin.'

Sherrin frowned as the super got into the rear seat. 'Then what happened, sir?'

'An Army Intelligence officer and a Republican are both dead, Sherrin. I had certain information but I am afraid I arrived here too late.'

'It was my fault, sir. For not driving fast enough.'

'No, Sherrin. I am the only one who is allowed to err.'

'Thank you, sir.'

'We shall report the incident at the nearest barracks. They can look after what has happened. And then I shall make my own report in the morning in Belfast. You also, Sherrin.'

'Yes, sir.' Sherrin frowned once more. 'Can I ask who the Intelligence officer was, sir?'

'A Captain Campbell.'

Unused to expletives, Sherrin was surprised at his own words. 'God Jesus, sir. The stories that's going round the Force about him.' Putting the car into gear, he turned the first bend at speed. 'You said about devils earlier, sir. I might be thinking devils sometimes come in quare packages.'

'I am a policeman, Sherrin. I do not allow myself to think other than that.'

'No, sir.' The map placed on the steering-wheel, Sherrin worked out the route to the nearest barracks, before saying: 'You have forgotten your gloves, sir.'

'No, Sherrin. I do not forget anything. That is not allowed me.'

'Well, sir, I was just— '

'Please do not think, Sherrin. To the nearest barracks. And then I said to the city.'

'To the nearest barracks, sir. And then to the city.'

In a transport depot on the Shore Road a warrior sleeps, Sam, Sam, Don Samuel, Shellshock Sam, Lieutenant Sam the Crazy Man, exhausted now after another day's battle, surrounded by the cold wheels of trams, technological beasts put to bed, quiet and still, long overhead arms clamped to their roofs—but quiet, Sam, an old hound lies by your side as part of your sacking and the homers gone wild are nesting in the girders and even a God-given wish in your dirty snattery beard—aye, something awaits now to snort and rumble across no-man's-land, Churchill's first tanks maybe quailing the enemy on the Western Front as they bump and slither through misty gloom—*Où sont-ils les Fritz? Nous sommes les hommes de l'Irelande du Nord*—over the top with Orange sashes on their battledresses seeking glory, finding death, Ulstermen annihilated, coming from the Shankill and Sandy Row, from the Falls too, dead men belching and farting, and now he turns, muttering—*Je voudrais le pinnard, le crapouillot*—resting now—running up the line—asking—*Savez-vous ce*

305

qui se passe en Irlande?—snatters on his beard wiped with a dirty sleeve, dreaming—*Je suis à la recherche de ma ville natale*—yes, dreaming now, Sam, of a city unseen . . .

V

Easter.

For the third time the bombers came in from the sea to circle the city and rain fire on the populace beneath. Within an hour it resembled a bowl of flames, the charred bodies already numbering hundreds. May, clutching Ruth yet frantic at the loss of Colm, escapes from a demolished house to seek refuge on the slopes of the surrounding hills. And Colm, at last struggling out from the choking rubble, runs and plunges with the fiery horses from a nearby stableyard which snort and scream their agony, his terror as theirs. Arms are held out to catch him but he eludes them all. And yet heightening terror as an old man appears before him, a demon bearded holding a glowing sack in his hands that he has brought with him from the furnaces deep below. Running running yet standing still he flees from this apparition also treading smoke and burning stone before crawling into the sanctuary of a cathedral where later he will be found safe.

And the old man turns, scales falling from mind and sight, feeling for his revolver, his Sam Browne, his helmet. What is a child doing in the front lines? Breaking into a clear area he sees a tall figure whom he instantly recognises, and he salutes.

'Captain Gordon, sir.'

'Lieutenant Ogilby?'

'Permission to take a raiding party across the lines, sir.'

Understanding what has occurred, Dalton salutes a second time. 'There will be no raiding parties tonight, lieutenant. You will please stand down.'

Puzzled, trying to think with a mind now over twenty years out of date, Samuel turns and, as the order is given to hold him, again vanishes into the smoke.

'Well, brother. At your policin' duties, I see.'

307

'And you?'

'Criminal ones, maybe.' Knapsack on his back, hat tilted on the back of his head, David stood laughing. 'I'll tell you a quare yarn. 'Member that job I told you I was thinkin' of takin'? Selling cars from a garage for some character? Well, I took it. But after the first raid didn't the yellow skitter up and away to the hills like a jackrabbit leavin' yours truly till burn. Till hell wi' you, says I. So didn't I sell his cars off for what I could get, pocket the money and throw a couple of them oul' incendaries intil his premises.' Still laughing, David added: 'You won't go and tell the peelers, will ye? Anyway, there's no evidence. And this isn't a bloody confession either.'

Hiding a smile, Dalton nodded. 'And where are you going now?'

'Lough Neagh. Norah's somewhere up there wi' her tribe. She's pregnant too. So I'd better go and see how she is and wait until the ba's launched. And then I'll take her south for some peace. De Valera in Dublin's the only one of the lot that's got any bloody sense. Maybe I'll take her to Donegal. That's a good one. It could only happen in Ireland that the northernmost county's in the south.'

'Am I to believe that you're guiding yourself straight by an Irish compass?'

'Well if the compasses of that bloody bombin' shower upstairs are anything till go by it might be the best one.' David held out his hand. 'See you, brother. And 'member the old sayin': Don't get your fingers burned.'

'See you, brother.'

Still the aircraft bombed and dived, guns chattering, as he walked through the city, busily wondering where he could commandeer a car or horse and working out the shortest route to Antrim and Lough Neagh, singing . . .

'October winds lament around the Castle of Dromore,
Yet peace is in its lofty halls, *a pháisde bán a stór.*
Though autumn winds may droop and die,
A bud of spring are you—
Sing hushaby, lul, lul, lo, lo, lan,
Sing hushaby, lul, lul, loo.

Bring no ill wind to hinder us, my helpless babe and me—
Dread spirit of Blackwater's banks, Clan Eoin's wild banshee,
And Holy Mary pitying, in Heaven for grace doth sue.
Sing hushaby, lul, lul, lo, lo, lan,
Sing hushaby, lul, lul, loo.

Take time to thrive, my Rose of Hope,
In the garden of Dromore;
Take heed young Eagle—till your wings
Are weathered fit to soar;
A little time and then our land
Is full of dreams to do.
Sing hushaby, lul, lul, lo, lo, lan,

    hushaby
      hushaby
        lul lul lul
          aby'